She's
My
DAD

Iolanthe Woulff

Outskirts Press, Inc.
Denver, Colorado

YESTERDAY'S GONE
By WENDY KIDD and DAVID STUART
© 1964 (Renewed) 1992 EMI UNITED PARTNERSHIP LTD.
Used by permission from ALFRED PUBLISHING CO., INC.

Rainbow photograph courtesy Mike Nencetti.

Outskirts Press, Inc.
Denver, CO
http://www.outskirtspress.com
v9.0

PB ISBN: 978-1-4327-4377-2
HB ISBN: 978-1-4327-4405-2

Library of Congress Control Number: 2009907565

Outskirts Press and the "OP" logo are trademarks belonging to Outskirts Press, Inc.

PRINTED IN THE UNITED STATES OF AMERICA.

With eternal love and admiration,
this book is dedicated to my daughter
Stephanie Alexandra.

I'll always be your Dad.

AUTHOR'S NOTE

All the characters in this book are purely fictional, and if names were used that may suggest a reference to any living or deceased persons, it was done inadvertently.

While the area of Northern Virginia known as "Hunt Country" remains beautifully real, Graymont County, Windfield College, and the surrounding locales have never had any existence save in the author's imagination.

PROLOGUE

May 1979
Graymont County, Northern Virginia

"Oh, my God. Wake up, Nick. Hurry! You've got to go."

Shaking the motionless naked male form sprawled beside her amidst rumpled bedclothes, the woman repeated, a note of urgency straining her voice: "Nick! Get up, it's almost six o'clock! You've got to leave now, his shift ends in five minutes. If he catches you here, he'll kill you. Nick, please, wake up!"

Still no response. Frantic, the woman, whose name was Luanne, grabbed for the other's crotch and squeezed, hard.

"Oww! Whassamatter? You trying to sterilize me? Geez, Luanne, that hurt." The young man tenderly massaged his bruised privates. "I feel like warmed-over death," he moaned, curling into a fetal ball. "Drank too much. Again." He grimaced. "What time is it, anyway?"

Luanne pointed at the red numerals of a cheap clock radio atop a dresser: 5:57. "See? You should've been gone an hour ago. Listen to me! Usually Jay-Bo hangs out at the police barracks for a while but sometimes he comes straight home. Get dressed, *please*. You don't know what he's like!" Luanne's pretty features were scored with lines of fear. She hopped off the bed and hurried about the dark room, gathering up scattered pieces of clothing and tossing them at Nick, who pulled himself upright, groaning and rubbing his eyes.

Struggling into a black t-shirt with 'WINDFIELD' blazoned across the front in pink block letters, he mumbled, "That'd be picturesque, wouldn't it? Getting my brains blown out by a psychotic state cop." He pulled on his blue jeans, began buttoning the fly. "Almost sounds like a plot line on my father's soap opera. Why'd you marry such a savage creep, Luanne? You had to know he was insane. What sort of a nut case would volunteer for two Vietnam tours?" Nick's long ginger hair fell forward as he leaned over to pull on worn Frye boots. "Screw him. He doesn't scare me."

"Don't be crazy, Nick," Luanne fretted. "Jay-Bo Skinner scares everybody. Everybody with a lick of sense, anyway. Hurry *up*," she begged.

Nick donned a weathered black denim jacket. A conspicuous American flag patch sewn on one sleeve might've looked menacing on a motorcycle outlaw but contrasted strangely with Nick's delicate frame and almost girlish looks. Ever since meeting him at the Knights Inn Tavern two months ago Luanne had wondered why her gentle sensitive lover tried so hard to project himself as a hard-edged tough guy, but there was no time to think about that now. "Here," she handed Nick his keys and wallet. "Have you got everything? Let's go."

She pulled Nick out of the bedroom, urging him along the hall toward the front door. As they passed the small extra bedroom that served as a nursery for Luanne's twins, Nick hung back, digging in his heels. He grinned and pointed. The two toddlers were standing side by side in their crib, grasping the rails and blinking large baby eyes at them. "Good morning, Lissa and Lloyd!" Nick waggled his fingers. "How's it goin', tiny people?"

Lissa's expression crinkled into a smile, but her brother returned a truculent stare, refusing to be charmed. Luanne's face softened. "Hey, guys. Mommy will be right back to feed you. Come on, Nick. There's no time."

By the front door, Nick gathered Luanne into his arms and kissed her softly with the odd tenderness she had never before experienced from a man. It was the same way he made love; not with the imperative thrusts of a male in heat, but patiently, with an unhurried sensual languor that felt almost musical. He hugged her close, nuzzling her neck. "I love being with you," he whispered. "I wish I didn't have to go."

"Me, too," Luanne hugged him back. "But you must. Please. It's too dangerous."

"Won't you at least think about coming to my graduation? I'll make sure you don't run into my family or friends. I don't care about them, anyway. It would mean everything to me if you could be there. Nobody will ever know, I promise."

"Oh, honey," Luanne sighed. It was impossible. Even if she hadn't been a mother and wife, married to a Virginia State Police trooper, local girls like her didn't dare set foot on the forbidden Windfield College campus. Nick knew that as well as she did. Time had finally run out on their glorious, reckless, mad love affair. By this time next week it would only be a memory. Luanne raised her hand and stroked his smooth cheek. "I'll try," she forced herself to fib. "If I can."

"Great." The young man smiled, and Luanne again experienced the delicious disorientation which had initially captivated her. Nick had two different-colored eyes; his left iris was a warm brown color, and the right was a gorgeous topaz blue. The discrepancy was caused by a genetic anomaly, he'd explained, and showed up more often in white cats than humans. Luanne found it irresistibly mysterious and sexy; so much so that upon first seeing those enthralling mismatched eyes she'd resolved to seduce the young Windfield prince to whom they belonged. And so she had; but now their time together was at an end.

"Goodbye, Nick." Refusing to cry, she opened the front door. "Now, shoo! I have to feed my babies."

"Wait," he said. "I want to give you something." Nick ran to his blue Pontiac GTO and retrieved something from the seat. He hurried back and handed Luanne a slim bound booklet. "Here. It's our senior class almanac, what we call the 'Face Book'. You keep it. That way you'll never forget what I look like."

Luanne clasped the book to her heart and stared at him with moist eyes. "I could never forget you, Nick. God, don't you know that?"

"Just making sure. Don't forget about graduation. I'll keep an eye out for you." He gave her one last quick kiss and went back to the car. With a rumble of heavy exhaust, he drove down the rutted dirt drive-way and disappeared into the surrounding trees.

Luanne stood for a moment watching a faint cloud of dust slowly dissipate into the morning air. All around the little cottage bushes and trees were bursting with springtime color: dogwoods, redbud, forsyth-ia, and lilac. She loved this time of year; everything seemed so alive, so full of possibility. Luanne breathed in the clean country scent. She heard the piercing whistle of a cardinal and spotted the bird sitting in a sun-dappled sycamore, singing his scarlet head off for the pure joy of it. Hugging Nick's senior class book she smiled to herself, secretly reviewing the passionate night they'd just spent together.

At that moment, the growl of an approaching car engine became audible. Luanne's serene expression melted into one of guilt and fear. She darted inside and closed the door scant seconds before a sleek blue-and-gray Virginia State Police cruiser pulled to a stop in the exact spot where Nick's Pontiac had been parked. Bristling with antennae, the patrol car was spotless. A multicolored light bar on top projected on both sides like a shark's pectoral fins. In front of the grille, heavy push rods jutted up in a chrome snarl. The blue-tinted windows were flat, cold and merciless. It was a vehicle designed from the wheels up to intimidate and terrorize.

In her bedroom Luanne buried the class book at the bottom of her sweater drawer. As she hastily straightened the bedclothes she heard the heavy *k-chunk* of a car door. Smoothing the bedspread with her palm, she fluffed a last pillow and scurried into the bathroom. Quickly she moistened a cotton square and wiped smeared traces of mascara from her lids. Dropping the square into the wastebasket, Luanne looked down and barely managed to stifle a scream. She heard the front door open and close, then the heavy tread of boots.

"Luanne!" A curt bark. "You up? I'm hungry. Where are you, woman?"

Kicking the bathroom door shut with her heel like a mule, Luanne fished a used condom out of the wastebasket and gazed at it in horror. It had obviously broken. There was no seminal fluid in the torn tip.

Feeling ill, she dropped the condom into the toilet and flushed just as a pounding came on the bathroom door.

"Hey! You gonna piss away the whole goddamn day in there, or can I get somethin' to eat?"

"I'll be right out, Sugar," Luanne answered, trying not to sound sick. "Go say hello to the twins, they miss their daddy."

"Yeah, like hell," she heard a growl as the boots clomped off toward the kitchen.

Luanne stared into the mirror. Impossible. She couldn't be pregnant. What were the odds? A hundred to one. Less. It wasn't even a fertile time; her period had only recently ended. But...?

Well, she'd cross that bridge if and when she came to it. One thing she knew for absolute certain: she'd never terminate any pregnancy, let alone this one. Abort *Nick's* child? She'd die first. No, if she became pregnant with her lover's baby then that was God's will for her and she would carry it out no matter the consequences. Somehow she'd have to find a way to let him know about it.

Or would she? Luanne inspected her face, noticing how spidery worry lines were beginning to erode the fresh-faced youthful beauty that had once made her the high school sweetheart. After all, she thought, why on earth would Nick ever want to know that he had fathered some bastard kid? He was young, free, with a rich father, and could do anything or go anywhere he pleased. The last thing he'd need would be a squalling reminder of his drunken fling with an ignorant redneck adulteress. It would completely ruin his life, and he'd end up hating and blaming her forever. She couldn't, she wouldn't let that happen. If necessary, the secret would accompany her to the grave.

So resolving, Luanne ran a brush through her hair, took a deep calming breath, and went out to make breakfast for her family.

She never set eyes on Nick Farrington again.

- Part One -

THE HATING

Chapter One
Family Secrets

September 2006
Near Stuarton, VA

T he narrow country road wound its way through rolling hills
ablaze with fiery autumn reds, oranges and yellows. Whirling eddies of fallen leaves marked the passage of a weather-beaten Chevy
Camaro as it rattled past stately equestrian estates and majestic cattle
farms delineated with pristine white fencing. On both sides, lush green
pastures were dotted with grazing herds of pedigreed Black Angus,
Charolais, and Simmental cows. Wrought iron gates on bluestone pi-
lasters guarded entrances to multimillion-dollar properties with names
like "Prosperity", "Damascus Farm", and "Foxwood". Set back in the
trees at the end of sinuous macadam driveways, stone mansions reared
their blue slate gables above the flaming foliage. "Hunt Country", they
called this part of Northern Virginia, after the red-coated foxhunting
gentry that still ruled with a well-bred society fist.

Collie Skinner kept his eyes pointed straight ahead, ignoring the
affluent acreage. He'd seen it all before, for twenty-five years, and resented every well-heeled inch. Rich snobs, the lot of them, with their
noses in the air and their damned horses worth more than a normal
man could earn in two lifetimes. Ordinarily he shunned these back
roads, but for some reason his mother loved to drive through the rural

opulence, especially during the springtime and autumn seasons when the colors were bright and beautiful. Collie didn't share her enthusiasm for what she called "God's natural beauty." It struck him as a bunch of useless sentimentality. He didn't care about leaves. They grew, became green, turned yellow, fell off and rotted, then reappeared and did it again, year after year. Big deal, and in the meantime the moneyed jerks got richer and regular guys like him sweated and got the shaft. For the most part, life sucked. His Old Man was a worthless son of a bitch, but he had that right.

"Isn't it all so fine-looking?" Luanne Skinner sighed. "Thank you for taking the time, honey. I know you don't care about this sort of thing. Just being nice to your silly old mother." She patted his leg. "Such a good son, always. Bless you."

"It's okay, Mama." The car descended around a sharp curve, past a bullet-pocked sign that warned: 'Single Lane Ahead'. "I'll bet Route 50 is backed up with all those city people driving around gawking at the leaves. Hell," he grunted, "if anyone should gawk, better you than them. At least you've lived here all your life."

At the bottom of the decline the road straightened and led onto a single lane stone bridge, where a crooked green sign on a rusty pipe proclaimed: 'Gander Creek'. Seeing a battered orange Chevy pickup truck entering the bridge from the other direction, Collie pulled off into a sandy area to wait. The truck clattered past, driven by a grizzled black man wearing a red mesh Bull Durham cap. Collie vaguely knew him as Blue Ridge Harry, an enigmatic local back-woods legend. Harry gave a two-fingered salute, which Collie coolly returned. As he started to pull the car back onto the road, his mother said, "Wait, please." She sat for a moment. "I'd like to look at the water for a minute. Do you mind, honey? I promise I won't make you late for work."

Collie swallowed his impatience. "Sure, Mama. No problem."

His mother got out and walked to the edge of the embankment, then continued a short ways out onto the bridge itself, running her hand along the low stone parapet. She stopped and gazed dreamily down at the creek rushing swiftly over the pebbled bottom.

"Mama? Be careful, that wall is kind of low," Collie called, leaving the car and hurrying to join her. He didn't like to worry so much, but lately he sensed that his mother's spirits had been fading. There was a worn-out melancholy air about her that made him uneasy. She'd led an unhappy life, he knew. Although Luanne didn't speak of it, the reality was that she'd never fully recovered from her heartbreak over Lissa. Plus, as he had for almost thirty years, the Old Man continued to treat her like shit. Collie's jaw tightened. That ungrateful bastard! She should've left him years ago.

"Uh-uh, I can't let you go swimming," Collie joked, putting an arm around her thin shoulders. "It's way too cold, y'know?" Luanne was rubbing her fingers over a spot on the stone wall, peering at it with a strange expression. "What're you looking at, Mama?"

"Oh," she replied, her voice strangely muted, "just trying to find if it's still here. Look there, can you see?"

Collie bent down and saw, barely visible in the late afternoon light, two letters gouged into the rough surface: 'L+N'. Squinting closer, he could distinguish a faint heart shape outlining the letters:

"Yeah, I see it." He straightened and grinned. "What's that? You and some old boyfriend?"

His mother slowly blinked, considering the inscription with a faraway look. "Something like that. It was a long, long time ago, before you were born. I was still young then. And not very smart. But... so happy, just that once." She looked up at her son, a tear tracking down one cheek. "It was love, you know. The real thing." Suddenly she wrapped her arms around him and hugged, clinging with a desperation he found frightening. "God, I love you, I love you so much. You're everything to me, do you know that? Everything!"

Mother and son stood for a moment in the middle of the bridge, embracing, the silence unbroken except for watery sounds from the rushing creek. Around them, autumn-colored leaves drifted down, some alighting atop the current to be swirled away forever.

"I love you too, Mama," Collie finally said, his voice unsteady. Womanly displays of emotion made him uncomfortable. Kissing the top of her head, "Come on, it's getting late, we better get a move on." He led her back to the car.

As they drove off Luanne Skinner cast a final look back over her shoulder at the narrow stone bridge fading into dusky shadows.

"The real thing, Nicholas," she repeated, using Collie's true given name, which her son permitted no one else on earth to use. "Oh, yes, my darling boy. It surely was."

———— ◉ ————

James Robert Skinner, universally known and unloved as Jay-Bo, sat slumped in a decrepit BarcaLounger and glowered over his spreading middle at the television, where a horse-faced blonde wearing a miniskirt and a smirk sat plugging her latest book, a collection of excoriating attacks against the evils of liberalism.

"Stupid bitch," muttered Jay-Bo, draining a Budweiser. He crushed the beer can in a hairy-knuckled fist and tossed it, like the first four, into a nearby sour-smelling wastebasket. Not that he didn't agree with the blonde's sentiments. Hell, he hated liberals, too. But would anyone pay him a million bucks to write books about it? Shit, no. Nobody wanted to listen to a decorated USMC Vietnam veteran and former Virginia State Trooper. They'd much rather watch this simpering twat flash her beaver at the bug-eyed interviewer. It wasn't fair. There she was, snotty, rich, on top of the world, while he, Jay-Bo Skinner, who'd killed in defense of his country and arrested hundreds of punks and criminals for the good of the citizenry, sat here in this seedy apartment, unemployed, broke, supported by a son he couldn't stand and shunned by almost everyone except his wife. Unfair? It was a goddamn outrage.

Jay-Bo stared morosely at a wall where framed photos, some hanging slightly askew, attested to past glories: A formal photo of the scowling young marine, fanatically spit-shined and creased, eager to go eviscerate gooks for the good old U.S.A. Another of himself and several comrades-in-arms over in Nam, faces smeared with camouflage paint, fiercely baring teeth and holding machine guns at the ready, their bandoliers sprouting grenades like deadly fruit. A photo showing him in his Virginia State Police Trooper uniform, immaculate as always, posing beside the beloved blue-and-gray patrol car he'd always prized as the "cleanest and meanest" police vehicle in Virginia.

"Damn," he muttered under his breath. In those days, life had been good: His authority had been unquestioned, his reputation had been ferocious, and everyone had accorded him deference bordering on fear. Jay-Bo had loved to hang around the barracks with the other officers while they all cleaned their service weapons. Polishing his jacketed hollow point rounds with an oily gun cloth, he'd boast about how he could easily reduce the most insolent lawbreaker into a terrified pussy cowering in the back seat of his patrol car. The other troopers would shake their heads and laugh, "Skinner, you are one hard-assed son-of-a bitch." And they'd been right. That's exactly what he was, and damned proud of it.

His gaze darkened as it fell upon a photograph of himself and Luanne on their wedding day. They stood arm-in-arm in front of the little country church, he resplendent in his Marine dress uniform, she a stunning vision in her white lace gown. Both of them wore sappy newlywed smiles. A muscle twitched along one bluish jowl as Jay-Bo clenched his jaw. Christ, what a fool he'd been! Getting married just because the supposedly untouchable high school beauty had swooned over his combat medals and bravery commendation. If only he had held out, she would've fucked him anyway and he could've escaped the marriage trap. But no, he'd been so addled with lust and a misguided sense of USMC honor that he'd gotten hitched. After a few weeks of screwing his pretty bride's brains out every night, he'd regained his senses and realized to his horror that he was stuck, like a prehistoric bug in amber.

He had escaped into the State Police Academy, breezing through the tough physical regimen and earning top marks for weaponry and high-speed pursuit. As an active-duty trooper, he could and did stay away from what he regarded as the prison of domesticity, sleeping at the barracks and sometimes not seeing Luanne for days on end. Within six months of his nuptials he'd been unfaithful three times, which he figured was his due for being a hard-working law-enforcement officer and combat veteran. His young bride seemed bewildered and forlorn at being so cavalierly abandoned, but Jay-Bo's conscience was clear. What did the little slut expect? That's what she got for suckering a red-blooded American man into matrimony way before his time. Officer Skinner devoted himself to the gun range, arrested more than his share of assorted speeders and lowlifes, and soon replicated the same gung-ho reputation he'd enjoyed in the service.

Then, of all the lousy luck, Luanne had somehow turned up pregnant. The lying bitch had claimed to be taking the pill, but whatever kind of pill it was had been a goddamn joke, since she'd conceived not just one but two kids. Before he knew it Officer Jay-Bo Skinner found himself the father of twins, being congratulated and handed cigars by the other troopers, who called him "Daddy" and assured him between guffaws that changing two sets of diapers was a double joy. As if that wasn't nightmare enough, within a year or so Luanne delivered her third child, another boy.

Jay-Bo got up out of the lounger and went to the kitchen for his last beer. He'd told Luanne to pick up another twelve-pack on the way home from church. Where was she, anyway? The worship service usually didn't take this long, even when that gasbag preacher got himself all wound up. Jay-Bo popped the tab, took a long swallow and wiped his mouth on his shirt. There'd be hell to pay if she didn't get her ass home in time to make his supper. Luanne had no business keeping him waiting while she drove all over the county with that cockeyed mutant of a son. Jay-Bo was damned if he'd be disrespected in his own home, even if it was a cruddy rented shitbox.

On the television the toothy blonde was gone, replaced by a bow-tied black man holding forth about affirmative action or equal opportunity or whatever else the damn coons were always bellyaching about. Jay-Bo Skinner wasn't fond of black people, except when it came to arresting them. That, he'd excelled at. The only downside had been remembering to call them "African-Americans." Regulations were very stern: an officer was in extremely deep shit if he ever uttered the so-called "N-word". But nowadays, thanks to the kangaroo court and his dismissal from the force, Jay-Bo didn't have to toe that politically correct line anymore. They could take away his uniform, his guns, his pension, but they couldn't deprive him of his free speech. This was still America, by God. He knew his rights.

"Shut up, you fuckin' nigger," Jay-Bo snarled at the television. "Go steal a white man's job, fuck a white woman, and then come talk to me about civil rights, you black faggot-lovin' monkey." He reached down the side of the lounger and from a magazine pouch withdrew a polished dark blue Colt Python .357 magnum revolver. Aiming the six-inch bull barrel at the television, he muttered, "Boom! Boom!" Jerking the handgun upwards in pantomime recoil: "See you in Hell, boy." He lovingly inspected the Python, which he'd taken from a outlaw biker years ago as the guy lay convulsing on the pavement from Jay-Bo's taser. Of course all such confiscated evidence was supposed to be turned in, but Jay-Bo had coveted the top-of-the-line weapon and surreptitiously kept it for himself. Now it was his sole remaining firearm. Part of the D.A.'s raw deal after the trial had forced him to relinquish his collection of guns, which he'd reluctantly done, all except for the illegal Python. Jay-Bo couldn't imagine life without access to a weapon; it was unthinkable, like not having a dick.

Hearing the front door open, he stashed the revolver as Luanne and Collie walked in. Jay-Bo greeted them with an irritated scowl: "About goddamn time. What took so long? Where's my beer?" Seeing his wife's sudden guilty glance at her son, he exploded, "Well, ain't that great. What the hell's wrong with you, Luanne? Do you even have a brain? Jesus Christ! I ask you to do one small thing, and you can't be fuckin' bothered?"

"I'm sorry, Sugar," Luanne stammered. "It's my fault, I did forget. Let me run down to the corner, I'll go get it right now. Give me the keys, Collie." She held out her hand.

Collie shook his head. "No way, Mom. You're tired. I'll go get his lousy beer."

Luanne wearily demurred, "Never mind, honey, you have to get dressed for work. It won't take me five minutes. Come on, now."

Collie started to protest again, but catching his mother's beseeching look he shrugged and handed her the keys.

As she went out the front door, Jay-Bo said with a crude mocking lisp, "Really, honey, you better go put on that thweetie-pie fag uniform for work. Muthn't be late."

"At least I have a job." Collie didn't disguise his contempt. "More than I can say for you, Old Man."

Father and son locked stares, silently daring each other to look away first. Both detested what they saw: Collie loathed the heavy-bodied thug with the military buzz cut and booze-reddened complexion, Jay-Bo hated the wiry red-headed punk with the disdainful sneer and damnable eyes.

Not breaking his gaze, Collie said, "You lay off Mama when she gets back. She doesn't feel good, got that pain in her stomach again."

Jay-Bo laughed. "Shit, there ain't nothin' wrong with her 'cept bein' a woman. Damn females always got a pain somewhere. Ain't you even learned that much yet? Go on, get out of here, fag-boy. You let me worry about your mother."

"Don't call me that," growled Collie. "Shut the hell up."

Jay-Bo snorted. "Why don't you come over here and make me shut up, you little chicken? Think you can take me?"

They glared at each other again. Collie finally said, "Just leave her alone." He turned on his heel and stalked out before Jay-Bo could think of a retort.

Letting his fingers drop down to feel the outline of the hidden Colt Python, Jay-Bo Skinner silently swore to himself. Someday that wiseass kid would get what he had coming to him. Jay-Bo would make sure of it.

———— ⫸⦿⫷ ————

In his cheerless small bedroom, Collie rapidly got dressed for work. As a waiter at the celebrated Foxton Arms restaurant he was required to wear black trousers, a formal white tuxedo shirt with studs, patent-leather moccasins and a maroon bow tie. He disliked the outfit almost as much as his father did, but for the kind of money he made serving the local gentry and Washington bigwigs who thronged to the restaurant in long limousines he would have worn a spangled tutu. It wasn't uncommon for him to receive a fifty-dollar tip or even, on rare occasions, a hundred. Collie was highly practiced at serving the wealthy clientele, presenting a respectful courteous manner without being obsequious. Many of the regular patrons asked for him by name when they made their reservations.

He pinned his little gold name tag in place, carefully combed his hair and turned to leave. As he passed by the shabby dresser his eye fell on an aging photograph taped in one corner of the cracked mirror. It was a snapshot of himself with his older twin siblings, Lloyd and Lissa. Sunburned and grinning, their arms around each other, the three of them mugged for the camera with all the mischievous exuberance of carefree youngsters. The twins had been around thirteen or so, Collie maybe ten or eleven. They'd gone to a lake somewhere and had the tousled sandy look of kids at the beach: Lloyd, brash and blonde; Lissa, also blonde, in that twilight time between girlhood and becoming a woman, sticking her tongue out and wearing her first bikini top over swelling breasts; Collie, the puny kid brother, wanting to be one of the gang but not quite making it.

Ignoring the rest of the photo, Collie studied the image of his older sister. The usual ache came into his heart, tempered as always with anger and confusion. He missed her desperately. Still, no one had forced Lissa to do what she did. It had been her choice. In the aftermath her father had blamed it on the corrupting influence of Windfield College with its liberals, queers, and socialists. How could a good Virginia girl be expected to grow up normally near such a pit of depravity? Collie despised Windfield like everybody else he knew, but whether it had played any part in what happened to Lissa…who could say? He just missed his sister. She had always been kind and sweet to him, standing up to school bullies, keeping Lloyd off his back, even shielding him from Jay-Bo's wrath when she could.

Collie briefly turned his eyes to Lissa's fraternal twin, and his mouth curved downward. Lloyd Skinner had always been a perfect clone of Jay-Bo: an outsized belligerent asshole. Lloyd had made a career of tormenting his little brother until the day Collie had buried a steel garden shovel in Lloyd's head to the tune of twenty-seven stitches. After that, correctly believing that Collie wouldn't hesitate to do it again, Lloyd left him alone.

But picking on Collie had only been a diversion for Lloyd Skinner. Practically from birth, his principal goal in life was to join the military. He hungered to earn a government-sanctioned authorization to slay people. It didn't matter who he got to kill: slants, commies, Hottentots, ragheads; if America wanted them riddled with bullets, Collie's brother was ready and willing to oblige. He contented himself in the meanwhile with shooting every living furry or feathered creature within range of his .22 rifle, and counted the days until he could join the Marines.

Unluckily for Lloyd, his dreams were shattered one humid Sunday afternoon when Jay-Bo, astride his beloved Wheel Horse side-discharge riding mower, carelessly ran over a can of motor oil he'd forgotten on the grass. The whirring blades spit out a cloud of well-lubricated aluminum razors, one of which neatly severed a good portion of Lloyd's right pinky.

It wasn't a life-threatening injury. Lloyd recovered in no time. But it was enough to get him rejected by the Corps. Lloyd begged and pleaded. He offered to take any physical test they might give him, shoot the eye out a gnat, anything. But the recruiters wouldn't budge. Lloyd's desire to serve his country was admirably patriotic, but regulations were regulations. Perhaps, they suggested, he could join the Peace Corps.

There ensued a bleak time in the Skinner household. Lloyd blamed his father, sulked all day, and wouldn't talk to anybody. Jay-Bo blamed everyone but himself for the accident, and spent almost all his time away from the house, on patrol or drowning his guilt in the local police taverns. Lissa made every effort to remain cheerful and raise Lloyd's spirits, but her twin brother met such attempts with sullen hostility.

Now, as he stood contemplating Lissa's old pixyish photo, Collie could recall the icy clench he felt in his gut the afternoon she came home and announced that she'd enlisted in the Marines. Jay-Bo had been stunned into silence, for once. Distraught, Luanne wept and begged her to reconsider. As for Lloyd, he fixed his twin sister with a glare of molten hatred and stormed from the house.

Collie remembered the day she left for basic training. Biting his lips, fighting back tears, he'd asked Lissa why on earth she was doing such a thing?

Her reply, "So things will be better," didn't make any sense to him. When she cryptically added, "For everyone," he couldn't think of anything to say, merely shuffling his feet in awkward silence until she finished packing and departed.

But of course things hadn't "gotten better." Instead the whole world soon came crashing down, and had never been the same again.

Collie reached out and sadly caressed his sister's face with the tip of one finger. "Lissa," he whispered in the silent room. Then he shook his head, expelled a breath and went out, closing the door quietly behind him.

=—■《◊》■—=

He found his mother in the kitchen, preparing one of Jay-Bo's preferred repasts: chili dogs and Tater Tots. From the other room he could hear the sound of gunfire and explosions as his old man, for the umpteenth time, watched John Wayne swagger all over Saigon in *The Green Berets*. (Subversive movies like *Apocalypse Now* and *Full Metal Jacket* were banned.) "Bring me another goddamn beer," came Jay-Bo's hoarse yell over the whine of an incoming mortar shell.

Ignoring him, Collie asked, "Are you feelin' okay, Mama? You look really beat."

"I'm fine, honey." Luanne shrugged. "Don't you worry about me.

Is it a double shift night?"

Yeah, I'll be at the Knights Inn after the Arms closes up. I won't get home till after two."

His mother nodded and slowly stirred the chili, her face drawn and weary.

"Mama?" Collie hesitated as his mother looked up. "That thing you showed me on the bridge…What I mean is, how come you didn't marry him instead of…?" He tipped his head toward the living room.

Luanne's expression grew fearful. "Sshh, please, he might hear you. I don't want to talk about it. I shouldn't have said anything." She dropped some chopped onions into the pot. "Just forget everything I told you."

"Come on, Mama." Collie persisted, "Please. Who was he?"

Luanne closed her eyes and a shudder seemed to run through her. "He was someone I knew for a very short while. It was never meant to be. All right? Now don't ask me any more. Go on, you're going to be late. Scat."

Collie bent and kissed her cheek. "Okay. I'll see you later, Mama. You take care of yourself."

Luanne managed a smile. "I will, I promise. Here, take your father his beer, that's a good boy. And Nicholas…?"

Collie stopped, the beer dangling in his hand.

"I love you, baby. Forever."

Chapter Two

Clashes

"Congressman Walters is here," the tuxedoed maitre d' told Collie when he arrived at his station. "Table Fourteen. He wants you, of course."

Collie nodded, pleased. The congressman, a Southern California Democrat, was a very generous tipper. Collie didn't know about his politics and didn't care. For a fifty-dollar tip he could be an anarchist.

The maitre d' added, "He has a guest. His daughter, I imagine. Better get over there."

"Right away, Mr. Foley." Collie gathered up a couple of ornately-bound menus and made his way across the crowded main room. The Foxton Arms stayed permanently busy; reservations were difficult to come by, being much sought-after by the sort of citizens who relished being seen at renowned restaurants. For certain high-society types, a pilgrimage to the elitist Middleville eatery was an existential must.

"Hello, Collie." Robin Thompson, one of the waitresses, whispered a greeting as she passed by on her way toward the bar. "Busy as a beehive tonight!"

"Good for us poor folks," Collie winked. Robin, who attended the same church as his mother, was a petite young woman, very pretty in a modest way, reserved but sweet-natured, who always tried to see the best in everything and everyone. In her maroon bow tie, formal shirt and black skirt, Robin managed to look fetching instead of dopey.

"Let's hope!" She returned a shy brown-eyed smile and hurried off.

When Collie arrived at the table, Congressman Walters hailed him in a hearty voice: "Well, Collie! Hello, my lad. Good to see you again. How have you been?"

"Fine, sir, thank you."

"Glad to hear it," replied the congressman. Indicating the young woman seated across from him: "This is my daughter, Heather."

Collie inclined his head. "Good evening, Ms. Walters. Welcome to the Foxton Arms."

The Infanta Walters sized him up with an imperious look while Collie maintained a well-mannered silence. She seemed to be all hair, attitude, breasts, and money. The congressman's daughter did a startled double-take when she noticed Collie's eyes, then tried to pretend that she hadn't.

"Heather just matriculated at Windfield," said the congressman. "Fine institution, of course. We're very pleased."

"Actually," said Heather, "Daddy wanted me to go to USC. But L.A. is totally putrid. Like I really want to go to school in the middle of Watts? Hello, I don't think so." Her eye fell on Collie's nameplate. "Isn't Collie a dog?" She giggled. "Like Lassie, or something?"

The congressman cleared his throat. "That will do, young lady." He flicked Collie an apologetic glance. "The usual for me, my lad. Filet *au poivre*, rare. And the white asparagus with Béarnaise. What looks good to you, dear?" he addressed his daughter, who studied the menu in horror.

"Omigod." She widened her blue eyes. "Don't you have anything that isn't so fattening? Look at all these *calories*."

This spoiled princess will fit in perfectly at Windfield College, thought Collie. "We have a signature venison dish that's quite lean, Miss. The chef prepares it in a scallion-peppercorn reduction with morels and—"

"Venison?" Heather gasped. Turning to her father: "These people eat *Bambi*." She sighed, with all the drama of Anna Karenina contemplating the train tracks: "Who knew Virginia was so…prehistoric."

Congressman Walters brusquely told his daughter to select an entrée. With a martyred air Heather finally decided that she could possibly tolerate the poached Arctic Char in parchment.

On his way back to the kitchen Collie saw Robin Thompson waiting on four young men, whose cocktail glasses and disdainful grins identified them as Windfield College upperclassmen. In a show of cheeky bravado they had all removed their ties in defiance of the restaurant's dress code. The discarded ties hung over the backs of their chairs like disdainful tails. Collie compressed his lips. These damned Windfield pests infested everything, like Japanese beetles in a tomato garden.

After placing the entrée orders Collie brought salads to the Congressman's table. Heather sniffed hers suspiciously and commented that the house wild currant vinaigrette smelled a lot like ant spray, but Collie's attention was drawn to Robin's table, where the Windfield men were indulging in a bit of collegiate fun. Sidling closer, Collie heard one of them address Robin with exaggerated patience, as though addressing a cretin: "Do you seriously expect us to drink such unspeakable rubbish?" He held up a glass of wine, wrinkling his nose at it. "Frankly, *Robin*, I wouldn't use this stuff to bathe a pig." Over the snickers of his tablemates he ordered: "Take that and throw it in the trash. Evidently you know nothing about classic vintages."

Robin flushed and quickly picked up the offending bottle. "Right away, sir. I'm sorry it isn't to your liking. Would you care to try something different? We have a fine selection of—"

"Your so-called selection is a bad joke," interrupted the Windfield student. "Bring me another Pinch on the rocks. Can you handle that?"

As Robin fled amidst a chorus of mocking laughter Collie heard one of them snigger something about "country bumpkins," provoking more merriment. Seething, he glared daggers at the foursome. But he knew that saying anything would put his job at serious risk, and these patronizing fools weren't worth it. As he turned away one of them suddenly snapped his fingers and called out: "You! Waiter! Is there something you want to say?" The Windfield boy was extremely handsome, with perfectly tanned angular features. "Well?"

Collie halted. "I hope you're finding everything satisfactory this evening, *sir?* "

"Actually, I'm not. But that's what comes of having unrealistic expectations," sniffed the other. "I keep forgetting that we're stuck out in the boonies." With an amazed squint at Collie: "Hey guys, check it out. This boy's eyes don't match."

At once Collie found his face being intently scrutinized by the other Windfield men, who grinned and nudged each other. "Oh, that is just too cute!"

Humiliated, Collie muttered an excuse and went about serving his other guests. At Congressman Walters' table Heather took a few bites of her Arctic Char, declared that it tasted like pure Crisco and refused to eat any more. Collie carried thirty dollars' worth of prime seafood away to the dumpster, silently swearing that he would never become a parent. Clearly embarrassed by his daughter's deportment her father slipped a fifty-dollar bill into Collie's hand as they departed.

But Collie's pleasure over the generous tip vanished when he saw the Windfield students, obviously well in their cups, berating Robin again.

"This is simply outrageous." The tanned pretty boy glared at the check. "How dare you charge us for that undrinkable swill? In all my life I've never endured such wretched service. Where do they recruit you people? Denny's?"

The others chortled. "Oh dear, Phillip, that is *so* cold."

Collie saw that Robin was close to tears and walked up beside her. "Is there a problem here?"

"You, again?" The Windfielder frostily looked Collie up and down. "What's up with you, Odd Eyes? Is this incompetent wench your girl-friend or something?"

Robin glanced at Collie, alarmed, and slightly shook her head.

Collie was five seconds away from launching a suicide attack when the maitre d' materialized at his elbow. "Mr. Skinner, I believe Table Seventeen is ready for dessert. Kindly see to it, please." From his clipped tone Collie could tell that a dressing-down was in the offing. Praying that he hadn't forfeited his job, he left the maitre d' and

Robin to smooth the ruffled Windfield feathers, and went to fetch Table Seventeen's tiramisus.

As it turned out, Conrad Foley's reprimand was not as severe as it might have been. The maitre d' wasn't blind. As far as he was concerned the Windfield boys were a stain on his eating establishment, insolently removing their ties and drinking to excess. Nonetheless, he sternly informed Collie, there would be no more town-gown confrontations in the Foxton Arms.

"Keep your temper in check, Mr. Skinner. Do I make myself clear?"

"Yes, sir. It won't happen again."

"See to it that it doesn't. You may go."

At closing time, after submitting his receipts, Collie quickly changed out of his uniform in the employee's back room. The Knights Inn Tavern, where he served late-night beers and pizza to a blue-collar crowd, was decidedly not a maroon bow tie kind of place. He exited the restaurant's rear entrance and almost ran into Robin Thompson, who stood softly weeping, her face in her hands.

"Hey, what's wrong?" Collie's immediate impulse was to hug her, but he didn't know how she might react. "Robin? What's the matter?"

Robin shook her head, sobbing. Then she held out one palm, and Collie could see a crumpled single dollar bill. "That's all they gave me," she cried. "How could they be so mean? It wasn't my fault about the wine. I tried to get it taken off the bill, but they'd already drunk more than half. And I really could use the money. I'm late on my school payments as it is."

"Those goddamned bastards," Collie cursed. Then, remembering that Robin took her Christian faith seriously: "Uh, I'm sorry. That's a lousy thing to do to somebody, but what do you expect? They go to Windfield."

Robin dolefully regarded her crumpled single bill. "I don't think it's the college's fault," she said. "Some people just have no kindness in their hearts."

Collie figured what the heck, and lightly put his arms around Robin. She didn't seem to mind at all, but leaned against him briefly before drawing back. In a worried tone: "Did you get into trouble? What were you thinking, anyway? You looked like were going to punch that boy. You can't lose your job, Collie. What would your family do?"

"Mr. Foley got mad at me a little, but it wasn't too bad. And I don't have a family, just my mother. The Old Man and my brother, wherever he is, can go to Hell for all I care."

"Don't say that! Even as a joke, Collie. It's not right. The Bible says we mustn't judge others."

Collie thought it best not to respond. He respected Robin's piety, even without sharing it. She was a modern rarity, a genuine old-fashioned "good girl". Knowing this made him feel very protective of her, since good girls seemed to be lightning rods for misfortune and calamity. After all, his sister Lissa had once been considered a good girl, too.

On a sudden impulse Collie reached into his pocket and pulled out the congressman's fifty-dollar tip. He held it out to Robin. "Here. This'll help make up for those jerks stiffing you."

Robin looked at the bill, astonished. "Collie! For goodness sake, I can't take that. Put it away."

"No, really. I want you to have it. It'll help pay for your school." He admired the way Robin was determinedly working her way through junior college. "C'mon, I know you can use it."

Robin's eyebrows rose. "That's not the point. I can earn my own way, thank you."

"Of course you can." Collie swallowed. "Look, Robin, I...God was very good to me tonight. Can't I share it with you?"

Robin studied his face for a moment. "All right, Collie. But only a loan, okay?"

"Sure. No hurry about paying me back, though." Collie handed her the fifty, which she carefully tucked into her purse.

"Thank you," said the girl. "You have a generous soul, Collie. Just like your mother." Robin's smooth features creased with concern. "Tell me, how is she doing? When I saw her in church she looked…I don't know, tired. Depressed. Like she's carrying some kind of burden."

"She is carrying one," Collie answered. "Being married to the Old Man is the worst burden I can think of. I wish she'd divorce his ugly… uh, butt."

"Your mother takes her marriage vows seriously, Collie. Not like most folks these days," said Robin. "You should be very proud of her for doing what's right."

"Is it right for her to stay miserable forever? How can that be what God wants?"

"I can't answer that." Robin shook her head. "I just know your mother is a godly woman, but something inside is really bothering her."

"She's been having pains in her stomach," Collie said. "She says it's something to do with going through…you know, the change."

Robin looked doubtful. "I don't think so. It's something else. Women can tell these things."

Collie didn't want to talk about Luanne anymore. He was worried enough about her as it was. "Well, Robin, you should go on home, and I better get to the Knights Inn. Mike can be pretty mean about showing up late." He paused, then: "I'm glad I got to talk to you."

"Me, too," said Robin, smiling at Collie in a way that made him suddenly forget about how much he loathed the Windfield creeps, and hated his Old Man, and missed his sister, and thought life sucked. A few dead leaves whirled about them in the deserted restaurant parking lot, making scratchy sounds on the pavement. The night wind carried an autumn chill, but Collie, looking into Robin's gentle brown eyes, felt cozy and warm inside. Maybe, he thought, there were some things in life that didn't suck after all.

—•《◉》•—

Luanne Skinner wiped her hands on a kitchen towel and peeked cautiously into the front room. Her husband lay passed out in the BarcaLounger, mouth open, his snores mingling with sports noise from the television. A few cold Tater Tots lay scattered on the stained carpet, and a Budweiser loosely clasped on his stomach rose and fell with every breath.

Luanne drew back and crept noiselessly to the bathroom. After closing and locking the door, she opened the under-sink compartment, which was jammed with assorted cleaning supplies, out-of-date grooming products, rolls of toilet paper, rust-streaked cans of Right Guard, and old toothbrushes with splayed bristles. Behind the bend of the sink trap was a large box of women's panty liners. Luanne carefully moved aside the clutter and drew it out. She saw that it hadn't been touched, which wasn't surprising, since Jay-Bo would sooner cut his throat than touch a box of panty liners.

Digging down past the top layers, Luanne drew forth a slim bound book. Stamped on the front cover was a shield of some sort and under it the words "Windfield College – Class of 1979."

Luanne sat on the worn linoleum floor and leaned back against the edge of the tub. She caressed the volume, running her fingers across the embossed words. Then she slowly spread apart the covers, and the book fell open to a certain place as if it had never been opened to any other, which it hadn't.

Bright young faces from a quarter-century ago filled the pages, but Luanne saw only one of them. A lump formed in her throat and her heart began to beat faster as she stared at the beautiful young man with the almost girlish looks. Full wavy hair falling down on both sides framed an impish smile. Even in black-and-white, his startling different eye colors were plainly evident. Underneath the photograph, a little box of text:

> Nicholas T. "Nick" Farrington; Born New York City, 1958.
> The Carleton School, class of 1975.
> Windfield College, 1979: Bachelor of Arts, English Literature.
> Gilbert & Sullivan society; Windfield Literati; Quadrangle Thespians.
> Career Goal: To be announced.
> Life's ambition: To have one.

Luanne held the open book to her breast, rocking slowly as tears leaked onto her cheeks from behind closed eyes.

"Nick," she wept, "Oh, Nick. He has no idea, but he's so much your son. And he's a good man, he has your heart. I think you would have loved him. Oh God, what did I do? I'm sorry, I'm so sorry."

Collie's mother cried and cried, crouched on the bathroom floor, the cold fluorescent light pitilessly highlighting the gray that streaked her hair.

⸺ ⦅◉⦆ ⸺

At the same time, some two hundred miles to the east, in a dark corner under the Ocean City, Maryland boardwalk, a beefy blonde man zipped up his pants as a young beach hustler climbed to his feet.

"Betcha liked that, huh?" Brushing sand from his knees, the kid grinned in the darkness. He was quite the expert at sucking off these lame pervs. It sure beat working. Now he could go score some Thai weed and spend the next day or so in a drugged stupor. Life was good. "That's fifty bucks, mister. A real bargain, doncha think?"

"Yeah, sure," replied the blonde man in a rough voice. He began to fumble in his pocket.

"C'mon, dude, I ain't got all night." The kid snapped his fingers and held out his hand. "Give it here."

"If you say so," said the blonde man, and smashed his fist into the kid's face with such force that he flew backwards several feet and lay motionless on the sand amidst the old cotton candy sticks and cigarette filters.

"Eat shit, you little faggot." The blonde man turned and picked his way among the creosote-covered pilings until he emerged back out onto the beach. Above, he could see lights and hear noises from the boardwalk. The summer season was long gone, but stragglers still came to stroll aimlessly and eat junk and waste money in the arcades. Until winter's freeze finally shut it down, Ocean City would keep flaunting its cheap pleasures like a painted whore on a street corner.

The blonde man walked along the beach until he came to an access stairway. He climbed up and bent his steps toward a seedy hangout known as the Chum Bucket Lounge. The bluish glare of the street-lights cast his sullen features into pasty relief. As the man walked along he shook his right hand to make sure nothing was broken, but it felt fine. An unpleasant smirk crossed his face. Even missing half a pinky, he could still punch out a queer's lights with one blow. Life was good.

Lloyd Skinner didn't notice the man in the brown leather jacket who followed at a discreet distance, watching his every move.

The yellowed wall clock showed one minute before eleven when Collie rushed through the back door of the Knights Inn Tavern. He quickly tied on a frayed apron and went out to the smoke-filled bar where, over a buzz of beery conversation, Leanne Rimes warbled about being blue.

"Cuttin' it close, Skinner," growled "Big Mike" Barlow. The saloon-keeper looked like a tattooed mountain bear. Everybody assumed he'd done prison time but no one was foolhardy enough to ask. Mike drew a frothy pitcher of beer from the tap and nodded toward a gloomy corner. "Take this to Deering and his boys."

"Right, Boss." Collie hefted the tray and wended his way among tables filled with local tradesmen, mechanics, and farmers. He returned a few nodded greetings and deposited the beer in front of Cal Deering, a venerable old-timer who managed the Stuarton Chevrolet dealership.

"We need a pizza." Cal Deering spoke around a Wolf Crook cigar, pouring beers for himself and his two sons, neither of whom looked like they needed anything except to lose a hundred pounds. "Bring us an extra large with sausage and onions, and no goddamn anchovies."

"Extra large sausage and onions, heavy on the anchovies," Collie repeated in a firm voice. "You got it, Mr. D." He sauntered away as Mr. Deering spluttered and pretended to be outraged. Good-natured joshing was an expected part of the Knights Inn atmosphere. After the formality of the posh restaurant Collie liked to come here and unwind. Unlike the Foxton Arms patrons the Knights Inn customers were ordinary folks. They didn't leave fifty-dollar tips, but Collie could appreciate a couple of bucks from a regular guy like Mr. Deering just as well as a hundred from some rich Middleville swell.

On his way to the kitchen Collie halted in dismay. Standing in the dart-playing alcove were the four Windfield students who'd earlier abused Robin. Jacketless, in rolled-up shirtsleeves, they laughed and took turns tossing the darts, exchanging high-fives and clinking their highball glasses after every shot.

Collie narrowed his eyes. It wasn't unheard-of for Windfield students to frequent the Knights Inn, although they mostly patronized the trendier Middleville pubs. But for whatever reason, the four musketeers had elected to show up here tonight.

As he slipped past them, averting his face, Collie heard one of them exclaim in a lilting taunt, "Pathetic toss, Phillip. Did anyone ever tell you that you throw like a girl?"

"Of course he does, silly," observed another. "He *is* a queen."

"Oh, no, you did *not* just call me a queen," retorted the one called Phillip in a prissy voice which Collie recognized as belonging to the tanned pretty boy. "Buy me another Tanqueray gimlet, you slut."

Back at the bar Collie muttered to Mike, "Did you see those damn Windfield fairies?"

Big Mike cast a disinterested glance at the chirruping dart players. "Their money's green. I ain't gonna stop 'em if they want to leave some of it here."

"But these guys are real pricks." Collie quickly told Mike how they'd mistreated Robin.

Big Mike shrugged. "So? They're lousy tippers. I don't give a shit. Never mind about them, Skinner. Get back to work."

Some time later Collie was carrying a couple of beers on his tray when he suddenly felt a painful sting at the base of his neck. Startled and hurt, he inadvertently jerked his tray and the beers fell to the floor in an explosion of suds. "Ow! Jesus! What the hell?" Wondering if he'd been stung by some nocturnal hornet he reached behind his head and with a yelp pulled loose a feathered steel dart. He stared at it in disbelief and rage as a voice behind him snickered, "Now look what you've done! Phillip, you ninny, don't you know that yokels are out of season?"

Collie whirled to see the four Windfield students trying, without success, to muffle their titters.

"Why, it's our ill-tempered friend from the restaurant," greeted Phillip the pretty boy, with a curl to his lip. "Oh, good, you found my dart. Give it here."

Collie saw red. In a flash he had the bigger man up against the wall, grasping him by the shirtfront, holding the dart up under his nose.

"How would you like to *eat* it, you pansy Windfield son of a b—"

"Back off, Skinner," Collie heard Big Mike say. "Now, boy. Get this mess wiped up."

Grudgingly Collie released his grasp on the other's shirt and took a step back. He realized he was still clutching the dart, and angrily slammed it down on a table. "The bastard did it on purpose, Big Mike! Damn right he did. Because of what happened at the restaurant."

"The boy is completely delusional," huffed Phillip. "He wasn't even our server."

"Go get the mop, Skinner. Move it." As soon as Collie was gone Mike addressed the Windfielders: "You boys need to call it a night. We're closin' up soon."

"But we haven't finished our drinks," objected Phillip. "Or our game."

"Yeah, you have." Big Mike jerked his head. "The door's over there."

Scowling, the Windfield foursome retrieved their jackets and filed out. The remaining customers shook their heads and exchanged low grumbles.

"Last call, folks," Mike announced, as Collie arrived and angrily began mopping up the spilled beer. His neck smarted and stung from the dart wound. He finished his cleaning and carried the pail and mop back to the utility sink. Dumping the filthy water, Collie felt drained and dispirited. The lift he'd gotten from talking with Robin Thompson was gone. Life was back to sucking again, and he doubted it would ever change. Not unless someone could figure out a way to make Windfield

College disappear.

With the last customer finally departed, Collie collected glasses, wiped tables, turned out lights and checked to make sure everything was locked up. Then he waved to Big Mike, who stood behind the bar, tallying up the night's take. "See y'later, Boss."

Mike grunted and went on counting. Collie closed the front door and headed across the darkened lot toward his Camaro. Reaching into his pocket for the car keys, he suddenly felt himself forcefully shoved from behind. He stumbled and fell, cutting his hands on the sharp gravel, and curled into a defensive crouch as a voice sneered: "All right, you cockeyed redneck, it's time for you to learn some manners."

Collie saw that he was surrounded by the four Windfield students. Phillip the pretty boy shook his head in disgust. "Did you really think I'd let you get away with putting your grubby hands on my shirt? It's from *Jos A. Bank*," he added, as if that explained everything. "You in-bred cretins need to be taught to respect your superiors." Pounding his fist into his hand: "Shall we proceed?"

Collie bounded to his feet and hurled a fistful of gravel straight at Phillip's head. The pretty boy howled, clawing at his face, and Collie unleashed a savage kick straight up into his groin. Phillip seemed to freeze for a second, then he violently threw up and collapsed, writhing and making gurgling noises.

Recovering from their surprise, the remaining three Windfielders charged. Collie managed to land one hard blow and felt something crunch, but then his feet were knocked out and he went down again. Knowing he couldn't fight three at once, Collie tightened himself into an armadillo-like ball, trying to protect his head from the vicious kicks. He could hear his attackers grunting and cursing, and wondered if he was really going to be stomped to jelly in the Knights Inn lot by some drunken Windfield homos. It was a dreadful thought.

He absorbed a ferocious boot to his ear that left him dazed. Then from out of the darkness came a sudden rumbling snarl: "*Get away from there.*" It was followed by the ominous click of a firearm trigger being cocked. "Don't make me tell you again."

The kicking ceased. Collie relaxed his tense body, trying to assess any damage. He slowly sat up and saw Big Mike pointing the largest handgun he'd ever seen at the Windfielders, who goggled at it in disbelieving shock.

"Seems to me like I already done told you boys to go home. I ain't big on repeatin' myself, see? Now get lost." Mike made a shooing motion with the gun barrel, which looked as big as a pipe bomb. "Don't let me catch you in my establishment again. Skinner, you okay?"

Collie scrambled to his feet. "Yeah, Boss," he answered, picking small bloody bits of grit from his palms. "Not a scratch."

The three who'd attacked Collie helped Phillip stand up. The pretty boy's fancy shirt was streaked with puke and gravel dust. He aimed a look of pure hate at Collie, then hobbled after the others and climbed into a silver BMW. Big Mike kept his pistol trained on them until the car started up and drove into the night, fishtailing slightly on the loose surface.

"I'm sorry about that, Big Mike," said Collie. "I didn't start it. Damn chickenshits jumped me..."

The owner snorted and uncocked the gun. "Hell, Skinner, I prob'ly shouldn't've rescued 'em, just let you finish the job."

Collie nodded, unsmiling. "I'd like to beat the shit out of every last one. I hate that goddamn Windfield."

Big Mike inclined his head at Collie's nearby Camaro. "Go home, Skinner. Enough fun for one night. Git."

He watched his employee climb into the old car and steer out of the lot. When Collie disappeared from sight the big man went inside to resume skimming the till. Although his customers had always assumed that Mike owned the Knights Inn, he did not. The true proprietor was a secretive tycoon with a reputation for being merciless and unforgiving. But Mike Barlow didn't care. He wasn't afraid of anybody.

It was an arrogance which would, in time, prove to be of fateful import.

Chapter Three
School of Controversy

Unlike most institutions of higher learning, Windfield College had its genesis not in time-honored gentlemanly academe, or solemn theological seminary studies, or agricultural research. It owed its existence to an eruption of livid homophobia. The circumstances surrounding this unique fact were already the stuff of legend, and for a relatively new school –the college opened its doors in 1969– Windfield had already provoked a remarkable amount of consternation among its detractors and an equal measure of delight among its proponents.

For generations and generations, stretching back to the earliest days of the commonwealth, the Windfields had been one of Northern Virginia's most prominent families. It all started when a hard-edged adventurer named Silas Windfield laid claim to as much of the rich rolling farmland as he could defend with his musket. Laying the foundation for a family tradition of ruthlessness, old Silas prospered like mad, aggressively farming the land and growing ever more powerful and rich. After he died his heirs continued to thrive, acquiring more and more of the surrounding countryside. In due course the Windfields became slave owners, and on the sweat of those unfortunates became enormously wealthy. The Civil War put a temporary crimp in their fortunes, but they quickly made up for their losses by expanding into armaments and coal. They made money hand over fist during World War One, wisely left the stock market to the city-dwelling suckers and breezed through the Depression.

As World War Two threatened civilization, patriarch-in-waiting Hendrix Windfield III made use of his engineering degree from the University of Virginia to patent a clever gizmo which quadrupled the efficacy of incendiary bombs. He patriotically sold it to the U.S. military for a titanic sum, thereby vaulting the Windfields to billionaire status. When his invention helped reduce Dresden and other European cities to hot gray powder, he celebrated by erecting an immodest replica of England's famed Belton House on a hillside overlooking the vast family domain.

After the war Hendrix fathered three children: Hendrix IV, known as "Drix", Susannah, and Randall; who, in the process of being born, somehow got turned got sideways in his mother Jeanette's womb and killed her. For the most part ignored by their tycoon daddy, the motherless young Windfields were raised by servants in southern opulence and splendor. Eventually they developed distinct personalities: Drix IV exhibited a precocious talent for drinking himself blind. Susannah, who was unluckily plain for a billionaire heiress, fretted constantly about being overweight, threw up everything she ate, and agonized that suitors would never be interested in anything but her money. Only Randall seemed relatively well-adjusted, although he showed little interest in the usual male Windfield pastimes such as fox-hunting, skeet-shooting, and riding steeplechase, preferring instead to read, paint, and spend time tending his prize hybrid tea bushes in the magnificent rose garden. When Randall elected to attend Berkeley instead of following Drix and Susannah to the University of Virginia, Hendrix III was apoplectic. In his view it was practically an act of treason for any southern gentleman to set foot in –let alone attend– a college like Berkeley. The old man seriously considered disowning Randall for having the impertinence to choose such a seditious rat's nest of druggies, darkies, and deviants.

But he had a problem. Of his three children, only Randall showed any potential at all. Hendrix IV was a reckless gambling souse. Susannah was a hopeless neurotic, addicted to Elvis and Ex-Lax. Only Randall, levelheadedly studying business and economics, seemed likely to develop the managerial acumen necessary to run the family empire. So, trusting that the Spirit of the South would in time restore his youngest son to sanity, Hendrix III looked forward to the day when Randall would return to the Old Dominion, take up the family banner, and carry on the Windfield tradition.

At Berkeley Randall excelled in his studies while enjoying the laid-back California existence, and didn't let himself get sucked up in the war protests and political brouhaha. Most importantly, after enjoying a few unexpected relationships with other young men, he came to the realization that he was not only gay, but very happily so. Refusing to remain closeted like so many of the others, he frankly embraced the lifestyle, began calling himself Randy, moved in with a boyfriend, had a wonderful senior year, was elected to Phi Beta Kappa, and graduated magna cum laude.

Returning to Virginia after his graduation, Randall was determined to tell his family the truth. He anticipated a very strained –doubtless heated– confrontation, especially with the old man; nonetheless, strongly believing that he was entitled to live his life as he chose, he refused to be cowed or demoralized by his family's narrow-mindedness.

But Hendrix Windfield had already gotten word about "Randy's" lifestyle. At a lavish lawn party the afternoon of his return, his father, under pretense of offering him a congratulatory toast, suddenly hurled the wine in Randall's face. As the guests stared in wide-eyed shock, Hendrix Windfield III unloosed a blistering verbal tirade, excoriating his youngest child as a cocksucker, a vile pervert, a goddamned Sodomite. He raged and cursed, his face a deep plum color, screeching that Randall had brought shame on his family, his friends, his church, his country, and all decent people in the Commonwealth of Virginia. After several minutes of this, during which his son stood unmoving, tears and champagne trickling down his face, the old man concluded by yelling that Randall was disowned, cast out, never allowed to set foot on the property again. Two robust groundskeepers were assigned to escort the young man to the front gate, which they did in terrible silence, slowly disappearing down the hill as the assembled company exchanged furtive glances and whispers.

Within the hour a tempest of tongue-wagging heated up every telephone line within twenty miles as those lucky enough to have witnessed the event recounted lurid details to those who had not. It was generally agreed that this stunning Windfield drama constituted the most spectacular scandal in recent memory. Speculation grew feverish as to what would happen next.

But of all the hypothesized scenarios, none came remotely close to predicting what actually occurred.

On the morning following the debacle, Hendrix III, Drix and Susannah boarded their new Beech King Air for a flight to Long Island, to watch the running of the Belmont Stakes. Not long after takeoff, the twin-engine aircraft went into an out-of-control spin and spiraled down, crashing into the waters of the Prettyboy Reservoir north of Baltimore. The pilot, executive secretary and all three Windfields were killed instantly.

An investigation by the newly-formed National Transportation Safety Board was able to determine that something, most likely a liquid, had shorted out certain critical avionics packages in the cockpit, leading to a loss of control. The exact nature of the liquid couldn't be verified, but the guess was an alcoholic beverage of some sort, since a silver mint julep cup had been found wedged behind one of the rudder pedals. The crash was ruled a preventable, and therefore especially unfortunate, accident.

The untimely demise of Hendrix III and two of his children left the family empire without a leader. The old man had been an absolute despot, retaining all executive power to himself and delegating only administrative work to his army of subordinates. There remained but one logical candidate to assume control: his sole surviving heir, Randall. But as everyone within a hundred square miles well knew, Randall had been publicly disgraced and thrown out of the family.

Except, as it turned out, he hadn't. Not officially. The necessary papers, although ready and waiting on his desk, hadn't yet been signed by the family patriarch. He'd meant to finalize the decrees upon his return from the horse race; but a spilled mint julep had prevented that. So, incredible as it seemed, in less than twenty-four hours Randall Windfield had gone from being an exiled pariah to a billionaire tycoon.

After the funerals, which Randall attended looking somber but dry-eyed, he directed one of the senior managers to look after things for a while, and vanished. No one knew where he had gone, or what his plans were. This mysterious disappearance supercharged the gossip mill to previously unheard-of levels. In the absence of any facts, endless rumors –some of them quite fantastic– popped up, were discarded, and popped up again. Most of these speculative scenarios had Randall squandering the Windfield fortune to construct a homosexual pleasure dome in some degenerate foreign country, where he and his fellow deviants would spend their days taking pleasure in unspeakable depravities that would put the antics of Emperor Tiberius to shame. It was an altogether appalling prospect, and eagerly anticipated.

But when Randall Windfield finally resurfaced and made known his true plans, the scandal-mongers were more aghast than if he really had commissioned a queer Xanadu. To their horror he proclaimed that the entire Windfield fortune was being liquidated. The proceeds, expected to be in excess of a billion dollars, would be used to establish a brand-new four-year institute of higher education. The new school would be built on the grounds of the former estate, which he was donating, and would be known as Windfield College. Randall intended it to be patterned after the most progressive colleges in the country, places such as Reed, Sarah Lawrence, Oberlin, Bryn Mawr and the like. It would be a forward-looking bastion of modern education, where open-mindedness and freedom of thought would be taught and encouraged. Windfield College's colors would be pink and black, and its motto would be a quote from Seneca: *TIMENDI CAUSA EST NESCIRE* (Ignorance is the cause of fear.) In short, Randall Windfield's seditious purpose was to erect, for all time, a living monument to *tolerance* on the bones of his dead father's heritage.

This announcement touched off a hue-and-cry of epic proportions. Local officials huddled, trying to find a way to stop the crazy homo's radical atrocity. Various *ad hoc* citizen groups held meetings, but accomplished little beyond a lot of impotent shouting. A few hastily-cobbled lawsuits were filed, only to be steamrollered by Randall's well-paid phalanx of elite Yankee attorneys. The protests and legal actions continued even as ground-breaking got under way, but they all met the same fate as a weevil under a combine.

Construction took two years, during which time Robert Kennedy and Martin Luther King were murdered, America's great cities were convulsed by race riots, Richard Nixon narrowly defeated Hubert Humphrey, the Vietnam conflict extinguished lives by the thousands, Neil Armstrong walked on the moon, the Woodstock concert defined a generation, and in New York's Greenwich Village the so-called Stonewall Riots marked the beginnings of the Gay Movement.

Windfield College officially opened its doors in the autumn of 1969. Amidst the spectacular colors of a Northern Virginia autumn, four hundred pioneering students and faculty took up residence. They were warmly welcomed by President Randall Windfield in the brand-new auditorium. In his speech, he thanked and congratulated them for having the courage and foresight to come share in his dream of a brighter future, one where all people, regardless of their differences, would respect each other and live in peace.

In the ensuing years, the college grew and prospered. Applications increased, enrollment grew, and the faculty attracted many defectors from other fine schools, drawn by the excellent pay, academic freedom and highly motivated student body. In time, Windfield graduates began to make their mark in the arts, in business, and especially in the dawning world of information technology, thanks to Windfield's cutting-edge computer center.

Randall Windfield served as president for four years, then resigned. Although extremely proud of the college which bore his name, as time passed he maintained an ever-lower profile, preferring to let the school find its own direction. In 1982, he suddenly fell ill with a strange pneumonia, and shortly afterward died, one of the early victims of the AIDS epidemic. With Randall's death, the Windfield line started by old Silas came to an end.

Although everyone associated with the college mourned his passing, many others didn't grieve at all. A great deal of entrenched antagonism toward the school continued to flourish in the vicinity, and many a beer was hoisted to commemorate the death of "that goddamn Windfield faggot", whose treachery had earned him a just retribution.

As the years passed, the antipathy between the college and the surrounding residents did not lessen. Windfield attracted a lot of smart but egotistical students, who tended to scorn a native populace they regarded as ignorant parochial rednecks. For their part, the local inhabitants felt occupied by an army of sneering immoral punks. There were periodic clashes, incidents, fights and confrontations. Perhaps the most notorious of these occurred when a State Trooper named James Skinner caught a Windfield sophomore smoking marijuana in some rich person's horse pasture and beat him into a near-fatal coma. The subsequent trial resulted in a hung jury, but anger and hatred on both sides lingered and festered. Randall Windfield had hoped that his school would pave the way for those of dissimilar backgrounds to live amicably together; but after more than thirty years, the fact was that Windfield College had arguably the worst town-gown relationship in the country.

———◦((◦))◦———

Joanne Markwith looked up at the tall well-dressed woman who had just walked into the English Department's reception area. "Hello, may I help you?"

"Good afternoon," greeted the woman in a husky contralto voice. "My name is Nickie Farrell. I believe I have a two o'clock appointment with Dr. Silverman?"

Jo (nobody ever referred to her as Joanne) checked her appointment book, and smiled at the newcomer. "Yes, you do. I'll let Dr. Silverman know you're here." She picked up her phone, hit a button. "Nickie Farrell is here to see you. Okay, I'll tell her." She replaced the receiver. "He'll be with you in a few minutes. Can I get you something to drink, Ms. Farrell? Coffee? A soda?"

The other woman politely declined the offer, and sat down to wait. Precisely crossing her long legs, she opened her cordovan attaché case, took out a hardcover book, and began to read.

The secretary pretended to focus on her computer screen, meanwhile furtively checking out Nickie Farrell. Jo's gay radar was picking up inconsistent signals, but in any case she liked what she saw. Ms. Farrell was a handsome forty-something lady with a clearly-defined jaw, high cheekbones, and a still-youthful complexion. Her eyes were obscured behind fashionably outsized sunglasses which had been tinted in unusual sunset hues of lavender, coral and pink. Long wavy red hair was combed back from her forehead and secured with a tortoiseshell band. Her outfit, a dark green blazer over a white silk turtleneck with pleated gray skirt and matching pumps, was perhaps a bit prim if not severe; but Jo didn't mind at all. Prim could be mighty sexy under the right circumstances, especially with legs like *that*. Ms. Farrell wore minimal makeup and no jewelry except for some pearl stud earrings and a small enamel hummingbird brooch on her lapel. Jo Markwith gratefully noted the absence of any wedding rings on Nickie's slender fingers. Of course there was no telling if Ms. Farrell was a lesbian sister, but it didn't seem out of the question.

At that moment Nickie glanced up from her book and caught Joanne Markwith looking. She lifted one eyebrow and faintly smiled.

Busted! Jo covered her chagrin by saying, "I love your glasses. Never seen any like that before. Very unique."

"Oh, thanks." With a little laugh: "They're an extravagance, but what can I say? I'm a pushover for accessories." She returned her attention to her book.

After a few moments, the phone buzzer sounded. Jo said, "Dr. Silverman will see you now, Ms. Farrell." She indicated a nearby entryway. "Right through there."

Nickie put away her book, stood and smoothed her skirt. "Well! Wish me luck."

"Not to worry," replied Jo, with a wink. To her delight Ms. Farrell returned her a mischievous grin, then disappeared through the doorway leading to Larry Silverman's office.

"Woo-hoo!" Jo giggled to herself, and went back to the computer.

Larry Silverman, the chairman of Windfield's English department, leaned back in his swivel chair and ran a palm across his bald pate. This was probably going to be a waste of time, but it was Larry's responsibility to explore all possible angles. He brought the chair forward as a knock sounded at his door.

"Come on in!"

He rose and came around from behind his desk as Nickie Farrell entered the office. His mood at once improved, as it always did around attractive women. He extended his hand.

"Ms. Farrell, I'm Larry Silverman. It's a pleasure to meet you. Thanks for coming on such short notice."

Nickie Farrell gave him a firm handshake. "Thank you for asking me, Dr. Silverman. I'm most appreciative."

"Not at all," said the chairman. "I apologize for the disarray," he waved his hands around at the cluttered office. "Start of the new semester, total chaos, you know how it is. Please, have a seat."

Ms. Farrell sat very straight in the wooden chair facing his desk, hands folded in her lap, knees and ankles together.

Well, thought the chairman, she's got the right look for a college instructor. He cleared his throat. "Now, as I told you on the phone, Ms. Farrell, we're in a bit of a bind here. One of our professors has unfortunately been stricken with a nasty cancer, and must take a prolonged leave of absence to undergo treatment. Of course we're all pulling for him, but obviously he won't be able to teach class for a while. We could cancel his courses, but we'd rather not do that if we can find someone to take over for a while."

Nickie Farrell nodded. "I understand."

"Our problem is," continued Silverman, "the semester's already begun. Most of the possible substitutes are already fully committed."

"Most," repeated Ms. Farrell with a slight smile, "but not all?"

Larry Silverman picked a folder up from his desk. "As it happened, we had your application in our files. I've been going over your CV. I must say, Ms. Farrell, it's somewhat out of the ordinary. I hope you don't mind, but I've already spoken with Dr. Martin over at Maryland. Don't worry, he was extremely complimentary, said your doctoral thesis was outstanding, if a bit incendiary. Apparently you caused something of a stir on the committee, defending Booth Tarkington from charges of racism in the Penrod trilogy."

Nickie Farrell smiled. "I imagine so. But someone had to do it. Tarkington has been unfairly vilified."

Silverman pursed his lips over the folder. "Prior to receiving your PhD, you were a writer for a soap opera?"

"That's right." Nickie brushed a stray hair back behind her ear. "Pure nepotism, Dr. Silverman. My father was involved with the production, and, well, you know how it goes. I wrote excruciating dialogue for the better part of a decade, and made a disgraceful amount of money. *Mea culpa!*" She shrugged. "That's one reason I went back to school and got a doctorate. Since my soap writing undoubtedly contributed to the overall decline of civilization, I hoped to repair some of the damage by teaching English Lit."

"I see." The chairman put down the folder, and picked up an onyx-handled letter opener. Tapping it against his palm: "I notice a number of intervening years between the television job and your doctoral studies. Were you not employed?"

After a tiny pause Ms. Farrell said, "I went through a difficult emotional time, Dr. Silverman. Family issues, psychological counseling. Took a while to resolve, but it's behind me now."

"Good, good. Well, in terms of the academic requirements I don't doubt that you could handle Hal's classes. Would you be averse to following his syllabus?"

"I'd prefer to chart my own curriculum, if possible. Within your departmental guidelines, of course."

Silverman nodded. "That can be arranged. Now, Ms. Farrell, I must ask you a somewhat...well, awkward question. May I?"

Nickie Farrell's face took on a guarded look. "By all means."

"It states in your application that you are a graduate of Windfield College. Class of 1979, I believe. Is that correct?"

"Yes, sir."

The chairman put down the letter opener. "I don't exactly know how to put this. To be blunt, there is no documentation of a Nickie Farrell in that class, or any other. We have gone over our records very thoroughly." His voice took on an edge. "If you know of a reason why this discrepancy exists, I'd like to hear it."

Nickie Farrell dropped her gaze for a moment, as if gathering her thoughts. Then she removed her sunset-colored glasses and looked directly at the chairman. "Dr. Silverman, is this conversation going to remain confidential?"

"Why, why...yes, absolutely." Larry Silverman was momentarily thrown off balance by the woman's remarkable eyes, which were of two different colors. "You may speak freely, Ms. Farrell."

"All right. In fact, I did graduate with the class of 1979. The reason there's no record…"

As she continued to speak, the chairman listened with growing amazement until at length he sat unmoving in his chair, gazing at Ms. Nickie Farrell in numb astonishment.

※

Joanne Markwith turned in her chair as Larry Silverman and Nickie Farrell emerged from his office. Ms. Farrell was all smiles, but Jo thought her boss looked a bit dazed.

The chairman said, "Jo, I'm pleased to say that Ms. Farrell is going to be joining the faculty. Would you be kind enough to begin the necessary paperwork? We'll need to get this done as quickly as possible."

"Right away, Dr. Silverman." Jo smiled at Nickie, her hazel eyes shining. "Welcome aboard, Ms. Farrell! If there's anything you need, just ask. I'll be more than glad to help."

"Please, call me Nickie. And thanks so much, I can't tell you how happy I am. It's like coming home, after all these years." The new assistant professor shook the chairman's hand. "Dr. Silverman, thank you for giving me this opportunity. I won't let you or the students down. Goodbye."

When the office door closed, Jo Markwith addressed her boss with a familiar grin. "Wow. I *like* her!"

"Do you?" Larry Silverman rubbed his forehead. "Jo, would you please bring me some coffee in my office?"

A minute later Jo placed a steaming Windfield mug on the chairman's desk. He sat tilted back in his chair, gazing out the high bay window at a broad courtyard which fronted the building. Students strolled singly or in groups along the crisscrossing walkways, where beds of late-season mums added an extra accent of color to the autumn foliage. Windfield College was always beautiful, no matter the season.

"Your coffee, sir," said Jo. "Will there be anything else?"

Larry Silverman hesitated. "Listen, if I tell you something, will you promise to keep it under your hat?"

"Why, Dr. Silverman. Don't I always?"

"All right. The thing is, about Ms. Farrell...you'll never believe this, but..."

As Jo Markwith listened her mouth fell open. "Are you serious? Good God! I never would have...She doesn't...I mean, holy *shit*."

The chairman of the English department solemnly nodded and took a sip of his coffee. "Inelegantly stated, Jo, but my sentiments exactly."

———————

Emerging into the late afternoon light, Nickie Farrell stopped and breathed deeply of the country air. How well she remembered that autumn smell! She stood on the stone steps, caught in memories of her own undergraduate years. From what Nickie could see Windfield hadn't changed very much. Several academic facilities and residence halls had been added along with a magnificent new theater, but for the most part it was still the same lovely campus. Three students walked by, chattering and laughing, as blithe and carefree as Nickie had been at their age. Watching them, she was suddenly chilled by an awareness of time's inexorable passage. Where had all the years gone?

"Quit your moaning," she reproached herself in a soft voice. "Like you'd really want to turn back the clock?" She gave her head a rueful shake. "Not even maybe."

Besides, she thought, setting out on the stone path, things really couldn't get much better. She'd been hired as an assistant professor at her own alma mater! Of course teaching was an awesome responsibility, but Nickie had worked diligently to prepare herself and now she couldn't wait to get started. Maybe she had finally discovered her niche, her purpose in life. After everything she'd been through, wouldn't it be wonderful to be at peace with herself and the world?

"Please," she silently prayed. "Let it be so."

The walkway skirted the edge of an expansive grassy hill which sloped from the old Windfield estate house down to massive stone gates framing the campus entrance. In the middle of the broad lawn a simple flower bed surrounded a small obelisk dedicated to the memory of Randall Windfield. Nickie had actually met the school's legendary founder once at a student gathering, and shaken his hand. But she couldn't remember any more than that because she'd been roaring drunk at the time. Nickie glumly stared at the distant memorial. Sometimes it was hard to believe that she had survived so many years of despair.

Turning toward the visitor's parking lot, Nickie found herself crossing the area known as Randall Quad, where every springtime the commencement ceremonies were held. She slowed, recalling her own graduation on that vanished springtime day: the bleachers filled with proud parents and friends fanning themselves with pink-and-black programs; the cap-and-gowned seniors stifling in the humid Virginia sunshine but too excited to care; the stage with its tables full of beribboned diplomas and academic trophies; the music piped over loudspeakers; the incessant click and clack of camera shutters.

A small stone bench beside the path caught her eye. Nickie put her attaché case down and slowly sat. She ran her hand along the weathered seat, remembering how she had stationed herself on this very bench, desperately scanning the crowd again and again, searching for the only face she wanted to see, gradually losing hope. She had gone through the graduation ceremony, received her diploma, flipped her tassel and dutifully smiled for the family photos, all the while feeling heartbroken and downcast. Overwhelmed by the memories, she hung her head.

"Ma'am? Are you not feeling well?"

Startled, Nickie looked up. A tall heavyset man with broad shoulders stood in the pathway. He had an appealing ruddy-cheeked face, lively blue eyes, a neatly-trimmed white beard, and a full head of snowy hair. Setting his old-fashioned briefcase down on the path, the man turned his palms out. "I do apologize if I alarmed you, ma'am. Please forgive me."

"No, no, I was just...woolgathering," Nickie said. "Really, there's no need to apologize." She pulled a tissue from her purse and touched her eyes.

"Woolgathering?" He smiled. "I haven't heard that in a while. Wonderful expression, isn't it? I'm Alex Steward. I teach English here at the college."

"Oh? That's too funny." Nickie thought the man looked like a cross between Kenny Rogers and Santa Claus. "As of a few minutes ago, so do I. My name's Nickie Farrell." She held out her hand. "I'm pleased to meet you, Professor Steward."

Kenny Klaus politely shook her hand. "Please, Ms. Farrell, call me Alex. Only the kids call me Professor Steward. Especially when they're begging for a deadline extension."

Nickie smiled. "I used to do that all the time. All right, Alex it is. And you'll call me Nickie, okay?"

"I'd be delighted to," replied Alex Steward. He pointed at the bench. "May I?"

Nickie made room and Alex sat next to her. "So, you've joined our merry band?"

Nickie nodded. "Yes. I'm to fill in for one of your colleagues, who's been taken ill."

"Hal Whitman. A terrible shame." Alex Steward looked grim. "Pancreatic cancer. Hal's a fighter, but he'll need a big helping hand from Providence, I'm afraid."

"I hope he gets it," said Nickie. "I'd much rather he got well than have his teaching position."

"You mean that?"

"Absolutely. I've no desire to benefit from the misfortune of others."

"Nowadays that rather puts you in the minority," Alex Steward observed. "You're an unusual woman."

"I've been told that before."

They sat silent for a moment. To her surprise Nickie found herself feeling a little bashful. Alex Steward seemed very…nice.

"What sort of courses do you teach, Alex?"

"Well, I try my best to impart an appreciation for the great British writers. Scott, Fielding, Richardson, and of course all the Victorian masters. I'm a bit nutty about Mr. Dickens."

"Oh, so am I!" Nickie enthused. "I love Dickens. Especially *Martin Chuzzlewit* and *Our Mutual Friend*…" Seeing Alex's wide grin, she dropped her eyes and blushed. "Geez, I sound like one of your sophomore girls."

"Don't I wish!" Alex laughed. "Hal Whitman teaches American Lit. Is that what you're going to cover?"

Nickie nodded. "Cooper, Melville, Hawthorne, Twain of course, and Booth Tarkington. I'm a bit nutty about *him*. And maybe Thurber and Clarence Day, if I can squeeze them in."

Alex Steward's eyes grew bright. "Wow! Clarence Day. Gosh, I almost envy your students."

"Let's hope they don't all run in the opposite direction. This is my first teaching position, you know. I'm as nervous as that long-tailed cat in a room full of rocking chairs."

Alex gave her hand a tiny pat. "I wouldn't worry too much, Nickie. I have a feeling they're going to love you. The students here are a joy. Well, mostly," he added with a chuckle.

"I know," said Nickie. "I was one of them." Seeing the other's puzzlement she added, "I went to Windfield, Alex."

"Did you really?"

"Yes. And I won't tell you when because then you'll know how old I am," Nickie laughed, "but I used to see dinosaurs running through Randall Quad."

Alex Steward threw back his head and chortled. "I love that!" He paused. "Ms. Farrell...Nickie, would you care to join me for a cup of coffee?"

"That would be nice, Alex, but it's a long drive into D.C. and I really should be going." Nickie stood up. "Rain check on the coffee?"

"As many as you want," Alex assured her. "May I walk you to your car?"

"I'd like that."

Setting behind the distant Blue Ridge Mountains to the west, the sun illuminated high cirrus clouds with a rosy tint, turning them into long pink sky feathers as Nickie and Alex made their way to the parking lot. They could hear laughter and music coming from the dorms, while a group of Windfield boys chased a Frisbee through the gathering twilight, shouting youthful taunts.

"Well," Nickie said, "here's my ride." She pressed her key pad and the door locks of her Honda Accord popped up with an obliging *blunk!* "Thank you for walking with me, Alex."

"It's been my pleasure," he emphasized, his blue eyes twinkling. "I'm so glad to have met you." He hesitated, then extended his hand.

Nickie shook it, then impulsively gave him a quick hug. "I'll be seeing you soon," she promised, "and I definitely want that coffee." As she tucked herself into the car her skirt rose, but she didn't immediately pull it down, and was rewarded by seeing Alex's admiring perusal of her stockinged thigh.

"Don't forget your seatbelt." Alex Steward held the door, reluctant to close it. "Promise you'll drive carefully? These country roads can be tricky, especially after dark."

"Oh, right. I don't suppose I need these any more." Nickie removed her colored glasses and smiled up at Alex. "I'll be careful, I promise."

He frankly stared, enthralled by her mismatched eyes. She let him look for a long moment then said, "I'd better go."

"What? Oh, yes, of course. Well, goodnight." He swallowed and closed the door.

With a final wave, she started the car and drove out of the lot. In her rear-view mirror she could see Alex Steward standing, briefcase in hand, watching her leave. Next to him a tall lamppost blinked to life.

Nickie glanced down at her hemline, still hitched high, and exclaimed out loud, "Are you proud of yourself? Acting like a forty-eight-year-old coquette. Oh, puh-*leez!* "

Still, she couldn't deny that Professor Steward's obvious admiration had given her a most agreeable feeling. Having men pay attention to her hadn't yet lost its novelty. But she needed to remain cautious for a host of reasons. Even minor flirting with Alex was probably imprudent.

Her cell phone suddenly began playing its electronic version of Ravel's "Bolero". Keeping an eye on the serpentine road, she blindly plucked it out of her purse: "Hello? This is Nickie."

"Hey, Nickie. This is Jo Markwith. From Dr. Silverman's office?"

"Oh, yes. Hello, Jo." Nickie felt a tickle of anxiety. "What's up? Please don't tell me he's changed his mind?"

"Gosh, no." She heard Jo laugh. "Don't worry. We're all very excited that you're joining us. In fact Dr. Silverman spoke with Fredericka Lindsey after you left, and she's anxious to meet you, too."

Now why, Nickie wondered, would the president of Windfield College be anxious to meet a lowly substitute English professor?

"Anyway, the reason I called, hon, I wanted to tell you again that if I can be of any help, anything at *all*, I'm just a phone call away. You know, finding a place to stay, getting settled in, sorting out the departmental stuff…whatever you need. Okay?"

"That's very thoughtful of you," replied Nickie as she maneuvered the Accord around a dark curve.

"My pleasure. When you come back, Nickie, how about we grab a cup of coffee or something? I'd really like to get to know you better. You seem like such an…interesting gal."

Immediately Nickie's instinct flashed a red alert: *She knows.* Dr. Silverman might have said something or conceivably she figured it out by herself, but Jo Markwith *knew.*

Damn!

Of course Nickie understood that it would all come out sooner or later, but maybe Jo could be persuaded to keep mum for a while, at least until Nickie got settled into her new position.

"Yes, that sounds fine. Jo, I'd better drive with two hands, this road is really twisty. Do you mind?"

"Oh, no, not at all. You take care, girlfriend. I'll see you soon, okay?"

"For sure. Bye-bye." Nickie closed her phone and dropped it in her purse as the little car drove on into the blackness, its twin headlight beams piercing the silent Virginia night.

Chapter Four
The Patriot

From the window of his walnut-paneled study on the top floor of an imperial fieldstone manor, a silver-haired elderly man wearing an eye patch glowered from one battleship-gray eye out into the darkness, following the far-off lights of a lone vehicle as it drove through the darkness. His face, carved into cruel lines from nearly eight decades of misanthropy, tightened into a mask of hatred. Coming from the damned college, he thought. With luck they'd end up in a ditch somewhere. As far as former United States Ambassador Eamon Douglass was concerned, anybody who had anything to do with that accursed place deserved whatever calamity befell them.

He let the heavy burgundy drapes fall back into place. Clutching a polished black thorn-wood shillelagh in one hand, he walked over to an antique mahogany desk set before a cavernous fireplace. Seasoned hardwood logs crackled in flames, scenting the room with wood smoke. The ambassador plucked up a medical report which lay on the green blotter, scanned it, then threw it down in disgust.

Goddamn pusillanimous doctors! Douglass would have preferred if they'd given it to him straight, man-to-man: "Ambassador, we regret to say that you are irrevocably fucked." That, he could have tolerated. Instead they'd subjected him to an hour of convoluted oncological gobbledygook about stage four this and pain management that until he felt like strangling them all. Spineless idiots! Did they think he was afraid of dying? Hell, everybody had to die sometime. His number had finally come up, and that was that. Damned if he'd snivel and whine and wring his hands. If necessary he'd end his own life before letting those parasites have their way.

Eamon Douglass went to a wheeled antique serving cart, poured himself a shot of sour mash whiskey from a crystal decanter and downed it. He was a reclusive feared tycoon, with no wife or children to mourn his passing. Not that he gave a damn. The ambassador knew he was regarded as an anachronism. Old-fashioned patriotic gentlemen such as himself were rudely mocked as quaint museum pieces while the world became overrun with Negroes, Jews, homosexuals and women. The way things were going, the entire planet would soon be one gargantuan version of Windfield College.

The ambassador went to the window and again drew aside the drapes. A gauzy glow emanating from the distant campus filled him with bitterness, as it had for the past thirty-six years. Windfield College was a pustular blemish on the face of his noble Virginia. The fact that it bore the name of his lost friend was even more unbearable. Eamon Douglass had been among the guests the day Hendrix III exposed his youngest son as a pervert. As Randall was being marched away Eamon had caught the father's eye and raised his champagne flute in a salute of approval, never imagining that the elder Windfield would shortly lie dead at the bottom of the Prettyboy Reservoir. And then the staggering gall of that presumptuous little fairy! Obliterating a noble family tradition, erecting a liberal snake pit nobody wanted, and adopting the motto *TIMENDI CAUSA EST NESCIRE* with its transparent insinuation that normal decent citizens were bigoted peasants like the mob in *Frankenstein*.

Ambassador Douglas clenched his teeth, dropped the drapes and moved to a deep red leather armchair by the fire. He stared over the gnarled head of his cane at the dancing flames, brooding. The medical nitwits wanted him to undergo radiation therapy. When he'd asked if it would do any good, they'd hemmed and hawed and said they couldn't guarantee anything. They did admit, however, that he would likely lose his hair, his appetite, his continence, maybe even his ability to think as he was cooked by the gamma rays, or x-rays, or whatever infernal rays they used. Well, he refused to play lab rat to their god complexes. He'd die as he chose here at his beloved Shamrocks, and those quacks could all go to blazes. If they wanted to fry a cancer, they could turn their ray guns on Windfield College.

Suddenly, the ambassador's single eye opened a little wider. The firelight reflected in his gray iris as he sat motionless, a vein in his temple twitching. His bony fingers drummed a tattoo on the leather arm of his chair, then suddenly stopped and formed a fist.

"By Christ," he muttered, "that would do it." His thin lips curled into a malevolent grin. "They'd never recover. And what a way to go! Quite a suitable epitaph for me, I should think. But how?"

He frowned in thought for a moment, then went to a wall of books and pulled out a heavy leather-bound copy of Tolstoy's *War and Peace*. He carried it to his desk and began riffling the pages. After a moment a small slip of paper fell onto the desk top. The ambassador picked it up. Written in black ink was the word "Volka", followed by a telephone number.

"*Gaspadin* Volka," Eamon Douglass smiled. "It's been much too long. Egor Antonovich, we must talk."

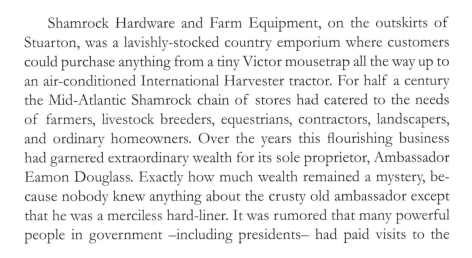

Shamrock Hardware and Farm Equipment, on the outskirts of Stuarton, was a lavishly-stocked country emporium where customers could purchase anything from a tiny Victor mousetrap all the way up to an air-conditioned International Harvester tractor. For half a century the Mid-Atlantic Shamrock chain of stores had catered to the needs of farmers, livestock breeders, equestrians, contractors, landscapers, and ordinary homeowners. Over the years this flourishing business had garnered extraordinary wealth for its sole proprietor, Ambassador Eamon Douglass. Exactly how much wealth remained a mystery, because nobody knew anything about the crusty old ambassador except that he was a merciless hard-liner. It was rumored that many powerful people in government –including presidents– had paid visits to the ambassador's stone-walled estate, Shamrocks. He was seldom seen in public, which suited the public just fine.

Luanne Skinner had a part-time job four days a week keeping the Stuarton Shamrock clean and well-organized. In five years of working there she had only seen Ambassador Douglass on one occasion. It had been a nerve-wracking experience to watch him prowl the aisles like a velociraptor, glaring at the gleaming tools, the bins of electrical fastenings and the neat rows of plumbing supplies. Luanne had nearly suffered a coronary when he marched up to her and demanded to know if she was the person responsible for maintaining the displays. She had meekly stammered an affirmative, whereupon the ambassador harrumphed that if all his stores were this orderly he'd be a damn sight more pleased. Then he stalked off, leaving Luanne with a case of the shakes which persisted even after the store manager awarded her a dollar-an-hour raise.

Naturally the extra money was welcome. Nonetheless, Luanne Skinner hoped that she would never come face-to-face with the terrifying ambassador again. One time was more than enough.

———»«◉»«———

In the big back lot behind the store, Luanne and her best friend Beryl Jamison lit up their Virginia Slims and settled themselves on a half-empty wooden pallet of cinderblocks. Around them were all manner of farm machines: tractors, lawnmowers, log-splitters, pesticide sprayers, bush hogs, and the like. Stacked to one side were piles of landscaping stones, slabs of varicolored slate, chunks of quarried granite, and an assortment of decorative garden ornaments, prominent among them an enormous pink granite sundial.

The feeble sunshine provided more light than warmth, and Luanne was glad she'd worn her sweater. Winter would be here soon, she thought. The trees were mostly bare now, their denuded branches stretching forlornly to the sky. Coming on the heels of autumn's exuberant colors, the drabness filled Collie's mother with melancholy. She puffed her cigarette, gloomily contemplating the sundial. The gnomon jutted up like a brass shark fin. If someone ever tripped and fell on that thing…Luanne shuddered.

Beryl Jamison was a shrewd big-boned woman who'd worked at Shamrock for nearly twenty years. In the wake of Jay-Bo's trial and dismissal from the force she had helped Luanne secure her part-time job. Beryl exhaled a blue tobacco cloud and glanced worriedly from the corner of her eye. She could always tell when her best friend was feeling low.

"What's wrong, Lu?" Beryl tapped her ash. "You look kind of down."

With a far-off stare: "Lissa. Tomorrow is eight years."

"Oh, Lu. Is it that long already? Eight years?"

"Sometimes I feel like it happened last week. I can see her as plain as–" Luanne's voice hitched, and she fell silent for a moment. "She would have turned twenty-eight in a couple of weeks."

"I'm so sorry." Beryl discarded the cigarette and hugged her friend. Lissa's suicide had almost destroyed Luanne. "She's with the Lord, honey. You know that."

Luanne remained mute, the Virginia Slim burning unnoticed in her fingers. Beryl said, "Such a terrible, awful thing. What became of the other girl?"

"We heard she got dishonorably discharged. Jay-Bo thought she should go to the brig, but the Corps just wanted it all to go away so that's what they did." Luanne's lip trembled. "There's no record. It's like Lis never existed."

Beryl angrily wondered how the military could cut a young female recruit down from an obstacle course tower where she'd hanged herself and pretend it never happened.

Luanne pulled away and hugged her elbows. "She was such a good person, Ber. Lis loved everybody. Not an ounce of hate in her. But when she got caught with that other girl…She knew what was going to happen, the disgusting things people would say. Lis couldn't face that shame, so…she did what she did." Luanne flicked away her cold cigarette stub. Covering her face with her hands: "Even if she was… that way, I wouldn't have cared. I loved her no matter what."

"Of course you did." Beryl had no children of her own. "Do you ever hear from her brother?"

"Not for a long time. Lloyd was somewhere down on the Eastern shore last I heard. He and I never had much of a relationship. He didn't even come to Lissa's funeral." Luanne grimaced. "His own twin sister."

Beryl had never liked Lloyd. He'd taken after his father; a surly, mean-spirited bully.

"Well, you've got Collie. He's a good young man."

"Yes." Luanne's eyes brightened a little. "I'm so lucky to have such a wonderful son."

"Amazing how different he is from his father and brother."

"Collie has always been his own person," said Luanne. "Even when he was little, he used to…oh…oh…" She gasped and pressed a hand to her stomach.

Alarmed, Beryl said, "That pain again? Lu, for God's sake, when are you going to see a doctor?"

"It's nothing, Ber. A little heartburn, I told you. And do I look rich enough to afford a doctor?"

"That's not just heartburn." More than once Beryl had caught Luanne clutching her abdomen, her face white. "Lu, I'll lend you the money for a doctor, I told you that. Or you could go to the clinic. It's free, y'know."

Luanne shook her head. "You know how Jay-Bo feels about that. He hates 'welfare people'. I might as well shoot myself in the head if he finds out I went to the free clinic."

Beryl's face reddened. "To hell with him. He's got no right." She detested Jay-Bo as much as she loved Luanne. "Let me give you the money. I've got enough, you know that. I could call Dr. Gordon over in Earlsville. Jay-Bo doesn't have to know you went. Please, Lu?"

Luanne shook her head. "No, Ber. I'll be fine." She stood up and pulled her sweater close. "It's getting cold." With a wan smile, "Frost on the pumpkins tonight, I bet. Come on. Mr. Holt will skin us if we don't get back to work. "

A cold rain fell the next afternoon, pooling in brown puddles on the dead grass and zigzagging in little rivulets down the headstones. Collie held an umbrella over his mother's head as she knelt before a simple marker, weeping. The plain inscription read: "Lissa Dawn Skinner – Home with God, October 29, 1998." Collie stared straight ahead, listening to her sobs and wrestling with his own conflicted feelings. He had adored Lissa. But he remained furious at her not only for taking her life but also because she'd lapsed into such shameful depravity. It sickened Collie to think of his beloved sister as a "dyke". As for her father, Jay-Bo made no secret of the fact that he'd rather have a dead daughter than a queer one and refused to visit her grave. While Collie and Luanne braved the cold rain to pay their respects, Jay-Bo was holed up in a squalid dive called Hamburger John's watching football and getting drunk on cheap beer.

Luanne struggled to her feet after laying a single sodden red rose at the base of Lissa's headstone. "Goodbye, my darling girl," she murmured. "Mama loves you." She latched onto Collie's arm, wiping her eyes. "Let's go, before we both catch our death."

In the Camaro Collie noticed his mother shivering, and turned the heat on high. "It'll warm up fast, Mama." Collie felt scared by how worn out she looked. Luanne was all he had left. He couldn't imagine what he'd do if something happened to her. He revved the engine, trying to accelerate the heating process.

Luanne slumped, staring listlessly. "Don't blow the engine up, Nicholas. I'm not that cold."

Collie lifted his hand to the vent, felt the hot air flow. "There, that's better." He put the car in gear and drove toward the cemetery gates. "Mama," he said after a moment, "do you ever wonder what made Lissa turn queer?"

Luanne's face contorted. "Why would ask something like that?"

"It's just that I don't get it. I mean, Lissa wore makeup, and dresses, and liked stuffed animals, all those girly things. She even went to the senior prom with Lonnie Calhoun, remember?"

"Yes, I remember. Why?"

"How come she decided to be a...a *lesbian?*" He choked out the word. "It doesn't make any sense, Mama." Collie paused. "Y'know, a lot of folks say it's because of all those fairies and pervs at Windfield College. Maybe Lissa got wind of that stuff, and–"

"That's plain ignorant," Luanne cut him off. "It's not something you catch, like measles. Don't you listen to that foolishness."

"But Mama, where did it come from?" He felt his anger mounting. "Are you saying she really was like that? A damn dyke? Jesus, my own sister, muff-diving like she was some *guy?*"

"Nicholas Colin! How *dare* you say something like that?! Pull the car over," Luanne scowled, pointing at the rain-soaked shoulder.

Collie muttered something unintelligible and kept driving.

"I told you to *pull over*," his mother almost shrieked.

The car splashed to a halt. "What, Mama?"

Luanne turned, her face a mask of fury. "You will never *ever* speak that way about your sister again! Do you hear me? I won't have her memory treated with disrespect by you or anyone else. *Is that clear?*"

Collie dropped his gaze. "I'm sorry, Mama." He had never seen his mother this angry. He could hear her breathing deeply, like a bull about to charge.

"Lissa was a wonderful person, a beautiful soul. You have no idea how much she loved you. She even loved Lloyd and Jay-Bo, Lord knows. Why do you think she joined the goddamn Marines? To try and please her dad, to make up for her brother not getting in. And Jay-Bo won't even visit her grave. His own dead daughter! Why? Because he's prejudiced and hateful like everybody else around here. Hating, hating, hating, that's all I ever hear. People are never just people. No, everybody's a faggot or a dyke or a nigger or a dirty Jew or a goddamn liberal or *something*." She clenched her fists and pressed them to her temples. "Oh, Jesus, I'm so *sick* of it. And now you're willing to forget everything that was good about Lissa and despise her memory just because she had something inside that made her love women instead of men?" Eyes ablaze: "Is that the kind of person you are?"

Before Collie could respond Luanne continued: "No. You're not a hater, you never were. I'm your mother, I know what you're like. You have a good, noble heart, like Lissa did. You've always been precious to me, Nicholas, more precious than you can possibly know."

Trying to lighten the mood a little Collie attempted a joke: "Aw gee, Mama, then why'd you have to give me a pansy name like 'Nicholas'?"

"Haven't you heard a word I've said? What's the matter with you? Nicholas is a great name, a *terrific* name. The most fantastic man I ever knew was named Nicholas. He was…" She abruptly stopped. "Never mind. Anyway, I want you to promise me that you will not fill yourself with hatred. Don't become like Jay-Bo. No hate. Please, Nicholas. I couldn't bear it. I'd rather die."

"You're not going to die, Mama," said Collie, nervously. "But all right, I promise."

Luanne leaned back in the cracked vinyl bucket seat and closed her eyes. "Can we go home now? I don't feel very good."

Collie pulled back onto the pavement and drove in silence. As the rain drummed on the roof and the thumping wipers made watery smears of the windshield, he uneasily wondered what had precipitated his mother's outburst. Luanne was always dejected after visiting Lissa's grave, but this had been out of character. Collie followed the bubbling black surface of the road in his headlights. And what could she have meant, that the most fantastic man she'd ever known had been named "Nicholas"…?

Then Collie remembered the faint letters he'd seen scratched into the Gander Creek bridge inside an outlined heart: L+N.

———— ((●)) ————

The tiny Caribbean island of Georgiana had long been an ignored dot in the turquoise liquid desert between the Lesser Antilles and the Grenadines. With a population of less than fifteen thousand and a land mass smaller than Nantucket, the tiny British colony had escaped the world's notice for over a century. Even the occasional hurricanes inevitably swept by to the north, ravaging more newsworthy islands.

Then, during the eighties, someone on the island concluded that they were being oppressed by the British imperialists and decided to organize a revolution. A handful of citizens marched on the governor's mansion and after a few *pro forma* threats with a corroded antique gun, politely asked him to go away. Delighted by this unexpected emancipation, the governor congratulated them on their new country and departed. The revolutionaries proclaimed that they were now the Democratic Republic of Georgiana, and that was that. Nothing much changed, except the Union Jack came down and in its place flew the new Georgiana flag, a blue-green affair bearing the likeness of a spiny urchin, known locally as a sea egg.

The island had little industry to speak of beyond a few papaya groves and was bypassed by tourists in favor of the well-established paradises in the Leeward and Windward island chains. Soon, deprived of its oppressive British welfare checks, the local economy took a dive. Things looked bleak until the Georgianans discovered money-laundering.

Prosperity returned overnight. The Georgiana banks multiplied like rabbits. Their vaults were immediately filled to overflowing with dirty cash from across the globe, and the profits were used to build a magnificent marina for a flotilla of smuggler's vessels.

When someone in the U.S. State Department noticed billions of dollars flowing to an unheard-of Caribbean flyspeck, the new country was promptly recognized by the United States, which further proposed to extend full diplomatic relations. Busy shoveling money, the Georgianans weren't opposed to receiving an American ambassador as long as they didn't have to build the embassy. That was no problem, they were assured, and in short order an American Embassy was constructed and staffed with spiffy gun-toting marines to protect it from the iguanas.

Some years later the recently-elected President summoned Eamon Douglass and offered him the Georgianan ambassadorship. Douglass had contributed heavily to the Chief Executive's campaign despite the fact that he considered the man an immoral imbecile because his opponent was a gibbering liberal with a vowel at the end of his name.

Upon thinking the matter over, Eamon Douglass decided that a few years of Caribbean vacation at the taxpayers' expense might not be all that terrible. The perks were endless, the responsibilities negligible, and he would forever after be addressed as "the Honorable Ambassador", which was fitting for a gentleman and patriot. So Douglass had accepted the immoral imbecile's appointment, and off he flew to the Democratic Republic of Georgiana.

Meanwhile, ever on the lookout for more ways to get rich, the Georgianan government had established a profitable sideline in granting asylum and citizenship to wealthy international criminals and thugs in exchange for mammoth donations to the local community chest. Many of these ne'er-do-wells erected lavish dwellings on the lush western slopes of the island, and the area soon became known as "Most Wanted Estates".

Within a month or so of his arrival the new American ambassador began to understand why the former British governor had fled with such alacrity. Once he'd gotten a tan, splashed in the sapphire lagoons, eaten enough raw coconuts to sink a container ship and re-read some moldering classics, Eamon Douglass began to go out of his mind with boredom. The Georgianan "diplomatic corps" consisted of himself and one shriveled Bahamian bureaucrat who spent his time coordinating the drug pirates' delivery schedules. The U.S. State Department had forgotten that Douglass existed, and so the ambassador found himself with absolutely nothing to do. Even to a taciturn loner like Eamon Douglass, Georgiana began to seem like a steamy land crab-infested *oubliette*.

Then one day an engraved note arrived at the embassy inviting the ambassador for cocktails aboard an elephantine Feadship which belonged to one of Georgiana's most distinguished new citizens, a German currency embezzler named Horst Jaeger. Grateful for the distraction Ambassador Douglass presented himself aboard "Horst's Vessel", as it had been christened by some island wag, and soon found himself conversing over Stolichnaya with a Russian expatriate by the name of Egor Antonovich Volka.

Volka was a powerful chunky man sheathed in wiry dark hair. The flat plane of his face, pierced by two unreadable black eyes, gave him the appearance of a coarse Cossack; but Douglass quickly discerned that in fact Volka was intelligent, shrewd, and fond like the ambassador of chess and the music of Modest Mussorgsky. When the ambassador spoke a few words in rusty Russian Egor Antonovich showed yellow teeth in a smile and invited Douglass to visit his tropical dacha in Most Wanted Estates.

Which the ambassador did; and soon discovered, over vodka and borscht, that *Gaspadin* Volka had a colorful history. Officially a university-trained chemical engineer, the Russian had been an undercover operative for the KGB, his mission being to insure the loyalty and patriotism of various high-level Soviet scientists. He accomplished this by way of threats, extortion, blackmail and the occasional frame-up. Volka carefully cultivated a reputation as the most corrupt brute in the entire KGB, until the mere mention of his name generated floods of illicit rubles from terrified potential targets. He squirreled the money away in illegal Swiss bank accounts, and in due course became obscenely rich. After the Chernobyl meltdown irradiated a good portion of Belarus, Volka exploited the catastrophe by selling flasks of tap water to the hordes of panicked peasants, flashing his fearsome credentials and assuring them that it was state-sanctioned "decontamination tonic." When the Soviet Union imploded Volka was forced to flee the Motherland for good. Stopping off in Berne long enough to collect his stashed millions, he flew to the Democratic Republic of Georgiana, bought a citizenship, built a seaside villa, and nursed his umbrage against freedom-loving democracies and capitalists.

Although startled by the frankness of these disclosures, Eamon Douglass didn't condemn the Russian. Volka's methods were somewhat unorthodox, but Douglass had a high regard for that sort of tenacity. The Soviet Union had been a Communist sump, yet Volka managed to thrive. The Russian was as hard-boiled as the ambassador. It was just random luck that Eamon had been born in Virginia and Egor in the U.S.S.R. In their own way, both of them were staunch patriots.

Ambassador Douglass and Egor Antonovich became friends. They spent many contented hours drinking and playing chess while listening to "Pictures at an Exhibition". Smoking Fidel's cigars, they bemoaned the wretched states of their respective countries, which both agreed had exhibited far more nationalistic health in the clarifying atmosphere of the Cold War. Thanks to Volka's presence, the ambassador began to find life on Georgiana tolerable.

Then, in an electoral upset, the American voters ejected the immoral imbecile from the White House and installed a former singing cowboy. Eamon Douglass was recalled and the Georgianan ambassadorship was bestowed upon a hog baron from Dubuque. Douglass was relieved to be home at Shamrocks, and he missed nothing about his Caribbean stint as ambassador except the comradeship of his Russian friend.

They'd briefly kept up a desultory correspondence, but the effort petered out. Years passed, memories faded, and after a while the ambassador ceased to think about the Russian. But that had changed the other night. Eamon Douglass needed some expert help with a great patriotic mission, and Egor Antonovich Volka was on his way to Virginia.

━━━━━⊰◦((◉))◦⊱━━━━━

Joanne Markwith and Nickie Farrell carried their coffees to a small table in the Windfield College faculty lounge. They pulled out chairs and sat facing each other.

Nickie tore open a packet of Splenda and stirred it into her cup. "Thanks for not saying anything, Jo." She set her spoon down. "I realize it's awkward for you."

Jo Markwith laid her hand over Nickie's. "Don't apologize, hon. This is your call. I'm sure you'll decide when it's time to let people know."

Nickie was aware of Jo's bright-eyed scrutiny, but she didn't let it bother her. People didn't mean to be rude, she knew, but they were invariably fascinated, and had a tendency to stare. It was one more facet of her new life that she'd learned to accept. "I don't make a point of being stealthy, Jo, but I do think it would be a distraction when I'm just starting out. It's hard enough getting my students interested in *The Deerslayer* without them inspecting me like I'm a two-headed llama."

Jo laughed. "You're so right. Still, our student body is pretty enlightened. They'll probably think you're da bomb, or whatever they're saying this week."

"I'll just be happy if they turn their papers in on time…what?" Jo was staring at her again. "Something in my teeth?"

"Nickie, I want you to know how much I admire your courage. I can't begin to imagine the kind of inner strength it must have taken to do what you did."

Nickie toyed with her spoon. "People say that a lot, Jo. It's a nice compliment, but for me it wasn't about courage. It was about not having a choice. I couldn't find any other way to be at peace with myself, so…" She shrugged. "*Voilà!* Nickie Farrell."

"And a mighty fine job of it, if you don't mind my saying so." Jo couldn't hide her admiration. "You look good, girl!"

"For a middle-aged schoolmarm, huh? Well, better late than never." Nickie wriggled happily in her chair like a little girl. "Yes, indeedy."

Joanne quelled a desire to pounce on Ms. Farrell like a wolf on a lamb chop. "Did you meet with Fredericka Lindsey?"

"I did," Nickie replied. "She's brilliant. Very understanding about my situation. I'm sure I was a lot more impressed with her than she was with me."

"Don't be so sure of that," countered Jo. "Besides, President Lindsey wouldn't be the only one you've impressed."

"What do you mean?"

With a wry grin: "I had to pull Alex Steward down off the ceiling after he met you."

"Oh." Nickie felt a blush rising to her ears. "Professor Steward. He seems like a nice man."

"Yes, he is," Jo laughed. "A little old-fashioned, but a very nice man." She added somberly: "He lost his wife about five years ago. She got caught in a rip tide out at Rehoboth Beach. By the time they pulled Paula in she'd stopped breathing. Alex made the decision to take her off life support."

Nickie cringed. "God, how awful."

Jo nodded. "For a while he was in really lousy shape. But he's managed to move on. Anyway, he certainly seems interested in you."

Nickie directed her gaze out a nearby window. "Well, I don't know about that."

"I do," said Jo. "Hey, can I see your eyes?"

"I beg your pardon?"

"Alex couldn't stop talking about your unbelievable eyes. Do you mind if I see them?"

"No, of course not." Nickie removed the multi-hued sunglasses and widened her eyes. "Ta-da!"

Joanne bent forward. "Holy cats. That's incredible, hon! Where does it come from?"

"A genetic quirk. It's called heterochromia iridium," Nickie explained. "A lot of people have it, although mine is more obvious than most. I don't notice anymore. It's just a part of me, like my nose. But folks do sometimes gawk, and since I'm still a little sensitive about being stared at..." She picked up her colored glasses. "I hide behind my magic sunset spectacles."

"Hey, I hear you. Nothing wrong with that. Elegant as anything, if you ask me." Joanne sat silent for a moment. "Can I ask one last question?"

"Sure," said Nickie. "What is it?"

"Do you date at all?" Jo looked embarrassed. "Well, what I really mean is, do you date men or women? Or both? It's none of my business, I know."

"Honestly? I've hardly dated at all since...since everything changed. I've been concentrating on school, writing my dissertation. Dating hasn't been a priority. Don't get me wrong, it's not like I want to be a nun or anything—"

"Thank God!"

"But as for men or women, I'm not entirely sure how I feel. I don't mean to sound evasive, but it takes a while to get that stuff sorted out."

"I'd love to go out with you, Nickie. If you're interested, we could drive into D.C., maybe go to the Kennedy Center." She reached across the table and touched Nickie's hand. "I'm *not* coming on to you like some pushy old lesbian. Well," she smiled, "maybe just a teensy bit. Okay?"

"Okay," said Nickie. The warmth of Jo's hand was a comfortable, familiar sensation. All the relationships in her life had been with women. It might be fun to go on a date with her.

"This was very nice, Jo. Thank you." Nickie pushed her chair back and stood. "Again, I'm very grateful for your discretion. I won't forget it."

"Not to worry." Jo gave Nickie a quick hug. "Your secret is safe with me, honey. I promise."

———— ◄◄◉►► ————

"*Zdravstvuite*, Egor Antonovich!" Ambassador Eamon Douglass greeted his old island companion. "Come in, come in. It's been far too long, my friend."

The Russian entered the ambassador's study. "Many, many years, Eamon. When we last played chess together, I was still a vigorous man. Now?" He sighed and shrugged. "I am shrunken and feeble, like a Red Square *babushka*."

Eamon Douglass thought Volka looked almost unchanged. His dark hair was peppered with gray and a few more lines showed in his face, but compared to the ambassador's level of decay the Russian had aged very little. Douglass said, "Your trip was uneventful, I trust?"

Volka rubbed his hands in front of the fireplace. "Of course. The American security officials have no interest in a retired grayhead named George Walker. They were busy searching a young woman's baby, examining the diapers for bombs." He uttered a harsh laugh. "Baby's diapers! Your countrymen have learned nothing from their past mistakes, Eamon. The future will bring many unpleasant surprises, I fear."

The ambassador nodded. "That it will. In fact, I have in mind just such a surprise, which is why I asked you here. No one else possesses your special abilities and knowledge, Egor Antonovich. In order for my surprise to work I need your expertise. Come, let us have a drink." Douglass poured vodka into two Baccarat shot glasses, handed one to Volka. "To a successful surprise." They clicked glasses and drank. "Now, I want to show you something."

Douglass led the Russian over to the window. Drawing aside the drapes: "Out there, beyond those low hills. What do you see?"

"Many buildings. An institute of some sort. A campus, perhaps?"

The ambassador placed one hand on his guest's shoulder. "Very good, Egor Antonovich. A campus called Windfield College. Do you know of it?"

"I have not made a study of your universities. What is special about this Windfield?"

"Windfield College is a plague, Egor Antonovich. A deadly plague, the likes of which has never before afflicted my country." Eamon Douglass yanked shut the drapes and led the Russian to a long leather couch. "May I tell you a story?"

Volka inclined his head.

"Many years ago, long before you and I met, a dignified and noble Virginia family made their home where that campus now stands…"

For fifteen minutes Douglas recounted Windfield's unique history. Volka listened with steepled fingers, his black eyes fixed on the ambassador.

"That, Egor Antonovich, is what I have been obliged to endure for the last thirty-six years. Every time I look out my window, there it sits, an academy built *for* sodomites *by* a sodomite, each year spewing forth another debauched cohort intent on spreading their depravity to every corner of my country." Eamon Douglass pounded his shillelagh on the floor. "And the bastards are *succeeding*."

Even for a nation which had long ago lost its moral compass, Volka conceded, this was a spectacular atrocity. "But the world as you and I knew it has ceased to exist, Eamon. There is no decency left anywhere. I am afraid we lack the power to effect any changes."

"That's where you're wrong, my friend." Eamon Douglass pointed his shillelagh at the draped window. "With your help, I can put a stop to the Windfield pestilence. Hear me out. Let us suppose for a moment…"

As the ambassador spoke the Russian's incredulous expression gave way to a thoughtful look.

When Eamon Douglas stopped talking Volka said after a moment's silence: "To do this thing will cost you your life."

"Yes. But I am a dead man already, Egor Antonovich. The doctors are certain of that." With a grim laugh: "The cancer is doing its work as we speak. But I refuse to waste away in some hospital with tubes up my ass, being spoon-fed by old women. I will die, true, but in a manner of my own choosing. Most importantly, my death can serve a great patriotic purpose by ridding the world of Windfield College. But I need your assistance."

"What you propose is quite bold. It will establish a whole new level of infamy, Eamon. Perhaps even more than the Trade Center attacks. The history books will not treat you kindly."

"Perhaps not. But then again, who knows? At first the shock will be enormous. But shock therapy can work wonders. What if my action makes people recognize the sickness that is destroying our society? Might not things change back to the way they were before everything became corrupt? Patriots have always sacrificed themselves for the good of their motherlands. How many of your countrymen willingly surrendered their lives to defeat the Nazi fascists? It is the noblest of traditions, and I shall simply be the latest."

Volka's black eyes shone. "Without question such an action would disrupt and panic the masses like nothing else. Your government lives in great fear of such an event." With a deep chuckle: "My compliments, Eamon. It is a grand strategy. Let us have another drink of vodka, and perhaps some dinner? Then we will talk more of this. I may have a few ideas."

＞•«(•)»•＜

After an elegant repast of Chateaubriands and Chambertin Eamon Douglass and Egor Antonovich Volka re-settled themselves in the ambassador's study, swirling snifters of Courvoisier as they reclined in deep armchairs before the fire.

"The first consideration," said Volka, "is what substance to employ as a contaminant."

Eamon Douglass took a sip of cognac. "In that regard, I must defer to your scientific expertise. I would prefer that the area be rendered uninhabitable for the briefest possible time. I don't want to permanently harm the land, Egor Antonovich. Virginia is sacred to me."

The Russian nodded. "In that respect, Cesium 137 is an excellent choice. Its half-life is only three decades. Your Virginia would be healed in less than a generation. Perhaps even faster. The supply I'm thinking of is already several decades old; its atomic decay is well underway, although the immediate lethality remains undiminished."

"Where does this Cesium 137 come from?"

"A secret project known as Gamma Kolos," replied Volka. "Back in the seventies, my government carried out extensive experiments to determine the effects of radiation on plant growth, especially crops. The purpose was to learn how our agriculture might fare in the aftermath of a nuclear conflict."

"Interesting," said Douglass. "Please continue."

"As part of the experiment, canisters containing Cesium 137 were buried in fields all across the country. Naturally, strict accountings were supposed to be kept about the exact placement of all these canisters. However, as so often happens, the record-keepers proved sloppy and inexact. Over time the Gamma Kolos experiment was abandoned and forgotten. When the Soviet Union ceased to exist, many of the Cesium 137 devices remained unaccounted-for."

"Unaccounted-for, but not lost?"

The Russian savored a sip of cognac. "A number of the devices were unearthed by farmers or vagabonds, who attempted to scavenge the metal canisters. They were severely burned by radiation from the Cesium 137. As for the rest, no one is certain what became of them. Many international watchdog organizations are apprehensive, their concern being that Cesium 137, while non-fissile, could readily be incorporated into a so-called 'dirty bomb' if it fell into the wrong hands."

"Well, imagine that!" Eamon Douglass slapped the arm of his chair and laughed. "More cognac?"

Volka resumed: "I have reason to believe that some of this missing Cesium 137 is possessed by entities of an extra-legal nature who might be induced to part with some of it for a sufficient monetary inducement." He directed a questioning look at his host. "Do you have any thoughts on the matter?"

"Would two million dollars be an adequate inducement?"

The Russian hooded his eyes. "My information is that these people calculate in multiples of five."

The ambassador sat silent for a moment. "Are you confident that they would deliver?"

The Russian's eyebrows rose. "They will deliver to *me*. That, I can assure you."

"It must be very compact," said Eamon Douglass, "with an initiating charge. Weatherproof, leakproof. I'll need a small remote detonator of some kind, and I want it here within three months. Possible?"

Volka smiled. "Technicalities. Of course. The method of delivery, timing…you have these in mind?"

"Not exactly. If possible I'd prefer not to drive in there with a truck and set it off like some primitive Arabian towel-head. But these details can be worked out. For now, just send me a nice explosive can of Cesium 137, Egor Antonovich. Enough to light up Windfield College and set it on the road to Redemption."

"So." Volka rose, and so did Eamon Douglass. They formally touched glasses. "Redemption," toasted the Russian. "I drink to yours, my patriotic friend."

———◦《◦》◦———

The following evening Ambassador Douglass watched from his study as a Lincoln Continental limousine glided down the long driveway, bearing Egor Antonovich Volka away to Dulles airport. The ambassador touched his shillelagh to his forehead in a salute. "Have a safe journey, my friend. Thanks to you, I am going to change history. The world will never be the same. *Da svedanya.*"

The limo disappeared through the gates. Douglass stared after it for a few seconds, mentally reviewing their plans. As he'd hoped, the former KGB operative had proved smoothly adept at this sort of scheming. They'd settled on the codeword "Redemption" for the event, and "Redeemer" for the Cesium 137 device.

The ambassador shifted his gaze toward the distant lights of Windfield College, which twinkled in the indigo twilight like fireflies. It was a lovely view, one which he had hated for many decades; but contemplating it now, his cruel lips twisted into a grin of lethal malice.

Chapter Five
Investigative Journalism

Heather Walters and another young woman entered the Foxton Arms foyer, which was seasonally decorated with a bountiful arrangement of pumpkins, Indian corn and baskets of colorful warty gourds. "Hi, reservation for Walters."

"Good evening, Miss Walters," greeted the maitre d'. Checking his book: "We were expecting you *and* the congressman?"

"Daddy got stuck in some committee meeting. He said to go ahead without him." Indicating her companion: "This is my roommate, Cinda Vanderhart."

The maitre d' took in Cinda's short spiky blonde hair, black leather jacket, cargo pants, boots, ruby nose stud, and pewter labrys pendant. "Delighted," he managed to enunciate. "If you ladies would follow me, please." He stiffly led the way.

"I think he's freaked," Cinda snickered to Heather. "Hasn't he ever seen a dyke before?"

"Sshh," Heather admonished. "You aren't exactly dressed like... well, like anyone else here."

"Can I help it if I forgot my Ferragamos?"

Heather rolled her eyes. "Omigod, Cinda." To the maitre d': "Can we have that waiter Daddy always gets?"

"Yes, Miss Walters." He seated them and hurried off, saying over his shoulder, "I'll send Collie Skinner over. Enjoy your meal, ladies."

Cinda Vanderhart wrinkled her nose at the opulent surroundings. "Jesus, a glass of water must cost five bucks."

"Never mind that. Here comes our waiter," Heather whispered. "Check out his eyes, it's like, so freaky."

"Good evening, ladies," said Collie. "Welcome to the Foxton Arms."

"Hello, *Collie*," Heather said. "I was here with Daddy a few weeks ago. Congressman Walters. I acted like a total brat, remember? This is my roommate, Cinda."

"It's always my pleasure to serve the congressman and his friends. I'll give you ladies a few minutes to look over your menus." Collie smiled politely and left.

"Did you see?" Heather whispered. "Is that not totally weird?"

Cinda squinted at her roommate. "Have you got crush on him, or what?"

"Don't be ridiculous," Heather sniffed. "He's a waiter, for God's sake. I just thought you'd be interested, that's all. How often do you see eyes like that?"

"He's a man, Roomie. I'm not interested in men whether their eyes match or not." With a puckish grin: "On the other hand, if *you* had one blue and one brown—"

"Shut *up*. Omigod, do you have to be so gay all the time?" Heather impatiently examined her menu. "Whatever you do, don't have the paper fish."

When Collie returned the roommates ordered Caesar salads and Chicken Marsala, then sat sipping iced tea, waiting for their food.

"So, what's your favorite class so far?" Heather asked.

Her roommate buttered a hot sourdough roll. "Oh, I like 'em all," she answered, and took a bite. Cinda Vanderhart was a fine-tuned academic machine, straight A's, perfect SAT's, attending Windfield on a full scholarship. Heather found it daunting the way Cinda absorbed knowledge like a sponge, studying to all hours of the night. Her stated ambition was to become the greatest investigative journalist of all time. "How 'bout you?"

"Well, my Poly Sci course is way cool 'cause Professor Daughtridge said I could do a term paper on Daddy," Heather giggled. "And I'm really enjoying Ms. Farrell's American Lit class. Aren't you?"

Cinda paused in tearing apart another roll. "Do you notice anything different about Ms. Farrell?"

Heather frowned. "What do you mean, 'different'? Like how?"

"I'm not sure, exactly." Cinda pursed her lips. "I get an unusual vibe. She seems a little…odd."

"Ms. Farrell, odd?" Heather scrunched up her face. "What does that make you?"

"Nothing odd about me," laughed Cinda. "I'm a perfectly ordinary twenty-first century lesbian who's going to kick butt and make journalistic history."

"Oh, I'm so sure."

"Wait and see," Cinda's eyes brightened. "And I'm going to figure out what it is about Ms. Farrell that's bugging me. I'm never wrong, y'know. There's something off-key about our American Lit teacher, and I'm gonna find out what it is. Just watch."

⚬

The Foxton Caesar salad for two was priced at twenty-five dollars, and for that sum the patrons were entitled to a full tableside production number. Collie gathered his ingredients, wheeled the special cart out to the girls' table and commenced the elaborate ritual. Heather and Cinda watched him mashing garlic and anchovies in the big wooden bowl, all the while chattering about classes, assignments and other scholastic esoterica.

As he worked Collie sneaked an occasional glance at the two Windfield girls. He took less notice of Heather than her friend, whose sharp demeanor put him on edge. There was a predatory intelligence in the way she talked and gestured that made him feel woefully undereducated. But what bothered him more was the fact that Cinda –an obvious lesbian– clearly didn't care who knew it. She wore her gayness like some sort of merit badge. Collie's sister Lissa had chosen to die rather than face condemnation as a homosexual, yet here sat this dynamic young woman openly celebrating the very thing that had destroyed his sibling. For the life of him he couldn't fathom why Lissa would have wanted to be like Cinda Vanderhart.

Collie garnished the finished salads with fresh croutons and served them on chilled plates. "Here you are, ladies. Enjoy." He wheeled the salad cart back to the serving station.

Robin Thompson greeted him: "Good, are you done with that cart? I don't know why, but suddenly everyone wants Caesar salad..." She stopped. "What's wrong, Collie?"

"*Nothing.*"

The petite waitress looked so taken aback by his curt retort that Collie felt ashamed. "I'm sorry, Robin." He hesitated. "Did...did you see the girl at my table? Black jacket, weird hair?"

"I know."

With a pained expression: "Why did Lissa want to be one of *those?*" You're a girl, Robin. How could any girl want that? I don't get it."

Robin moved closer. "I don't understand it either. But I have no right to judge. Remember, God made Lissa the way He saw fit."

"Mama and I visited her grave a couple of weeks ago. I made some stupid comment and she jumped all over me. Said she was sick of everybody hating each other and made me promise not to do it."

"There *is* too much hate. It eats you up inside. Don't ever forget that Lissa was a good, kind person." Robin squeezed his palm. "Just like her little brother." She abruptly dropped his hand. "Uh-oh, here comes Mr. Foley."

The maitre d' halted and peered at Collie, then at Robin, who was busily arranging her Caesar salad cart. He hoisted his eyebrows, said "Ahem!" and went about his business.

Collie whispered, "Thanks, Robin, you're the best," and hurried off to the kitchen to pick up his orders. He didn't see the way she looked after him, but if he had, it would have warmed his heart.

⟫⟪⟫

Luanne Skinner sat at her chipped Formica kitchen table, sipping a hot cup of Celestial Seasonings Cinnamon Apple tea. A beat-up old boom box was playing one of her music cassettes, a collection titled "British Invasion: 1964". Luanne loved the innocent tunes from her girlhood, when she and her friends used to spend afternoons playing 45rpm records and squealing over such cute songsters as Chad and Jeremy. Now she sang along with them to one of her favorites, their sweet-sad tune called "Yesterday's Gone":

> We had such happiness together
> I can't believe it's gone forever.
> Wait till summer comes again
> I hope that you'll remember when
> Our love had just begun.
> But that was yesterday, and yesterday's gone.

Luanne sighed. The tea wasn't making her tummy feel much better. The pain felt like a little rat gnawing away at her innards. Collie and Beryl Jamison were right; she really did need to see a doctor. Maybe a stealthy trip to the free clinic...

Luanne jumped, spilling her tea, as the front door crashed open and then shut with a bang. Her husband appeared in the doorway, a surly expression on his face.

"Why do you always have to listen to those goddamn faggotty songs? I hate that shit. If you wanna to listen to old music, play Elvis."

Luanne turned off the tape player. "I'm sorry."

"Sure you are," Jay-Bo grumbled. "I gotta put some gas in my truck, goin' to Hamburger John's. Gimme twenty bucks. You got any idea what the gas prices are like? Fuckin' Ay-rabs. Better make it thirty."

Luanne only had about forty dollars. She hesitated, and her husband's expression darkened. "Something wrong with your ears? I said *gimme* thirty dollars. Or do you want me to get it myself?" He frowned at her worn purse and approached the table.

Luanne snatched it away. "Fine. Here. Take it," she snapped, extracting some bills and dropping them on the table. "Take it and go."

Jay-Bo scooped up the bills and stood by the table, towering over her. "Quite an attitude you got there, Lu. Think you're better than ol' Jay-Bo, ain't that right?"

Luanne shivered, wondering if she was going to be hit. It wouldn't be the first time. "Please," she implored, not looking up. "Just leave me alone."

Jay-Bo didn't move. "Think I don't know how it is? You and that freak kid of yours, actin' like your shit don't stink. What a joke. Nothin' but white trash, both of you. *I'm* the one who served his country, *I'm* the one who put his ass on the line with the force for twenty fuckin' years, *I'm* the one who got burned for doin' his duty and arrestin' that drugged-up Windfield fuckstick, and now you're whinin' about giving me a few dollars, you cheap bitch?" Luanne, cowering in her chair, could see the hand holding her money clench into a meaty fist.

"I gave you the best damn years of my life, but what did I get? Three kids, sure. One of 'em was a lesbo carpet muncher, one was a screw-eyed runt, and one was too goddamn stupid to move his ass out of the way while I mowed the lawn. Well, Miss High-n-Mighty, from where I sit, you owe me. So you better not sass me again next time I ask you for a few lousy dollars. You hear what I'm tellin' you? Or you'll be sorry you were ever born."

Luanne whimpered in a trembling voice, "What makes you think I'm not already sorry?"

She flinched as Jay-Bo raised his hand, but instead of striking her he stormed into the living room and immediately rushed back into the kitchen, holding up their framed wedding photograph.

"You want to know how sorry *I* am?" he bellowed, and smashed the picture down on the kitchen table, shattering the glass and frame into small fragments which flew in all directions. Luanne averted her eyes as several small pieces hit her in the side of the face.

Breathing heavily, Jay-Bo leaned over her as she sat with bowed shoulders, weeping in fear. "Goddamn you, Luanne. You and your stinkin' kid can go rot in Hell." He straightened up and without an-other word left the kitchen. Collie's mother sagged in relief when she heard the front door slam, the tension pouring out of her like blood from a ruptured spleen.

Still sobbing, she got a broom and dustpan, carefully cleaned up the mess and dumped the glass shards and wood splinters into the garbage pail. The wedding photo had been creased and nicked, but she smoothed it on the Formica as best she could. Luanne stared at the beautiful bride she had been, wondering how her life could have turned out so differently than she'd planned. Then she got a scissors, cut away the image of her husband and threw the piece in with the other trash. Maybe, Luanne thought, it was time to think about leaving. Collie would take care of her, she knew, and together they'd make out okay. She had remained with Jay-Bo despite his cruelty because of her shame at letting him raise another man's child. But how much suffering did she have to endure? Was her punishment to stay until he killed her?

After a few moments she pressed the button on her tape player, closed her eyes and imagined the beautiful youthful face of Nick Farrington. She hugged the torn bridal picture to her bosom as Chad and Jeremy began to sing:

> Wait till summer comes again
> I hope that you'll remember when
> Our love had just begun
> I loved you yesterday
> But yesterday's gone.

⌒◉⌒

In the crowded high-tech Windfield College gymnasium, Heather Walters and Cinda Vanderhart puffed and pumped on side-by-side Cybex elliptical climbers. Both girls were shiny with perspiration; they had programmed their machines to maximum settings. Heather wore an eye-popping chartreuse leotard with snowy white leggings while Cinda had on a camo tank top and gray sweatpants. They made a colorful if contrasting pair.

"Y'know," offered Heather, "I could lend you this lavender unitard I have, the legs are high-cut to *here*. With those buns you would look seriously hot."

"Turn myself into a sex object, you mean? Okay, it's a deal. On one condition."

"Oh, no. Don't even say it. I am not going to be a lesbian, so you can just go bark up some other tree."

"I didn't say I want you to be a lesbian," countered Cinda, furiously working her legs. "But I really think you should sample one. Me."

"Well, it's never going to happen, so...Hey, look who just came in!" Heather pointed toward the gym entrance. "Isn't Ms. Farrell kind of old to be working out? I hope she doesn't have a stroke or something...Why are you looking at her like that?"

"Like what?" Cinda protested, not taking her eyes off their American Lit professor. Nickie Farrell wore an outsized pink-and-black Windfield T-shirt over plain black gym shorts, with her signature multihued sunglasses. Her hair was fastened back in a ponytail, bracketed by a pair of iPod headphones.

"Come off it," Heather said in an accusing tone. "You always get that determined look when you're trying to figure something out. And you've got a bug up your butt about Ms. Farrell. Really weird, Cinda."

"It's weird, all right." Cinda pushed her machine's kill switch. "Enough."

"But we haven't even done an hour yet," protested Heather, still climbing. "Hold on...where are you going?"

"I gotta check something out," replied Cinda, wiping her face with a towel. She kept her gaze on Nickie Farrell, who had stationed herself at a cable pull machine and was performing a set of triceps extensions.

"Omigod, will you wait a sec?" Heather stopped her machine. "This is so like stalking or something. You need to chill, girl. Leave Ms. Farrell alone."

"Don't be absurd," Cinda replied. "This isn't stalking, it's investigative journalism."

"Like there's a difference?"

As soon as Nickie Farrell finished her set and moved on to another apparatus, Cinda hurried to the cable pull. "There! Look at that," she said to Heather, pointing at the weight stack.

"Yeah, so?"

"Are you kidding? Try it. Go on."

"This is totally lame." Heather grabbed the T-bar. "I don't know what...*unh!*" She grunted, but the weight didn't move.

"Eighty pounds." Cinda emphasized, "*Eighty*. And our lady prof was pulling it down easy as pie. There are guys in here that can't do that much."

"Some guys are total wussies. Anyway, since when can't women be strong? I thought you're so liberated."

"That's not all." Cinda tipped her head toward Nickie, who was draped over a nearby hamstring curl machine. "Check out her thighs."

"So? Ms. Farrell has great legs. I hope mine look that good when I'm an old lady."

"You need to be more observant, Roomie. When was the last time you saw a middle-aged woman with no cellulite? I mean *none*. Zero. Even liposuction can't make it that smooth. Anyway that's not lipo, that's pure gluteus farrellus." Cinda cocked an eyebrow. "Still don't get it, huh?"

"What is up with you?" Heather pushed her lips in a pout. "Have you got some kind of lesbian itch for Ms. Farrell? That is so perverse. She's my mother's age."

"Perverted," Cinda corrected. "Perverse means stubborn. And I doubt Ms. Farrell is gay, if she even knows what she is. I have to go ask her something. I'll be right back."

"Wait a sec," Heather urged, but Cinda walked to an adjacent hamstring machine and pretended to fuss with the bar adjustment. When Nickie glanced over Cinda grinned in counterfeit surprise: "Hey, Professor Farrell! I didn't know you like to work out."

Nickie removed her iPod headphones. "Hello, Ms. Vanderhart. I don't feel quite ready for the trash heap, so I make some small effort to stay in shape. Not that I can compete with you young hardbodies..."

well, and here's Ms. Walters. That's quite an outfit."

"Thanks," said Heather, with an uncertain look at Cinda. "I'm really enjoying *Benito Cereno*, Ms. Farrell."

Nickie looked pleased. "I'm glad to hear that. I realize it's a bit off the usual Melville track, but I thought we'd take a chance on—"

Cinda interrupted: "Ms. Farrell, I've been meaning to ask, for our midterm papers didn't you say we could choose any American author?"

"Within reason," Nickie confirmed. "Do you have someone in mind?"

"Yes. I'd like to examine a work by L. Frank Baum."

"The *Wizard of Oz* fellow? Interesting choice, Ms. Vanderhart. Any particular reason?"

"Oh yeah," affirmed Cinda. "But I'm still doing the research."

"Well...why not? No one can say that Mr. Baum hasn't had a profound influence on popular culture. I'll look forward to reading your paper. I loved the Oz books when I was a little...young thing." Nickie reached for her headphones. "I'd best finish up here, ladies. See you in class."

"Okay, bye," said Heather.

Cinda added, "Have a good workout, Mr. Farrell."

Nickie stared at Cinda, her face frozen behind the sunset-colored glasses.

"I mean *Ms.* Farrell," amended Cinda with an embarrassed simper. "Like, duh." She allowed herself to be dragged away by her red-faced roommate.

In the women's locker room Heather exploded: "*Mister* Farrell? What on earth is wrong with you? Are you out of your mind?!"

Cinda raised her hands and slapped herself a high five. "I knew it," she crowed. "I just knew it! This will get me on the *Spectrum*, for sure. My first big exposé. Didn't I tell you I was going to be an investigative journalist?" She snickered, "Oh, I am so good."

"I don't see how offending Ms. Farrell is going to get you on the school paper," Heather fumed. "But it may get you a failing grade in American Lit."

"Calm down, girl. Auntie Cinda has everything under control. C'mere." She began whispering in her roommate's ear. At first Heather scowled, but gradually her blue eyes grew wide and her jaw dropped.

"No way," she spluttered when Cinda finished. "You're wrong. It's not possible."

"It's possible, all right." Cinda's eyes glittered. "I'm going to make *her* admit it. And when I'm the most famous journalist around, you can tell everybody how you were right there when I broke my first big story."

⊸⊸⊸≋⊸⊸⊸

An hour later, showered and back in her office, Nickie Farrell tried to concentrate on grading some papers, but she kept hearing Cinda Vanderhart's voice saying "Have a good workout, *Mr.* Farrell." At length she threw down her red pencil and softly swore to herself: "Damn."

Of course the girl simply might have misspoken. But Nickie sensed that young Ms. Vanderhart wasn't the sort of person who made casual slips. Cinda was a perspicacious go-getter. Although it didn't happen very often, Nickie suspected that she had been "read", as the expression went, by her discerning young student.

So now what? If Cinda asked her straight out, Nickie decided, she wouldn't lie. She didn't *want* to lie. There was no reason for her to feel ashamed. Maybe the time had come to let everyone know. Still, even in a place as open-minded as Windfield there were bound to be some negative reactions. Nickie had seen the leers, the smirks, the expressions of disgust when people found out the truth. She pulled a small hand mirror from her purse and studied her face, feeling the old insecurities flood in. Was it really all that obvious? Nickie put away the mirror with a sigh, picked up her red pencil and bent over her papers.

She had just gotten absorbed in a surprisingly keen analysis of Taggart's sadistic homosexuality in *Billy Budd* when her cell phone rang. "Hello?"

"Hello, Nickie. It's Alex Steward. Am I interrupting anything important?"

"As a matter of fact you are, Professor Steward," Nickie smiled. "Bless you for distracting me from a pile of essays."

"Glad to be of help," she heard him laugh. "I'm behind on a bunch of those, too. The reason I'm calling, are you by any chance free this evening?"

Nickie leaned back in her chair and looked out the window. On the underside of a nearby sycamore limb a small grey nuthatch was gravely walking upside-down toward a seed-filled feeder. "I don't have anything planned," she answered. "Why?"

"There's a freshman dance tonight in the conference hall," Alex said. "It's not a big deal like the proms, more of an informal mixer. The powers-that-be always like to have a few adults there, just to keep an eye on things, and I volunteered."

"You, a chaperone?" Nickie watched the inverted nuthatch cautiously stalk the feeder. "Hard to picture."

"I think 'chaperone' might be a slightly outdated term," suggested Alex, "when the kids can go back to the dorms and get free condoms."

"Um. I see your point."

"In any case, I was wondering if you'd like to come with me?"

"Why…why…" Nickie suddenly felt flustered. "You mean to dance?"

"I think that's the general idea," said Alex. "Are you game?"

"Gee, Alex, I don't know. Have you seen the way the kids dance these days? I can't do any of that. Can you?" She had a sudden vision of Professor Steward doing a frenzied hip-hop jig. "Lawd have mercy!"

"Well, maybe we can convince them to play one or two dusty old songs for us ancients. What do you say?"

Nickie watched as the nuthatch conquered its fear and nabbed a sunflower seed from the feeder. It immediately flew off. "Professor Steward, are you asking me for a date?"

There was a pause. "Yes, Nickie, I am. Will you please come with me to the dance?"

Nickie Farrell suddenly felt warm all over. "Yes, Alex, I will," she accepted. "Thank you for asking me. But no break dancing. You promise?"

"Deal," agreed Alex Steward, sounding elated. "I'll meet you there at eight-thirty."

Nickie closed her cell phone, bemused for a moment. Then her brows contracted. What if she ran into Cinda Vanderhart at the dance?

"No. I'm not going to live in fear," Nickie stated out loud. She picked up her red pencil. "I am *not*."

<hr />

Several hours later, just inside the conference hall doors, Nickie stood blinking at the pounding music and massed gyrating bodies, feeling acutely aware of being forty-eight years old. Perhaps she had once been this young and full of energy, but if so it was very ancient history.

She felt a hand touch her arm.

"Nickie!" Joanne Markwith stood beside her, holding a can of soda and beaming. "Geez, do you look cute." She admired the other's maroon skirt, gray sweater, high-heeled black boots and jaunty black beret. "Where on earth did you learn to dress like this?"

"My mother's catalogues." Nickie grinned. "Needless to say, Mom wasn't exactly thrilled."

"I can't imagine why! So, what brings you here? Got a date or something?"

"Uh, well, Alex Steward asked me."

"Oh. Well, what can I say?" Joanne's smile seemed a shade forced. "Lucky him."

Nickie felt awkward. "It's not really a *date* date…"

Jo waved her silent. "No, no. Alex is a sweetheart, really." She put her hand under Nickie's chin. "No rainbow glasses tonight! Let's see those gorgeous eyes…"

"Good evening, ladies!" Alex Steward unexpectedly materialized and executed a courtly bow. "Ms. Markwith, Ms. Farrell. How delightful to see you both."

"He's half-truthful, at least," Jo winked at Nickie. "This one might be a keeper."

"Hello, Professor Steward." Nickie thought he was very handsome in his dark sport coat with a pink-and-black Windfield club tie. "You look quite the gentleman."

"Quite the anachronism, too," Alex swept a hand at the crowd of dancing students, none of whom wore jackets or ties. "Thank you, Professor Farrell. You look charming as well."

"I think Nickie and I are the only women here without exposed midriffs," observed Joanne Markwith. "I don't know why these girls bother to wear anything. Well, I'll see you two later. Have fun." She shot Nickie a quick glance and walked away.

Alex Steward took both of Nickie's hands in his own. "I don't mean to be unduly effusive, Ms. Farrell, but you look not only charming but absolutely breathtaking."

"That's very sweet, Professor. Whatever happened to calling each other Alex and Nickie?"

"Oh, right." His blue eyes sparkled. "I'm so glad you came, Nickie. Even though this probably isn't exactly your cup of tea. The Freshman Follies."

"I was their age once, too." Nickie looked around a bit wistfully. "They're entitled to have their fun. It doesn't last very long, does it?"

"No, it sure doesn't. *Tempus fugit*, and all that."

"Oh, that's much too gloomy a sentiment for the Freshman Follies." Nickie grabbed Alex's hand and pulled him toward the dance floor. "Come on. As long as we're here, let's give it the old college try."

On the opposite side of the hall Cinda Vanderhart stood leaning with one foot bent back against the wall, arms crossed, thoughtfully watching the two English professors dance in their preposterous middle-aged way. She found it fascinating. First Ms. Farrell had been talking chummily to that gay broad from the English office, and now she was dancing with a straight old professor. Which way would she eventually go? Boy? Girl? Both? Too cool, really.

Cinda uncrossed her arms and took a drink from a bottle of Evian water. "When Tip becomes Ozma," she murmured. "How's that for a title? Just wait till you read my midterm paper, *Ms*. Farrell."

⸺◈⸺

"Okay, kids, for our last song tonight we're going lower the lights and wind things down with an oldie from the Eagles. To honor the Class of 2010, here's "New Kid in Town"."

"Oooh, one of my favorites," Nickie exclaimed. "Did you like the Eagles, Alex?"

"Very much. I saw them in concert once." He held his arms out. "May I have the honor?"

"Of course." Alex gently enfolded her as the music began. After a moment he stopped. "Er, Nickie...Not to be a chauvinist, but isn't the guy supposed to lead?"

"Oh, lord. Forgive me." Nickie colored to her ears, then rested her head on his shoulder. Alex hugged her, savoring every moment until the song ended.

The lights blazed up and the crowd began to disperse. Nickie disengaged herself and glanced at her watch. "This was fun, Alex. Thank you so much." She smiled at him, her different-colored eyes vividly evident. "I should get going, it's after eleven. I have a ten o'clock class tomorrow."

"Take a little walk with me first...please?" Alex Steward entreated. "Just for a few minutes."

"All right. For a few minutes."

They exited into the night. Despite the November cold, which chilled their breath into white plumes, the stillness was peaceful and soothing. In the blue-black sky overhead, a three-quarters moon played shadow tag with some passing clouds. After a short walk they arrived in front of Randall Windfield's memorial obelisk.

Nickie hugged her camel-hair coat tight. "I met Randall Windfield once, you know. Just to shake hands." In the clear moonlight Alex could see her staring off into the distance. "I was so young, so conceited. I thought I had all the answers. And I didn't know a thing."

Alex embraced her with one arm. "Couldn't the same thing be said of the kids back there? We were all once filled with the folly of youth. But we survived."

"I almost didn't." Nickie shivered. "My life hasn't followed the usual paths. It's been…complicated. I went through some very difficult times."

Alex Steward bowed his head. "I have, too."

"I'm terribly sorry about your wife, Alex. She must have been a wonderful person."

"After I lost Paula I didn't think I could go on living. But my boys helped me get through it, and…" Alex shrugged. "Like I said, we survive. Somehow."

Nickie leaned against him. "You have children, then."

"Two sons, Craig and Neil. They're grown, have their own kids now. I'm a grandpa three times over. Do you have any?"

"No," Nickie sadly shook her head. "My ex and I tried, but it didn't happen. Eventually we got divorced and that was the end of it for me." She paused for a moment. "I used to wish for a little boy. It would have been so wonderful to love him and play with him and watch him grow up!" She dreamily added, "And of course he would have excelled at all those boy things I was never any good at."

Alex smiled. "Why should you be any good at boy things?"

Nickie abruptly pulled away. Alex saw that her eyes were wide with alarm. "*What* did you say?"

"I…I don't know," he stammered in surprise. "Did I offend you? If so, I'm sorry."

Nickie stared at him, then dropped her face into her hands. "No, I'm the one who's sorry. I don't know what came over me. I'm just very tired, Alex. I need to go home. Please."

"Of course. It's late."

They made their way across the moonlit campus to the faculty parking lot. Neither of them spoke until they stood by her car.

"Alex, I apologize for the way I acted back there. Please don't think it's anything you did or said. You are a kind, thoughtful gentleman." She looked up at him. "I like you very much. I really do."

"I like you very much, too."

"What I need to say…" Nickie hesitated. "There are things about me you don't know. Important things, which might make a difference in how you feel." She searched his face. "You don't understand."

"No," he admitted. "But it won't matter. I'm starting to care for you a great deal, Nickie. Maybe that's not something you want to hear, but you should know it anyway. I haven't felt this way since Paula died."

"Oh, Alex." Nickie's eyes filled. He held her and they kissed; not forcefully but gently, with the tentative awe of a nascent coupling.

"I have to go," she whispered when they parted. "Good night, dear Professor Steward." Nickie kissed him again, then tucked herself in her little car and drove away into the night.

Alex Steward stood where he was, listening to the receding sound of her car. When the last echoes faded away he murmured aloud, "Well, Paula. You won't mind, will you? I'll never stop loving you, you know that. But I don't want to be alone any more. Time's passing, and I'm not getting any younger. If Nickie and I can be happy together, I'd really like that. Okay?"

Alex gazed up at the brilliant moon for a moment. Then he buttoned his jacket and went on his way, humming a melody from an old Eagles song.

———— ⊸《◈》⊷ ————

A week later Joanne Markwith sat working at her desk in the English department. She broke into a grin as Nickie Farrell entered.

"Good afternoon, cutie! How's my favorite assistant professor?"

"Frazzled," grumped Nickie. "Don't I look it?"

"Not a bit. Impeccably put together, as always. You go, girl."

"Don't fib," scolded Nickie. "Anyway, here are my attendance sheets for last week. Oh, and today's the deadline for midterm papers, so I told the kids to drop them off with you."

"Not a problem, I'll put 'em in your box. How did it go the other night? Did you and Alex have a good time?"

"We did. Very nice. Although dancing next to those youngsters made me feel older than the Blue Ridge Mountains." Nickie hesitated. "He asked me out again. I said yes."

"Does Alex know about...?" Jo didn't finish the sentence.

With a guilty look: "No. I haven't gotten up the nerve to tell him yet. I'm afraid of how he might react."

"How do guys usually react?"

"I don't really have much experience, but it's unpredictable," replied Nickie. "Some are okay with it. Others say they'll call and never do. A few get totally freaked. I know one girl, her supposed boyfriend threw her out of the car at night in the middle of nowhere then drove off and left her alone."

Jo grimaced. "Alex isn't like that, Nickie. I mean, he's the sort of guy who rescues bees from hot tubs." She tried to sound reassuring. "I'm sure it'll work out okay."

"Maybe." Nickie's face registered doubt. "But I have to tell him soon, before he hears it from someone else."

"Nobody else knows, do they?"

"No," answered Nickie. "At least, I haven't confided in anyone besides you and Dr. Silverman and President Lindsey." With a slight frown: "But I have this one student...I'm not positive, but I think she suspects."

"Uh-oh."

"Yeah. Uh-oh. That's why I need to level with Alex. Oh hell," Nickie lamented, "I don't know anything about having relationships with men. Isn't that pathetic?"

"Nope," Jo grinned. "I don't, either."

Nickie impulsively reached across the desk and clasped the secretary's hand. "Thanks for being my friend."

"Bless you, honey. I hope you know how much I'm rooting for

you." Jo paused. "What are you doing for Thanksgiving? Family?"

Nickie's face fell. "No. I'm not welcome in my family. Dad won't speak to me. Mom thinks I'm disgusting, and my brother Bennett tells everyone I'm mentally ill. I've tried explaining that I'm still the same person inside, but…" She dropped her eyes. "Anyway, no. I don't have any plans."

"You do now. You're coming with me to my mother's house. She lives in Bethesda, it'll just be us and my sister and her kids. An all-girl Thanksgiving. We'll sit around and eat ourselves silly and have as much dessert as we want. Mom makes a world-class pumpkin pie. How's that sound?"

"Pumpkin pie?" Nickie smiled. "Yummy! I'd love to join you, Jo. But I don't want to intrude on your family. Are you sure no one would mind?"

"Sweetie, my mom is used to *me*. She'll love having a classy lady like you join us. It will make her day, guaranteed."

"Then I accept with pleasure. I'd better get to class. Thanks again, Jo. For everything." Nickie blew a quick kiss and left.

Perhaps a quarter of an hour later the door opened and Cinda Vanderhart sauntered into the office. With a rhetorical "Hey, whas-sup?" she held out a green binder. "Here's my midterm paper for American Lit 104. You know, Ms. Farrell?"

Jo took the binder and set in on her desk. "I'll make sure she gets it."

"I think she's going to find it really interesting."

Thinking that Cinda was trying hard not to look like the cat that ate the canary, Jo glanced down at the binder. A thrill of alarm raced down her spine as she read the title:

TIPPETARIUS TO OZMA:
THE TRANSSEXUAL DENOUEMENT IN L. FRANK BAUM'S
"MARVELOUS LAND OF OZ".

Cinda Vanderhart smirked, "Way cool, huh? Bet she gives me an A. Well, see ya."

She pranced out of the office. As soon as the door closed Joanne snatched up the binder and rapidly scanned a few pages.

"Oh, no," she groaned after a minute. Dropping the binder: "Oh, shit, Nickie. Go tell Alex. Tell him before it's too late."

Chapter Six
Storm Fronts

Hearing his desk intercom's tactful buzz, Ambassador Eamon Douglass set aside a biography of Nathan Hale and stabbed the button. "What is it now?"

"Doctor Greenwold for you, Ambassador. Line two."

Douglass grunted. Damn pesky Jew wouldn't leave him alone. He plucked up the receiver: "Yes?"

"Hello, Ambassador," he heard the irritating voice say. "And how are you feeling today?"

"I'm feeling busy. What's on your mind?"

"I hadn't heard from you regarding those options we discussed. Have you given it any thought? The sooner we initiate a treatment protocol, the better."

"I do have one question," replied Eamon Douglass, idly pushing a glass wolf figurine around on the desktop with the tip of his shillelagh.

"By all means," the doctor answered in a pleased voice.

"Assuming I decline treatment, how long will I have?"

Sounding far less pleased, the doctor replied that he would strenuously advise against any such approach.

"How long, damn it? Weeks? Months? Years?"

"Ambassador, it's impossible to say. The disease progresses differently in each patient. You are in reasonable health otherwise. With proper treatment the probabilities are that you would have a goodly length of time left."

The ambassador glowered. "What is it about doctors that makes you so blasted reluctant to give a straight answer? I need to know whether I'll be dead before spring. If you won't tell me, Greenwold, by Christ I'll find someone who will."

After a strained silence the doctor stiffly replied, "It's unlikely that the disease would run its full course that rapidly. But your comfort level might well be compromised to a severe degree. I urge you to reconsider this—"

"Never mind my comfort level. You just make damn sure I stay functional until..." He thought for a moment. "Memorial Day. After that, you're off the hook. Do I make myself clear?"

The doctor whined, "Ambassador, please, this is terribly unwise. I recommend that you come in at the earliest opportunity so we can outline your course of therapy..."

"That'll be all, Doctor. Goodbye." Douglass hung up the phone. Damned Hebe doctor was a sniveling fool, but at least he'd confirmed that the ambassador would live long enough to carry out his plans for Windfield College.

"Excellent," he muttered, and went back to his biography.

Some while later a brief knock on the study door interrupted his reading.

His executive secretary entered and held out an express overnight envelope. "This just arrived, sir."

Douglass took it and saw the return address: "Redeemer Ministries, Johns Harbor, Georgiana".

"Very well, Holmes. That'll be all."

Douglass ripped the opener strip sideways and extracted a single typewritten page. He flung the envelope aside and read:

Honorable Ambassador Eamon Douglass:

We at Redeemer Ministries would like to acknowledge receipt of, and humbly express our gratitude for, your magnificently generous contribution. Please rest assured

that the funds will be used to help bring an end to the
anguish of which you have so eloquently spoken. It is
through the dedication of charitable individuals such
as yourself that our world can and will be changed for
the better.

In service before the Eternal,
Your humble servant,
Father George

P.S. With regards to the special plaque for your planned
cenotaph: It will be crafted by our artisans to your
precise specifications. Further details concerning delivery time and location will be forthcoming as they
become available.

Ambassador Eamon Douglass roared with amusement. Redeemer
Ministries! Father George! Egor Antonovich had always exhibited a
keen wit. He re-read the letter, laughed some more, then got up and
poured himself a shot of whiskey. He raised his glass in the air: "To
the Redemption!"

The liquor went down in a smooth fire fall. He'd never felt more
alive. A perfect time, he decided, to set things in motion. He went to
the desk and buzzed his secretary.

"Get me Fredericka Lindsey. Yes, that's what I said. The President
of Windfield College. Now, Holmes."

⸺⸺◉⸺⸺

Luanne Skinner's eldest son Lloyd sat at the bar of a ramshackle
Ocean City eatery called Dockside Dave's Grab-A-Crab, drinking long-
neck Budweisers and chewing his way through a bowl of free pretzels.
During the summer season Dockside Dave's was packed with tourists
gorging themselves on Chesapeake Bay's famous blueclaws; but now
in November only a few customers sat picking at their steamed crustaceans. The remains of a hamburger sat in congealed grease on a nearby
plate; after so many months in Ocean City Lloyd would no more eat

a fucking crab than a pelican. Even the smell of Old Bay seasoning made him sick.

Lloyd drained his bottle and motioned to the bartender, who interrupted his bored perusal of a racing form long enough to serve up another beer.

"And gimme more of those," Lloyd indicated the empty pretzel dish. The bartender complied and went back to his paper. Lloyd stared morosely out the salt-crusted windows at the windswept bay, where a few boats motored along under slate-colored skies. He needed a change of scenery. Ocean City was entering its winter hibernation and jobs were non-existent. For a month or so Lloyd had made decent money working on a dredging barge, but now there was nothing to do. Even the beach hustlers had departed. He needed to move on. South, maybe. Somewhere warm, with no goddamn crabs.

On the wall-mounted television a comedy rerun provoked howls of canned laughter from an unseen audience. Lloyd had seen the show before. It was all about a twat who lived with a faggot. All the jokes seemed to be about how the twat was desperate to get laid but the faggot wouldn't do it because he'd rather wear her clothes. Lloyd shook his head. Some asshole out in Hollywood got paid a million dollars to write that crap. It was unbelievable.

"Hey, partner. Mind if I sit down?"

Lloyd swiveled at the sudden voice and saw a dark-haired man pointing to an adjacent barstool. The man added, "Unless you'd rather drink alone. Been there, done that."

"It's a free country." Lloyd turned back to his beer.

"Think so? Could've fooled me." The man perched on the stool and flipped a few bills onto the bar. "What're you drinking?"

Lloyd Skinner warily examined the newcomer. The fellow was well-built, of moderate height, maybe a few years older than Lloyd. He wore a red plaid shirt tucked into snug blue jeans and a brown leather jacket festooned with zippers and epaulets. His masculine features were regular enough to be considered good-looking but not pretty, topped by a head of conservatively-cut black hair. But what Lloyd noticed most were the other's eyes: very dark blue, approaching navy.

The man extended his hand. "I'm Cale. Cale Pittman. Seriously, if you want to be alone, I respect that." He smiled easily, and Lloyd noticed that Cale Pittman's dark blue irises were shot through with amber flecks.

"Nah." Lloyd grasped the proffered hand. "Lloyd Skinner."

"Glad to meet you, Lloyd. Ready for another round?"

"Always." Lloyd tipped up his bottle and drained it.

Cale Pittman snapped his fingers until the bartender looked over with an annoyed expression. "Two more." He glanced up at the television and his expression darkened. "Do you like this sort of stuff, Lloyd?"

"Are you kiddin'? Goddamn faggot bullshit."

Cale's eyes widened. "Damn right." When the bartender brought two frosty bottles Pittman pointed up at the television: "How about getting rid of that? We don't like degenerate filth."

"Degenerate filth, huh?" The bartender grabbed the remote and flipped channels to a baseball game. "Pure enough for you?" He dourly made change and stalked away.

"Dickhead," observed Lloyd. "Prob'ly a gay boy himself."

"Never know these days. Damn fairies are everywhere, like roaches. Cheers," Pittman saluted, and drank. "You live around here?"

"Just a room." Lloyd paused to light a generic cigarette with a yellow plastic Bic. "You?"

The other nodded. "Motel up by the inlet. For now. I move around a lot."

Lloyd blew a stream of smoke. "I gotta be movin' on, too. Ocean City is fuckin' dead. No good jobs. And I ain't about to flip burgers."

"The burger joints would never hire someone like you, Lloyd. Corporate bastards can't exploit intelligent white men. That's why they only employ niggers and mental defectives."

"You got that right." Lloyd regarded Cale Pittman with new respect. "Not too many guys tell it like it is anymore. They're afraid of this political correct shit."

Cale fixed his blue eyes on Lloyd. "Exactly. Weaklings and cowards. Arnold Schwarzenegger called them 'girlie men'. The whole country is awash in sissies. Even those who aren't faggots all want to *act* like faggots, so they call themselves 'metrosexuals'." Pittman made a gagging sound. "What the fuck is a metrosexual?"

"I dunno," admitted Lloyd, "but if I ever see one I'll pound his ass into the sidewalk."

"Spoken like a true *Übermensch*," Cale said. "We think alike, my friend."

Lloyd frowned. "Uber-what?"

"*Übermensch*. Nietzsche's so-called Overman. It's usually translated as Superman, but that makes me think of a homo in blue tights. I prefer the term *Superiorman*." Seeing Lloyd's bewildered expression he continued: "Friedrich Nietzsche was a German philosopher, probably the greatest. His writings are little complex, but the basic idea is quite clear."

"Yeah?" Lloyd grumbled, feeling dumb as a post: "What is it?"

Pittman solemnly recited: "He who has the power, makes the rules."

"Like the government."

"Not exactly. The government is really nothing but a zookeeper for cages full of sheep. I'm talking about men, Lloyd. Strong, superior *men*. Men who don't allow religion or society to tell them what's good or what's evil. They determine that for themselves."

"Huh." Lloyd signaled the bartender. "I'll get this round."

"A Superiorman doesn't pity or put up with weaklings. Power is everything. You see," Cale explained, "soft heartedness is a profound failing, because it allows the feeble to hamper the growth of the powerful. All this sensitivity crap is turning America into a nation of pantywaists."

The bartender placed two fresh bottles in front of them and retreated to the far end of the bar, where he slouched on his stool chewing a toothpick, eyeing them suspiciously.

Lloyd polished off half his bottle in three swallows. "I think that jerk heard you." He wiped his mouth with the back of his hand. "Looks kind of pissed. I guess he's not a Superiorman."

"Him?" Pittman laughed. "He's just a useless drone, following the rules because he can't think for himself."

"Well, I dunno much about Nitchie and stuff," Lloyd conceded, "but I damn well think for myself."

"Yes, you do. It isn't necessary to read Nietzsche to be an *Übermensch*, you know. I've watched you in action, Lloyd." Cale raised his bottle. "Admirable. Very admirable."

"Watched me?" Lloyd repeated, frowning. "When?"

Cale Pittman leaned closer and spoke in a low voice: "That night under the boardwalk?"

Lloyd gripped the beer bottle so hard that veins popped out on the back of his hand. "I dunno what you're talkin' about. Musta been someone else."

"It was you," Pittman reiterated. "The way you laid out that little piece of faggot trash…magnificent. Right then I recognized that you were a genuine Superiorman, one of a select breed. I decided I had to meet you. And now that I have…well, Lloyd, let's just say that I'm thrilled and honored."

Lloyd's head whirled with fear, anger, and uncertainty. It was bad enough that this stranger knew of the episode beneath the boardwalk. But the idea that Cale Pittman had made a point of tracking him down was downright scary. Lloyd wondered if the other man could be an undercover vice cop. The prospect infuriated him. On the other hand, if Pittman was a police officer, cracking a bottle over his head and fleeing would land Lloyd in deeper shit than he cared to imagine. He squirmed nervously on his stool.

"I'm not a cop, Lloyd, if that's what you're thinking." Cale's dark eyes gleamed. "But you're smart to be suspicious. An *Übermensch* must be eternally vigilant. Everybody's a snitch these days. There's no integrity left in the world. But I can tell you are a man of integrity, Lloyd."

"That creep tried to hold me up," Lloyd muttered. "It was self-defense."

"Of course it was," Cale concurred. "A man's got to defend himself from these damn perverts, and…" Jerking his head toward the bartender: "What do you say we go somewhere else, Lloyd? I don't like the way that prick is staring at us."

Lloyd gulped the rest of his beer, banged the bottle down and rose off the stool. "Let's get outa here."

The bartender, whose name was Pete, watched the two men scoop up their change. There would be no tip, but Pete didn't care. After twenty years of serving drinks he considered himself a shrewd judge of human character, and his instincts told him that these clowns were trouble. The blonde brute was just another stupid redneck, but that guy in the bomber jacket gave off some disturbing vibes. Pete thought the departed pair had the potential to be bad news. Very bad news indeed.

Cale Pittman accepted Lloyd's proposal that they head for the Chum Bucket Lounge. They hadn't walked more than two blocks when a lilting nasal voice suddenly addressed them: "Hellooo, boys! Enjoying our lovely seaside town?"

From a recessed doorway emerged a slight young man, dressed all in black except for a flowing pink scarf of some silky material. Pinned to his black denim jacket was a yellow smiley face button. The young man held a large multicolored all-day sucker. He slowly licked it, his pinkie extended. "I'm Sandy, the good witch of the Delmarva. You gentleman looking for a fun time?"

About to lunge, Lloyd felt a restraining grip on his arm. He glanced at Cale Pittman, who grinned at Sandy and exclaimed, "A witch! Does that mean that you can perform all sorts of magic tricks?"

"Tricks?" With a slow lascivious lick of his lollipop: "Honey, I wrote that book. I can be positively enchanting."

Cale Pittman laughed, his eyes sparkling. "Oh, that sounds fabulous. Doesn't it, partner?" With the quickness of a striking python he grabbed Sandy and encircled his neck in a vicious headlock, twisting one arm halfway up his back. Sandy dropped the lollipop, which shattered on the pavement. In a strangled whine: "Let me go, you shithead!"

"Shut up," ordered Pittman, "or I'll pop out both your eyeballs."

He forced the arm up even higher. "Understand?"

The young man managed a weak nod against the powerful arm around his windpipe.

Cale Pittman hissed in his captive's ear: "Sandy, you have disrupted a pleasant walk I was having with my partner. That's unacceptable, especially since you are such a despicable piece of shit. It's diseased little flits like you that have disgraced the noble tradition of manly love with your twisted perversions. You are lower than the lowest streetwalking cunt, Sandy. I see no reason to let you live. A mealy bug is more worthwhile than a faggot, and do you know why?" He tightened the elbow until Sandy's head looked ready to separate from his neck. "Because you faggots have ruined everything. Men aren't men anymore, they're all pansies like *you*, Sandy. Gutless girlie men who can't do anything except whore around and spread disease like rats and flies."

Lloyd stood by, delighted. Clearly Cale was no undercover cop. He glanced up and down the street, but they were alone. Lloyd leaned over and snarled in Sandy's blood-engorged face: "You hear what my bud's tellin' you, asshole?"

Pittman's dark blue eyes gleamed. "Like I said, Sandy, the proper thing would be to snuff you right now. You're nothing but a germ, and germs should be eradicated. But I'm in a great mood, and killing a turd like you might ruin it. So I've decided to let you live. Would you like that?"

A faint keening issued from the helpless young hustler.

Lloyd uttered a derisive laugh. "I think the scumbag said yes."

"All right. When I let you go, Sandy, I suggest that you run, fast, before I change my mind. And make very sure that I never see you again, because if I do you are faggot toast. Got that?"

He released his grip so abruptly that Sandy crumpled to the ground. He lay there for a second, gasping and crying, then staggered to his feet and began to lurch away. Cale Pittman let him take a few steps and then suddenly barked: "Boo!"

Sandy jumped like he'd been zapped with a cattle prod. Fleeing down the street without looking back, he rounded a corner and disappeared.

"Holy shit, Cale." Lloyd couldn't hide his admiration. "That was fuckin' awesome."

Pittman straightened his jacket and kicked the broken remnants of Sandy's lollipop into the gutter. "Coming from you, Lloyd, I consider that a real compliment." He grinned. "You'd do the same thing, of course. I just happened to grab him first."

"Sure I would," agreed Lloyd. "I think you scared that little fruit into the next county."

"Good. Hey, what do you say we forget the bar and head over to my place for a while? I've got bourbon, beer, stuff to eat if you're hungry. I'll show you that Nietzsche book, where he talks about guys like us."

Lloyd thought for a minute. "He who has the power, makes the rules?"

Pittman's face lit up. "That's right, Lloyd. As our friend Sandy found out, it's a bad idea to fuck with us *Übermenschen.*"

"Sure, let's go." Lloyd smacked his fists. "*Übermenschen*...damn right."

"My car's parked on the next street," said Cale Pittman. He gave Lloyd a comradely pat on the back. "Come on, partner."

Lloyd fell in with his new friend. Only after taking a few steps did it hit him that he'd become powerfully aroused.

Some hours later Lloyd Skinner reclined on Cale's bed, smoking a cigarette and loosely grasping a tumbler of Jack Daniels. He felt giddy, perplexed, hung-over, and sexually spent to a degree he'd never imagined possible. Nothing in the world could have prepared him for the experience; it hadn't been "making love", or a "sexual encounter", or anything else he'd ever heard about or read. It had been raw, savage, hard fornication; two dynamos generating a male mating energy so extreme it threatened to tear them both apart.

Lloyd drank some bourbon and puffed on his cigarette. Sounds of running water emanated from the bathroom where the other

Superiorman was taking a shower. Very few individuals had ever impressed Lloyd Skinner. He thought most people were frauds, losers or assholes. But Cale Pittman had mesmerized him with stories about Alexander the Great, Richard the Lionhearted, Lawrence of Arabia; mighty warrior men who not only scaled heights of historic achievement unimaginable by today's puny standards, but understood and practiced the ancient hallowed acts of masculine bonding. Who in their right mind would dare to label Richard as a "fag" or Alexander as "gay"? Why, the man had conquered the known world in his mid-twenties! That wasn't "gay"; it was *strength*, a manifestation of pure manly *power*. Lloyd had listened spellbound as Cale explained how the modern-day queers perverted the ideal of manly love with their effeminate ways and sordid lechery until it came to be regarded as an ugly sin against nature. That was why, he said, *Übermenschen* like Lloyd and himself had a solemn duty to cleanse the world wherever possible of gay vermin like Sandy. Lloyd had drunk it all in, feeling charged and virile. Then Cale had made some moves, and before he knew it Lloyd was helplessly swept away.

Pittman emerged from the bathroom, a white towel wrapped around his middle. He came over to the bed, took the other's bourbon and set it on the nightstand. "So, partner," he inquired, dark eyes glistening impishly, "are we sleepy yet?" He looked down, and his grin widened. "I didn't think so. Hail Caesar!"

It never did occur to Lloyd Skinner that he had been seduced as easily as a young girl.

⸻ ◉ ⸻

Fredericka Lindsey sat at her magnificent colonial cherrywood desk in the Windfield College President's office, perusing figures for an upcoming scholarship committee meeting. Due to a high matriculation rate of "full ride" students this fall, the scholarship fund, although securely in the black, wasn't quite as robust as she preferred it to be. She studied the numbers through some half-glasses perched part way down her long nose. When it came to her school's finances, President

Lindsey liked to have fat safety margins in place. She was writing a couple of notations in the margins when her intercom beeped.

"Sorry to interrupt, Ms. Lindsey," came the voice of Maudelle Chesterfield, her long-time administrative assistant, "but I have a call for you from an Ambassador Eamon Douglass."

Fredericka Lindsey laid down her pen. "Are you certain, Del? Ambassador Douglass?"

"Yes, ma'am. Shall I put him through?"

Taken by surprise, President Lindsey didn't immediately reply. Although she'd never met him, she knew that Eamon Douglass was one of several reclusive business tycoons who lived in guarded estates dotted about the surrounding countryside. None of these gentlemen harbored any amicable feelings toward Windfield College. She couldn't imagine why a crusty old reactionary like Ambassador Douglass would be calling her.

"Ms. Lindsey?"

"I'll take the call, Del."

She heard a brusque voice: "Hello?"

"This is Fredericka Lindsey. Am I speaking with Ambassador Douglass?"

"Yes, Eamon Douglass here. It's cordial of you to take my call, President Lindsey. I'm most grateful."

Fredericka Lindsey recognized the peremptory tone of someone who was more used to giving orders than expressing gratitude. "Not at all, Ambassador. How may I help you?"

"You're a busy woman, Madame President, so I'll not waste your time. I would like to come see you." The ambassador added, "At your convenience, of course."

Horsefeathers, thought the president. She was a tough seasoned pro, well acquainted with cantankerous dinosaurs like Eamon Douglass. He didn't give a damn about her or anyone else's convenience. "May I ask, Ambassador, what this is regarding?"

"I don't wish to discuss it over the phone," she heard him say. "Let's just say that it's a matter of considerable philanthropic interest to your institution."

President Lindsey sat up suddenly and uncrossed her legs, snagging her hose on the underside of the desk. Biting off an unladylike expletive she replied, "I feel compelled to admit that I'm somewhat perplexed, Ambassador. Frankly, sir, you have not been in the vanguard of those who support this college, financially or otherwise."

"That is so," acknowledged Eamon Douglass. "However, Madame President, certain recent events related to my health have brought about a change in my perceptions. I now believe my thinking has been wrongheaded. To be blunt, I've been a horse's ass. I'd like to make amends while I am still able to do so. Will you see me?"

Fredericka Lindsey swiveled her chair to face an enormous window that commanded a spectacular view of the broad hillside fronting Windfield College. In the distance she could see Randall Windfield's memorial obelisk. She was far too shrewd not to realize that something was afoot with this old buzzard. But what harm would it do to hear him out in person? After all, the scholarship fund could never be too plump.

"It would be my pleasure, Ambassador Douglass. Shall we say next week some time?"

<hr />

After closing, Collie Skinner walked Robin Thompson to her car in the Foxton Arms parking lot. Her little second-hand Kia Sephia wasn't much to look at, but he admired the way she kept it spotless and neat. One day, he thought, Robin would make some lucky guy a terrific wife.

Fishing in her purse for her keys Robin asked, "Did your mother come right out and say she wanted to leave Jay-Bo?"

"Not exactly," Collie shook his head. "But she said that she wanted to talk to me about what we're going to do."

"That could mean anything. Maybe you just heard what you want to hear, Collie." Robin placed her hand on his arm. "I know it's what you'd like to see happen, but only your parents can make that decision. Whether they decide to split up is their private business. You just have to let them work things out."

"But I hate him, Robin! I hate him enough to kill him. The way he treats Mama..." Collie couldn't go on.

Robin set her purse and keys on the hood of her car. "Don't. Remember what your mother told you? Hatred is a poison. But you're not like that, Collie. I see a lot of Luanne in you, but there's something else, too. Something different and special, and it doesn't come from Jay-Bo Skinner. Please, don't hate. You don't want to end up like him." She pulled his arms around her, laid her head against his chest and whispered, "*I* don't want you to."

Collie hugged her. Robin felt delicate but also warm and very alive. He gently rested one cheek against her soft brown hair, and suddenly realized that his feelings for Robin Thompson ran deep; so deep, in fact, that he could barely catch his breath. Heart pounding, he tried to speak, but for some reason his voice wasn't working. Robin looked up into Collie's face, her expression one of complete serenity.

"Sshh," she smiled. "I know. Me, too." Then they were kissing, and for a glorious interval both of them forgot about everything else in the world.

⚬«❍»⚬

"You no-good *cunt.*"

Jay-Bo Skinner flared his nostrils and glared at Luanne, who sat across from him at the kitchen table, her chin up in a show of defiance. "I knew you'd finally get around to runnin' out on me. Well, guess what, Lu? You ain't goin' anywhere." He drained his beer and deliberately crumpled the can in front of her nose. "You got anything else to say?" He threw the crushed can past her face to fall clattering in the kitchen sink. "Bring me another goddamn beer."

Luanne rebelliously shook her head. "Get it yourself. I'm tired of being your slave. You've been treating me worse than a dog for all these years. I'm sick of it, and I want out."

"I don't give a rat's ass what you want," retorted Jay-Bo. "Like I said, you ain't leavin'. Get that thought outa your head. West Virginia trailer trash," he sneered, going to the refrigerator and extracting another beer. "I always knew you were a dumb bitch."

Luanne bristled. "Who are you to call me trash? Your people were nothing but hicks and no-account drunks. Just because you joined the service and got to kill a bunch of foreign people, that makes you some kind of hot shit American hero? Not by me, mister."

"Your memory ain't working so good, Luanne. It was you that came after me, so damn hot to trot your pussy almost caught fire. I blew it, though. Marryin' you ruined what should've been just a nice cheap fuck."

"You bastard," breathed Luanne, hot tears in her eyes. "I *am* leaving you, and you're not going to stop me. Collie and I will thank God every day that we've gotten away from such an asshole."

"Collie. I shoulda known. That back-stabbin' little fairy is the one who put you up to this, ain't he?"

"No," snapped Luanne. "You leave him out of it, Jay-Bo Skinner."

"That runt has been nothin' but trouble since the day he was born." Jay-Bo's neck began to swell and redden. "At first I thought you'd gone and fucked the mailman or somethin', he was such a messed-up little freak with those damn eyes. Except no one around here would be stupid enough to screw *my* missus. It was just rotten luck that you had such a butt-ugly pup."

"Collie is my beautiful boy," cried Luanne. "You shut your mouth about him."

"That's right, stick up for the brat," growled Jay-Bo. "Always Collie this, and Collie that. You'd think *he* was the man of the house."

With a shrill laugh: "He is the man of the house! Collie is a hundred times more of a man than you are. *He* has the job, *he* pays the rent, *he* makes sure there's enough beer for you to sit on your fat ass and get drunk all the time…"

Too late, Luanne realized her peril. Jay-Bo Skinner leaped up and in a flash had her by the throat. He tightened his fist until she could hardly breathe. Collie's mother struggled in vain, as helpless as a kitten in the clutches of a gorilla. Jay-Bo dragged her out of the kitchen, over to the

BarcaLounger where he swiftly extracted his Colt Python. Slamming her against a wall, he forced his wife's head back with the gun barrel, shoving it up into the soft area under her chin. Overwhelmed with terror, certain that she was about to die, Luanne squeezed her eyes shut. All she could think about was her son.

"Okay, now you've gone and made me mad, so here's how it's gonna be." Jay-Bo nudged the gun for emphasis. "No more talk about you leavin'. If I hear one more word out of your damn mouth about that, you know what happens?"

Pinned to the wall with a loaded .357 magnum jammed beneath her chin, Luanne didn't make a sound.

"You think I'll waste good ammo on you?" Jay-Bo shook his head. "Nope. I'll kill Collie boy instead. Two bullets, one in each of those fuckin' eyes. And then I'll shoot myself. Think I give a shit? I don't. But you'll have the rest of your life to think about how you got your precious Collie's head blown off. Am I gettin' through to you?"

Paralyzed in his grip, Luanne remained silent.

"AM I GETTIN' THROUGH TO YOU?!" Jay-Bo screamed, and cocked the trigger.

A mere feather's touch separating her from eternity, Luanne felt a wet warmth spread in her groin. She faintly nodded her head.

After several interminable seconds Jay-Bo lowered the gun and uncocked it. "That's real good, Luanne. Maybe you ain't so dumb after all." He released her throat and she slowly slid down the wall onto the floor, gasping to regain her breath. "Damn, woman," he jeered, waving the gun at her stained jeans. "Looks like somethin' scared the piss outa you."

Crushed and humiliated, Luanne turned away and slunk to the bathroom. She undressed, put her soiled clothes in the hamper and got in the shower. After a few moments of standing under the hot flow, the shakes hit. She hugged herself in the steamy stall, teeth chattering and limbs quaking. All thoughts of leaving Jay-Bo, of trying to find a peaceful life with her son, had vanished from her mind. Only one thing mattered: the boy's safety. To the exclusion of all else, her life from now on would be devoted to keeping Nick Farrington's son out of harm's way.

The shaking finally subsided. Weeping steadily, Luanne began to wash herself, as her tears went swirling down the shower drain along with all her hopes.

Collie was still thinking about Robin Thompson as he steered his Camaro into the Knights Inn parking lot. How amazing it had been to hold her and kiss her! He couldn't wait to tell his mother. She thought the world of Robin. Maybe this romantic development would help cheer her up.

Collie had just locked his car door when to his surprise he saw a gleaming black Continental limousine pull into the lot and brake to a stop. Opulent chariots like this were a decided rarity at the Knights Inn. Collie glanced at the illuminated license plate: "SHMRCKS". He pocketed his keys and waited.

One of the blacked-out rear windows hummed down and a gray-haired man wearing an eye patch peered out. Spying Collie, he imperiously gestured with one hand. "You! Come over here." When Collie moved closer the old man looked him over with his one good eye. In an authoritative rasp: "Do you know who I am, boy?"

"Mister Douglass?"

"*Ambassador* Douglass," snapped the man. "What makes you think so?"

"Your license plate," Collie answered, pointing.

Eamon Douglass grunted. "What's your name?"

"Collie Skinner, sir."

"Did you say 'Collie'?"

"From Colin. It was my mother's maiden name. She works for you, Ambassador. In the Stuarton Shamrock. Luanne Skinner."

"Skinner…yes. Her husband was pilloried for arresting some damn Windfield dope fiend." The old man rested his hands atop a thorny-looking black cane. "Your father?"

Collie shrugged.

"He should've been given a medal. Instead he got screwed by homosexual lawyers. Outrageous." He indicated the Knights Inn. "Do you work in there?"

"Yes, sir. Couple of nights a week, after my regular job at the Foxton Arms."

"You know Mr. Barlow?"

"He's my boss," replied Collie, wondering what this interrogation was all about. "Everybody around here knows Big Mike."

Eamon Douglass's single eye narrowed. "Go in there and inform Big Mike that Ambassador Douglass wants to see him."

"Okay, but he's usually pretty busy," said Collie. "I don't know whether—"

"If he isn't out here in sixty seconds neither you nor your mother will have jobs by sunrise."

"Yes, sir. Right away." Collie didn't doubt for one second that the man would make good on his threat. He ran inside and quickly made his way to the bar. "Boss, Ambassador Douglass is outside in some huge limo, he said he wants to see you. He's kind of impatient."

To Collie's surprise Mike at once stopped what he was doing and wiped his hands on a bar towel. "Take over. Don't fuck it up."

"I won't. I didn't know you knew the ambassador. He's one of the richest guys in the state. How do you..." Seeing his boss's expression Collie abruptly closed his mouth.

"Skinner, do I pay you to know things?" Mike Barlow didn't wait for a response. "No, I don't. Forget about everything except serving drinks. I mean *everything*. You got that?"

"Got it." Collie began rinsing some dirty glasses as Barlow lifted the bar door and went out. If his boss and the ambassador were somehow connected, Collie didn't want to know. He felt positive that those two could serve up a world of hurt to anyone who didn't stay out of their business.

Collie had no way of knowing how right he was. "Big Mike" Barlow wasn't just a saloonkeeper. Unbeknownst to anybody, for a long while he had also served as Eamon Douglass's personal enforcer. This unlikely pairing had come about by accident many years earlier.

Mike Barlow had been the only child of a raging alcoholic father and a religious nut mother. Almost from the day he was brought home to their battered old Airstream trailer Mike had been beaten by his dad while his mother quoted Scripture and sprinkled water from the Holy Land in all directions. Most babies would have succumbed to the ceaseless pummeling, but Mike had been born tough, and he not only survived but grew, and grew, until by the time he turned ten he stood as tall as most seventeen-year-olds. He was sent to school but merely slouched in back of the classrooms, ignoring his teachers. When anyone disturbed him he knocked them senseless. One of the athletic coaches attempted to exploit young Barlow's toughness for the football squad, but abandoned the effort when Mike nearly paralyzed a couple of teammates during a practice scrimmage. The school officials fervently prayed for the adolescent giant to drop out, which to their relief he did at the age of fourteen.

Tiring of his father's unrelenting assaults, Mike had just about decided to kill him when Amos Barlow resolved the issue by falling off his tractor drunk and running himself over with a bush hog, thereby saddling a local funeral director with the problem of how to respectfully inter one hundred and eighty pounds of ground meat and thistle. Buoyed by his Old Man's demise, Big Mike embarked on a career of boosting cars, poaching, and vandalizing vending machines. In due course he was arrested and jailed, which he didn't mind since the meals were regular and everyone treated him with respect.

Upon being released he reluctantly returned home to the corroding Airstream. During his absence, however, Ma Barlow had begun seeing religious visions and before long became convinced that she could discern the divine countenance of Paul the Apostle in a large yam. She carried it to a tent revival one night and so inspired the congregation with her faith that the itinerant preacher convinced her to accompany them on their blessed travels, and Mike never saw her again.

For years he performed odd jobs and lived by himself in the

decaying trailer, with intermittent sojourns in the county lockup. He made no friends because he didn't want any. Every so often he'd screw a backwoods whore, although he regarded women as shrill pests. Mike had little use for the human race and was content to let life pass him by. He didn't go out of his way to bother anybody, and nobody in their right mind ever thought of bothering him.

One day, between jobs and looking for work, Mike wandered into a big Shamrock farm equipment store. As it happened, the store manager was in the process of firing the yard forklift operator, a rat-faced glue-sniffer named Moley Fescue. Since Big Mike knew his way around machinery and looked as powerful as a forklift himself, the manager hired him on the spot. Quivering with resentment and glue fumes, Moley Fescue began spewing vile epithets and threats in Big Mike's face, windmilling his arms and vowing retribution, whereupon Mike picked Fescue up like a rag doll and slung him over the yard fence.

Two days later, after huffing several baggies of industrial adhesive, Moley Fescue charged into the equipment yard, his red eyes bulging. He jumped onto a forklift and began driving around crazily, trying to skewer his successor with the giant steel prongs. He failed to harm Big Mike, who could move with great speed when necessary, but he did cause a grievous amount of damage to the pricey tractors, mowers, and cultivating attachments. Eventually the police came and hauled him off, kicking and foaming at the mouth. Big Mike stood by silently, watching the store manager groan and curse as he surveyed the wreckage.

Fescue was released on bail, but when the date for his court appearance arrived, he didn't show up. Nobody could recall seeing him. An arrest warrant was issued and the police conducted a search, but Moley Fescue had disappeared. Suspecting foul play, the cops questioned everyone at the Shamrock store, especially Big Mike; but having nothing to go on, they finally consigned Moley Fescue to the missing persons file and forgot about him.

Not long afterward Mike received a summons from Eamon Douglass himself. Presenting himself at the huge estate known as Shamrocks, which beggared his wildest imaginings, Mike was escorted up to Douglass's private study. Without preamble, not even a handshake, Eamon Douglass demanded to know if Mike had disposed of Moley Fescue.

Seeing no reason to deny it, Mike shrugged his massive shoulders and told Douglass how he had waylaid and throttled Fescue, then thrown his corpse into a remote West Virginia lake known to be inhabited by Volkswagen-sized snapping turtles. Eamon Douglass listened, nodded, said that he was damned appreciative, and wondered if Mike would consider working for him as a "special consultant" from time to time. Mike liked the important-sounding title of "special consultant", and agreed at once. Eamon Douglass handed him ten hundred-dollar bills and dismissed him.

And so it began. Over the ensuing years Mike Barlow performed all kinds of consulting work for Eamon Douglass: arm-twisting, intimidating, threatening, bullying, maiming, firebombing; whatever the ambassador deemed necessary. It was fulfilling employment, paid well, and gave Big Mike a heretofore unknown sense of purpose. After a while Eamon Douglass bought the Knights Inn and installed Barlow as the putative owner, which provided a nice cover and kept him on a handy leash. It was a mutually satisfactory association, and both gentlemen benefited from the relationship.

⸺ ◆ ⸺

While Eamon Douglas talked Mike Barlow kept his eyes on the shivering driver, who'd been ordered out of the limo and told to wait by the tavern. When the ambassador stopped speaking Mike shook his head. "Damn."

"Windfield must be wiped out before it's too late. The task has fallen to me, and I won't shrink from it."

"This'll kick up a bigger ruckus than those Ay-rabs up in New York," guessed Big Mike. "*Damn.*"

The ambassador scowled. "Those deluded Mohammedans were driven by religious fanaticism, which is the purview of criminal imbeciles. I am motivated solely by a patriotic desire to cleanse my state and country of the immoral degeneracy that is destroying everything good and decent."

"But radiation ain't clean. Everything 'round here is gonna end up poison." Big Mike gestured out the limo's window at the Knights Inn. "Whole place'll probably start to glow in the dark."

Eamon Douglass impatiently waved aside the concern. "The dangerous contamination will be confined to a small area and be gone in less than fifty years. Goddamn it, Barlow, do you suppose I would allow permanent harm to come to the hallowed soil of Virginia? That would be an act of madness." He glowered. "Do I seem insane to you?"

Mike shrugged. "So what do you want me to do?"

"I'll be finalizing certain arrangements soon. In the meantime, keep yourself available. Things may happen quickly and I'll need you in a hurry." The ambassador studied him. "You do understand that this will bring an end to your consulting career."

Big Mike nodded, none too happily.

"In consideration of the extraordinary nature and historical significance of this event, your final consultation fee will be one million dollars."

"A *million* bucks?"

"All cash, deposited for you in an overseas bank," lied the ambassador. "After you retrieve it I suggest you lose yourself somewhere. I suspect things may turn a little hot hereabouts." He emitted a nasty cackle. "Well, that's all. Tell my driver to get over here."

Big Mike watched the limo drive away, then pushed inside the Knights Inn and wordlessly resumed his station behind the bar. Collie went to wait tables, refusing to give in to curiosity about what had just transpired outside. It was none of his business.

———— ((◉)) ————

By the time he drove home Collie had put Big Mike and the ambassador out of his mind. He was busy reliving the details of his earlier encounter with Robin: the scent of her hair, the warmth of her lips, and the loveliness of her petite figure under her winter coat.

Collie let himself into the darkened apartment and tiptoed to his room. He flipped on the overhead light and started at the sight of

Luanne lying curled on his bed, facing the wall, legs drawn up almost to her chest. She wore a faded pink terrycloth robe over a flannel nightgown, and despite the chill her feet were bare. Collie saw that her hair had been washed but not combed; damp strands dangled in her face. He approached the bed and softly called, "Mama? Are you okay?"

At the sound of Collie's voice she rolled over. "Nicholas?" Her voice was a weak wheeze. "Thank God. You're all right, aren't you?"

"Sure, I'm fine." Collie sat on the edge of the bed. "Mama, what's wrong? Why are you in here?"

Luanne struggled to sit up. "I'm sorry, baby, I didn't mean to take your bed. I'll go out on the couch..."

"Mama, no, don't worry. Take it easy. Is it the pain again?"

When she shook her head Collie noticed an angry red mark under her chin. "What happened to your neck, Mama?" He reached out to touch her but Luanne shrank away. "Did you bump into something?"

"That's right. I...I accidentally ran into the edge of the medicine cabinet mirror. It's nothing." She put her hand over the red mark as her eyes flooded with tears. "Nothing at all."

The truth hit Collie like a punch in the face. "Did that son-of-a-bitch do this to you?!" He stood up, shaking with rage, fists clenched. "I'll kill that worthless piece of shit!"

"Nicholas, *no*." Luanne grabbed his arm. "It was an accident, I told you! Don't make so much noise, he'll hear you," she pleaded. "Please, baby, sit down, for the love of God."

Collie allowed her to pull him down even as he yearned to run into the next room and smash the brute who had done this to his mother. His heart felt on the edge of exploding. He put his arms protectively around Luanne: "Don't cry, Mama. I'll take care of you." Collie felt his own tears spill over. "We're going to get out of here, I promise. Far away, California or China or anywhere, it doesn't matter, as long as I get you away from that dirty scumbag..."

Collie felt his mother stiffen. She pushed free and glared at him, her eyes white with panic. "Don't you talk about that, you hear me? Don't you even think it, Nicholas!"

"But we can leave, just you and me. I hate his guts, Mama! That fatass prick drinks up half of every paycheck I bring home. He won't even let you go see a doctor. Well *fuck him*," Collie snarled. "We'll start packing tonight, take off before he can–"

Luanne Skinner slapped her son. He stared at her, his mouth hanging open in shock. "Why, Mama?"

Her face crumpled. Luanne embraced Collie, her thin frame wracked with sobs. His cheek stinging, Collie hugged her back, trying to control the firestorm in his heart. Finally she expelled a shuddering breath and moved back so she could look at him.

Holding both his hands in a tight grip: "Nicholas, I'm sorry I hit you. Hitting is never an answer, baby, and I hope you'll forgive me. But I want you to listen to your mother now, all right?" She waited for him to nod. "If you love me, my sweet boy, you must promise that you will *never* talk about leaving again. It doesn't matter if you don't understand. That's what I want. As for your fath…as for Jay-Bo, just stay out of his way. Leave him to me. I know you're feeling awfully angry, sweetheart, and I wish I knew how to make it stop, but only you can do that." She tried to smile. "Do you have any idea how much I love you?"

Unable to speak, Collie slowly nodded his head.

"No, you don't. Not yet, but you will someday, when you become a daddy. Now promise me. I want to hear you say the words, Nicholas."

"I…I promise I won't talk about leaving anymore." The words felt like barbed wire in his mouth.

Luanne closed her eyes. "Thank you." She waited a moment, opened them again. "Isn't there anything happy we can talk about? I'd like that so very much, honey. Please."

"All right, Mama." Collie pulled his mother close and kissed her temple. "I wanted to tell you anyway. Something really nice happened to me tonight."

Luanne's sad features brightened. "It did?"

"Uh-huh. I think…What I mean is, I'm pretty sure Robin Thompson likes me." He added with a shy smile: "A lot."

"Oh, sweetie, that's wonderful!" Luanne's face regained a measure of animation. "I love Robin, she's precious. You and her? How long has this been going on? It's so exciting! Tell me everything."

So Collie did, and for a little while mother and son were able to laugh together, to feel glad, and not think about the dark cruel corners of their world. They spoke of young love, of kisses in the frosty air, and of a future filled with hope. Neither could know that the time was drawing near when Luanne Skinner would enjoy no more such moments.

Chapter Seven
Gathering Shadows

Cinda Vanderhart paused outside Nickie Farrell's office, gave two firm knocks and cracked the door enough to peek inside.

"Ms. Farrell? It's me." Cinda waved the summons note she'd found in her dorm mailbox. "I came right over."

"Come in, Ms. Vanderhart."

Cinda walked into the small room, noting the shelves crammed with books, the potted plants on the window sill, and a large framed Save the Tigers poster on one wall. Her midterm paper was lying before Nickie on the desk.

"Have a seat." Nickie pointed with a pen to a wooden chair.

Cinda settled herself and waited, one arm dangling over the seat back.

Nickie leaned forward on her elbows and studied her student for several seconds.

"Well, Ms. Vanderhart. About your midterm paper."

Cinda's mouth twitched. "What did you think of it?"

Nickie picked up the green binder, read the title, and put it down. "If I assigned grades based on subtlety, you'd be getting an F."

"But you're not."

"No. So let's forget about grades for a moment. What is it, exactly, that you want from me?"

"The truth," replied Cinda. "Ms. Farrell, you're a T-girl, aren't you?

A transsexual?"

Nickie shrugged. "I think you already know the answer to that."

Cinda persisted: "*Are* you?"

"Yes," Nickie surrendered. "I'm a transsexual woman. Now may I ask *you* a question?"

"Sure," grinned Cinda, savoring her triumph.

"What business is it of yours?"

"Not business, Ms. Farrell. News. Transsexuality is a hot-button issue these days. Movies, television, books. I'm a journalism major, and I'm going to be an investigative journalist. Your story is going to get me onto the *Spectrum*."

"What do you mean, 'my story'?" Nickie frowned. "You're not intending to publish this so-called news in the school paper?"

"Get real, Ms. Farrell. If I don't, somebody else will. Do you seriously think you can keep something like this a secret? Don't kid yourself. I figured it out, didn't I? The others will, too." With a smug grin: "It'll just take them longer. Anyway, I think it's totally cool. We have lots of trannies back in Indy."

Nickie whipped off her sunglasses and glared at her pupil. "Ms. Vanderhart, I consider 'trannie' a patronizing and disrespectful term. I'll thank you not to use it around me."

"No problem...Oh, wow!" Cinda leaned forward and stared intently into her professor's face. "Do you have relatives around here, Ms. Farrell? I mean, in this part of Virginia?"

"No, my family is from New York. What does that have to do with anything?"

"I'm not sure. I was in town the other day and saw someone with the same kind of different-colored eyes as yours. Pretty unusual coincidence, don't you think?"

"Hardly." Nickie replaced her glasses. "Lots of people have some degree of heterochromia. Ms. Vanderhart, what you are planning to write about me, and when? I have a right to know."

"Actually, I'm not sure you do." Cinda contemplated the Siberian tiger cubs on Nickie's poster. "There are certain First Amendment considerations..."

"Ms. Vanderhart, I am not in any way attempting to censor or interfere with your journalistic endeavors. I would never do that. But I'd like you to consider something." She gestured at Cinda's labrys pendant. "As a gay woman you must be aware that 'outing' people against their wishes can have damaging, even tragic consequences. Isn't that so?"

Cinda lifted her shoulders. "Oh, well."

Nickie held her tongue for a five-count. Heaven protect us from ambitious teenagers, she thought. "What if I told you that I'm not ready to let everyone know about my circumstances? Would that make the slightest difference to you?"

Cinda shifted uneasily in her chair and remained silent.

"Because if not I'll save my breath and you can just go do whatever you feel you have to do."

"How long before you're going to feel…ready?"

"Well…" Nickie hesitated. "Would you be willing hold off until after the Thanksgiving break? Let's say the first of December?"

"Mmm," said Cinda in a dry noncommittal voice.

"If you will, I'll make you a deal."

"What kind of deal?"

"If you agree not to publish anything before December –which includes keeping mum to your friends– I'll grant you an exclusive interview."

Cinda perked up. "No kiddin'?"

"Really. That way your story won't be exploitative tabloid gossip but a real journalistic coup." Nickie forced a wry smile. "You'll be a shoo-in for the *Spectrum*."

"And you promise not to talk to anyone else first?"

"You have my word," Nickie stiffly said. "Will you give me yours?"

"You got it. No story until December first." Cinda gleefully rubbed her hands together. "Awesome! When can I have that interview?"

"Sometime next week. I still have midterm papers to grade." Nickie flourished Cinda's binder. "Starting with this. What do you think you deserve?"

"Um, I…" The younger woman's cocksure attitude wavered a bit. "That's up to you, Ms. Farrell."

"No constitutional issues you want to raise first?"

Cinda shook her head.

"Truthfully, Ms. Vanderhart, for a GG of your abilities this was a bit facile."

"GG?"

"Acronym for Genetic Girl," Nickie clarified. "What you are and I can never be."

Cinda blinked. "Oh."

"On the other hand, the passage you discuss is one that I read a hundred times as a child. Good heavens," Nickie laughed at Cinda's surprised look, "did you think I wasn't familiar with Ozma's transition?" She laughed some more. "You have a lot to learn about people like me, Ms. Vanderhart." She opened Cinda's binder and inscribed a B+ in red ink. "Never let it be said that I don't admire a woman with balls."

"Thanks, Ms. Farrell," Cinda grinned. "I'm sorry if I came off like a blackmailer."

"Now that you've gotten what you want, huh?" Nickie sighed. "Apology accepted. You may go, Ms. Vanderhart. Oh, one more thing."

Cinda halted with her hand on the door. "What?"

"I expect serious questions." Nickie gave her a stern look. "If you ask what color underwear I prefer the interview will be terminated. Understand?"

"Oh yeah," Cinda giggled. "You're too much, Ms. Farrell." She pulled the door shut.

Nickie rubbed her temples and glumly stared out the window. So, it was all going to come out soon. Which meant that, for Nickie, the blessed anonymity of being just another middle-aged lady was about to be taken away forever. Henceforth she would be Windfield's "trannie" professor, and all she could do was handle it with as much dignity as possible.

But above all else, she had to tell Alex Steward the truth. The thought of doing so gave her a sinking feeling, but there was no postponing it. Alex had a right to know. Whatever the consequences.

————)((()((————

Walking from the parking lot to the defiled family mansion where President Lindsey now held court, Eamon Douglass found it unbearable to see how Hendrix Windfield's once-proud estate had been violated by these liberal locusts. It was horrible enough when some longhair stopped to admire his shillelagh with an impertinent "Whoa, dude, bitchin' stick." But the final straw had been when he spied two hand-holding sodomites strolling along billing and cooing. He'd itched to hurl curses at them but contented himself with hoping that they would be present at the Redemption to receive a nice thick coating of Cesium 137.

The ambassador frostily announced himself to the professionally-attired black woman behind the reception desk: "Ambassador Eamon Douglass. President Lindsey is expecting me."

Maudelle Chesterfield sized up the ambassador then lifted her phone. "He's here," she announced in an unimpressed way. "Right away, Ms. Lindsey." She stood up. "Follow me, Mister Douglass."

Eamon Douglass didn't need to be shown the way. He'd been a regular visitor to Hendrix Windfield's inner sanctum when this uppity shine had still been crapping her diapers in a tarpaper shack somewhere. But mindful of his mission he inclined his head and followed the woman's lead. Ms. Chesterfield swung the carved wooden door inward and gestured him through.

The ambassador strode into the ornate space. A quick glance around showed him that not much had changed in three decades. The trophy animal heads were gone from the walls, of course, replaced by effete seascapes and still lifes. A state-of-the-art computer center occupied the corner where Hendrix had displayed his shotguns in a custom-built zebrawood case. The elaborate mirrored bar with its tiers of crystal decanters had been removed and the drapes and carpeting were different, but in Eamon Douglass's view the office remained Hendrix

Windfield's domain, despite the current enemy occupation.

The occupation leader, a robust power-suited woman with her grey hair pulled back in a severe bun, came forward to greet him with an outstretched hand. "Welcome, Ambassador Douglass. I'm Fredericka Lindsey."

"Madame President." Eamon Douglass shook her hand with formal courtesy. "It's gracious of you to receive me."

"Windfield College is always pleased to extend hospitality to our distinguished neighbors." With a keen look: "Especially those whose interest is so…unanticipated."

The ambassador immediately discerned that he was not dealing with some lily-livered academic administrator. Fredericka Lindsey was a damned liberal but also a seasoned battleaxe with an obvious load of skepticism about the Honorable Eamon Douglass's agenda in being here. He would have to play his cards with great care.

"President Lindsey," the ambassador crafted a tone of humility, "I am neither surprised nor offended that you harbor reservations about my sincerity. Were our situations reversed I would doubtless feel as you do. Nevertheless, permit me to tell you what I propose, then feel free to evaluate the authenticity of my motives and proceed as you see fit."

"By all means, Ambassador. Shall we?" They settled themselves on a brass-studded black leather couch angled in front of the enormous window. Douglass recalled sitting here with Hendrix Windfield, savoring exquisite French brandy and smoking cigars as they gazed out over the lordly property. Fredericka Lindsey crossed her legs. "Please continue."

"Thank you," said Eamon Douglass, leaning his shillelagh against the front of the couch. "Madame President, I recently received some disagreeable news from my doctors. To put it bluntly, I have cancer, and I am dying. The precise time frame remains uncertain, but in any case I am not long for this world."

The president of Windfield nodded. "I'm sorry to hear that, Ambassador. Is there nothing they can do?"

"I do not wish to be subjected to a lingering demise at the hands of the medical practitioners. Consequently I have declined their recommended courses of treatment. The prospect of dying holds no fear for me, Madame President. My life has been long and full, and my enterprises have prospered. I have no regrets." He coughed. "That is to say, I didn't believe I had any regrets. But now, faced with my own mortality, I am beginning to find certain aspects of my past…well, rather bothersome."

"And what might those be, Ambassador?"

Eamon Douglass stared broodingly out the window. "I have been intolerant, Madame President. Intolerant of people I considered different, intolerant of new ideas, intolerant of those who wished to move our society in directions I found repellent."

"As exemplified by Windfield College?"

"I won't deny it," acknowledged the ambassador. "Over time this institution has come to represent, in my mind, everything that is wrong with the world." He looked down at the carpet for a long moment. "I am not a man who finds it easy to admit being wrong. But I believe my adamant opposition to Windfield College has been not only wrong, but shameful."

"Well, Ambassador," the college president observed, "what person hasn't at some point been guilty of errors in judgment? Shame, I think, is misplaced."

"Your forbearance is humbling, Madame President. But the truth is that few will mourn my death or remember me as anything but a mean-spirited old reprobate unless I can somehow make amends before I go. And that is why I have come to see you, Madame President, to beg you for the opportunity to redeem myself."

"Please go on, Ambassador." Fredericka Lindsey carefully re-crossed her legs. "Of course I'd like to help if I can."

Eamon Douglass smiled. "Thank you, Madame President. Please correct me if I'm mistaken, but I've been led to believe that Windfield College is fortunate to have a substantial fiscal endowment."

"We are quite fortunate, yes," conceded Fredericka Lindsey. "But no institution of higher learning can ever afford to be complacent in that regard."

"Certainly not," agreed the ambassador. "I imagine that you are required to deal with budgetary complexities on a frequent basis."

"That, sir, is an understatement. There are days when I do little else."

"A constant challenge, I'm sure." Eamon Douglass reached into his jacket pocket and produced a folded piece of paper. "Madame President, if I may?"

He handed her the paper and was pleased to note the woman's astounded expression. "Ambassador...two *million* dollars?"

"An initial grant, Madame President, to be allocated where you believe it will most benefit the students here at Windfield."

"This is...extraordinarily generous." Fredericka Lindsey stared at the certified check. "I don't know what to say."

"As I told you, Madame President, over the years I have amassed great wealth. However, the time has come to utilize it for a nobler end than simply enriching me further. Besides," he allowed with a little chuckle, "even I haven't been able to figure out how to take it with me."

"You do understand, Ambassador, that I can't simply accept this on my own authority. A donation such as this must be approved by the trustees."

"Yes, of course," The ambassador paused. "I have another proposal I would like to discuss, with your permission."

Somewhat warily President Lindsey replied, "Certainly."

The ambassador stood the shillelagh upright between his knees and rested his two hands on it. "Money is a useful fuel, Madame President. Like any other fuel, however, once it has run the engine for a while it's gone forever. No trace remains."

Fredericka Lindsey's puzzlement showed in a quizzical frown. "Oh?"

"Impermanent, Madame President," clarified Eamon Douglas. "Two million dollars will vanish like smoke. Therefore, I would also like to present Windfield College with something of a less ephemeral nature. Perhaps a monument or a commemorative of some sort." He rose to his feet and stood before the window. Pointing at a distant object on the broad knoll, "What is that?"

"The obelisk? It's the Randall Windfield memorial," responded Fredericka Lindsey. "In honor of our school's founder."

The ambassador nodded slowly, and then smiled. "It may surprise you to know that I was acquainted with his father, Hendrix Windfield. In fact, Madame President, I met young Randall on one or two occasions. My recollection is that he was an extremely able and bright fellow."

"He was a visionary, Ambassador Douglass. Far ahead of his time."

"Which is why a gentleman of his caliber deserves the finest possible tribute." Eamon Douglass pointed at the distant obelisk. "Isn't that marker somewhat…minimalist? I would have thought that Randall Windfield's memorial would be a bit more imposing."

"We've talked of constructing something a little more stately," admitted the president, "but somehow there were always other priorities, such as those budgetary concerns you mentioned." She fluttered Douglass's two million dollar check. "The students' immediate needs must always come first."

"Madame President, what would you say if I offered to underwrite such a project?"

"I beg your pardon?"

"I'd be honored to build your school a new Randall Windfield Memorial," proposed Ambassador Douglass. "No expense spared, using only the finest materials. I'll hire the best architect available, have him design a magnificent monument to the founding patron of Windfield College. Then, Madame President, after I'm gone at least something will remain to show that in the end I wasn't just a hateful old s.o.b."

At a loss for words, Fredericka Lindsey sat in silence. The ambassador's eye patch, the shillelagh, the certified check…it all struck her as exceedingly strange. Still, she couldn't detect any obvious catch. Maybe Eamon Douglass was exactly what he seemed: a lonely dying man trying to buy some acceptance and forgiveness after a lifetime of prejudice and arrogance.

"I will present your generous offers to the trustees at the earliest opportunity." The president stood up. Offering her hand: "I don't imagine it will take them long to reach a decision. Thank you very much for coming, Ambassador Douglas."

"President Lindsey," Douglass assured her with a little bow, "I assure you, the pleasure was entirely mine."

As he exited Hendrix Windfield's former office, the ambassador's grin resembled that of a man-eating shark.

———————

"I wouldn't trust him," Maudelle Chesterfield firmly stated, "if he'd handed you a check for *five* million dollars."

The Windfield College president had called her administrative assistant into the office for a post-mortem on the meeting with Eamon Douglass. After twenty years of working together, Fredericka Lindsey considered Maudelle her closest confidante and advisor.

"I'll grant you, the ambassador does come off as somewhat… prickly. But Del, he's just been diagnosed with terminal cancer. That would abrade anyone's spirit."

"Prickly, my foot," scoffed Ms. Chesterfield. "That old man is slick and cold as a copperhead. If he's dying, the Devil best start worrying about him moving into the neighborhood. Something doesn't feel right about this, Freddie."

"What doesn't feel 'right', Del? He handed me a check for 2 million dollars and offered to build the school a new memorial to Randall Windfield! Why on earth would he do that if he wasn't sincere?" President Lindsey tapped her high heel, frowning. "I grant you it's a most unusual turnaround, but we mustn't forget that people can change. It does happen."

"Like a leopard changing its spots, you mean," sniffed Maudelle. "Except this leopard wants you to believe he's changing his whole self into a kitty cat. Mean old Eamon Douglass finds out he's going to kick so he has a spiritual epiphany and decides to dump millions of dollars into Windfield's lap. Oh, and build us some kind of lah-de-dah new memorial.

Reminds me of all those death-row inmates who accept Jesus and start preaching fit to beat the band. Sorry, Freddie. I'm not buying."

Fredericka Lindsey grumpily observed that no one could accuse Ms. Chesterfield of lacking a cynical streak. "What am I supposed to do? Not relay his offer to the board? You know I can't do that. Two million dollars isn't chicken feed, Del, even for us. I just don't see any reason to refuse the ambassador's generosity. And the trustees won't, either."

The administrative assistant shrugged. "Then let's hope I'm wrong. But it might be a good idea to have someone keep an eye on this Ambassador Douglass. Make sure he doesn't dedicate that new monument to Beelzebub."

"Honestly, Del," Fredericka Lindsey chuckled. "But I already had the same notion. Actually I'm thinking about giving the job to our new assistant English professor. Nickie Farrell."

"The sex-change gal?" Maudelle smiled. "That would put the ambassador's new-found love of Windfield to the test, wouldn't it? Perfect."

"No one is supposed to know about Professor Farrell's gender transition," stressed the president. "We're keeping that confidential, remember?"

"Something like that won't stay hidden for long, Freddie, no matter what Ms. Farrell wants. Secrets have a way of leaking out. Look at our own government."

Fredericka Lindsey grimaced. "Don't talk to me about the government. In any case I'll contact Ms. Farrell about this, assuming we get the go-ahead. Meanwhile, please take that," she pointed at Douglass's check, "and find out from the bank if it's legitimate. I would prefer not to tag myself as a horse's behind by running to the trustees with a two-million-dollar piece of rubber."

"Yes, ma'am." Maudelle Chesterfield picked up the ambassador's check, holding it between two fingers like a dead bug, and went to the door.

"And, Del?"

Her executive secretary halted.

"Let's have a little faith for once, can we?"

The evening chill was beginning to sting when, several days later, Nickie Farrell let herself into the small cozy apartment she'd rented on the outskirts of Middleville. She hung her coat in the closet, draping the pink-and-black Windfield scarf around the collar, then went into the tiny kitchen and brewed herself some tea. Carrying the steaming cup into her living area, she kicked off her pumps and curled up in a comfy wing chair.

The interview with Cinda Vanderhart had gone surprisingly well. To Nickie's relief the girl hadn't inquired about messy anatomical details. Instead she'd wanted to know at what age Nickie had first begun to suspect that she was transsexual, and about the difficulties of deciding to transition, and whether she thought transsexuality was accurately presented in the media. Good insightful questions, which Nickie did her best to answer honestly. It wasn't a stretch to believe that her gifted student would someday become a first-rate journalist. Assuming Cinda wrote her article with the same intelligence and moderation that she'd exhibited during the interview, it could help make the disclosure of Nickie's secret less stressful than it might've been.

Most importantly, Cinda had reiterated her promise to delay publication until the end of the month. Nickie still had time to tell Professor Steward the truth, but she had to hurry. Less than a week remained before the start of the Thanksgiving recess, and Alex had plans to visit his sons in Atlanta. Nickie clicked through her cell phone's menu until she found Alex's programmed number, then hesitated with her thumb poised over the send button. Professor Steward had complimented her, kissed her, made her laugh; in short, done all the things men do when they find a woman attractive. How on earth would Alex react when he found out that he'd been courting a man?

"You're *not* a man," Nickie angrily muttered. When, she wondered, would the insecurities ever end? She'd completed her gender transition with consummate patience, by the book, never cutting corners like so many others, and had emerged as a nice-enough-looking lady to catch the eye of a gentleman like Professor Steward. Nickie stared at the phone in her hand, contemplating her choices. She could chicken out and wait until Cinda Vanderhart's article outed her, which would likely trash any chance she had with Alex, or she could tell him the truth and hope that he would care more about who she was than what she was.

"So what's it going to be, Farrell? Do you know what you want?"

Of course she knew. She wanted to continue dating Alex. She wanted to walk by his side, listen to him talk, and hold his hand. She wanted to feel his arms around her. She wanted him to admire her legs. She wanted to kiss him, and in time, explore womanly intimacies with him that she'd yet to experience with a man. She wanted all these things; but if she succumbed now to her fears she'd never know what might have been.

She pressed the button, and held the phone to her ear.

"Hi, Alex. It's Nickie. I was wondering...would you like to have lunch with me next Tuesday?"

———⸻«◊»⸻———

Ambassador Eamon Douglass frowned at a crude sketch he'd drawn on a yellow legal pad. He tore off the sheet and crumpled it into the wastebasket, then grabbed his pencil and started over. After a few moments he threw it down in disgust. He'd been attempting to come up with a design for the Windfield memorial, but his ideas were too complicated or grandiose or ugly, like some overwrought Third Reich monstrosity. Douglass considered himself a man of considerable talent, but clearly he wasn't enough of a flit to conjure up a charming saccharine vision of marble and daisies and other limp-wristed rubbish.

The phone buzzed. He snatched up the receiver, listened and bared his teeth wolf-fashion at the window which faced Windfield College. "By all means, Holmes. Put her on."

"Ambassador, Fredericka Lindsey here. I trust I'm not disturbing you?"

"Not at all, Madame President. To what do I owe the pleasure of this call?"

"Ambassador, the trustees are honored to accept your most generous donation, and to express their gratitude on behalf of everyone at Windfield College."

Eamon Douglass struck his fist on the desktop, causing the glass wolf to jump sideways. "Excellent! That is splendid news. I couldn't be more delighted, Madame President."

"Your bequest will enable many deserving students to realize their dreams," enthused Fredericka Lindsey. "Through them and their future achievements, Ambassador Douglass, your legacy will live on for generations."

Impatient with her rhapsodizing, the ambassador responded, "Let us hope so. And what decision regarding the new memorial?"

"To tell you the truth, Ambassador, that was a bit more... complicated."

Making a concerted effort to keep the dismay out of his voice: "Oh? In what way, Madame President?"

"Several of our trustees are, shall we say, purists. They expressed reluctance to tamper with a venerable icon. Surely you can relate, Ambassador. I don't imagine that you are particularly fond of change, either."

Get to the goddamn point, woman, Douglass silently fumed.

"There was a rather energetic discussion concerning your proposal. Those opposed defended their viewpoint with considerable vigor."

Son of a *bitch*, seethed the ambassador. Screw it, I'll stick the Redeemer in the trunk of my limo with a crate of dynamite and blow everything to kingdom come like some raghead fanatic.

Fredericka Lindsey continued: "But in the end, Ambassador, I won them over. We gratefully accept your generous offer and look forward to the new Randall Windfield memorial."

Eamon Douglass sat bolt upright in his chair, swept up the glass wolf and kissed it on the snout. "Thank you, Madame President! I promise that this will be remembered for a very long time. That is my commitment to you, and I will not fail."

"I'm sure you won't," replied Fredericka Lindsey. "The trustees did request that it be completed in time to have the dedication ceremony during our annual spring picnic, which will take place this year on Sunday the first of April."

April Fools Day? The ambassador winked his eye at the glass wolf clutched in his hand. What a delicious bit of irony! "Of course, Madame President."

"Also, I plan to assign one of our professors to be your Windfield liaison during this project. Her name is Nickie Farrell. I'll ask Ms. Farrell to touch base with you after the Thanksgiving recess, if you approve."

"Splendid idea," replied the ambassador. "I'll expect Ms. Farrell's call. Enjoy your holiday, Madame President, and rest assured that I will construct the new Randall Windfield memorial in time for a dedication ceremony at your spring picnic. I daresay it will be an April Fools Day to remember."

———⊸«()»⊶———

At the conclusion of her Tuesday morning class Nickie Farrell closed her notes. "Let's stop here. I imagine everyone's concentration is compromised by thoughts of turkey and pumpkin pie. Mine certainly is." She smiled at the restless students. "I wish all of you a very happy Thanksgiving. Oh, wait, there's one more thing," she added to a chorus of groans. "Relax, I'm not sadistic enough to assign homework over the break, but if anyone feels like taking a quick peek at *The Innocents Abroad* they might find themselves with a head start on our next assignment. Okay? See you next week."

Heather Walters jumped up, hurriedly gathering books and shouldering her purse. "I gotta run to the gym, Cinda. If I don't get signed up for next semester's spinning class I'll totally kill myself. See you back in the room." She rushed off.

Cinda Vanderhart left the classroom with the other students. In the corridor she bent to drink from a water fountain and overheard a nearby girl giggle to her companion, "You want to hear something totally weird? Pastel Horowitz says he thinks Ms. Farrell used to be a man."

Cinda felt her blood turn as icy as the fountain water.

"He says *what?* "

"Pastel thinks she had one of those sex change operations. He knows all about that stuff from living in New Orleans. He's positive that Ms. Farrell is one of them. You know. A trannie."

Cinda slowly straightened, thinking, *shit!*

"Puh-leeze. You're gonna listen to someone who changed his name from Irving to Pastel? Shut up," scoffed the other girl. "Besides, Pastel is so girly he's the one who needs a sex change. Ms. Farrell is no more a man than, I don't know, J-Lo. He is *so* pulling your chain."

They chattered off. Cinda stood rooted, her thoughts in a tumble. Calamity! Disaster! If word leaked out about Ms. Farrell before Cinda's article appeared in the *Spectrum*, her triumphant scoop would be akin to reporting that someone had just invented the wheel.

Lips set in a determined line, she hastened from the building. No way. Her journalistic aspirations were not going to be derailed. She wouldn't let it happen.

———— ◆ ————

After a quick stop in the English department office to touch bases with Jo about Thanksgiving, Nickie Farrell drove home to get ready for her lunch date with Alex Steward. She was grateful for the upcoming holiday break. Naturally she hoped that today's talk with Alex would go well; but either way, it would be good to have some free time afterwards to sort things out.

Back in her apartment, she briskly scrubbed herself in the shower. Ever since the reassignment surgery Nickie had been extra-scrupulous about her personal hygiene; the nurses at the clinic had stressed how important it was to keep her new anatomy clean. After toweling dry she stood for a moment before a full-length mirror, studying her still-wondrous image reflected in the glass. As always she wished that her hips were wider, her tummy flatter, her shoulders not quite as broad. But the breast augmentation had helped even out her proportions, and overall it was an acceptably pleasing body, especially for her age. With her slight frame, even as a five-foot nine-inch male she had seldom weighed more than one hundred and forty pounds. Over time the estrogen therapy had supercharged her hair growth, producing a full wavy mane which was her secret pride and joy. That and her legs, which were unquestionably her best feature. Nickie stood on tiptoes and turned slightly, inspecting her firm rounded calves and smooth thighs.

"Oh yeah, babe!" Assuming things ever got that far, she thought, the good professor wouldn't be too displeased.

After making sure that her makeup was exactly right, Nickie put on her underwear and dressed in a demure outfit calculated to emphasize her femininity: a cream-colored cashmere sweater, blue wool skirt, pearl-colored hose and slingback spectator pumps. She added a silk scarf wonderfully patterned in blue, lilac, and green, then finished by carefully securing her hair with a faux pearl head band. A quick spray of Jessica McClintock Number 3, one final inspection in the mirror, and she nodded, satisfied. Whatever else happened, at least Alex wouldn't be able to accuse her of looking like a drag queen.

"Okay, Ozma," Nickie donned her sunset shades. "Let's go see how the wizard reacts."

When Heather Walters returned to her dorm room she found Cinda Vanderhart busily typing on her laptop, squinting at the screen.

"Omigod, don't you ever stop working? It's vacation, Cinda! You're allowed to take a break."

"Sshh, I've got to finish this. Gimme a minute."

Heather threw up her hands. "Whatever. But could you hurry? I want to leave soon. The traffic around Washington is almost as bad as L.A." Cinda was spending the Thanksgiving holiday in Washington with Congressman Walters and his family. "We'll drop our stuff at Daddy's then head into Georgetown. There's a new boutique on M Street I've *so* got to check out."

"Okay, that oughta do it." Cinda hit a button and pages began spitting out of her printer. "I've gotta hand-deliver this, then we can take off."

Heather paused in packing a Louis Vuitton cosmetics case. "What is that, anyway?"

"My *Spectrum* article about Professor Farrell," Cinda replied, picking pages out of the printer. "It's dynamite, too." She stapled the sheets together and slipped them into a brown envelope.

"Wait a sec," Heather frowned. "I thought you promised her it wouldn't be in the paper until December first? That's not till the end of next week. You can't give it to them yet. It's too soon."

Cinda shrugged. "I need to move the deadline up. We're only talking about a few days, anyway."

"But Cinda, you promised. That's the only reason Ms. Farrell let you interview her in the first place."

"I know, but I can't hold off." Cinda quickly related what she had overheard by the water fountain. "Someone's going to figure this out any second, Roomie. I can't take a chance that my exclusive will be blown. Ms. Farrell will understand."

"Like, give me a break." Heather's tone took on a biting edge. "You don't care about Ms. Farrell. This is all about you. You and your oh-so-important career. Except it's the wrong thing to do and you know it."

"Oh, for Chrissake." Cinda began pulling on her coat. "Look, sweetie. Journalism is unpredictable. Sometimes situations arise which necessitate an improvised course of action. Since when is it *my* fault that Ms. Farrell decided to be stealthy? If she'd been honest about herself in the first place there wouldn't even be a story. Don't blame the messenger. It's very pious of you to stand there and preach about what's right, but your entire future isn't on the chopping block, y'know?"

"Oh, gag me. I haven't heard such a crock of rationalization since Daddy voted in favor of the war. Except this is worse. You gave her your *word*."

"Fine. Remind me from now on to check with you for the ethical angle. But this can't wait. I'll be back in a flash."

"At least call Ms. Farrell and let her know," Heather insisted. "Give her a heads-up."

Cinda returned a condescending look. "Journalists don't do that. You just finish packing, and don't forget to bring all thirty-seven of your lipsticks. And quit worrying about Ms. Farrell. Those trannies are tough, believe me."

Alex Steward stood when the Foxton Arms maitre d' escorted Nickie Farrell to one of the secluded booths.

"Hello, Nickie. You look beautiful."

"Thank you." Nickie planted a quick peck on his cheek, then slid in across from him. "I hope you don't mind," she gestured at the booth. "I wanted a little privacy."

Alex's eyes shone. "My gosh, you get prettier all the time."

Nickie removed her sunglasses. Gazing straight at him: "You have no idea, Alex, what a compliment that is."

"Well, I'm sure you've enjoyed a lifetime of compliments."

Nickie's hand tingled as Alex took it in his own. "Not so many as you might think."

A discreet cough interrupted their reverie: "Sir, ma'am, welcome to the Foxton Arms. My name's Robin. I'll be your server this afternoon."

They quickly released hands, and Nickie smiled up at the pert waitress. "Hello, young lady."

Transfixed by the sight of eyes that were an uncanny replica of Collie's, Robin stared in mute astonishment.

"Aren't they remarkable?" Alex chuckled. "Knocked me out the first time I saw them, too."

Robin gulped. "I'm sorry, ma'am. I don't mean to be rude, it's just that a very dear friend of mine...his eyes are *exactly* like yours."

"Oh?" Nickie retrieved and donned her glasses. "That's nice."

Still flustered, Robin asked if they would care for anything from the bar.

"I'd like a cranberry juice and tonic, please," requested Nickie, "with a piece of lime."

"I'll have the same," said Alex Steward. When Robin left he asked: "Your special libation?"

"Yes, since I quit drinking. I call it a 'Sigh of Relief'," replied Nickie. "Silly, huh?"

"No. There's nothing remotely 'silly' about you, Nickie Farrell." He paused. "Do you abstain completely?"

"Yes, for many years. If I hadn't stopped I doubt I'd be here." She spoke haltingly, eyes downcast. "I couldn't control my drinking, Alex. I stayed sloshed most of the time." She shuddered. "Thank goodness those days are over."

"It takes great inner strength to overcome something like that, Nickie. I so admire you." He added with a smile: "But perhaps you suspected that already?"

"La, sir, you make me blush," Nickie laid a hand on her bosom. "You are a rogue, Professor Steward."

"I am?" Alex looked surprised, then grinned. "I am. You seem to have that effect on me, Professor Farrell."

When the drinks arrived Alex raised his glass. "Happy Thanksgiving, Nickie. I'm sorry we won't be together, but I promise I'll be thinking about you."

Nickie thought, ain't that the truth! "Happy Thanksgiving, Alex. I hope you have a wonderful time with your family in Atlanta."

"Oh, I will. The boys like to run Grandpa ragged, but that's what I'm for. Especially Craig Jr. He's a turbocharged six-year-old version of me."

"How sweet." Nickie sipped her drink. "Does he have the same lovely white beard?"

She smiled as the professor chuckled but inside Nickie uneasily wondered how Alex's face would change when she told him the truth. Would his blue eyes lose their sparkle, become flat and distant? Would his cheerful expression give way to an appalled glare? Would his natural warmth dissolve into aloofness? Would the thought of kissing her suddenly fill him with disgust? When Alex realized that he'd fallen for a surgically-designed woman who still had XY chromosomes he might very well take off and never look back. The hard truth was that many men —in fact most— simply couldn't make the leap. Nickie didn't know what she'd do if he rejected her. The mere thought made her ill. Please,

God, she prayed, give Alex the ability to understand. Please let him love me.

"Nickie?"

Nickie realized she had been staring unseeingly at nothing. She began an apology but Alex reached across the table and gently laid his finger across her lips.

"Woolgathering. I remember." He smiled and handed her a menu. "Let's have some lunch."

While their Nicoise salads were being prepared, Robin sneaked a peek in the maitre d's reservation book. Booth number four had been reserved by "Ms. N. Farrell", and since Robin had heard the white-haired gentleman address his companion as "Nickie", she concluded that the lady with Collie's eyes was named Nickie Farrell.

Robin still couldn't get over the similarity. Curious about Collie's genetic trait, she had researched heterochromia on the Internet, discovering that it was an uncommon oddity but not all that rare. Many famous celebrities had it, among them the actress Jane Seymour and the comedian Dan Akroyd. On the other hand both Collie and Ms. Nickie Farrell had starkly distinct color differentiations, which occurred far less frequently. Robin thought that Nickie Farrell could easily be mistaken for Collie's mother, so identical were their ocular patterns. Which was ridiculous, of course; Luanne Skinner was his mom. Still, Robin wished that Collie had worked the lunch shift so he could have gotten a peek at Nickie Farrell. She made a mental note to tell him about it later. It really was an interesting coincidence.

Nickie tried to eat, but the tension she felt quashed her appetite and she set down her fork. "I don't seem to be very hungry," she confessed. "I'll take it home for dinner."

"Good idea." Alex's eyes showed concern. "Nickie, you seem…a bit preoccupied. Are you feeling unwell?"

"No, no." Nickie shook her head. "I'm fine, really."

"Why don't you tell me what's on your mind? Whatever it is." He softly urged, "Come on, pretty lady. I'm a good listener."

Nickie studied Alex's face and saw nothing but openness and affection. She took a shaky breath. "All right. I told you once before that there were some things about me you weren't going to like. Alex, please," she cut him off as he tried to protest, "hear me out. This is terribly difficult." Professor Steward fell silent, watching her. "It's hard to know where to begin. I was a very unhappy person for a long time, Alex. Practically from the day I was born. And I was a completely different person than I am today."

"Different in what way, Nickie?"

"In every way imaginable. And in ways unimaginable, too."

"I don't think I follow," said Alex, his confusion evident. "How could you be so different?"

"I've told you that I had a severe drinking problem. Well, my alcoholism was a symptom of a larger problem, Alex. Much larger. One which couldn't be fixed by simply going on the wagon."

"Can you tell me about this other problem?"

"It had to do with…how I thought about myself. How I fit in. My self-image. I never felt comfortable in my own skin, Alex. I never felt *right*." She saw his look of bewilderment. "God. You really have no idea, do you?"

"I guess I don't." He turned his palms up on the table. "I'm sorry if I'm being opaque."

Nickie closed her eyes for a moment, then: "Alex…do you know what TS means?"

Alex looked startled, then amused. "Um…I think so."

"You *do?*"

"Sure. It stands for 'Tough Spit'. Well, not 'spit', something a lot more vulgar. It's a snappy retort. You know, a come-back. 'TS!' I didn't know anyone still used it, though."

Nickie covered her eyes. "No, Alex. That's not what I'm referring to. The TS I'm talking about stands for..."

Alex suddenly held up a finger. "One sec, Nickie. Doggone phone is buzzing." He reached into his breast pocket and pulled out a cell phone. "Let me turn it off...uh-oh." Frowning: "That's Craig's number, in Atlanta." He looked at her. "He usually doesn't call me like this. Do you mind? Just in case."

Feeling suspended in midair like the luckless cartoon coyote, Nickie managed to articulate, "Of course not, go ahead."

"Hello?" Nickie saw his face go pale. "What? When did it happen? Oh, Christ. Oh, no." Alex put a hand to his brow. "Is he at the hospital? Jesus. All right. I'm going to leave for Dulles right away. I'll catch the next plane. I should be there in a couple of hours." He snapped shut the cell phone. In a shocked trembling voice: "It's my grandson, Nickie. Craig Jr. He was playing in his friend's tree house, and somehow he...he fell. They think he might have a spinal injury, he's unconscious. I have to leave, Nickie. I hate to run out on you like this..."

"Don't worry about me. Do you want a ride to the airport?"

"No, I'll take my car." He slid from the booth, his face frightened and disbelieving. "Craig Jr...oh my *God*."

"He'll be all right, Alex. I know he will." Nickie put her arms around him. "I'll pray for the boy. Please, please be careful driving."

"I'm dreadfully sorry, Nickie." Alex returned her hug. "I promise I'll call you the minute I know anything. Take care of yourself."

He kissed her once and was gone. Stunned, Nickie sank back down and didn't move until Robin approached. "Can I get you anything else, ma'am?"

Nickie pointed at her untouched salad. "I'd like to take that home. And I'll have the check, please."

A few minutes later she walked out of the Foxton Arms, clutching the small carryout bag. Alex was gone, and she still hadn't told him the truth. Her stomach hurt. The air felt icy, and a few snow flurries drifted down. Nickie blinked up at the lowering sky, her face a mask of loneliness. She shivered, found her car in the parking lot, and slowly drove home to her empty apartment.

The traditional Thursday of giving thanks was again celebrated across the land. Fifty million turkeys were slain and devoured as people contemplated their reasons for feeling grateful. Many did so in a spirit of appreciation, while others merely conceded that things could be worse. Some used the occasion to disparage the holiday, stuff themselves with food and lapse semi-comatose in front of the television. But not a one could claim to know what lay in store for them before the next Thanksgiving would arrive.

Alone in his study at Shamrocks, Ambassador Eamon Douglass ignored a barely-touched turkey dinner growing cold on a serving tray beside his chair. He stared at the dancing flames in the fireplace, pondering what things would be like a year from now, after the Redemption. He would be gone, but so would Windfield College. He lifted a brandy snifter from the tray and drank to the patriot Nathan Hale. Like Captain Hale, the ambassador regretted that he had but one life to give for his country; but he was damn well going to make it count.

Big Mike Barlow didn't give a shit about eating some stupid barnyard fowl, but he was more than happy to feast upon the simian gobblers that crowded into the Knights Inn for a night of boisterous boozing after being cooped up with their families. He kept the beer and whiskey flowing, all the while skimming from the till as he had for years. Though generally not a grateful sort, Barlow felt thankful that the ambassador wasn't aware of the skimming. He was wrong, of course; but secure in his ignorance, Big Mike didn't worry.

In one of Atlantic City's glittering casino hotels, Lloyd Skinner and patron *Übermensch* Cale Pittman celebrated their good fortune at the craps table by gorging themselves on a sumptuous Thanksgiving buffet dinner, then went cruising through unsavory neighborhoods in Cale's Mustang until they picked up an unwary male prostitute. After driving him to a remote location they beat him bloody, breaking his arm and jaw, and left him unconscious. Afterwards, in a festive mood and feeling gratefully superior, they went back to their hotel room and drank Jack Daniels while Cale read Nietzsche aloud until they flew at each other and indulged in a long night of warrior-style bonding.

Coiffed and elegant in a new designer frock, Heather Walters held court in her father's elegant Georgetown row house, savoring the attention of several handsome congressional interns who hovered around her like bees, humming with flattery. She felt deeply thankful that her outspoken lesbian roommate was far on the other side of the room assuring the Congressman that any politician who supported a Constitutional ban on gay marriage would surely end up enshrined in history's Hall of Infamy alongside Torquemada, Himmler, and the President. As for Cinda herself, she was grateful not only for the fact that Heather hadn't insisted she wear a dress, but also because the feature editor of the Windfield College *Spectrum* had been so jazzed by her exposé of the transsexual professor that he'd immediately offered her an internship on the newspaper.

As was her custom, Robin Thompson helped prepare and serve her church's Thanksgiving dinner for the less fortunate. Her warm presence went a long way toward cheering those who might otherwise have given in to despondency over their troubled circumstances. As she did every day, Robin gratefully counted her blessings. She had many close friends in the church who shared her commitment to a morally decent way of life. She thanked the Almighty for her job, her modest apartment, and her college studies. Most of all she thanked Him for her new relationship with Collie Skinner, for whom she was developing a deep emotional attachment which, if God willed it, would blossom into a lifelong love.

Unlike Robin, Collie found it difficult to keep disturbing thoughts at bay even as he tried to maintain good spirits for his mother's sake. Luanne had insisted on cooking a complete Thanksgiving dinner despite her obvious abdominal pain; a dinner which her husband mockingly refused to eat, instead driving off to watch football with the other drunks at Hamburger John's. Collie helped his mother put away the uneaten food, then sat with her for the rest of the long evening while she played her beloved old songs. The sadness on her face as she tiredly sang along broke his heart. He swore to himself that he would take his mother to a doctor. Collie thought about Robin's faith in God, and offered a silent prayer asking Him to please help Luanne get better.

Seated between Joanne Markwith's mother and one of Jo's bright-eyed nieces, Nickie Farrell felt deeply grateful that she could enjoy Thanksgiving in the company of such kind and accepting people. She humbly thanked her Higher Power for allowing her to be at peace with herself. And she was supremely thankful to have heard from Alex that his grandson had escaped serious injury. The professor had apologized a dozen times for leaving in such haste. He insisted on taking her to dinner as soon as he returned so that they could finish their conversation. Nickie had accepted at once, greatly relieved that Cinda Vanderhart wouldn't publish her article before the end of the month. There was still time to tell Alex the truth, and all might yet be well.

Afternoon light faded to lavender dusk, which gradually gave way to black night. Another Thanksgiving Day began a recession into memory as the hours began inexorably ticking away toward unguess-able events that lay shrouded in the future.

Chapter Eight
Unravelings

The following morning Collie Skinner begged his mother to call in sick so she could rest, but Luanne wouldn't hear of it. Didn't Collie remember that the Friday after Thanksgiving marked the start of the busy holiday season? Skipping work would likely get her fired.

Collie doubted that hordes of shoppers would flood the Shamrock store to buy pliers and beetle traps as Christmas presents, but not wanting to subject his mother to additional stress he held his tongue. Evincing no such concern, Jay-Bo endorsed his wife's determination to work, pointing out that someone had to make up for the money they'd wasted on that stupid Thanksgiving shit.

Collie forced himself to suppress his rage. Mindful of Luanne's –and Robin's– warnings against hating, he was making a conscious effort not to give in to such feelings. They left the apartment without a word and got into the Camaro for the short drive to her workplace.

Collie drew to a stop in front of the Shamrock store. As he leaned to kiss his mother he caught sight of a long black limousine pulling to the curb a few car lengths behind him.

"Uh-oh, Mama. Looks like the Man is here. That's Ambassador Douglass's limo."

Luanne looked out the rear window and visibly sagged. "Oh, no. Not today."

"What's the matter, Mama?"

"He frightens me." Luanne threw another fearful glance at the limousine. "I don't know why, but...I get a bad feeling."

"Mama, just because he's rich doesn't mean we should be afraid of him." Collie spoke with more bravado than conviction. "So he's got a billion dollars. Big deal."

"Nicholas, it's smart to be afraid." Luanne put her hand on the door handle. "People with that much money always do whatever they want to whoever they want. Remember that. Now I've got to get in there. I hope I don't have to see him." She opened the door and scurried across the equipment yard into the store.

Collie sat for a moment scowling into his rearview mirror. Thinking of how his poor mother had darted into the store like a frightened mouse, Collie realized that he very much disliked Ambassador Eamon Douglass.

He watched the chauffeur open the rear door. The old man emerged and made his way toward the Shamrock store. He was crossing the equipment yard when Collie saw him halt and peer attentively at a large object on the ground. Collie couldn't make out what it was, but Douglass suddenly nodded, knocked his cane against the object several times, then threw his head back and laughed. Collie felt a chill. Whatever had just amused Ambassador Eamon Douglass, it almost certainly boded no good for anyone else.

⊷⊷≈«◉»≈⊶⊶

In the store office, Ambassador Douglass sat behind the manager's desk while the manager himself, Chuck Holt, stood fretfully turning a green-and-yellow John Deere cap in his hands.

"How long have we had that thing?" Douglass demanded. "Where the hell did it come from?"

"It was a special order from the Pomfrey estate," answered Chuck Holt. "For a fancy rose garden they were building. Then Adelia Pomfrey fell off her horse and broke her neck, remember?"

"Only sensible thing that social-climbing halfwit ever did," snorted the ambassador. "They cancelled the order?"

"Yes, sir. We kept their deposit, but it's been sitting out there ever since. Not much demand for that kind of thing. No one else wants it."

"*I* want it," Eamon Douglass corrected him. "That's *my* sundial. I've decided to incorporate it into a monument I'm having commissioned. Remove it from the inventory. Right now, Holt. If anyone sells it I'll bury them. And you."

Chuck Holt gulped. "I'll take care of it, sir."

The ambassador leaned back in the store manager's chair. "Go find that Skinner woman and send her in. Make it quick, I haven't got all day."

The manager hurried out of the office. Delighted with his inspiration, Eamon Douglass rocked in the chair, gleefully envisioning the fearsome destruction which would ensue when the Redeemer set off a huge quantity of dynamite under a half-ton granite sundial. It would transform the entire Randall Windfield Memorial into a giant radiological fragmentation grenade, something the world had never seen. The towel-heads would turn green with envy.

A timid knock sounded.

"Come in," barked Eamon Douglass.

Luanne Skinner sidled into the office, her face pale with apprehension. "You wanted to see me, sir?"

"Close the door, Mrs. Skinner." Her evident fright pleased him; fear was an excellent motivator. He pointed at a scarred wooden chair. "Sit."

Luanne sat on the edge of the seat, hands clasped in her lap. She found it gruesome to be scrutinized by Douglass's single gray eye, but didn't dare look away.

"You don't know why you're here, do you?"

"My work, sir? I'm sorry if I haven't been keeping up the way I should..."

Douglass silenced her with a brusque wave. "If your performance was substandard you'd already be fired." He contemplated her in silence for a moment. "Mrs. Skinner, you owe me."

Luanne blinked and stammered, "I...I'm very grateful for my job, sir..."

"Not that." The ambassador eyed her. "Your husband was formerly an officer with the Virginia State Police?"

"Yes, he was."

"And several years ago Officer Skinner became embroiled in some serious legal difficulties, did he not?"

Shamefaced, Luanne gave a tiny nod.

"Excessive use of force in the course of arresting one of our local college students, as I recall. He was charged with aggravated assault."

Luanne dropped her eyes. "Yes, sir."

"Officer Skinner had every right to apprehend that trespassing Windfield dope fiend. The little bastard was smoking his filthy drug in one of *my* pastures! Your husband was treated abominably. The man fought for his country, but those yellow hounds in the D.A.'s office were out for his blood. It was outrageous. That's why I paid for his attorney."

Luanne momentarily forgot her fear. "*You* paid for the lawyer? I always wondered who put up the money..." She caught herself, and fell silent.

"It was necessary for me to remain anonymous. I couldn't allow my involvement to prejudice the course of justice. The hung jury should have been the end of it except for that damned kid's family. They were obsessed with ruining your husband. That spineless district attorney caved in to everything but incarceration. Still, at least you didn't have to pine away without your spouse."

"No." Luanne's expression was unfathomable. "I didn't."

"That, Mrs. Skinner, is why you owe me. I kept your husband free to be with his loving family."

"Yes, sir." A tear spilled down Luanne's cheek. "You surely did."

"You needn't cry about it."

"I'm sorry, sir." She brushed away the tear.

"Never mind," frowned the ambassador. "In return for the kindness I did your family, Mrs. Skinner, I require you to do something for me. It's a simple task, but very important, and extremely confidential. You cannot breathe a *word* about this to anyone. Is that clear?"

"Yes, sir."

"It had better be." From his jacket pocket Douglass pulled out a square floppy disk. He held it up. "Recognize this?"

Luanne knew nothing about computers. She shook her head.

"It's called a floppy disk. Damned if I know why, since it is neither a disk nor floppy." Douglass set it down on the desk. "What I want you to do is take that," he pointed at the floppy, "and keep it safely hidden where no one will find it. Can you do that?"

Luanne immediately thought of the Windfield college senior book hidden in the box of panty liners. The disk would easily slip between its pages. "Yes, sir."

The ambassador glared from his single eye. "You're positive it won't be found?"

"No one will find it, sir." The gnawing pain in her abdomen was back.

"I am placing enormous trust in you, Mrs. Skinner. That disk is the only copy of some top-secret details for a hostile takeover I am planning." His sudden grin made Luanne's blood run cold. "Do you know what that is?"

Luanne swallowed. "Is it about the stock market?"

"Something like that." The ambassador cackled. "My plans will doubtless have a profound effect on the market. Now, pay attention: Four months from now, on the morning of April first, at precisely ten o'clock, you will take this," he tapped the disk with one gnarled finger, "and deliver it to the offices of the *Middleville Gazette*. Do you know where that is?"

"On Garretson Lane?"

"Exactly. You will ask for a man by the name of Mr. Gerard DuPree. He is the editor of the paper. Hand the disk to Mr. DuPree, and inform him it's from Ambassador Douglass, on a matter of extraordinary urgency. Understand?"

Luanne didn't understand at all, but she was desperate to get away from Eamon Douglass. "Yes, sir. I'll give it to Mr. DuPree, like you say."

"At the same time you must deliver a message. Two simple words."

"Sir?"

"Doublecross Dingbats."

Nonplussed, Luanne said, "*What?*"

"It is imperative for you to inform Mr. DuPree that Eamon Douglass said 'Doublecross Dingbats'," stressed the ambassador. "Say it."

"Sir, I…" Luanne gulped. "D-Doublecross Dingbats."

"Again," he commanded her. "Three times."

Feeling insane, Luanne did as she was told: "Doublecross Dingbats, Doublecross Dingbats, Doublecross Dingbats."

"Excellent." The ambassador picked his shillelagh off the desk and rose. "When and where will you deliver the disk?"

"April first, ten in the morning, to the *Middleville Gazette*. Mr. DuPree."

By George, I think she's got it." Douglass picked up the floppy disk and held it out. "Guard it with your life."

Luanne shakily stood up, accepted the disk and put it in her pocket. "I'll do everything exactly like you told me, sir."

"That's right, Mrs. Skinner, you will." The ambassador bent and snarled in her face through clenched teeth: "*Because if you fuck this up you will be the sorriest piece of white trash that ever had the bad luck to find out what happens to people who piss me off!*" He straightened. "Now get back to work."

Eyes big as saucers, Luanne stumbled from the room. Watching her panicked exit, Eamon Douglass nodded with satisfaction. The woman was thoroughly terrorized; she would do his bidding or die trying. As for that jackass newspaperman, Douglass rather regretted that he wouldn't be able to see DuPree's expression when the *Gazette's* editor saw what was on the floppy, but by then little would be left of the ambassador but a patriotic scatter of damp radioactive specks.

Feeling altogether pleased, Douglass headed for the yard to examine the sundial more closely. On his way out he passed by the ladies' room where inside Luanne Skinner was bent over the toilet, retching and vomiting in a misery of fear and pain.

She had no way of knowing, of course, that the floppy disk in her pocket contained Eamon Douglass's ingeniously coded "Death

Declaration" celebrating —and claiming credit for— the annihilation of Windfield College.

———————»«(●)«————————

The following Monday morning, Nickie Farrell hummed to herself as she drove to work. Alex Steward had telephoned her upon his return from Atlanta and insisted that they resume their interrupted date at the earliest opportunity. Not wanting to delay her confession any longer and mindful of Cinda Vanderhart's impending newspaper exposé, Nickie had suggested they meet that evening at the Foxton Arms for dinner. Alex had promptly agreed. And tonight, Nickie swore, before she took so much as a sip of water she'd make a clean breast of everything.

She parked in the faculty lot and set out for the English department. Halfway across Randall Quad Nickie encountered two of her students heading in the opposite direction.

She nodded a pleasant greeting: "Good morning, Mr. Carpenter, Mr. Fine."

The young men exchanged swift looks and one of them replied, "Hey, Ms. Farrell."

Nickie smiled. "Did you gentlemen have a nice Thanksgiving?"

"Yeah, y'know." Again they traded the knowing sardonic glances that seemed to be a favored mode of collegiate male communication.

"That's good. Well, see you in class." Nickie continued on her way as behind her the boys snickered and high-fived each other.

Nickie unlocked her office door and bent to pick up her folded issue of the *Spectrum*, which was delivered free to all the academic staff. A half-seen word on the cover caught her eye. Suddenly overcome by a horrible premonition, she dropped her attaché case and unfolded the paper. The headline screamed up at her:

WINDFIELD'S TRANSSEXUAL ENGLISH PROF:
"JUST ANOTHER WOMAN"?

Cinda Vanderhart's article dominated the entire right-hand column. Momentarily overcome, Nickie leaned against the door frame. When the lightheadedness subsided she went into the office, dropped the *Spectrum* on her desk and sank into her chair. After scanning the article she removed her glasses and dropped her head onto crossed arms. With a defeated moan: "Oh, God. Alex."

She stayed that way until a hesitant knock sounded on her door. A low voice said, "Nickie, it's Jo. Can I come in?"

Nickie raised her head. "Jo? Yes, sure." Her hair band had fallen askew and she adjusted it as Joanne Markwith entered the office and closed the door.

Seeing the paper Jo frowned. "That over-eager little witch jumped the gun, didn't she?" She circled the desk and put her arms around Nickie. "I'm so sorry, sweetie. Are you okay?"

"I guess so." Nickie swallowed. "I mean, it's not like I didn't give Cinda the interview. This was already in the works. I am what I am, and blaming her for saying so won't change anything. Actually," she forced a brave smile, "it's a well-written piece. And now I'll find out how accepting my students are. Nickie Farrell, trannie professor extraordinaire. Ought to be interesting, don't you think?"

Joanne Markwith gave her a quick squeeze. "You have more guts than anyone I've ever known. I absolutely love you. So does my whole family. Mom still hasn't stopped talking about how much she enjoyed your company."

"It was the nicest Thanksgiving I ever had, even if I did gain two pounds from your Mom's pie. I still haven't taken it off. I'd better not eat anything tonight..." Her face fell. "If there even is a tonight. I was supposed to go out with Alex." She groaned. "Lord knows how he'll feel after reading that. What if he hates me?"

"No one could possibly hate you, Nickie."

"I was a damn fool. I should have let Alex know right up front. Before we ever started going out. Now he'll think I was hiding the truth, being dishonest. But I *did* try to tell him, Jo!" She spread her hands in despair. "If only he hadn't left so suddenly..."

"Alex is a decent guy, Nickie. Why anticipate the worst? Everything can still turn out okay."

"I need to speak with him." Nickie looked at her watch. "Do you think I should?"

No, Joanne Markwith selfishly thought. In fact she wished that Nickie Farrell would forget all about Alex Steward. But she couldn't tell her that. "There's only one way to find out, right? Call him. Listen, I better get back to the office now. If there's anything I can do to help, I'm here for you. You don't have to face this alone, Nickie." She put her hand on the doorknob.

"Jo, wait." Nickie came and enfolded Joanne Markwith in a hug. "You're my best friend, and I love you, too."

"It'll all work out, sweetheart." Jo briefly savored Nickie's closeness then broke away. "Gotta run," she said in a muffled voice, and slipped from the office.

Nickie returned to her desk, thinking that she'd have to be blind not to recognize Joanne's feelings for her. Nickie had been truthful in telling Jo that she loved her. In fact, she'd searched her soul for any romantic element to that love; but it just wasn't there. Yes, she loved Jo; but she was in love with Alex Steward.

Nickie took out her cell phone, called Alex's number, and was directed to his voice mail. She considered not leaving a message but decided that under the circumstances Alex might misinterpret that in the worst possible way.

"Alex, it's Nickie. I was wondering…are we still on for tonight? I'm sure you have a few…no, a lot of questions. I'll be glad to tell you whatever you want to know, if you'll give me a chance. I've got to go to class now, so please leave a message if I don't answer. I hope I'll see you later. Bye, Alex."

Nickie closed the phone and collected her class materials. Summoning up a look of serene self-assurance, she went out to face her new notoriety.

━━●》●━━

Joanne Markwith hadn't been back ten minutes when the door

opened and Alex Steward came into the office, his face uncharacteristically somber.

"Hi, Joanne," he greeted in a dull voice. Not 'Jo' but 'Joanne'. Oh, hell, she thought, he's seen the damn newspaper.

"Good morning, Professor Steward," she replied. "Did you enjoy your holiday break?"

"Holiday?" Alex echoed. "Oh. I suppose. You?"

"Wonderful, thanks." Joanne paused. "Nickie Farrell joined us. She mentioned that you had a scare with one of your grandsons."

"Yes, well, we're very lucky. The little guy is tough as nails. He's going to be fine." Before Jo could say anything else he asked, "Did you get those Congreve excerpts printed out?"

"Right over there," she pointed to a neat pile on a nearby table.

"Great." Alex gathered up the printouts. "See you later." He moved towards the door.

Jo blurted, "Have you seen that article about Nickie in the *Spectrum?*"

Alex halted. "I saw it."

"What did you think?"

Staring straight ahead he hoarsely replied, "Right now I'm better off not thinking."

Jo thought the resentment in his voice boded ill for Nickie. "Look, Alex, I apologize if I'm speaking out of turn, but this really shouldn't make any difference. She's exactly the same, you know. Nothing's changed."

"That's where you're wrong. Everything's changed." He stared down at the papers in his hand. "Everything."

"But why? Listen to me, Alex..."

"I don't want to discuss it. Thanks for these." He waved the printouts at Jo and exited.

Joanne Markwith quelled the urge to run after Alex, shake some sense into him. But it wouldn't do any good. She had seen the look on his face, like an animal in a trap.

"*Damn* it." Sometimes, Jo thought, life could be really, really, rotten.

When Nickie Farrell walked into her classroom the hubbub cut off as if someone had thrown a switch. She set her attaché case on the desk and swept the room with her gaze. "Good morning, ladies and gentleman. I imagine that many of you have read this morning's *Spectrum*." A few uneasy chuckles broke the silence. "Well, it's all true. I am a post-operative transsexual woman." She scanned the rows of students, making eye contact wherever she could. "I know you have a lot of things you'd like to ask me. That's perfectly natural, so I'm going to make myself available at a time to be announced, and then I'll try to answer as best I can. But not this morning."

A low rumble of disappointment as a male voice protested, "Why not?"

"Because, Mr. Sorrentino, the people who are paying to have you educated would be displeased to find out that precious class time had been taken up by a protracted show-and-tell session with your trannie professor." Nickie smiled. "*Capisce?*"

The class erupted in laughter, breaking the tension. Nickie noticed Cinda Vanderhart sitting with her roommate in their usual seats off to one side of the room. Cinda's facial expression showed a complex mix of pride, defiance, and embarrassment. To her own surprise Nickie felt a twinge of sympathy for the girl.

"This morning's piece in the *Spectrum* was written with my cooperation. It's important for you to know that I wasn't 'outed' against my wishes. Furthermore, the article is an accurate presentation of the facts as I told them to Ms. Vanderhart. So at least in this instance you can believe what you read in the paper." Nickie opened a book. "Now then, about Mr. Samuel Clemens…"

The class went off without a hitch. Afterwards a number of her students came forward to offer support and encouragement, which warmed her heart. When the room finally emptied Nickie dug out her phone to see if Alex had left any messages.

"Uh, Ms. Farrell?"

Cinda Vanderhart had come back into the classroom. She stood by the front row of seats, hands jammed in the pockets of her outsized military surplus jacket.

Nickie held herself very straight. Even in low heels she stood several inches taller than the younger woman. "Well, Ms. Vanderhart? What is it?"

Cinda shifted her weight, looked at the floor, then back up. "I just wanted to say that I'm sorry for putting out the story a few days early. I know we agreed not before December first, but the thing is, Ms. Farrell, people were beginning to talk about you. I heard them, okay? I figured you'd rather have the story come from me than a bunch of stupid gossips. Anyway, I'm sorry."

"Explanations and apologies can't erase the fact that you deliberately chose to break your promise to me, Ms. Vanderhart."

"I know. I hate that I did that," Cinda mumbled, looking away. "Sometimes I hate myself, too."

"Don't." Nickie moderated her tone. "Beating yourself up won't accomplish anything. Believe me, I know. Look at me, Ms. Vanderhart."

Cinda complied, with a hangdog expression.

"Life is about learning from our mistakes. Perhaps you'll approach things differently the next time. Because there will be a next time, and a time after that. Journalism is a demanding and harsh field, fraught with opportunities to hurt people, and you'll have to weigh your choices very carefully. Which will be more important, getting the story or keeping your word? Frankly, Ms. Vanderhart, it's not a profession I would ever want. It's too cutthroat for my taste. But if that's your goal, go for it. The only thing I ask is that you don't advance your career at the expense of others. Play it straight. If you do, your accomplishments will shine much more brightly. All right?"

"Yes, Ms. Farrell." Cinda added in a rush: "I think you're a class act. And I honestly do apologize. If I can ever make it up to you, I will. I hope I didn't cause you any trouble." She scurried up the aisle and out of the classroom.

Nickie watched her go, with the forlorn thought: If you only knew.

Heather stood waiting for her roommate outside the classroom. "Well," she demanded, "so what happened? Did Ms. Farrell tear you a new one?"

"Not at all," Cinda answered. "She is one cool lady."

Heather nodded. "That's what most of the other kids think, too. Except some of the boys were being, like, kind of gross about...you know. Her operation and everything."

"When are you going to get it through your head that boys are always gross?"

Heather bit her lip but said nothing.

"All I know is, I feel kinda shitty," said Cinda. "Like I bushwhacked her, or something."

"Hello, you *did*. Of course you should feel bad. Didn't I say it was the wrong thing to do? But nooo..."

"Thank you very much, Mother Theresa, for that entirely predictable I-told-you-so. I feel a hundred percent better now."

"Sorry. I don't mean to get on your case. I'm not exactly perfect either."

"Really? Coulda fooled me."

"C'mon, don't be mad," Heather begged. "Hey, I know, let's do lunch. The Foxton Arms. My treat, okay? I feel like having some ice cream."

"Ice cream?" Cinda snorted. "Yeah, right. You just want to flirt with that waiter, the one with the different..." Her voice trailed off. She glanced back toward the classroom, and a thoughtful frown crossed her face. "Different colored eyes. Hmmm."

"I do not," Heather protested. "In case you don't remember, I'm going out with Lamar Trent. He...why are you looking like that?"

"Like what?"

"Like *that*," said Heather. "It's the same way Daddy's German shepherd looks right before he puts his nose on the ground and goes crazy sniffing after something."

Cinda laughed. "I have no idea what you're talking about."

"I know you, Cinda," retorted Heather. "You're up to something."

"I'm not," her roommate solemnly declared. "Look, Roomie, if you want to treat me to ice cream, hey, I'm so there. Let's bounce."

Buttoning their coats, they exited the building into a cold drizzle and headed for the student parking lot, where Heather kept her white Scion XB with its "BOX4FOX" license plate.

As they climbed into the car Heather counseled her friend: "Seriously, Cinda. Don't go looking for any more trouble. Can't you please just chill for once?"

"For sure," Cinda promised. "Chill. You bet."

————)(())((————

Back in her office, Nickie pounced on her cell phone before the first chords of "Bolero" had finished playing. "Alex?"

"Hello, Professor Farrell. This is Maudelle Chesterfield speaking, from President Lindsey's office."

Trying to cover her frustration Nickie answered: "Yes, Ms. Chesterfield. How may I help you?"

"President Lindsey would like to see you, Professor."

What now, Nickie wondered. "Certainly. When would be convenient for Ms. Lindsey?"

"A week from today. Around nine o'clock, if that fits your schedule."

"Fine." Nickie scribbled a notation in her appointment book. "Do you know if this will be a lengthy meeting?"

"I didn't get the impression it will take up too much of your time."

"All right. Goodbye, Ms. Chesterfield." No sooner had Nickie laid her phone on the desk than it rang again. "Hello?"

"Alex Steward here. I got your message."

He sounds different, Nickie thought. Formal, almost distant. As calmly as she could: "Thanks for calling me back, Alex."

"Yes. Um…about tonight."

Nickie waited, conscious of her pulse pounding in her temples.

"I don't think I'd be comfortable at the restaurant. Sorry if that strikes you as rude, but it's how I feel."

Nickie leaned on the desk, her forehead propped on a fist. "All right," she replied. "Can we meet somewhere to talk?"

A painful silence. "I don't know," said Alex Steward. "What's there to talk about, really?"

"Alex, for pity's sake." Nickie spoke softly, but there was no hiding the desperation in her voice. "Don't just cut me off. *Please*."

"Well…Are you familiar with the Reflection Garden? Behind the chapel?"

"Yes, I've been there."

"I'll meet you there at five."

"Thank you, Alex. I appreciate…"

But the phone had gone dead. Nickie slowly closed it, thinking, I'm not going to cry. There's no point, and it won't help anything.

For emphasis she repeated aloud: "I am *not* going to cry."

But even as she said the words her voice cracked, and Nickie Farrell did start to cry.

———— ((◊)) ————

Despite their casual attire and lack of reservations Congressman Walters' daughter and her roommate were shown to a table at once, attracting censorious looks from a predominantly female crowd of well-dressed luncheon guests.

"It's like *so* useful having a Capitol Hill daddy," whispered Heather. "We could come here dressed as bag ladies and they'd still seat us."

"Let's do it," Cinda agreed. "These broads need to get over themselves."

"I was kidding, Cinda," Heather reproached her roommate. "Geez, do you always have to be so confrontational?"

"Without confrontation society stagnates. Look around you."

"Welcome to the Foxton Arms, ladies. I'm Robin, your server." The waitress handed them menus. "May I bring you something to start?"

Heather declined. Cinda asked for some hot tea, then casually inquired, "Hey, where's that red-haired waiter? With the bitchin' eyes? Does he still work here?"

Despite her gentle spirit Robin Thompson possessed a well-developed sense of feminine territoriality. Bristling a little, she replied that Mr. Skinner wasn't working the lunch shift.

The roommates exchanged wise glances.

"So you guys are hooking up, huh?" Heather twitched her nose. "Daddy thinks very highly of him, y'know."

"Why don't I get the tea and come back to take your orders," said Robin, and departed.

"I think she feels threatened." Heather grinned. "It must be you, because I'm sure not interested in her waiter boyfriend. Why do you care where he is, anyway?"

"Oh, just making conversation." Cinda yawned. "No big deal."

"As if." Heather eyed her companion. "You've got something up your sleeve. Well, I don't want to know what it is. Leave me out of it."

Robin returned with Cinda's tea, silently took their orders and stalked off.

"Omigod, you'd think we insulted her mother or something. Some people are too insecure." Heather bit into a breadstick. "When you interviewed Ms. Farrell, did you find out what her name used to be? I mean, back when she was a boy?"

"I asked, but she wouldn't tell me," replied Cinda. "Said she never gives out her family name. Something about protecting their privacy, but I think it's something else. I have a feeling they don't accept her gender transition. As in, total rejection."

"Can you blame them? It must be totally bizarre," mused Heather. "I mean, what on earth would Daddy do if I told him I was really a guy?"

Cinda lifted eyebrows at her roommate. "Somehow, I can't picture it."

"Thank God," giggled Heather. Suddenly a furtive look crossed her face. She muttered, "Oh, crap. I've got to go to the ladies. Those Depo Provera shots make me bleed like crazy. Be right back." She grabbed her purse and rushed off.

"Thanks for sharing," Cinda muttered. She sat idly toying with a fork, lost in thought, until Robin appeared with their entrées. Cinda lightly touched the waitress's arm. "Listen, uh, Robin? I'm Cinda, Cinda Vanderhart. I'd really like to talk to you about your boyfriend. Could I call you some time?"

Robin stiffly drew away. Cinda persisted: "Okay, you locals don't like us Windfield people. I get that. But I'm not trying to move in on you, I swear. I don't even *do* boys. But Robin, there's something weird going on. I've seen your boyfriend's different-colored eyes. Pretty unique, right? Well, one of my professors has the exact same eyes, but she keeps them hidden most of the time. I'm an investigative journalist. Coincidences like that...well, they just make me itch, y'know?"

She must be talking about that lady I served last week, Robin thought at once. Although the lady's name had slipped her mind, she did recall mentioning it to Collie, but he'd been too preoccupied with his mother to pay attention. Besides, talking about Collie –or anything else– with this brazen lesbian made her very uncomfortable. Robin said, "Coincidences sometimes happen. Your professor can't possibly have any connection to Mr. Skinner." She offered a large wooden grinder. "Fresh pepper?"

"Listen to me, Robin. This professor of mine went to Windfield a long time ago. Probably around the time your boyfriend was born. Only she wasn't a 'she' back then."

"Huh? What are you talking about?"

Cinda spied Heather approaching the table. "Not now. I'll call you. Give me your pen, quick."

Robin hesitated.

"*Give* it to me. Aren't you even a little bit interested? What's your number?"

Robin reluctantly handed the Windfield girl her pen and said, "Six two eight, four nine two three."

Cinda hastily jotted the numbers on her wrist and returned the pen just as Heather arrived. Cinda winked at Robin and turned to her roommate. "Hello, gorgeous. Did everything come out all right?"

"Shut *up*. Honestly, sometimes you are cruder than the boys."

After the meal, as Heather was signing the check Cinda said, "Leave her a good tip."

"Well, duh. Twenty percent, always." Heather narrowed her eyes. "Why?"

With a foxy look: "She's way cute, don't you think? Give her a little extra."

Heather made a show of being exasperated. "She's got a boyfriend, Cinda! The waiter, remember?"

"Yeah, but still. You never know."

From across the room Robin watched the two girls get up and leave. She wished she hadn't given Cinda Vanderhart her phone number. Too late now, but if the Windfield girl did call, Robin decided, she'd just hang up. Even though a faint curiosity lingered in the back of her mind about the lady with Collie's eyes, they really had nothing to discuss. The similarity was an odd fluke. Nothing more.

⟫⟪◍⟫⟪

The Reflection Garden was a secluded courtyard which abutted the rear of Windfield's chapel. A few stone benches and leafless shade trees were interspersed among neat flower beds which in season contained masses of colorful blooms, but were now bare save for some straggly stalks. Rose bushes, their branches pruned short, lay dormant under winter cloaks of shredded mulch. In springtime the garden was a refuge of serenity and solitude, but this late autumn evening, under gray clouds threatening rain, it seemed still and lifeless as a mausoleum.

Nickie Farrell walked into the deserted enclosure a few minutes before five. She felt certain that Alex Steward had chosen to meet here because he didn't want to be seen with her in public. The thought made her insides hurt. Nickie walked to a stone bench and sat. She rewound the pink-and-black scarf around her neck, wondering if she'd ever feel entirely at home in her new gender. Sitting here alone, shivering in the cold, waiting for a man who probably considered her some sort of freak, Nickie found it difficult to believe that she would ever be completely happy. And if not, she thought, what use had it all been? The years of therapy, the agonizing electrolysis treatments, the costly surgeries, the long recuperation, the spiteful rejection by her family; why had she endured all that, if only to end up unhappy anyway? Her life would've been much less complicated if she'd remained a man, gotten drunk all the time, drifted about aimlessly and lived in secret misery until the end.

She checked her wristwatch. Almost ten after five. Was it possible that Alex wouldn't show up? It seemed inconceivable; he was too decent a person. On the other hand, it always amazed Nickie how incredibly cruel people could be to one another...

She heard footsteps on the gravel path, and looked up as Alex Steward slowly approached. He stopped a few feet away and stood still, hands shoved deep in his jacket pockets, his face as gloomy as the sky. From the way his blue eyes roved, Nickie could tell that it was difficult for him to look at her.

Nickie yearned to stand up and hug him but she remained seated on the cold stone bench. "Hello, Alex."

"Hi." His voice sounded old, drained. "I didn't mean to keep you waiting."

"I know you didn't. Thank you for coming. I...I wasn't sure you would."

Alex shifted his weight. "Neither was I."

There was an uncomfortable silence. At length Nickie said in a small voice, "I am so sorry that you had to find out about me by reading that story in the *Spectrum*. I didn't want it to be that way, Alex."

"Didn't you?" His tone wasn't friendly. "Then how come you couldn't find some way to tell me yourself?"

Nickie met his gaze. "Alex, I tried. I was right in the middle of telling you when you got that call about your grandson. Don't you remember? I asked you if you knew what TS meant."

"Oh, hell, Nickie. That was five days ago! How long have we been going out? A month? You should have said something right at the beginning."

Nickie hugged herself. "I know. You're right. But I was afraid.

Damn it, Alex, I was afraid you'd react just like *this*."

Alex Steward didn't reply. He began a slow pace back and forth before her bench.

"Tell me something," Nickie said after a moment. "If you'd found out the truth any earlier, would it have made a difference in how you feel about me?"

"I don't know the answer to that."

"I think you do, Alex."

He stopped and faced her, an angry look on his face. "Maybe it wouldn't have made any difference."

Looking down at her lap, Nickie quietly asked, "Do you really find me so repulsive?"

A pained expression replaced his angry one. "No. *No.* Don't say that."

"What, then? Why don't you want to be with me any more?"

Alex placed his hands on both sides of his head as if to keep it from exploding. "Jesus Christ, Nickie! You are...you were a *man*. Like me! With all the same parts! I don't know how to deal with that."

Defensively Nickie snapped, "I am *not* a man. Those *parts* are all gone. You couldn't tell the difference between me and any other woman." Her expression hardened. "Want to see?"

Alex winced. "For God's sake, Nickie."

"Do you think it's been easy? I went through years of hell trying to discover some way to be at peace with myself. Nothing worked. In the end this was the only solution I could find. So I did it, carefully, patiently, with all the required medical supervision, and what did I get? My own family slammed the door in my face. Why? What did I do that's so unforgivable? I just wanted a chance to be happy." She began to weep.

Alex Steward made a sound as if he'd been punched in the stomach. "I don't belong here," he moaned.

"What do you mean?" Nickie cried. "Don't leave. Please."

"I don't belong at here Windfield," groaned Alex. He moved to a nearby bench and sank down on it, his head in his hands. "I always thought I was a reasonably hip old guy, y'know? Liberal arts, modern outlook, all that."

"I don't understand," Nickie sobbed. "What are you saying?"

Alex raised his head and looked at her. "Me, a liberal? What a joke. I'm an old-fashioned square. Don't you see? I am so damned conformist and puritanical that I can't handle being attracted to a...a transsexual woman," he choked out the words. "Which means that I'm in no position to be teaching these young folks. They need to be guided by people who have open minds, who aren't bound up in knots by their own prejudices. People like you. Not like me." He dropped his head. "Maybe I'll talk to Larry Silverman about resigning."

Aghast, Nickie sprang to her feet. "Alex, *no*. Windfield is your school. Everyone here respects you. You're tenured, for heaven's sake! If anyone should go, it's me. I've never belonged anywhere. Windfield doesn't need me. But you can't leave. I won't let you!"

Alex Steward heavily got to his feet. "It's not your decision, is it?" They stood mere inches apart. Nickie could feel the powerful magnetism of their physical attraction. She ached with longing to throw her arms around his neck, to plead for Alex to stay and love her as she loved him. But in seconds the opportunity was lost as he turned from her and began trudging away with bowed shoulders.

"Alex," she implored, "don't let us end like this. *Please*, Alex! Come back."

He stopped. For a brief instant Nickie hoped he would turn around. But then she heard him say in a defeated voice: "I'm sorry. I can't."

She watched him walk out of the Reflection Garden, then disappear from sight around the side of the chapel without once looking back. A light rain began to fall. Nickie stood motionless, heedless of her hair becoming soaked. A nearby lamppost flickered to life, but still she made no move, just standing there, a solitary figure in the wet lamp-lit darkness.

Chapter Nine

Yesterday's Gone

The following week at the Stuarton Shamrock store, one of Beryl Jamison's co-workers called out: "Ber? Phone, line three. Some guy."

Beryl frowned in puzzlement. Her friends knew better than to call her at work. Mr. Holt didn't like his employees wasting valuable business time on personal phone calls. She lifted the receiver. "Yes?"

"Mrs. Jamison? It's Collie Skinner. I'm sorry to bother you, ma'am..."

Beryl immediately sensed his distress. "Collie, what's wrong?"

"My mother's really sick, Mrs. Jamison. Can you tell Mr. Holt that she won't be in today?"

Beryl thought, *damn.* She'd been afraid this was coming. Luanne had looked like death ever since Eamon Douglass called her into the office. "Forget about Mr. Holt, Collie. Is it her stomach again?"

"Yes, ma'am. Mama was hurting all night. The pain got so bad this morning that she threw up. Right now it's hurting less, but she's sweating and shaking. There's no way I can let her go to work."

"God almighty. Listen to me, Collie." Beryl spoke urgently. "You have to take your mama to the emergency room. Pain like that, and a fever...She's got to see a doctor. Take her over to Graymont Community Hospital, *now.* I don't care if she doesn't want to go, just get her there." Beryl added, "If you run into any trouble with you-know-who, call me back and I'll come right over there with my shotgun. There's no time to waste, Collie. Your mother needs help. You get going, hear? Be sure to keep her as warm as possible."

"Yes, ma'am, I will."

"Good. And call me as soon as you can, will you?"

"I will, Mrs. Jamison."

She heard the phone click off. Beryl Jamison was a tough-minded woman, but she suddenly felt terribly afraid for her friend.

"Luanne, baby, please hang in there," she whispered, and went off to find Mr. Holt.

⸺◈⸺

At the same time, a few short miles to the west, Nickie Farrell was being shown into President Fredericka Lindsey's office by Maudelle Chesterfield.

"Good morning, Professor Farrell," greeted the president. "How nice to see you again." She nodded at her assistant, who withdrew and closed the door.

Nickie shook the president's outstretched hand. "Good morning."

"I appreciate your coming in so early," said Fredericka Lindsey. "I hope it isn't too much of an inconvenience." She indicated the black leather couch. "Please, sit."

Nickie settled onto the couch. Fredericka Lindsey appraised her visitor with a practiced eye.

"Is everything all right, Professor?"

"Yes, ma'am." Nickie looked down at her folded hands. "Everything's fine."

"That was quite an article in the *Spectrum* last week," observed Fredericka Lindsey. "I assume it wasn't written without your consent?"

"Not at all. I spoke with the young woman at length."

"I see." The president paused. "Professor Farrell...may I call you Nickie?"

"Of course."

"Nickie, have you encountered any inappropriate responses? Unwarranted comments, snide remarks, anything like that? Because such things will not be tolerated at this school so long as I'm president." She placed a gentle hand on Nickie's arm. "Feel free to confide in me, dear. Nothing you say leaves this office."

"Actually," said Nickie with a smile which the president thought looked rather artificial, "my students have been quite supportive. Naturally they're very curious, but the general consensus seems to be that their transsexual English professor is, if you'll forgive the expression, way bitchin'."

"Good heavens. A double-edged compliment, to be sure."

"Considering the possible alternatives," Nickie gave a small shrug, "I'll take it."

"Hm, I suppose so." The president studied her in silence. "But I'll not permit you to be disrespected or mistreated. If anything untoward does happen, Nickie, anything at all, I want you to let me know right away."

"I will, President Lindsey. Thank you."

"Good. Now, the reason I asked you here this morning..."

Fredericka Lindsey briefly related the circumstances surrounding Ambassador Eamon Douglass's proposal to upgrade the Randall Windfield Memorial. "Needless to say, we were more than a little surprised. Ambassador Douglass has not been known as a friend of Windfield. Quite the contrary. But he demonstrated his commitment with an exceptionally generous financial gift to the college, and the trustees have decided to accept his offer regarding the memorial. And that's where you come in."

"How so?"

As the president outlined her proposal Nickie listened, expressionless.

"So," Fredericka Lindsey concluded. "How does that strike you?"

Nickie Farrell didn't answer for a long moment. Finally she said, "And when this Admiral Douglass—"

"Ambassador Douglass."

"When Ambassador Douglass finds out that his Windfield College liaison is a transsexual woman, then, depending on how he reacts, you'll know for certain what his true feelings are. Am I right?"

Fredericka Lindsey couldn't bring herself to lie. "Well, now that your situation is public knowledge...I suppose that's not out of the question."

"I get to be a litmus test for the sincerity of some dying reactionary's sudden reformation." Nickie stared out the large window, a remote look on her pale face. "I'll never be just a normal person, will I? No matter what I do, how hard I try, I'll always be different, and people will always treat me differently."

The resignation in her voice made Windfield's president flinch. "You mustn't think like that, Nickie. You're a fine woman, an admirable and courageous woman."

"But I'm not like other women." She added in a barely audible voice, "No one ever lets me forget it."

President Lindsey reached out and took Nickie's hand.

"If you'd rather not do this, I understand completely. You've already been through so much. I don't want to add to your burdens. Let's forget it."

"No, Ms. Lindsey. Windfield College is my alma mater, and if I can be of help I want to do it." She grimaced. "I haven't brought much credit to my school in the past quarter century."

"That's not true, Nickie. You came back." President Lindsey spoke gently but firmly. "You took charge of your life in a way that few can, you did what you had to do, and you returned to teach a new generation of students. That isn't merely commendable. It's the single finest thing you could do for your school. Don't ever forget that, my dear, because I can assure you that Windfield won't."

Nickie managed a smile.

"Now, if you're quite sure you want to take this on, here is Ambassador Douglass's private number." Fredericka Lindsey handed her a business card. "He's expecting your call."

"I'll attend to it right away." Nickie stowed the card in her purse. "I really do appreciate this opportunity."

The president rose from the couch. "I'm sure you'll do a splendid job. Keep me informed, though. We don't want our benefactor constructing some godawful *thing* out there."

"That wouldn't be good," Nickie agreed, with a small laugh.

"Ah, much better. Laughter suits you. You are such an attractive lady, Professor Farrell. Different, yes. But so very, very special. And I'll tell you something else: The day isn't far off when everyone at Windfield College will recognize just how fortunate we are to have you here."

Bleary-eyed and hung over from a night of downing Sore Losers at Hamburger John's (a Sore Loser consisted of rotgut whiskey in cheap beer), Jay-Bo Skinner stumbled to his BarcaLounger and stretched out with a groan. He clicked on the television, wishing that he had a glass of Clamato juice and vodka to numb the banging in his head.

He was scanning the channels for a conservative talk show when he heard a noise, and looked over to see Collie supporting his mother with one arm, helping her walk toward the front door. White-faced and shaking, Luanne had a blanket draped around her shoulders. She seemed to be on the edge of fainting.

Jay-Bo scowled. "Where the fuck do you think you're goin'?"

"None of your business, Old Man," snapped Collie. He encouraged his moaning mother, "Come on, Mama. We're going to get you some help."

"The hell you say." Jay-Bo heaved himself out of the lounger, and stood glowering in his stained boxers. "You ain't takin' her anywhere, boy, except to work. That's where she's been all night, huh? In with you, snivelin' about a little tummy ache." He snorted. "Damn weakling. Hell, I was half-dead once with jungle fever and still took out a machine gun nest full of gooks. Nobody ever coddled my ass."

"Yeah, you're a real hero," Collie retorted. "Shut your mouth and sit down."

"Or what, you damn pissant?" Jay-Bo took a menacing step forward but stopped when Collie whipped up his free hand and pointed an aluminum baseball bat at his face.

"Back off," he ordered. "Or I'll smash your brains out. I swear I will." Collie warily moved toward the front door, awkwardly supporting Luanne and holding the bat out. Jay-Bo knew that he could disarm Collie and break his arm in two seconds flat, and he sorely wanted to do it. But then what? If Jay-Bo put him out of commission, the rent wouldn't get paid, the beer money would stop, and things would suck even worse than they did already. Thwarted, Jay-Bo's anger and hatred boiled over.

"You cockeyed little fuckstick! I always knew you were a Mama's-boy. So go on. Take that complainin' ungrateful bitch and sit on your ass all day in the nigger clinic until some fuckin' Jew doctor gives her an aspirin and charges you two hundred bucks. That's real smart, boy. Get the hell outa here. I can't stand the sight of you."

Luanne made a feeble attempt to speak, but Collie said, "Sshh, Mama, never mind," and maneuvered her out the door. Turning to Jay-Bo he spat, "Go to Hell, *Daddy*."

Coming from him, it sounded like the vilest epithet in the language.

<hr>

The day had not started out well for Ambassador Eamon Douglass. He'd noticed some discomfort in his nether regions; after he used the bathroom, there was blood in the toilet, which presented a stark reminder that the disease was steadily working its malignant business in his bowels. Not that it had shaken his resolve in any way. Hell, no. The doctors continued to remonstrate and yowl about initiating treatment, but Douglass brushed them off. The Hippocratic Oath somehow caused physicians to develop a parasitic imperative to firmly attach themselves to their patients, like sea lampreys, and the simplest course was to ignore them.

Besides, this morning he was more determined than ever to eradicate Windfield College. He'd sent for a copy of the *Spectrum*, hoping to read something about his magnanimous donation, and instead found the article about their transsexual professor. Of course he immediately recognized the name. It came as no surprise that Fredericka Lindsey was an underhanded bitch; still, the idea that she would appoint a side-show freak to be his liaison on the memorial project was beyond belief. This Nickie Farrell was doubtless a hulking grotesque with beard bristles sticking out from under a slather of pancake makeup, clomping along in gunboat-sized high heels. The thought made him ill. But the ambassador knew he was trapped. If he objected, it might call into question his supposed liberal rebirth, and he couldn't chance that. His only recourse was to make damned sure the transsexual monster was standing right next to him when the exploding sundial blew them all to Perdition.

That was another bothersome thing. There had been no further word from "Father George" Volka, and Eamon Douglass was beginning to feel a bit antsy. He trusted Egor Antonovich, of course; nonetheless, until the Redeemer arrived safely his plans were so much hot air. Barely four months remained until the April first Redemption. Things needed to start happening, and fast.

The ambassador stared morosely at the glass wolf on his desk, irritably tapping his shillelagh on the carpet. When the intercom buzzed, he growled, "What is it?"

"A Ms. Nickie Farrell, sir. She says you are expecting her call."

"*She* says that, hey?" Douglass snorted. All right, put her on." After a pause: "Hello? Eamon Douglass here."

"Good day, Ambassador. This is Nickie Farrell, from Windfield College. President Lindsey requested that I get in touch with you."

The ambassador's eyebrows lifted. He had expected a syrupy baritone lisp, but Nickie Farrell's voice, while on the lower range, was lilting and womanly. Still, Dustin Hoffman had made himself sound feminine in *Tootsie*. Anyone could change their voice. It didn't mean a damn thing.

"Yes, Ms. Farrell. So good of you to call. I assume President Lindsey has filled you in on my proposal?"

"Yes, she did. An extremely generous gesture, Ambassador. I'm ready to assist you in whatever capacity you deem appropriate."

At least he has some manners, thought the ambassador. But then, homosexuals did tend to be polite.

"Excellent." Eamon Douglass grinned unpleasantly at the glass wolf. "I have a feeling that with your help my little project will be a smashing success."

"I'm sure it will, Ambassador. How do you wish to proceed?"

"We should meet, Ms. Farrell. What is your schedule like?"

"As you know, Ambassador, we are near the end of the semester, and finals are starting soon. I am going to be a bit busy with my academic duties for another week or so, but after that I will make myself available at your convenience."

The ambassador frowned. More delays. "But won't you be leaving for the Christmas holidays?"

"As it happens, sir, I have no plans for the holidays. I won't be going anywhere."

"Good," replied Douglass. "We have to get the ball rolling, Ms. Farrell, and the sooner the better."

"I understand. Shall I call you when my schedule clears?"

"Do that. I have a feeling that we will accomplish great things, Ms. Farrell."

"I'll try my best to make sure of it, Ambassador. Goodbye."

"Goodbye, Professor Farrell." Eamon Douglass set down the receiver. "You perverted Windfield freak. Cut your cock off and run around in petticoats, will you? Well, enjoy it while you can, mister. Enjoy it while you can."

———⚬———

By the time they arrived at Graymont Community Hospital Collie's mother was so weak that he had to half-carry her into the Emergency Room. He carefully lowered her into an unoccupied seat. Luanne propped herself against the wall, eyes closed, her breathing ragged and shallow.

"I'll be right back, Mama." Collie made his way toward the reception desk. Only a few others were waiting to be seen: An elderly woman with a bloody bandage on her arm, a couple of mothers with rheumy-eyed sniffling children, and a scabby-faced homeless man. Collie said to the receptionist, "Please, I need someone to take a look at my mother. She's sick." He indicated Luanne slumped in her chair. "I mean, really sick."

The receptionist, a stout lady with piled magenta hair, handed Collie a clipboard. "Sign her in, and take a seat. We'll call you. Do you have medical insurance?"

"No, ma'am."

The receptionist nodded, wrote something on a form and repeated, "We'll call you."

Collie went back and sat by Luanne. "They'll see us soon, Mama. You're going to be okay. Here, lean on me." Under the blanket he could feel her shivering. He put his arm around her, rubbing with his hand to generate some warmth. "Just hold on, Mama."

Luanne faintly spoke through chattering teeth, "I'm s-sorry to b-be such a problem, N-Nicholas, b-but I'm so c-cold."

"I know, Mama." Collie heard the receptionist call out: "Terrell?"

The old lady with the bloody arm rose and followed a green-smocked assistant through some swinging doors.

After fifteen minutes crawled by, Collie began to panic. Luanne's whole body was shaking like an out-of-alignment car; he could hear her teeth clicking together as she was wracked by chills. He placed his palm on her forehead, which felt damp and hot.

A piteous whimper: "Oh, God, Nicholas, I d-don't f-feel good."

"I'll be right back, Mama." Collie half-ran to the reception desk. "Ma'am, please, somebody's got to take a look at my mother!"

The receptionist frowned. "We're working as fast as we can, young man. You have to wait your turn. Your mother will be taken care of when—"

Collie burst out, "Ma'am, she's shaking and burning up and I want someone to help her right now!"

The receptionist's mouth compressed. "Take a seat, young man, and don't create any more disturbance or I'll have to call security."

A calm voice at Collie's elbow inquired, "Is there a problem here?"

A white-coated tall bald man with a stethoscope draped around his neck peered more closely, and said in a surprised voice, "Collie Skinner?"

Collie blinked, then recognized the man as one of his regular customers at the Foxton Arms. "Doctor Roberts!"

The doctor held his hand up at the indignant receptionist. "It's all right, Mrs. Horn. What seems to be the problem, Collie?"

"It's my mother, Dr. Roberts. Something's really wrong. She's in terrible shape. Can you come take a look?"

"Of course."

Collie led the doctor over to where Luanne sat collapsed against the wall. Dr. Roberts knelt down and after one look snapped his fingers at the watching receptionist. "I'm Dr. Roberts, ma'am. We're going to take you in back now, see if we can make you feel a little better. Okay?"

Luanne whispered, "Thank you." The green-smocked assistant helped her into a wheelchair and began rolling her away.

Collie started to follow but Dr. Roberts laid a restraining hand on his arm. "Talk to me, son," he said. "How long has this been going on?"

"It got really bad last night, but she's been having this pain in her stomach for a long time. She said it was heartburn or something to do with...you know, the change. Woman stuff."

"How long a time? Weeks? Months?"

"A couple of months, I guess."

"Show me where she said the pain was."

Collie pointed at an area below and to the left of his navel. "Down around here. It was really killing her last night, but now she says it doesn't hurt as much."

Dr. Roberts gravely inquired if she'd been seen by a doctor before now.

"No, sir. We...we can't afford it, Dr. Roberts. "And my Old Man... well, he doesn't much like doctors."

"I see." Dr. Roberts wore a grim expression. "All right, Collie. I have to go examine your mother...what's her name?"

"Luanne," Collie told him. "Can I come?"

"Let me see where we're at, okay? I'm going to do everything I can to help her." Dr. Roberts put his hand on Collie's shoulder and added in a serious voice, "She's a very sick lady, son."

Fear clamped an icy claw on Collie's neck. "But you can help her, right? She'll get better, won't she?"

"We're going to do our best," promised the doctor, and disappeared through the swinging doors.

Collie unsteadily made his way to the chair where Luanne had been sitting and collapsed into it. He put both fists to his forehead and squeezed his eyes shut. She *had* to get better. The thought of living without her was too frightful to contemplate. He'd never make it alone.

But...he wasn't alone. Collie rose from the chair and approached the reception desk. Mrs. Horn regarded him with a mixture of compassion and mistrust.

"Ma'am, I'm sorry for losing it. I know you have a hard job, and I didn't mean to make it any harder."

The receptionist's expression softened. "I understand how worried you are about your mother. But Dr. Roberts will take good care of her. He's the best."

"Yes, ma'am. Is there a pay phone somewhere I can use? I'd like to call my girlfriend."

"Of course. Down that corridor, past the gift shop." She added, curiously: "I heard Dr. Roberts call you 'Collie'. Is that your name?"

"It's just a nickname." Collie looked at the swinging doors where his mother had disappeared and felt his eyes fill. "Mama named me Nicholas."

Inside the warm cabin of a black Mustang GT cruising south on the New Jersey Turnpike, Cale Pittman and Lloyd Skinner drank Red Bull energy drinks and discussed where to go next. New York City hadn't been to their liking. Although the streets were swarming with every variety of deviant prey, Cale, pointing out the ubiquitous surveillance cameras, had reluctantly concluded that post-9/11 New York was too risky a place for Superiormen to hunt freely. So they'd departed and now, driving through the infernal stink from the Elizabeth chemical works, they chugged high-caffeine beverages and considered their options. Money wasn't a problem thanks to Pittman, who'd won several thousand dollars in Atlantic City and had a wallet full of limitless bank cards. With all their possessions packed in the trunk the two *Übermenschen* were free to go wherever and do whatever they pleased; an agreeable situation for them, if less so for the unsuspecting citizenry.

"Hey, partner," Cale proposed, "what would you think about heading down to New Orleans?"

"New Orleans?" Lloyd shrugged. "I dunno. Isn't it all tore up from that hurricane?"

"It's a mess," Cale nodded, "but that means there's tons of construction work. The government's pouring our tax money in there to rebuild those nigger slums, y'know."

"I thought they all drowned." Lloyd snapped his fingers. "Damn."

"Don't worry, they will. That storm was big, but it wasn't the biggest. When the real monster hits everyone there will be swept away like rats. But in the meantime we can have ourselves a pretty good time." Pittman gave Lloyd's shoulder a playful squeeze. "They have a saying: '*Laissez les bon temps roulez.*' Let the good times roll." With a wink of one deep blue eye: "Want to give it a try?"

Smiling like a worshipful teenage girl Lloyd replied, "I'm with you, Cale."

"Okay, good. We'll head for Richmond then decide which route to take from there. *Laissez les bon temps roulez!*" Cale switched on the radio and hit the auto-scan button. An ad for health insurance, an oldies station, a sports talk show, Mariachi music, a blithering woman psychologist, a snatch of Haydn, and then a strident voice: "Hi, folks. Welcome to this hour of *Take Back America*. I'm your host, Mitchell Hannigan. Let's go right to the phones and find out from our listeners what the liberal homosexual lobby is doing this week to destroy our beloved country."

Cale stopped the auto-scan. "This I'd like to hear."

"First caller is Mack from Stuarton, Virginia. What say you, Mack?"

"Stuarton?" Lloyd Skinner sat up in surprise. "That's my home town."

"Mister Hannigan, it's an honor, sir. You're a great American."

"Thank you, Mack. What are the secular progressives up to in your corner of our proud land?"

"Mister Hannigan, you ain't gonna believe this. There's a college here, it's called Windfield, and it's a super-liberal socialist ACLU kinda place, see?"

Cale glanced over as Lloyd popped another Red Bull and leaned forward, listening intently. "You know what he's talking about?"

"Oh, yeah," responded Lloyd. "Fuckin' Windfield."

The caller continued: "Turns out they done hired one o'them tran-sek-shool preverts to be an English perfesser and teach all them kids. A tran-sek-shool! Right in my own back yard! This here's a good Christian town, Mister Hannigan. We don't go for all that sick stuff. Y'all know what them tran-sek-shools do? They dress like gals and pay doctors to chop off their..."

"Outrageous!" Mitchell Hannigan hastily thundered. "Thank you, Mack, for that alarming report. You see, folks, this is the kind of deadly moral rot we're faced with every day in our country, thanks to godless politicians and activist judges who subvert and defile the Constitution. And now our universities are encouraging *sexual deviants* to educate our innocent children! My friends, we cannot continue to sanction this brazen desecration of our Judeo-Christian heritage..."

Cale switched off the radio. "A shemale college professor." His knuckles showed white where he gripped the steering wheel. "Unbelievable!"

"Not so unbelievable." Lloyd took a long pull of his drink. "Windfield College is worse'n you could imagine."

"Is that right?" Cale's dark eyes narrowed. "Tell me about it, partner."

Fueled with enough caffeine to resurrect a mummy, Lloyd recounted the history of Windfield College. He told Cale how Windfield's malign influence had caused his twin sister to turn queer and hang herself in Marine boot camp, and how his father's law enforcement career had been sabotaged and ruined because he'd arrested some rich Windfield pot-head. By the time Lloyd wound up his tale of woe they had driven across the Susquehanna River into Delaware.

"It's a scandal. A tragedy, even." Cale lit a cigarette. "How could an upstanding American family like yours be so badly treated by these degenerate pseudo-intellectual faggots? And to think that they got away with it...makes me sick, partner."

"Yeah, well, those assholes always get away with it." Lloyd leaned back against the head rest. "Plain folks like us don't stand a chance. We never get any payback."

"Perhaps we should remedy that."

"Yeah, sure. How?"

"Oh, there are ways. When was the last time you paid a visit to your home town?"

"I dunno. Three years, maybe." Lloyd stared gloomily out his window. "Why?"

"How about we detour through there on our way to New Orleans? Stop in and surprise your family. I'm sure they'd be glad to see you. And I'd be interested to check out that transsexual professor. *Extremely* interested."

Cale's smooth silky voice ignited Lloyd's warrior passions. He hooked one finger through Cale's belt loop. "Sure," he said. "Let's do it. But first can we find someplace to rest? I'm sorta tired." Lloyd ran his tongue across his lips. "I want to hear some more Nietzsche." Playfully twisting the belt loop: "Besides, I just love how you read."

<hr />

Twenty minutes had passed with no word from Dr. Roberts. Maybe, thought Collie, that was a good sign. On the other hand, it might mean that his mother's condition had gotten even worse. Without any information all he could do was mentally ping-pong between hope and despair. He'd spoken with Robin, who encouraged him to stay calm and maintain a positive outlook. She promised to join him at the hospital as soon as she arranged for someone to cover her shift at the restaurant.

Another quarter of an hour went by. Collie sat, drumming one heel on the floor in a nonstop tattoo. Where was the doctor? Why hadn't he heard anything? When would they know what was wrong with his mother? Would they be able to help her? How long was it going to take? Non-stop questions, and to each the same maddening answer: "I don't know."

Finally deciding that he couldn't stand it any longer, he got up and approached the reception desk, determined to extract some information from Mrs. Horn even at the risk of angering her again. As he opened his mouth to speak he saw Dr. Roberts peer through the swinging doors and beckon to him. Collie joined the doctor, who led him down a short hallway to a small empty examining room. The doctor closed the door and indicated a beige plastic chair. "Sit down, son."

Collie complied. The look on the physician's face was anything but reassuring. "How's Mama, Doctor Roberts?"

"I'm afraid she's in very bad shape, Collie." The doctor faced him squarely. "I wish I had better news but I'm not going to hand you a bunch of baloney. You're her son, and you deserve the truth."

"How...how bad?" Collie could barely force the words out. "What's wrong with her?"

"She has peritonitis. Do you know what that is?"

Numb, Collie shook his head.

"Well, basically it means that a highly aggressive bacterial infection has spread inside her abdomen. It's a nasty business." The doctor rubbed his brow. "Very difficult to fight."

"But...how could she catch something like that?" Collie stammered. "I don't get it."

"She didn't 'catch' it, Collie. It's not a contagious thing, like a cold or the flu. I'm pretty sure the pain she's been having all this time was caused by a condition called diverticulitis," explained Dr. Roberts. "I did an ultrasound examination, and from what I saw it seems likely that she suffered what we call a ruptured diverticulum. That means that there was a big pocket of infection on the wall of her descending colon," he pointed to his lower left abdomen, "and when it burst it released all kinds of bacteria into her abdominal cavity. Our problem is that the infection has spread everywhere and taken hold, and it's putting a terrible strain on her immune system. That's why she's so weak and feverish. Her body is fighting back as hard as it can, but it's an uphill battle."

"You have drugs to fight infections, don't you?"

"Yes, we do," nodded Dr. Roberts. "But we have to find out exactly which bacteria we're dealing with. There are dozens of different varieties, and no single drug is effective against all of them. I've already ordered a blood culture. That's how we pinpoint the exact bug, but it takes about 48 hours. Until then we'll give your mom a broad-spectrum antibiotic. Sort of a pharmaceutical shotgun approach. With luck the infection will respond to that treatment. But if not..." He stopped, weighing his next words. "Collie, I'm sorry, but I have to be straight with you. Right now, it doesn't look promising."

"Are you saying Mama could *die?* " Collie gasped. "No. She can't, Dr. Roberts. There must be something you can do. *Please!* "

"I've scheduled her for surgery tomorrow morning. I'm hoping she'll be more stabilized by then. We have to go in and remove the damaged part of her colon. We're giving her the best care we know how, son. That's the most we can do."

Collie ground his fists into his eyes, trying to staunch the tears. "This is all my fault. I should've told the Old Man to fuck off and taken her to a doctor."

Dr. Roberts gripped Collie's shoulder. "Don't think like that. Trying to assign blame won't do you or your mother any good." His voice was sympathetic but firm. "Just let it go."

"If Mama dies," Collie stuttered, "I swear I'll kill him." He looked up at Dr. Roberts with red-rimmed wild eyes. "I'll kill him if it's the last thing I do. He *hurt* her."

Sternly Dr. Roberts stated, "I didn't hear that." Then in a gentler voice: "We've taken your mother up to the intensive care unit, so someone will be monitoring her all the time. I'll let you go up there, but only if you promise not to upset her with this kind of talk. That's the worst thing possible, Collie. I mean it. No threats, no recriminations, nothing that might agitate her. I want her as strong as possible for surgery. Okay?"

Collie bowed his head and nodded. "Okay, Dr. Roberts. I promise. Does Mama know how bad this peritonitis is?"

"I explained things. Luanne understands her situation. Now, you'll see she's hooked up to some machines, but don't be alarmed. Those are to help us track her blood pressure, heart rate, and so on. We've given her some medication to bring down the fever. She may seem a little out of it, Collie, but that's to be expected. She's fighting for her life." The doctor paused to let his words sink in. "You need to step up, be strong for her sake. Can you do that?"

Collie stood up. "Yes, sir. I will."

"Good." Dr. Roberts patted him on the back. "Come, I'll take you up to ICU."

Overcome with dread, Collie stumbled after the doctor. There was nothing he could do for his mother now but wait by her side to see whether she would live or die.

———⟫⟨⟪⟩⟫⟪———

Unlike Collie, Robin Thompson had previously visited an intensive care unit when her father was felled by what eventually proved to be a fatal stroke. Afterward Robin had prayed that a long time would pass before she ever found herself in one again. Although the ICU was intended to provide the highest levels of care and healing, she knew that what a lot of people did there was decline and die. Like that ominous valley in the Twenty-third Psalm, the intensive care unit served as a haunt for the Shadow of Death.

The charge nurse directed Robin to the fourth cubicle from the door. She found Collie seated by his mother's bed, unmoving, staring at her with an expression that put a lump in Robin's throat. Dressed in a pale blue hospital gown, Luanne lay with her head slightly to one side, hair matted, chin sunken on her chest, her face haggard and pale. An intravenous drip snaked into one arm. From beneath the sheets wires ran back to various monitors which vigilantly beeped and hummed, their screens tracing a progression of green lines and numerals.

Robin gently laid her hand on Collie's shoulder. He glanced up with a frown, then seeing who it was, stood up and clung to her like a lost child. Robin held him tightly. Although he made no sound, she could feel him shaking with suppressed sobs.

"Sshh," she whispered. "We'll watch over her together."

Collie led her a short way from Luanne's bedside. "Thank God you're here. Mama's sick, Robin. Really sick. Dr. Roberts said she might not–" He broke off and mutely stared at her, his different-colored eyes dulled with anguish.

"Tell me what he said."

Collie summarized what he knew. "So there's nothing more they can do, at least for now. The operation is tomorrow morning, but then they have to wait for the blood culture to come back so they can decide which medicine to give her. Dr. Roberts said there's no way to rush it because the culture needs time to grow. Mama just has to hang in there, but..." His voice caught. "She looks so weak. Did you see?"

"Yes," Robin said. "But she's resting, that's the most important thing. This is the best place for her, so let's be thankful she's here. Do you like Dr. Roberts?"

Collie nodded. "He's a straight-up guy, laid it on the line without any goddamn bullshit." He bit his lip. "Sorry, Robin. I hate it when I cuss. I don't want to be anything like my Old Man."

"You're not." Robin lifted his hands and kissed them. "You're so much like your mother. You have her heart and spirit." Her brown eyes lit with a soft glow. "That's one of the main reasons I'm in love with you, Collie."

He stared at her. "You...you are?"

"Yes." Robin pulled his arms around her and embraced him. "Very, very much."

Swept up in a maelstrom of contradictory emotions, Collie's heart felt like a transmission slammed into reverse at sixty miles an hour.

The most wonderful girl in the world had declared her love for him while ten feet away his mother struggled to live. He rested his forehead against Robin's. They held each other while around them the noises of medical equipment punctuated the ICU's somber quiet.

"Nicholas?"

They looked up to discover Luanne watching them. Incredibly, she was smiling.

"Mama!" Collie hastened to her bedside. "We didn't mean to wake you up. How do you feel?"

His mother ignored the question, instead lifting her arm toward Robin. "Hello, dear. I'm so glad to see you."

Robin gently grasped the sick woman's proffered hand. "Hello, Mrs. Skinner. I came as soon as Collie told me you were here."

Luanne's eyes showed concern. "But what about your work?"

"Mr. Foley said it was okay. Collie too. Please don't worry about that."

Luanne closed her eyes, then opened them and addressed her son: "Honey, why don't you go get a snack or something. I'd like to talk to Robin." Seeing Collie's unwillingness, she quietly chided, "Now, do what Mama asks. I'm not going anywhere."

"Okay, but I'll be right outside." After a stricken look at Robin, Collie left the ICU.

Luanne watched him leave. "My poor baby," she sighed. "This is going to be awful hard on him."

Robin knew better than to ask pointless questions. She felt tears sliding down her face.

"Don't cry, sweetheart." Robin felt a weak pressure on her hand. "I know the doctors are trying their best, but it's my time to go. I don't mind, really. I'm so very, very tired. It'll be nice to rest." She paused. "Did you ever have a pet, Robin? Like a kitty, or a dog? Animals can tell when it's time to die, so they go off somewhere quiet and wait. I always wondered how they knew. Now I think I understand. It's like the last days of summer, when the leaves start to turn. Everything is just...ending. But it's okay. That's a part of life, too."

Robin blinked her overflowing eyes, unable to speak.

Luanne studied her for a moment. "Do you love my boy?"

"Yes, Mrs. Skinner," Robin whispered. "I love him a lot."

"Are you going to marry him?"

"If he asks me, I will."

"Thank God." Luanne exhaled in relief. "He'll be all right, then. You'll take good care of him?"

"Yes. I promise."

The duty nurse suddenly appeared. She checked Luanne's monitors, took her pulse, made sure the IV was dripping at its prescribed rate. "Now, don't talk too much," she cautioned. "You need your rest."

"I know, but this is my future daughter-in-law. There are things I have to tell her about my son."

"If I'd done that for my daughter-in-law," the nurse ruefully observed, "it might've saved her from a few surprises." She patted her patient's shoulder, and left.

Luanne lay silent, staring up at the ceiling. At length she said, "I'm going to tell you a secret that I've never told anyone. It's about Nicholas. You know that's Collie's real name?"

"Yes. I think it's lovely, but he doesn't like it."

"Many years ago I sinned terribly." Luanne searched the younger woman's face. "I broke one of God's commandments, Robin. I committed adultery."

Robin swallowed. "None of us are without sin, Mrs. Skinner. That's why we need Jesus's forgiveness."

"I don't know how Jesus can forgive me. We're supposed to repent, but I never did. I've never been sorry for my sin," Luanne hesitated, "because that's how I had Nicholas."

"I don't under...oh, no." Robin stared at Collie's mother, eyes wide. "Oh, my God."

Luanne averted her gaze. "Please don't hold it against my son. He has no idea. I'm the one to blame. All these years I've been a liar, a cheat." She began to cry. "I hope God does send me to Hell. It's where I belong."

"No!" Robin bent over Luanne, smoothing her hair, kissing away her tears. "You mustn't say things like that, Mrs. Skinner. God would never punish you for bringing Collie...Nicholas into the world. You're a wonderful mother. Jesus loves you. Everyone at the church loves you. *I* love you."

"I couldn't ever tell him the truth, Robin." Luanne's eyes clouded. "I could never tell anybody. Everyone around here hates Windfield College so much, Jay-Bo would've killed us both for sure."

"Windfield?"

"My son's father was a Windfield student." Luanne's eyes shimmered beneath the tears. "The most wonderful, gentle and loving young man in the world, Robin. Nicholas is just like him."

"Oh, Mrs. Skinner." Robin's head was spinning. She couldn't imagine how this revelation might affect Collie, especially if Luanne died. It could push him over the edge into depression or worse...

No, thought Robin, setting her jaw. I promised I would take care of him, and I will. "What was the Windfield student's name?"

"Nick," answered Luanne. "Nick Farrington. Such a beautiful man, Robin, you have no idea. He had two different-colored eyes. That's where Collie got them. Another thing I've lied about all these years."

Something tugged at the edge of Robin's consciousness. "Do you know what became of him?"

"No. He graduated and I never saw him again. There was no way for me to let Nick know I was pregnant. He came from a rich family, and...oh, God." Luanne winced in pain. "It's starting to hurt again."

"I'll call the nurse." Robin started to rise but Luanne held onto her hand.

"Wait, wait, please. Can I ask you a favor, Robin? A really big one?"

"Of course. Anything at all."

"I need you to go to my home and get something. I can't ask Nicholas. If he ran into Jay-Bo with the way things are..." She left the thought unsaid. "There's a Windfield College senior class book I've kept hidden all these years. It has a picture of Nick Farrington. I...I'd like to have it with me."

"All right," Robin answered. "Are you going to tell him the truth?"

"Yes." Luanne bitterly added, "It's about time."

"I'm glad, Mrs. Skinner. He deserves to know. Is there anything else you want me to bring?"

"Do you think they'll let me listen to music?" Luanne's lip trembled. "I'd really like to hear my old songs again. There are some tapes in my kitchen..."

"I'll find them. And I have a Walkman you can use. I'm sure it'll be okay," Robin assured her. "Now tell me where the book is."

Luanne described the hiding place under the bathroom sink. "Please hurry, honey. I don't know how much time I have left...agh," she writhed under the sheets, gasping. "Tell Nicholas you're going to get me some personal things, he'll give you the key." She kissed Robin's hand. "God bless you. Go, now."

Out in the waiting room Robin found Collie slouched in a battered armchair, a half-eaten candy bar dangling in one hand, frowning dully at nothing. Seeing her approach he tossed the candy remnant into a nearby receptacle. "How is Mama?"

"She asked me to bring her some things," Robin said. "Let me have your house key."

"Huh? No way, I can't let you go over there. What if you run into the Old Man?"

"Don't worry about him," Robin flatly stated. "He won't hurt me, and I can take care of myself. The key, please."

Collie shook his head. "It's too dangerous. He's a psycho drunk. Besides, Mama doesn't need–"

Robin's brown eyes flashed. Holding out her hand: "I *promised* your mother. *Give* me the key!"

"All right. But if you see his truck out front, don't go in there. Whatever Mama wants, it's not worth getting yourself killed."

Robin stood on her tiptoes and kissed him. "I'll be back soon. Go to your mother. I love you...Nicholas."

She hurried from the waiting room. Collie looked after her, wondering why "Nicholas" sounded so much better when Robin said it. Maybe it wasn't such a dumb name after all.

When Robin pulled up in front of Luanne's shabby complex, Jay-Bo Skinner's beat-up Ford pickup was nowhere to be seen. Feeling very thankful —bravery aside, she preferred to avoid confrontation— Robin rang the bell several times. Receiving no response, she let herself into the apartment with Collie's key.

She quickly skulked to the bathroom and opened the under-sink cabinet. The Windfield book was right where Luanne had described, stuffed deep into the box of panty liners. Too rushed to glance at it, Robin shoved the slim volume deep into her shoulder tote and found her way to the kitchen. Trying to ignore the empty beer cans scattered everywhere, she spied a small stack of audio cassettes by an old tape player, and added them to her tote bag. She went out, locked the apartment and hastened back to her car. Slinging her tote on the seat, she drove away as fast as possible, only then becoming aware of how rapidly her heart was beating.

A glance at her watch revealed that forty minutes had elapsed since she'd left the hospital. The light was dwindling, and she was anxious to be there for Collie —Nicholas— when he learned his mother's shocking secret. She left the main thoroughfare and turned onto a narrow winding county road which would halve the distance of her return trip.

She negotiated the shortcut in record time. Less than a mile from where the road reconnected with the highway, Robin rounded a sharp curve and to her horror saw two large whitetail deer frozen in the headlights. They stared at the onrushing car, ears up, obsidian eyes glistening.

Robin screamed and instinctively slammed down her clutch and brake pedals. She felt her seatbelt lock as she was hurtled forward. The little Kia shuddered, rocked, and began to fishtail. Her tote bag went flying off the seat, spewing its contents everywhere. Startled by the screeching tires, the whitetails recovered their wits and in two enormous bounds disappeared into the trees. Finally the car skidded to a stop sideways across the road, its rear wheels half off the shoulder, engine still running.

Robin sagged over the steering wheel, whimpering with fear and relief. After a few seconds she realized that her feet were still jammed on the pedals. She let up the pressure, feeling her muscles quivering with adrenalin, and painstakingly steered the car back onto the pot-holed asphalt. She drove the remaining short distance out to the main highway at twenty miles an hour and turned toward the hospital, still shaky and unnerved by her close call.

Once safely parked in the hospital's lot, Robin turned on the in-terior light and began collecting the scattered items from her purse: lipstick, address book, hairbrush, coin purse, wallet. She recovered Luanne's tapes, replacing the ones which had been knocked out of their plastic cases. She discovered the Windfield class book lodged upside-down between the passenger seat and the car door. At length, satisfied that she'd retrieved everything, she locked the car and rushed into the hospital.

There was no possible way that Robin could have seen Eamon Douglass's floppy disk caught up in the springs under her seat.

⟶ ((◉)) ⟶

Quaking, white-faced, confounded beyond coherent thought, Collie gaped at his mother in disbelief. "No," he choked out in a stran-gled voice. "Can't be. No way."

"It's true." Tears flowing, Luanne watched the emotional train wreck unfold on her son's face. "Can you ever forgive me, Nicholas? I should've told you long ago, but I was too afraid."

Collie held his head in his hands, trying not to hyperventilate. The enormity of it felt like a crushing weight on his soul. "Jesus Christ, Mama! Are you telling me I was a *mistake*? A mistake you made screw-ing around with some *Windfield* prick?"

"It wasn't like that," wept his mother. "Your father was a brilliant, incredible person. We loved each other! I didn't plan to get pregnant, it just...happened. But you were conceived in the only pure love I ever knew. And I swear there was never a single minute that I didn't want you. You've got to believe me! You have always been the greatest blessing in my life, Nicholas."

"*Don't call me that.*" Collie hunched forward in his chair, hugging himself. "How could you give me his goddamn name? Everything I am is a lie. Even my name is a lie." He felt a horrible dissolving sensation, as if his entire identity was coming unglued like a cardboard box in the rain. "I'm nothing at all, just an accident from some shitty little fling you had with Nick *fucking* Farrington." He spat the name, and jumped to his feet. "How am I supposed to live with that, Mama? *How?*"

Luanne cringed and covered her face, moaning, "I'm so sorry. Jesus forgive me! I never meant to hurt you. I love you more than life, my precious son, don't hate me, please don't hate me."

"*No.*" Collie clapped his hands over his ears. Suppressing a scream, he turned and fled from the ICU, certain that he would go mad if he stayed a moment longer. Rushing out of the waiting room toward the elevators, he ran into Robin so hard he almost knocked her down.

Instantly divining what had happened, Robin grabbed his arm as he tried to rush past her. "Wait! Where are you going?"

"I don't know. Away. Let me go," he choked out, trying to shake free.

Robin kept her grip on his arm. "You can't run away from this." She spoke in a soothing but unwavering voice. "You mustn't abandon your mother, especially now. You have to know that."

"I don't know *anything*," cried Collie, glaring at her with the whites showing around his different-colored irises. "I don't know why I was born. I don't know who my father was. I don't know why Mama lied all these years. I don't know who I *am*."

"I know who you are." Robin gathered him into her arms, held him as his struggles gradually ebbed. "You are the man I love. You're *you*, the same as you were a few minutes ago. By whatever name, you are my sweet, thoughtful, generous, good-hearted man. None of that has changed. I realize that the things your mother told you must be terribly confusing and I won't pretend to understand how you feel, but I'll help you in any way I can. The important thing is that you've heard the truth now. Is that so horrible? Would you rather *not* know?"

"Don't ask me that." Collie pulled away from her, but didn't try to leave. He put one hand on his stomach. "God, I think I'm going to throw up."

"No, you're not." Robin brushed a stray lock off his forehead. "You're coming with me to see your mother." She hesitated. "I brought her something that I'm sure she'll want to show you. It's important. Please. Don't make her suffer any more than she already is."

Grief-stricken, deflated, Collie nodded and allowed Robin to lead him back to the intensive care unit.

Once inside, the charge nurse frowned and motioned them over to her station.

"I realize this is a stressful situation for you," she told Collie, "but if you upset my patient again I will have to ask you to leave. Your mother is gravely ill. Do you understand what I'm telling you?"

"Yes, ma'am."

"Very well."

Luanne's tear-streaked face was ashen, her eyes sunken and blood-shot. "Forgive me, Collie," she feebly croaked, trying to smile at him. "I promise I'll never call you Nicholas again."

In that instant, the terrible certainty that his mother was dying descended on Collie like an icy black cloak. Tears ran down his face as he bent over her, kissed her, caressed her hair with his hand, desperate to preserve the memory of what her living warmth felt like, knowing it would soon be gone forever. "Mama, Mama," he sobbed, "I'm sorry I got angry. It's okay. You named me Nicholas. I...I'm glad you told me the truth. But please don't die, Mama. Don't leave me alone."

Luanne shook her head. "You won't be alone, my darling. I'll always be watching. And God has brought you and Robin together. She's so beautiful, Nicholas." Luanne shifted her gaze to the younger woman. "Did you bring it?"

"Here it is." Robin drew the old Windfield class book out of her bag and laid it near Luanne's hand.

"Could you open it for me?"

Robin carefully lifted the cover, and the book at once fell open to the one page that had ever mattered.

"There," Luanne whispered, pointing a trembling finger. "There's your father, Nicholas. The only man who ever really loved me."

Collie and Robin peered in wonder at the black-and-white senior photo of the smiling young collegian. Robin discerned a resemblance to Collie in a fullness of lips, high cheekbones, the set of the nose. But one unmistakable feature stood out above all else.

"You have his eyes," she breathed. "You really do. *Exactly* the same."

Collie stared spellbound at the picture. This stranger was his *father?* Thoughts whirled about his consciousness like bits of paper in a dust devil. His psyche ached with the sudden realization that half of who he was –his blood, his genes, his brains, his eyes, everything– came from this mysterious man whom his mother hadn't seen in over twenty-five years. A man who didn't even know that Collie existed.

After an interval he tore his gaze away from the Windfield year-book. Luanne and Robin were watching apprehensively. "It's okay. I'll be all right. Really, I will." He leaned over, nuzzled and kissed his mother's cheek. "Those initials you showed me on the Gander Creek bridge, Mama...That was you and Nick, wasn't it?"

"Yes, Nicholas. On the most beautiful springtime day I ever saw. I was never that happy again...except on the day you were born." She closed her eyes as more tears fell. "I wish Nick could have been there to see his son. He would have been so proud."

Collie pressed his mother's hand to his breast. "Maybe he still can be, Mama. I'm going to try and find Nick Farrington. After all, he's my dad."

———

Collie was awakened by some disjointed sounds coming from the bed. Groggily checking his watch he saw that it was just past four-thirty in the morning. After sending Robin home at one o'clock despite her protests, he'd maintained a watchful vigil in Luanne's darkened cubicle. Intending not to fall asleep himself, he'd eventually succumbed to crushing fatigue and passed out. Now, stiff from hours of slumping in the hard plastic chair, he leaned over his mother, who was restlessly muttering something over and over.

"What, Mama?" Collie spoke softly. "What are you trying to say?"

"Dingbats," Luanne mumbled, eyes shut. "Doublecross Dingbats. Mr. Douglass...disk...Dingbats."

"Oh, God." Terrified, Collie felt his mother's forehead. It was burning, slick with perspiration.

"Dingbats," Luanne repeated. "Mr. DuPree...the disk...Mr. Douglass...Doublecross...Dingbats."

"Mama, you're not making sense. Dingbats? What about Mr. Douglass?"

Collie was about to run and get the nurse when Luanne suddenly opened her eyes. "Nicholas? Is that you?"

"Yes, it's Nicholas. I'm here, Mama." Collie tenderly combed aside the wet strands of hair clinging to his mother's face. "Were you having a bad dream? You kept saying something about Mr. Douglass and Dingbats. Do you remember?"

"It doesn't matter anymore." Luanne slowly blinked her eyes, and Collie perceived a distance in them he'd never seen before, as if she was receding away from him even as she tried to focus. His stomach contracted into a frozen knot. Luanne blinked again, and a peaceful expression warmed her drained face. "I saw Lissa," she whispered. "My beautiful girl. She's waiting for me."

"Will you tell her how much I miss her, Mama? How much I love her?"

"She knows, honey." With great effort Luanne raised a trembling hand to touch her son's cheek, then let it fall back. "She knows." Her eyes closed, then opened again. "Don't hate, Nicholas. Hate destroys everything. Don't let it destroy you. Will you remember?"

"Yes, Mama. I'll remember. I promise." Collie stared with agonized intensity into his mother's dimming eyes, trying by force of will to keep the light from going out.

"Good boy." She smiled. "I'd like to listen to my music now, Nicholas. Can I?"

"Of course you can, Mama." Collie retrieved Robin's old Walkman from the bedside table, gently placed the headphones over his mother's ears, lowered the volume and pressed the play button.

Luanne lay with her eyes closed, the ghostly smile still in place. Collie sat in the chair and held his dying mother's hand as she haltingly began to sing in an almost-inaudible voice:

> Wait till summer comes again
> I hope that you'll remember when
> Our love had just begun
> I loved you yesterday
> But yesterday's gone...yesterday's gone...yes...ter...day...

Collie felt Luanne's hand go slack in his own. Her head fell sideways, knocking the headphones awry, as a shrill tone erupted from one of the monitors behind her bed.

Collie barely had time to cry "Mama!" before the charge nurse arrived and in a strict no-nonsense voice informed him that he had to leave the ICU immediately.

With one final look back at the motionless form in the bed, Collie stumbled from the room.

⸺◈⸺

Luanne was indistinctly aware that things were happening around her, but it all seemed very far off and not of any consequence. There was noise, and movement, but none of it made sense and soon faded to nothing. A great feeling of tranquility enveloped her like a delicious warm bath, and she felt safe and loved. The soothing darkness comforted her, taking away all hurt and sorrow. With one final flickering thought she recalled how nice it had been to be tucked into bed and kissed goodnight by her mother.

And then the gentle spirit that had animated Luanne Skinner departed on its prescribed path, and the last of her yesterdays was gone for all time.

- Part Two -

REDEMPTION

Chapter Ten
Sequelae

"What?!" Eamon Douglass's face reddened, his foul mood grown fouler by several degrees. "God *damn* it, Holt! When did this happen? Who told you?"

He listened for a few moments, fuming. "All right. Find out when they're having the blasted funeral and call me back."

The ambassador slammed down the phone with a curse. Everything seemed to be going south at once. He'd been shitting blood for days, the internal pain was becoming a constant, there was still no word from Volka, and the transsexual Windfield deviant hadn't yet called. Now, to top it all off, that idiotic Skinner woman had come down with peritonitis and *died*. Jesus Christ on a bicycle! Cancer was one thing, but peritonitis only struck down dimwits who didn't have enough brains to take care of themselves. He paced back and forth across his study, scowling, swatting at the carpet with his shillelagh. This was what came of dealing with peasants. They were all ignorant and backward, no better than third world savages, and relying on them for anything was as foolhardy as putting your faith in a pet cat. He should never have entrusted the delivery of his disk to a white trash imbecile like Luanne Skinner. God only knew where she'd hidden it. Probably in a goddamn sugar bowl or something equally inane.

On the other hand, he reassured himself, even assuming the disk was discovered, the likelihood of it being decoded was virtually nonexistent. The ambassador had taken great pains to disguise his "Death Declaration" in an obscure and bizarre font known as Doublecross Dingbats. Without that information, it would take a cryptographic specialist to decipher the thing. Ambassador Douglass saw no need to fret about his scheme prematurely coming to light. Nonetheless, he wasn't the sort to leave loose ends. He intended to ascertain for himself whether or not the bereaved family knew about the missing disk. Doing so wouldn't present a problem. These rural boneheads were easily awed by the likes of Eamon Douglass. The rogue cop husband was a sodden thug, and the son who worked for Mike Barlow was a trivial punk. If they had his floppy, he'd get it back. If they didn't, so much the better. He'd simply make a new one and have it delivered by a more reliable dupe.

The phone rang. He snatched it up. "This Saturday? All right, Holt. Call that limp-wristed florist in Middleville, tell him to send flowers to the church. Lots of goddamn flowers. An elaborate funeral display... what? Christ, who cares? 'Condolences from the entire Shamrock family', something like that. Use your imagination, Holt. I don't have time for details. Just get it done."

The ambassador seated himself in the big leather desk chair, wincing a bit at the discomfort in his bowels. "I'm surrounded by cretins," he complained to his glass wolf. "It's a miracle I get anything accomplished."

In response to a knock at his study's door, Douglass issued a curt, "What is it now?"

Holmes entered and handed him a flat oblong Federal Express box. "For you, sir."

The ambassador took the box, saw the sender's address, and lit up with such a pleased smile that the secretary inquired, "Good news, sir?"

"I do believe so, Holmes. From an exemplary charitable institution with which I am philanthropically involved. Redeemer Ministries. They provide corrective direction for wayward youths."

"Most commendable, Ambassador. I trust the wayward youths are suitably appreciative of your kindness."

"Some of them are quite incorrigible," replied Douglass. "But I am endeavoring to make certain that they all find redemption. You're excused, Holmes."

The instant the door latch clicked, the ambassador ripped open the box and extracted a typewritten page and a small bubble-wrapped cell phone. He cautiously hefted the phone, wondering if it concealed a detonator. He carefully set it down by the glass wolf and picked up the page:

Honorable Ambassador Eamon Douglass:

I am delighted to inform you that the special memo-rial plaque you ordered has been completed. You will be pleased to know that our artisans have assiduously followed your precise design specifications. I feel most confident that your desire to provide a lasting remembrance will be more than fulfilled.

For reasons of economy and weight, the plaque will be shipped to you by sea. The transport specialists we've chosen are highly knowledgeable mariners with considerable practice in delivering precious cargoes. Based upon their navigational and other experience, they intend to sail up the Chesapeake Bay to a point near the mouth of the Choptank River, on Maryland's Eastern Shore. Barring unforeseen weather delays, the estimated time of arrival will be sometime before Christmas. On Christmas Eve they will contact you on the enclosed phone to arrange final rendezvous details. Their exact words of greeting will be: "The Redeemer is come." You must respond: "Blessed be the Savoir." Any deviation from this formula and contact will be permanently broken off.

I wish you great success with your memorial. May it be an enduring tribute to all that you hold dear. I pray that the Savior will watch over you at all times.

Blessing God's bounteous Grace,
Your humble servant,
Father George

Eamon Douglass laid down the sheet, grasped his shillelagh in two hands and pumped it in the air like a drunken football fan, chortling with glee. "There's no stopping it now. Redemption! Redemption!"

Then the former United States Ambassador to Georgiana hopped from his chair and began dancing a little jig, tapping his cane and cutting strange capers in front of the roaring fire. Behind him, sinister shadows cast by the flames wriggled on the study's book-lined walls, mimicking his jubilant boogie.

———◦《◦》◦———

Nickie Farrell entered the English Department office and deposited a neat stack of blue exam booklets on the counter. "Hey, Jo. Here's the last of my exams, all graded and recorded. I survived my first semester. How about that?"

"Exams graded already? Holy cats, Nickie." Joanne inspected her friend, noting the circles of fatigue beneath her eyes. "I hope you didn't stay up all night doing this. Final marks aren't even due till next week. What's your hurry, hon?"

"No hurry, but why put it off? The kids are glad to be finished, and this way I'll have extra time to prepare for next semester's courses. Also I have to get started on that business with Ambassador Douglass about building the new memorial." Jo sensed a melancholy undercurrent beneath the upbeat tone, and she knew why. Nickie still bore a raw wound from Alex Steward's rejection. Now she was trying to elude her unhappiness by burying herself in work. Poor girl, Jo thought with an ironic pang. Having crossed the gender line Nickie was learning that womanhood represented a mixed bag of realities: mostly wonderful, but some bad. Even, occasionally, very bad. Again Jo wondered how anyone could voluntarily subject themselves to such a monumental upheaval.

"Why don't you take a break, Nickie? Seriously. You've been working non-stop since you came to Windfield, and then with everything else..." Joanne paused. "If I can hunt up some tickets to a concert at the Kennedy Center, would you like to go with me?"

For an instant Nickie looked tentative, then she smiled. "That is a great idea, Jo. I'd love to. We'll split the cost, of course. Hmm," she mused with a pensive frown, "I don't have a thing to wear."

"You have got to be kidding, girlfriend," Joanne giggled, feeling thrilled as a schoolgirl. "You do like classical music, I hope?"

"Oh, yes. I'm no connoisseur, though. Mostly I like the standard stuff. You know, Mozart, Bach, Haydn. I love Rossini, too. Such beautiful melodies!" Checking her watch: "Oh gosh, I'd better run along. This evening is my long-awaited question-and-answer session. The kids have been really patient and I promised them I'd schedule it as soon as exams were done."

"Are you sure you're up for that? They're liable to be pretty blunt."

"As long as they're not crude or vulgar they can be as blunt as they like." With a keen look: "Despite what you might think, I'm a pretty tough cookie."

"That you are," Jo conceded. "I'd like to listen in, if you don't mind."

"Not at all. Five o'clock, in my regular classroom. Who knows, maybe you'll be the only one that shows up. I really can't see what's so interesting about me, anyway." Nickie waggled her fingers and left the office.

"Can't you," Joanne Markwith murmured. "Nickie, Nickie. You're such an innocent thing. I hope it lasts, hon. I really do."

———— ((●)) ————

The classroom was almost full by the time Joanne arrived. Clearly the students found their professor far more fascinating than Nickie imagined. Jo took a seat in the rearmost row where her presence wouldn't prove distracting.

Nickie sat perched on the edge of her desk, regarding the multitude with a mildly amused expression. She was more casually dressed than usual in jeans, a white cable-knit sweater, and athletic shoes. Like most of the younger women she wore her hair in a ponytail, secured in back with a lime-green scrunchie.

"Okay, guys." Nickie clapped her hands. As the noise subsided: "Before we start, I want to express my gratitude to each and every one of you for making my first semester such a pleasure. You've made me realize how much I love teaching. So again, thanks a lot. You're the best." She grinned. "Oh, and I apologize for making you read *The Deerslayer*. I've already taken it out the syllabus." There was an appreciative titter. "Well, now, does anyone have a question?"

A forest of hands shot skyward. "Oh, my." Nickie pointed to a girl in the front row. "Alyssa?"

"What would you say is the biggest misconception people have about transsexuals?"

"Wow, good question." Nickie thought for a moment. "Unfortunately, thanks to a certain exploitative television show, a lot of people think that we all look like demented crack whores, shrieking obscenities and throwing torn-off wigs at each other. But that's not true. I don't even own a wig." She allowed the laughter to subside. "Beyond that, I think the biggest misconception people have is that we are all gay. But in fact, GID –Gender Identity Disorder– has nothing to do with sexual preference. GID is about how you *feel*, in here and in here." Nickie pointed to her heart, then her head. "There are only two choices: Blue, or pink. On the other hand, sexual preference is about who you like to sleep with. Three choices there: the opposite sex, the same sex, or bring 'em both on." More giggles. "I guess it can be a little confusing, but the bottom line is that trans folk are just like everyone else: straight, gay, or bi."

Joanne tensed as a male voice called out, "Which are you?"

Nickie smiled and replied, "Forget it, Andrew. I'm way too old for you." She pointed. "Yes, Thomas?"

A slim effeminate young man stood up. "Do you remember how old you were when you first...when you began to feel different?"

Nickie nodded. "Do I ever. One summer at the beach, when I was around four years old, I was hanging out with a couple of the other little boys and for some reason I just blurted out, 'Oh, I wish I'd been born a girl!' "

"So what happened?"

"Exactly what you'd expect." Nickie shrugged. "They laughed like crazy and made fun of me and went around telling the entire gang that I was a sissy. This happened long before GLBT liberation, back when it was *fatal* to admit something like that. In those days men were men and women were...irrelevant." Nickie looked around at the solemn faces. "Naturally, the lesson I took away from that experience was to keep my mouth shut and stuff my feelings. I went deep into the closet, locked myself in with denial and substance abuse, and stayed there for almost thirty years."

In the back row Joanne envisioned a delicate red-headed little boy being teased ragged, crying, ostracized, not understanding why his playmates had turned on him with such vicious glee. God almighty, she thought, that poor child! Then, from the corner of her eye, she caught a glimpse of someone slipping into the classroom. It was Alex Steward. The professor edged to a shadowy corner, where Jo couldn't make out his expression. He stood with crossed arms while Nickie continued to field questions from her students. Jo felt a rush of anger. How dare Alex show up here? He'd been a complete idiot to reject Nickie, but too damn bad. Now he should just leave her alone. Joanne prayed that Nickie wouldn't see him. She realized that her fists were tightly balled and forced them to unclench.

The question-and-answer session continued for the better part of an hour. At length Nickie pointed and said: "Cinda. Goodness, girl, don't you ever quit?"

"Not a chance," rejoined Cinda, joining in the general laughter. "Ms. Farrell, what was your name back when you were a man?"

Why, thought Jo, that little snip is trying to put Nickie on the spot. The nerve!

"I admire your perseverance, Cinda," said Nickie, "but as I told you before, I'd rather not divulge that information. I don't wish to compromise my birth family's privacy. Besides, my former name has no bearing on anything in the present. It's in the past and forgotten."

"But what if it isn't?" Cinda persisted. "Forgotten, I mean?"

"Then it should be, because the individual who went by that name has ceased to exist." She paused. "Okay, one or two more and then I think we'll wind it up. Let's see...Rob?"

"Do you have sex?" The questioner, a very tall lanky youth, faced her with a smart-aleck grin. The other students shifted in their seats and snickered.

Unperturbed, Nickie responded: "Well, Rob, I think the appropriate phrasing for your question should more properly be '*Can* you have sex'. And yes, I certainly can. However, as to whether I *do*, well, that's no more your business than it's mine as to whether *you* do."

"He doesn't, Ms. Farrell," piped up Rob's neighbor. "His libido went in the tank ever since Aubrey Hazelton told him he screwed like a chipmunk on speed."

The room erupted into hilarity as Rob began to scuffle with the other boy. Nickie clapped a hand over her mouth. Laughing in the back row, Joanne was relieved to note that Alex Steward had slipped from the room.

"All right, one last question." Nickie motioned for quiet. "Anyone? Okay, Rachel."

"How did you change your voice, Ms. Farrell? Did you have an operation?"

Nickie shook her head. "No. There's a procedure they can do which involves shaving down the vocal chords, but I met a girl who'd had it done, and she could hardly speak above a whisper. Too scary for me. I just practiced a lot, same as everything else I've had to learn."

"Can you still sound like a man?"

"Gosh, I don't know. It's been a long time." Nickie stood up from the desk. "Let's see." She took a deep breath and let out a booming imitation of James Earl Jones' famous bass tag line: "THIS is CNN." She grinned and said in her normal voice, "Like that?"

The class erupted into applause and cheers. Joanne watched the students milling around their transsexual teacher offering thanks and good wishes. It warmed her heart to see Nickie being admired and loved by so many fresh young faces. Perhaps, thought Jo, there really was hope for the future. These kids could make it happen.

After the last of the students had departed Nickie walked up the deserted aisle and sank into a seat by Jo. "Well, that's that. How'd I do?" With a shy smile: "Did you see? I think they like me."

Joanne put one arm around Nickie and drew her close. "You were terrific, hon. Wonderful. I've never seen anything like it. And of course the kids like you. In fact, they love you." Jo lightly caressed her friend's cheek with two fingers. "After all, what's not to love about Nickie?"

———⸺((●))⸺———

When Cinda Vanderhart returned to her dorm room she found Heather scowling over a thick psychology textbook.

"Hey, girl." She gestured at Heather's book. "So, how many personality disorders do you have?"

"Hah, hah." Heather shot Cinda an irritated glance. "At least I'm not a narcissist like you." She petulantly tossed aside the book. "God, I was such a stupid dork to take psychology. Like, who *cares?* " But if I don't ace tomorrow's final I'll get a C and Daddy will go completely postal." She puffed her cheeks and sighed. "I wish I didn't have to cram, I wanted to hear Ms. Farrell. How did she do?"

Cinda kicked out of her shoes and peeled off a sock. "Oh, the usual thing. Managing to be straightforward and evasive at the same time." She tossed the sock onto an overflowing laundry basket.

"What do you mean, 'evasive'?"

"She still won't say what her boy name used to be. Supposedly to protect her family's privacy."

"That's considerate, not evasive. Besides, if she doesn't want to tell, why should she? Maybe the old name reminds her of when she was unhappy. Stop being so nosy about Ms. Farrell. It's turning into, like, an obsession or something. You got your story, you're on the *Spectrum*, you'll get an A-plus in her class...what more do you want? Leave her alone, Cinda. Seriously. You're going home for vacation in a couple of days. Kick back, chill, have a good time."

"A good time? In Indy? Get real." Cinda unfastened her studded belt and let her baggy black pants fall around her ankles. She kicked them aside and stood in her boy's boxers, hands on hips. "Here's the deal with Indianapolis, Roomie. It's flat. It's gray. It's boring. The people there are Bible-thumping Republican fundamentalists who have Jesus and Rush Limbaugh on the brain and think the whole world revolves around the fucking Colts and the Indy 500."

"C'mon," Heather rolled her eyes. "It can't be that bad."

"Oh, no?" Cinda snorted. "In downtown Indy you can actually find a parking space in the middle of the day, right on the street. Does that sound like a happening place to you?"

"Don't ask me," Heather shrugged. "I'm from California. I've never even *seen* a parking space."

"My point exactly. So don't tell me to have a good time, because it isn't going to happen." Cinda plopped on the edge of her bed, face glum. "I wish I didn't have to go home."

"Won't your family be glad to see you?"

With a bitter laugh Cinda said, "My family? Let me tell you about my family. Dad pushes paper for a company that manufactures cinder blocks. Mom works in a Christian book store. My older sister Tammy is a former kiddie pageant princess who doesn't have the brains of a pea fowl. She's engaged to a bald perv who probably wants her wear to her old cheerleading uniform into the sack. Nobody really likes anybody else and they disagree all the time, except for one thing."

"What's that?"

"Me," answered Cinda. "I am the Great Abomination around which they can all rally. Cinda the Hell-bound homosexual witch who's lost her way and must be prayed for twenty-four seven so she can be saved before Yahweh casts her down into a lake of fire with all the other godless dykes. Don't laugh, girl. I can't remember the last time I went to bed at home without finding some sort of pamphlet on my pillow about how being gay is a choice, and all I have to do is accept Jesus back in to my heart to be cured and live happily ever after."

"But that's ridiculous. Everyone knows being gay isn't a choice."

"Maybe everyone in California," countered Cinda, "but not in my part of the country. Where I come from, there's nothing worse than a queer. *Nothing.*" She paused. "Why do you think I've worked my ass off since I was a little kid, always studying and getting perfect grades? Because I knew it was the only way I could break free from all that fundamentalist bullshit and earn the right to live my own life. Now that it's finally beginning to happen, the idea of going back there –even for a few days– makes me nauseous. I *detest* it, Heather."

"Then why do they even want you to come home?"

"Oh, because it's their Christian duty to browbeat my sinful lesbian soul back into the fundie fold. After all, they love me so much."

"I'm really sorry, Cinda." Heather sat by her roommate and hugged her. "Parents are so lame sometimes. They should be incredibly proud of you."

Cinda shook her head. "Maybe that's why I find Ms. Farrell so... admirable. I identify with her. Gay isn't the same as trans, I know. Still, she had to completely escape her old life in order to be happy. That's exactly how I feel. I guarantee you Ms. Farrell's family gave her holy hell. I'll bet that's why she won't talk about them. But she stayed true to herself, and she made it. Well, so will I. People can't stand it when you're different, so they attack. Fags, dykes, trannies, we're all targets for the world's moronic assholes."

"It totally sucks," agreed Heather. "But Windfield's not like that."

"No, it isn't. I could've gone to Princeton, Stanford, you name it. But I chose Windfield because...well, because it's the kind of place that would hire someone like Ms. Farrell. They don't just squawk a lot of pious liberal slogans. They actually *practice* equality and inclusion. It doesn't get any better than that. I love Windfield." With a lopsided grin: "I'm surprised somebody hasn't tried to blow it up yet."

"That's silly. Why would anyone want to blow up a college? This isn't the World Trade Center."

"Listen to me, Roomie." Cinda looked Heather in the eye. "Don't *ever* underestimate the power of hate." She stood up, pulled off her top and grabbed a bathrobe. "The haters never let up. As soon as you forget it, they'll nail you. If you think I'm wrong, you'd better study those personality disorders again." Affectionately running her fingers through her roommate's blonde mane: "Damn, why do you have to be so straight?" She exhaled heavily. "This narcissist is gonna go take a shower. A cold one."

The gray winter light was dying. Stinging pellets of freezing rain dropped from a dreary sky to hiss through bare tree branches and bounce among the markers of the small cemetery where Luanne Skinner had been laid to rest beside her daughter. The memorial service had ended and only Collie, Robin, and Beryl Jamison remained, staring down at the fresh grave.

Beryl broke the silence. In a voice hoarse from weeping: "I'd better get Mrs. Greene home before this sleet gets any worse." She placed a consoling hand on Collie's shoulder. "Your mother is at peace, honey. She isn't suffering any more, and Heaven is a brighter place now that she's there with Lissa."

Frozen-faced behind black wrap-around sunglasses as he had been during the entire funeral, Collie acknowledged her words with a silent nod. Beryl and Robin exchanged mute worried looks. Since his mother's death Collie had withdrawn into a state of taciturn non-communication, speaking to no one but Robin and leaving the burial arrangements to Beryl Jamison and Luanne's church friends. His only input had been to request that his mother's last favorite oldie be played.

"Thank you, Mrs. Jamison," said Robin. "For everything. You and all the others have been so kind. Please thank Mrs. Greene also. Mrs. Skinner was truly blessed to have so many wonderful friends."

"I should have been a better friend." Beryl felt her throat closing up again. "I loved Luanne so much." She wiped her eyes. "Well...God bless you both."

Walking away, she glanced back and saw Collie and Robin still huddled together over his mother's grave. "Jesus have mercy," she muttered, and tucked herself into the idling car.

"Those two best be on their way before they freeze to death," observed Beryl's passenger in a gravelly smoker's voice. "This storm ain't quittin'. Look at you, you're turnin' blue. Crank the heat up."

Carlotta Greene was a wizened red-faced woman in her seventies. Nobody –including her deceased husband– had ever referred to her by any name other than "Mrs. Greene." Acerbic and impatient, Mrs. Greene had lived in the surrounding countryside all her life. For twenty-some years she had been the chief housemistress of an elegant equestrian estate owned by a curmudgeonly old retired general named Jack Parker. Since Mrs. Greene was every bit as irascible and iron-fisted as the old bachelor general and kept his mansion fanatically spit-shined and neat, they got along famously. When the general finally expired, Mrs. Greene bought a boxy little cottage where she kept busy making war on the dandelions in her lawn and ceaselessly polishing every square inch of her home, meanwhile smoking carton after carton of generic cigarettes down to the filter. In her considerable spare time Mrs. Greene pursued a lifelong favorite pastime: keeping track of other people's doings. Possessing a mental catalogue of county-wide indiscretions, affairs, double-crosses, swindles, scandals, back-stabbings and assorted skullduggeries stretching back over fifty years, Mrs. Greene —like the infamous J. Edgar Hoover— knew where most of the bodies were buried. Critical and sharp-tongued, she had few friends, which didn't bother her in the slightest since she held most of the local populace in extremely low regard. There were occasional exceptions: Beryl Jamison, Robin Thompson, and Luanne Skinner were all included on Mrs. Greene's short list of "quality folks"; a list which, with Luanne's death, had just been diminished by one.

"Robin's a sensible girl." Beryl steered her Monte Carlo out the cemetery gates. "She'll make sure they're all right."

"Somebody better take care of that boy." Mrs. Greene's pessimism never wavered. "He ain't holdin' up so good."

"Collie and Luanne were close, Mrs. Greene. He's taking it very hard."

The older woman pursed her lips. "Youngsters lose their parents. It ain't easy, but they need to tough it out. Hell, Momma up'n died when I was eleven. Did I stand around like a garden statue in sunglasses?"

Being acquainted with Mrs. Greene's rhetorical style Beryl knew that a response was neither expected nor desired. She kept her eyes on the road.

"I've been to a mess of funerals in my time, but this one was mighty strange, if y'ask me."

This time a reply was expected. "What do you mean, strange?"

"Things didn't feel right." Mrs. Greene squinted out at the icy precipitation. "Collie never said one word to his father. Sat by hisself with Robin on t'other side. Jay-Bo Skinner is a no-good sumbitch, everyone knows that, but still..." She paused. "And how 'bout that other son, whatzisname, Lloyd, suddenly showing up after all this time?" Mrs. Greene readjusted her purse on her lap. "Don't make sense."

"It was just one of those things, Mrs. Greene," said Beryl. "I heard that he and his business partner were driving through for a little surprise visit, and...found out about Luanne. Lloyd never got a chance to see his mother. It's sad."

"Sad, my foot. I never seen such phony tears, a-blubberin' and pretendin' to be heartbroke." Mrs. Greene pointed a finger at Beryl. "That Lloyd is exactly like his daddy, rotten to the core. He'll come to a bad end, mark my words. And his so-called business partner? Gave me the willies, that one did. Slick as a black racer."

"I didn't talk to him." Beryl knew better than to contradict Mrs. Greene outright. "But he did seem respectful."

"Respectful?" Mrs. Greene snorted. "He didn't fool me. I know a damn snake when I see one."

Again Beryl chose to keep mum. Mrs. Greene's opinions were inflexible, like rebar in concrete.

"And you want to tell me what in the hell old man Douglass was doin' there? That damn skinflint never gave a diddly-whoop about anyone in his life. Did you see those flowers he sent? You can bet they cost a pretty penny. Actin' all courteous and sorrowful-like with Jay-Bo Skinner. I ain't buyin' it. He musta been after somethin'."

"I don't know, Mrs. Greene." The ambassador's sudden appearance at the funeral had astounded Beryl as much as anyone else. "But I remember one time in the store he actually complimented Luanne, told her that she was doing a good job. She even got a raise. Maybe he just wanted to do something nice."

Mrs. Greene loosed a derisive laugh. "Beryl Jamison, Eamon Douglass ain't no more interested in bein' nice than a damn crocodile.

Ain't you been workin' for the old buzzard long enough to know that?"

Beryl admitted to herself that Mrs. Greene had a valid point, but she wasn't heedless enough to say anything negative about her employer to the queen wasp of gossip.

"Did you see the way Collie Skinner stiffed him?" Mrs. Greene gleefully cackled. "Refused to shake his hand, left him standin' there like a dope with his paw stretched out."

"Collie's not himself, Mrs. Greene. I don't think he meant to offend the ambassador."

"Sure he did. Clearer'n if he'd told him to go shit in his hat."

Beryl turned her car into the little driveway which led to Mrs. Greene's cottage. The headlights illuminated scattered white patches of sleet mounded in the gravel. After a short ways she drew up next to the front door. "Here we are, Mrs. Greene. Might be a good night to turn up the furnace."

Mrs. Greene made a dismissive gesture. "Ain't got money to burn." She frowned. "Speakin' of money, you want to tell me how Jay-Bo Skinner managed to pay the funeral home? Had to be a couple thousand dollars."

"That's the family's business, Mrs. Greene." Beryl tried not to sound as annoyed as she felt. "The important thing is that Luanne had a decent Christian burial, God rest her soul."

"Hmph." Mrs. Greene put her hand on the door handle. "Did you ever turn over a rock? All kinds o' ugly things a-crawlin' around under there in the dark. That's how it felt today, like there's this big ol' rock just waitin' to be turned over. I don't know what's goin' on, Beryl Jamison, but it's all gonna come bustin' out. Wait an' see." She opened the door and exited the car. Beryl saw her stop by the front door and remove her boots, oblivious to the icy wind. She saluted Beryl with the boots in her hand, went inside and slammed the door.

Beryl sighed with relief as she drove away from the little cottage. Only Carlotta Greene could take a poor woman's funeral and whip it into some sort of creepy plot from a conspiracy novel. The old lady was really losing it.

Absentmindedly throttling his shillelagh with bony fingers, Ambassador Eamon Douglass glowered from his limousine out at the inclement weather. He detested sleet, freezing rain, any sort of precipitation involving ice. There was something annoyingly indecisive about it, as if the damned atmosphere couldn't decide whether to snow or rain and instead vomited a frozen mess all over everything.

Although Llewellyn the chauffeur was a practiced professional, the ambassador knocked his cane against the glass partition. When it whirred down Douglass growled, "Are you watching out for ice? Goddamn sleet. See to it that this boat doesn't end up in a ditch."

"Yes, Mr. Ambassador." The chauffeur raised the partition.

Eamon Douglass slumped with his head between his shoulders, brooding. The Skinner woman's memorial service had been a dreadful ordeal. The ambassador abhorred funerals, regarding them as little more than staged exhibitions of lachrymose hypocrisy. This one had been exceptionally vulgar, with the mourners bleating and carrying on as if Luanne Skinner had been Saint Joan instead of an inconsequential rustic. Even worse, he'd been subjected to wide-eyed stares from the assembled yokels, who gawked and whispered as if Old Scratch himself had materialized in their midst. Douglass could hardly have been more discomfited if he'd suddenly awoken in a madhouse full of lepers.

He'd only gone to the funeral to sniff out the whereabouts of his coded floppy disk; however it soon became clear that Jay-Bo Skinner –who may once have been a patriot but was now a dissolute yahoo– had no idea what Douglass was talking about. The ambassador was disappointed but not alarmed. Even if Jay-Bo did stumble across the floppy, Douglass figured he'd have as much chance of deciphering it as a boozed-up ape. The sullen blonde son and his putative business partner were irrelevant. Whatever that enigmatic pair's interests were –the ambassador sensed he'd rather not know– they had zero to do with anything involving Luanne Skinner.

But that other son, the one called "Collie"...It was bad enough that he had silently ignored the ambassador's probings, but then the little bastard had embarrassed him in front of the gaping mob by refusing to shake hands! Douglass tightened his grip on the shillelagh until his knuckles cracked. No one insulted him that way and got away with it. *No one.* Bereaved or not, the insolent pup would pay dearly for disrespecting Eamon Douglass.

Listening to sleet rattle on the limo's roof, the ambassador wondered if he should simply order Mike Barlow to dispose of the kid. But that might be imprudent. A lot of witnesses had seen what happened, and if Collie Skinner vanished into thin air even the dimwitted rubes might suspect something. It was too bad Luanne's brat didn't attend Windfield College, where the Cesium 137 Redeemer could blow him to atoms along with everybody else.

On the other hand, Douglass mused, perhaps a way might be found to ensure that he'd be at the picnic anyway. Collie Skinner had once mentioned that in addition to the Knights Inn he worked at that overpriced Middleville restaurant, the Foxton Arms. Lost in thought, the ambassador repeatedly tapped the head of his cane into his open palm. Then he suddenly closed his fist, trapping it.

"Of *course*," he grated through clenched teeth. "Perfect! The impertinent bastard will be *right there*. And we'll draw an even bigger crowd."

Eamon Douglass laid aside his shillelagh, opened the compact bar and poured himself two fingers of Rebel Yell sour mash whiskey. Everything was going to be just fine. The missing floppy disk didn't matter. His grand design could no more be undone by country scum like the Skinners than the Earth's rotation could be perturbed by an errant gnat. He was Ambassador Eamon Douglass, and his patriotic will would bring them all to the day of Redemption.

He raised his shot glass in the dark limo, toasted "April Fool!" and tossed it down.

For the first time in a great while, Jay-Bo Skinner felt that his lousy luck might be starting to improve. His headache of a wife had expired and could no longer be a perpetual whiny pain in the ass. Even better, her fag son Collie had been so overcome with grief that he'd moved out of the apartment, thereby elevating Jay-Bo to undisputed lord of the manor. This welcome development might've proven a bit problematic since Jay-Bo had no means of paying the rent himself; but salvation had already arrived in the form of long-absent son Lloyd, who'd miraculously dropped from the sky with his business associate, Mr. Cale Pittman. They set themselves up in Collie's old room, and Cale —who struck Jay-Bo as an exemplary fellow— had assured Jay-Bo that he needn't concern himself with monetary trifles like the rent. Pittman stocked the refrigerator with food and beer, paid the funeral home to dispose of Luanne, bought mourning suits for them all at JC Penney and treated Lloyd's father with the deference and respect he hadn't enjoyed since his state police days. Jay-Bo could scarcely believe his good fortune. Still, it'd been a long goddamn time since he caught a break. He wasn't about to complain.

Jay-Bo watched Cale Pittman twist the cap off an unopened fifth of Wild Turkey 101 bourbon that the bartender had brought to their grimy booth in the rear of Hamburger John's, where they'd driven immediately after the interment.

"Damn, that's some high-class whiskey," he grinned as Pittman poured out three shots. "Can't remember the last time I had any."

"It would be unseemly to drink to your wife's memory with anything less. I wasn't privileged to know her, but she must have been a good woman to have had a son like Lloyd. Gentlemen," Cale raised his glass, "to the late Mrs. Skinner."

They touched glasses and drank. Jay-Bo sighed with pleasure as the tawny liquid warmed his gullet, thinking that he'd gladly bury his good woman a dozen times over in order to enjoy such superb liquor.

"Ma was okay, I guess." Lloyd refilled the glasses. "Kinda weak when it came to pussies and feebs, though."

Cale nodded regretfully. "Females don't grasp the necessity for ruthless selectivity, partner. It's a defect in their genetic makeup. They're programmed to coddle everyone, even the ones who should be culled. The ancient Spartans were aware of this, of course. By exposing the weaklings at birth, they bred themselves into a fierce noble warrior race. Maybe someday it will happen again."

Jay-Bo knocked back the rest of his Wild Turkey. "Agghhh," he smacked his lips. "How do you know about this stuff, Pittman?"

"Cale reads books." Lloyd glanced at his business partner. "A lot of 'em. He knows all kinds of things."

"Yeah? Well, I ain't big on readin' books. Waste of time, if y'ask me. Unless you wanna be like one o'them pointy-head Windfield faggots."

"Lloyd has told me some things about this Windfield College," said Pittman. "Sounds like it's been nothing but trouble for your family."

"That fuckin' place has been more than just trouble," Jay-Bo scowled. "It's ruined everything around here. Somebody oughta burn it to the ground. Did Lloyd tell you about his twin sister?"

"Yes, he did. I can't think of a more despicable crime against an innocent young woman than to corrupt her into a lesbian dyke." He added, with a sorrowful shake of his head: "In my opinion, sir, the queers are responsible for undermining our civilization."

"Damn right, Cale," Lloyd concurred. "Every last one of 'em should be rounded up and hung. Fuckin' pansy homos."

Watching his eldest offspring toss back another shot, Jay-Bo experienced an unfamiliar surge of fatherly pride: "That's my boy!"

Cale Pittman looked from father to son. "You have every reason to be proud, sir. Lloyd is a superior man, and I am honored to be his partner."

The bourbon had spread a mellow glow throughout Jay-Bo's extremities. It was a pleasure to share company with two such enlightened men. With a magnanimous gesture: "Well, Mr. Pittman, you've been mighty helpful to Lloyd and me in a rough time, and I ain't too proud to say thank you."

"You and your family have been victimized by the immorality which is poisoning our society. The least I can do is share my resources with a father and son in their time of grief." He refilled their glasses. "I've had my share of family tragedy, too."

"Yeah? Like what?"

With a somber expression Pittman told them how both his parents had been killed in a house fire when he was only sixteen. The family Christmas tree had somehow spontaneously ignited and the resulting conflagration enveloped the house so rapidly that only Cale managed to escape by jumping from an upstairs window. Trapped in their bedroom, his mother and father had been incinerated alive while he listened to their screams.

"Jesus Christ," said Lloyd. "You didn't tell me about that."

"It's a painful memory, partner." Cale sipped his bourbon. "You see, the insurance investigator —an evil homosexual named Norman Hennisey— tried to convince the police that I had deliberately started the fire. It turned out that my father had purchased an accidental death policy for a half a million dollars. Double indemnity. The insurance company didn't want to pay it, naturally, so they did their best to frame me for arson. In the end they failed, and I got the money." He shrugged. "Being on my own was very difficult for a while, but I learned a lot of valuable lessons, and it made me tough."

"It sure did." Lloyd Skinner gave his business partner's back a manly slap. "Too bad that insurance faggot didn't burn up in a fire, too."

"Y'know, it's a funny thing." Cale's teeth showed in a smile. "A couple of months after the fire some juvenile delinquent booby-trapped his mailbox with an M-80. It blew up in his face and blinded him."

Jay-Bo chortled, banging a meaty fist on the table, "Whoo! I'll drink to that."

"What I wanna know," Lloyd said to his father, "is what Eamon Douglass was doin' there today. What's all that bullshit about some computer disk?"

"Hell, I dunno. He said it wasn't anything really important, just some inventory thing from the store Luanne was supposed to be keeping for him." Jay-Bo poured himself another shot. "Who gives a shit? One more thing she managed to fuck up."

"Figures." Lloyd shook his head. "Did you check out how Collie wouldn't even shake the old fart's hand? Little scumbag needs to have his ass stomped."

"His neck broke, more like." Jay-Bo's face flushed deep red. "That cockeyed geek never showed an ounce of respect, not for me or Douglass or anybody. He and Luanne were like two snotnosed girl-friends. Most sickenin' thing I ever seen." He emptied his glass, and set it down with a bang. "How long you boys plannin' to stick around?"

Lloyd looked questioningly at Cale, who said: "Well, sir, if you wouldn't mind putting up with us for a while, I've a notion to stay and find out a bit more about this Windfield College. If it's as bad as you say –and I'm sure it is– I'm thinking of writing an article for a maga-zine. People need to know what's going on, don't you think?"

"Hell, yes," agreed Jay-Bo. "Y'all stay with me as long as you like." And keep on paying the rent, he silently added. "Better company than what I've had lately. Mighty nice to have some right-thinkin' men around for once."

In the dim booth Cale Pittman's dark blue eyes gleamed like pol-ished onyx. He held up his glass: "To right-thinking men."

With a jovial triple click and nary a thought of the late Luanne Skinner, the three right-thinking men heartily consummated their ca-maraderie with another round of Wild Turkey 101.

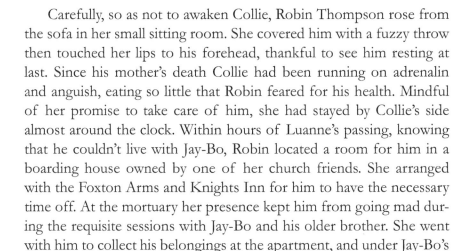

Carefully, so as not to awaken Collie, Robin Thompson rose from the sofa in her small sitting room. She covered him with a fuzzy throw then touched her lips to his forehead, thankful to see him resting at last. Since his mother's death Collie had been running on adrenalin and anguish, eating so little that Robin feared for his health. Mindful of her promise to take care of him, she had stayed by Collie's side almost around the clock. Within hours of Luanne's passing, knowing that he couldn't live with Jay-Bo, Robin located a room for him in a boarding house owned by one of her church friends. She arranged with the Foxton Arms and Knights Inn for him to have the necessary time off. At the mortuary her presence kept him from going mad dur-ing the requisite sessions with Jay-Bo and his older brother. She went with him to collect his belongings at the apartment, and under Jay-Bo's suspicious glare boxed up Luanne's meager possessions for donation to the needy. Then today, at the church and later the cemetery, she'd steadfastly stood beside him, holding his hand as he buried the mother he'd loved. It had been a wretched five days. Robin was nearing exhaustion herself, but her sole focus remained on Collie, making certain that he felt safe and above all loved. Now, hearing his deep regular breathing, she allowed herself to hope that he'd weathered the worst of the emotional storm. His grieving would persist for a long while, she knew, but at least the grim procedures of laying Luanne to rest were finished. The oldest and least comforting cliché in the language happened to be the truest: Life goes on. For both their sakes, Robin was determined to make sure that Collie's life would not merely go on, but be better than ever before.

Carrying her heels, Robin padded noiselessly on stocking feet to her bedroom. She removed her mourning outfit and indulged herself in a long hot shower, washing her hair twice and scrubbing her skin pink with a loofa sponge. Emerging much refreshed, she put on a pair of comfy jeans and a gray sweater. Peeking into the living room, she saw that Collie hadn't moved. She watched him sleep for a moment, then her affectionate look gave way to a thoughtful expression.

Fluffing her damp hair with her fingers, she went to a tiny desk, sat down and opened a second-hand Toshiba laptop that she'd purchased from an infatuated nerd in one of her classes. She got on the Internet and typed "Windfield College" into the search window. In an eyeblink Google presented her with one million seven hundred and twenty-six thousand choices.

"Gee, that's all?" Muttering to herself, she narrowed her search and found the listing she wanted: www.windfieldcollege.edu/alumni. She clicked on it and found herself looking at a website overlaid on an aerial photograph of the college in full springtime bloom. She scanned the various hyperlinks, saw one that read "Find a classmate" and found herself looking at a list of all the graduating classes. She clicked on "1979", and a window opened with two blank spaces for her registered username and password.

Robin made a face at the screen. No doubt any self-respecting hacker could have breezed right in, but she neither possessed nor desired such skills. Tracking down the whereabouts of Nick Farrington '79 wasn't going to be a simple matter. Collie had made it clear that he wanted to search for his genetic father, and she could certainly understand why he felt that way. But that didn't necessarily make it a good idea.

Robin bit her lip, worried. More than anything she wanted Collie to be at peace, but even assuming that they somehow found Nick Farrington, what then? Collie couldn't just stroll up to him and say, "Hey, Pop!" It was far from certain that Farrington would welcome an unexpected bastard son with open arms. Many other possibilities loomed, none of them pleasant. After the trauma of losing Luanne, what would happen if Collie found himself spurned –possibly even hated– by his natural father? Nick Farrington would be a forty-something man by now, undoubtedly settled into contented middle age with all the trappings of an educated gentleman: surgically-sculpted wife, children, wealth, career, Mercedes, titanium golf clubs, and liposuctioned abs. Was it likely that he'd be delighted to see a forgotten indiscretion from his oat-sowing days turn up on his doorstep in the person of Collie Skinner? No, Robin decided, it wasn't likely at all. Stories abounded about similar situations ending very badly. Finding Nick Farrington could easily backfire into something awful. With a twinge of guilt because she knew Collie felt otherwise, Robin nonetheless nurtured a hope that he would never find his lost parent. Sometimes it was smarter to leave the past undisturbed, and this was one of those times. Instead, she would help him concentrate on the future. Robin clicked the little 'X' in the computer window, and the pretty view of Windfield College vanished. Let it go, she thought, and closed the laptop.

The jangle of her house phone fractured the silence. Robin snatched it up before it could ring again, hoping that the noise hadn't woken Collie.

"Hello?" She listened for a moment. "I don't know anyone named Cinda...oh. It's you."

Robin glanced uneasily toward the other room. In a low voice: "Listen, I can't talk right now. This isn't a good time. There's been a death in the family, and...What? Well, that's not my problem." She turned her back to the door and spoke more firmly. "I'd rather not talk about this any more. There's no point...So? It's a weird coincidence, but some people have eyes like that...Look, his mother just died, all right? Go home on your vacation and leave us alone. Please. Have a merry Christmas. I'm hanging up now. Goodbye."

She hastily replaced the receiver and jumped as Collie's sleepy voice said from the bedroom doorway, "Who was that?"

"Nobody important," answered Robin. She went and encircled him with her arms, smiling up into his haggard face. "Are you hungry? Can I fix you something to eat?"

"I don't think so, but thanks. You've done so much for me already. No wonder Mama loved you. *I* love you, Robin."

Seeing his faint smile, the first in a long while, Robin felt joy in her heart. "I love you too, Collie. Oh, I do, so very much."

They kissed for a long moment. "Robin, would you do me a favor?"

"Anything."

"Now that Mama's gone, and I know the truth about...my real father, I'd like it if you would call me Nicholas. The way she always did. Not everywhere, but when we're in private, like now. Would you do that?"

Robin looked into Collie's different-colored eyes, the genetic legacy of a man she secretly hoped he would never meet. "Of course I will. Nicholas. A beautiful name for my beautiful man."

"You're the beautiful one," he said, and kissed her again. Then: "I want to find my father, Robin. He's got to be out there somewhere."

"Well, Nicholas," Robin bravely smiled, "there's plenty of time to think about that. What you need now is to catch up on your sleep. There's no rush, you know." She blinked big brown eyes at him and declared in a surprisingly good Scarlett O'Hara drawl: "Aftuh all, tomorrow *is* anothuh day."

Chapter Eleven
Love and Hate

Sitting in the first tier of the Kennedy Center's Concert Hall, Joanne Markwith tried to stay focused on Rossini's "Semiramide" overture, but couldn't resist an occasional peek at her lovely companion. Hands folded in her lap, Nickie Farrell sat listening with the spellbound expression of a little girl seeing Disneyland for the first time.

Jo quietly sighed. Nickie was everything she loved: charming, considerate, smart but not pedantic, good-humored, even on occasion a little mischievous. Plus, of course, she looked good. So good, in fact, that Jo almost couldn't stand it. This evening Nickie had decided to "put on the Ritz", as she said, and the results were spectacular: She wore a dark green velvet evening jacket over an ivory chiffon skirt, with green satin dress sandals and a matching evening clutch. A double-strand pearl necklace, pearl drop earrings and a malachite-pattern hair band completed her look of elegant femininity. The Kennedy Center audience always included numbers of high-gloss cosmopolitan ladies; but even among such Nickie attracted her share of once-overs from the gentlemen. Not that she took much notice. In fact, Joanne found it rather paradoxical that Nickie, having gotten herself up in a fashion certain to make men look, seemed more-or-less oblivious when they did. Like all genetic women Jo had been born with female radar which could detect male interest from afar; but evidently her friend hadn't yet developed that sixth sense. Since Nickie had only been a woman for a short while it wasn't surprising that she lacked many fundamental feminine instincts, including some which were much more vital than an awareness of men's glances. Jo had already felt compelled to lecture an oblivious Nickie about the hazards of deserted parking lots and other isolated areas. In many ways Nickie was a woman who hadn't learned to think like a woman; it was an unsettling but endearing facet of her unique young-girl naïveté.

As the concert hall swelled with Rossini's music Jo noted with secret amusement that Nickie was unobtrusively conducting the overture with one French-manicured forefinger in her lap. The transcendent melodies of "Semiramide" resounded in her ears as Jo closed her eyes, fighting the feelings, but denial was hopeless. Whether she wished it or not, Joanne Markwith had fallen very much in love with Nickie Farrell.

⸺ ((◦)) ⸺

The audience erupted into applause as the overture concluded and the house lights came up for intermission. Nickie bubbled to Joanne, "Oh, wasn't that *incredible?*" With an excited wriggle in her seat: "What fun! Shall we go get something to drink?"

"Sure," Jo acquiesced, smiling at Nickie's enthusiasm. "I'm glad you're having a good time, hon."

"I really am. This was the best idea. You're a lifesaver."

They made their way with the other patrons out into the grand foyer. In her high heels Nickie stood six feet tall, and again Jo noticed several men giving her the eye. How would these smug Casanovas react, she wondered, if someone informed them that the lady they were ogling had once been a man? She pressed her lips together and stayed protectively by Nickie's side. No point in such idle speculation, and she didn't care what men thought, anyway.

No sooner had they taken their place in the refreshment line than they heard a male voice behind them say, "Well, ladies, are we enjoying the evening?"

A well-built fortyish fellow wearing an expensive dark suit and a self-important Washingtonian air smiled easily as they turned around. Ignoring Joanne he pointedly addressed Nickie: "How did you like the Rossini?"

Nickie took in his precisely-trimmed mustache, thinning hair, silk tie, and pocket handkerchief. "Truthfully," she replied, "the tempo was a bit faster than I prefer, but I've heard that Toscanini used to conduct it that way. Besides, how can 'Semiramide' ever be anything less than divine?"

The man chuckled with a faintly patronizing air, as if Nickie had said something unexpectedly coherent. "Exactly, exactly."

Yuck, thought Jo. She could see that the guy was fixated on Nickie's eyes. This irresistible specimen had to be part of the local political fauna, perhaps a legislative aide or a lobbyist. Double yuck.

"So," he inquired, "are you a regular subscriber to the concert series?"

"I'm afraid not," Nickie shook her head. "We're just giving ourselves a treat. My partner and I are on the staff out at Windfield College. We thought it'd be nice for a change to come into the city for an evening of music."

"Partners? Are you ladies in business together?"

"Well," Nickie arched one eyebrow, "I suppose you could put it that way." She coyly batted her eyes at Joanne. "Wouldn't you think so, darling?"

Without missing a beat Jo smiled and said, "Whatever you say, my love."

As they locked gazes the man stared, flushed pink, and with a muttered excuse hurried away.

"Lawd, girl, you are so bad," Joanne gleefully admonished. "I think that guy just aged a few years."

"You think?" Nickie looked pleased. "Good. That'll teach him not to hit on someone when she's with her girlfriend. Men are such primitive organisms." She tossed her head. "I should know. I used to be one."

"No kidding?" Jo feigned amazement. "Gee, you don't look it."

"Trust me, honey, it's a constant struggle."

Giggling, they finally reached the bar and gave the harried bartender their orders. They'd barely had time for a few sips when a chime signaled the end of intermission.

"Oh, for heaven's sake." Joanne put down her club soda. "Well, let's go in. You're going to love the second half. It's Dvorak's Ninth, the 'New World' Symphony."

"Never heard it. I'm definitely having a Philistine moment. So this is a perfect opportunity to broaden my modest musical horizons." Nickie smiled and took Joanne's arm. "Shall we?"

⸺ ((◉)) ⸺

From the moment the music started Nickie listened with the entranced intensity of a dog on point. Watching her, Jo couldn't imagine that anyone else in the concert hall was deriving more enjoyment for their money.

A few moments into the second movement, as the famously poignant melody echoed through the hushed concert hall, Joanne felt a warm hand slide gently into her own. Not daring to move, her heart hammering, Jo intertwined her fingers in Nickie's. They remained that way until the movement ended. Then with an unfathomable little smile Nickie sighed and pulled her hand away.

Not knowing what to make of the hand-holding interlude, afraid to even speculate, Jo heard the rest of the symphony in a daze. When Dvorak's towering opus thundered to a conclusion Nickie was on her feet applauding before the conductor turned for his first bow.

"Omigod," she exclaimed, clapping briskly, her face luminous. "What a fantastic piece of music!"

"I thought you might like it," Jo smiled.

"I'm going to run right out and buy the CD. I can't wait to listen to it again." Nickie continued her ebullient chatter all the way out of the hall. "Did you hear how the fourth movement started? Jo, it's exactly the same two chords as the opening theme from *Jaws*. I wonder if that's where John Williams got his inspiration..."

After retrieving their coats they were heading for the escalators when Jo caught sight of the man from the refreshment line smirking in their direction and whispering to a fellow establishment clone. Nickie followed her gaze and saw them grin and snicker. The happy expression faded from her face.

"Never mind." Joanne shepherded her onto the escalator. "They don't matter."

Nickie muttered, "It's never going to change, Jo, is it? Prejudice will never go away."

"Don't think that, sweetie. Things do get better. It just takes a long time. Remember, someday those students of yours will be the ones in charge. And they'll be more enlightened, partly because of your example. *Timendi causa est nescire*," she quoted the Windfield motto. "The cause of fear is ignorance. But not forever, hon. As we used to say, keep the faith."

"You're right." Nickie gathered her skirt and tucked herself into Jo's shiny black RAV-4. "No way am I going to let a couple of cretinous bozos ruin the evening."

"Nothing could possibly ruin this evening." They drove away from the Kennedy Center, merging onto Interstate 66 to cross the Potomac River into Virginia. The myriad lights of Washington twinkled reflections on the placid surface. "I haven't enjoyed myself this much in forever, Nickie. Thank you so much for coming with me."

"It's been wonderful. I hope you know how special you are to me, Jo. I'm so grateful to have you in my life."

They drove without speaking for several miles. "Nickie," Joanne finally broke the silence, "do you mind if I ask you something kind of personal?"

"I don't mind at all," Nickie answered at once. "Ask away."

Jo hesitated. "Before you...I mean, back in the days when you were still male, did you ever have a gay experience? With another man?"

Nickie stared out at the night with an unreadable expression. "One time."

Jo nodded, keeping her eyes on the highway.

"It happened when I was still in the throes of my alcoholism, long before I had any concrete consciousness of being transsexual. I was at some resort in the Catskills, I can't remember why, but anyway one night I met a man in the bar. Dark blonde hair, blue eyes, white teeth, tanned, just gorgeous, white sweater knotted around his shoulders, GQ all the way. Of course I could tell he was gay, but I lived in New York City, gay men were nothing new to me. Anyway we started talking, you know how it is in a bar, and Jo, he was so nice. I mean, a real gentleman. Great sense of humor, thoughtful, intelligent, the whole nine yards. He was a guidance counselor at some small New England college. And the tennis coach. Can you imagine?" She paused. "His name was Jamie."

"Jamie the gay GQ tennis coach." Jo let out a soft whistle. "Oh, boy."

"Mm-hm." With a sidelong glance Nickie continued: "Well, I was dazzled and flattered that he seemed so interested. The next day I couldn't wait to run into him. He showed me the tennis courts, and we went to lunch, and..." She stopped for a moment. "I realize now that Jamie was actually *courting* me, Jo. It wasn't some crude hit job like that fool tonight. He was polite, and attentive, and considerate...like something out of a romance novel. At least that's how it struck me at the time. And I absolutely loved it, because Jamie made me *feel like a woman.* It was the most intoxicating, the most right feeling I'd ever had. I was living every girl's fantasy of being wooed by a handsome prince."

Not every girl's fantasy, thought Joanne Markwith, but remained silent.

"This went on for a couple of days. Luckily Jamie had plenty of practice at being discreet because I certainly had no clue. To this day I have no idea whether people suspected anything, and it doesn't matter. We would go for walks through the woods and hold hands, and he would put his arm around my shoulder, and I would pretend I was Jane Eyre, and it was all romantic beyond belief. Well, one night I got myself really swozzled and somehow we ended up in this hidden grassy area by the lake. Before I knew it we were kissing and necking and making out." Nickie swallowed. "I remember Jamie asking me, 'Where on earth did you learn to kiss like that?' I was so drunk, God knows what I said. But suddenly he...he wanted to go farther, and started going for my belt and zipper."

Jo heard the tightness in her friend's voice. "Nickie, you don't need to tell me any more. It's okay, hon. Really."

"No, I want to." Nickie took a breath. "We didn't have sex, Jo. Drunk as I was, I couldn't do it. The fantasy broke apart, don't you see? I wasn't a woman, and I couldn't make love like a woman. Besides, Jamie didn't want a woman. But I wasn't a gay man, either. I didn't know what the hell I was. It was awful. I felt like the cheapest tease in the world. Poor Jamie was the consummate gentleman, of course. He stopped right away, never protested, was as sweet as ever. I never saw him again after that night. But I'll never forget him, or the way he made me feel." She passed a hand across her eyes. "Anyway, that's the story of my gay experience. Pretty lame, huh? We trannies sure know how to make a mess out of everything."

Joanne reached out and stroked her friend's cheek, felt the wetness. "Oh, Nickie. You've endured enough heartache to tear apart a dozen people. But you made it, girl. You really did. And I'm glad." Jo blinked the mist from her eyes. "So very, very glad."

<hr />

By the time they arrived back in Middleville, Joanne's dashboard clock showed twenty minutes past midnight.

"Well," she said. "Home again, home again, jiggety-jig."

"Would you like to come in for a little bit? Not much to look at, but it's cozy."

Jo had a feeling it might not be such a good idea. But she didn't want the evening to end yet. Who knew when she'd have another date with Nickie? Besides, they were both big girls.

"Okay, but just for a few minutes. If I don't get my beauty sleep I turn into a frightening hag."

"Oh, stop." Nickie unlocked her door and beckoned Jo inside. "Welcome to my tiny corner of the world."

She flipped a wall switch and a floor lamp came on, illuminating the room in a warm pinkish light. Joanne looked around the small neat space, noting the freshly-vacuumed beige carpet, the carefully-tended houseplants in shiny brass containers, the white eyelet curtains, and the floral-patterned love seat. Against one wall two free-standing shelves were filled with books lined up according to size. A small side table displayed a grouping of porcelain cat figurines. One played with its tail, another licked itself, and a third was curled in a tight sleeping ball.

"They're Royal Copenhagen," Nickie said with fond pride. "My special kitty collection. Here, give me your coat. Sit, sit."

"They're precious." Joanne settled herself on the love seat, suddenly becoming aware that there were no family pictures anywhere. It made her feel sad for Nickie. "This is lovely, hon. Just what you said. Cozy."

"Thanks. Actually, you're my very first guest. You really don't think it's too...masculine?"

"No, dear." Jo couldn't help but smile at Nickie's anxious tone. "Perfectly girly. You can relax."

"Thank goodness." Nickie sat next to Jo and bent over to unfasten the straps on her high heels. "I must get out of these cripplers. To coin a phrase, my feet are killing me."

"Hey, no complaining. You wanted to be a girl. Comes with the territory. Unless you're a dyke like me." Joanne wore low-heeled black loafers. "Anyway, it serves you right for wearing CFM shoes."

"CFM?" Nickie dropped the green sandals next to the sofa and curled her legs up, massaging her toes. "What's that?"

Joanne forced her eyes up from Nickie's nylon-clad legs. "Come on, don't tell me you never heard that. CFM? Come-fuck-me?"

Nickie scrunched up her face. "That's awful." She readjusted herself, revealing more leg. "I never heard anything so...so...classless," she sniffed.

"Maybe," Joanne conceded, "but pretty descriptive. Those sexy shoes of yours sure did a job on that creep in the drink line."

Nickie opened her mouth to protest, then closed it. With a foxy look: "Gee, y'think?"

"You damn well know it, Miss Prim-and-Proper. You're not that innocent."

"Oh, but I am." Nickie extended her leg and lightly traced a toe along Jo's thigh, purring in her contralto voice, "I'm as innocent as the dawn. As the driven snow. Innocent as a newborn lamb..."

Joanne reached down and grasped Nickie's ankle. She could feel the warmth of the other's skin through the sheer hose. "You saucy minx!"

"A minx, am I?" Nickie widened her eyes and smoothly slid herself closer on the love seat. Jo opened her arms to receive her and then they were kissing, slowly at first, gradually with more ardor as their embrace grew more heated. Joanne surrendered to the rapture of the moment, feeling Nickie's exploring tongue, inhaling the scent of her perfume, hearing her amorous whimpers and growls. She ran her hand up Nickie's leg and discovered that she was wearing thigh-high stockings instead of pantyhose. With mounting fervor Jo began to nip and lick along her friend's neck and heard herself breathlessly exclaim, "Good god, woman, where did you learn to kiss like that?"

Nickie's different-colored eyes were almost glowing. "Gee, I dunno. Some guy named Jamie? Mmm, c'mere." She opened her mouth and began to plant little soft kisses on Joanne's eyes, her ears, her chin.

Giggling, Joanne pulled Nickie closer, feeling her breasts press against her own. Jamie! How funny that she would say that...except...except...Joanne felt Nickie's hand sliding inside her blouse. In a matter of seconds, she knew, there would be no going back.

"Nickie, wait," she gasped, trying to think clearly. "Sweetheart, I don't know if this is such a good idea."

"It's a fabulous idea," Nickie panted, her voice muffled in Jo's curly hair. "Just wonderful."

"No, I don't think so." Trying to push free, Joanne suddenly became aware of how much stronger Nickie was. With a twinge of alarm she braced herself and thrust with both arms. "*Stop.*"

Nickie fell back, staring at Jo uncomprehendingly. "What's the matter? Did I do something wrong?"

"No, no, of course not. It's just...Honey, we shouldn't do this. It isn't right."

"Why not?" Nickie's wounded expression cut into Jo's heart. "How can you say such a thing?" She abruptly jumped to her feet and glared. "Is it because I'm not a real woman? That's it, isn't it? When you get right down to it, I'm nothing but a trannie freak with an artificial pussy. I should've known." She clenched her fists and laid them against her breastbone. "Oh, God, why doesn't *anybody* want me?"

Appalled, Joanne rose and tried to hug her friend but Nickie sidestepped her and took refuge in the wing chair. "*No.* Stay away."

"Nickie, listen to me. *Listen.* I do want you. I want you so much it's driving me crazy. Do you hear me? For God's sake, I'm soaking wet. You are so damned sexy I get turned on just thinking about you. I could make love with you forever and it wouldn't be enough for me." She knelt down beside the chair. "But this isn't about me, sweetheart. It's about you. And despite what you think, this isn't what you really want."

"You don't know that." Nickie hugged herself in the chair, legs drawn up, hair mussed, eyes red and swollen.

"Yes, I do." Jo laid a hand on Nickie's knee. "You're not a lesbian, sweetie. If there was the slightest chance of it, we'd be down and dirty right this minute. Or maybe if you were bisexual. But you're not even bi. Your story about Jamie proves that, doesn't it? You're a straight woman, Nickie, and you want a man, the same as other straight women. Don't you suppose I can tell? That's just who you are. It's perfectly fine, and my lousy luck. But the last thing you need in your life right now is more confusion. If we made love it would be a terrible mistake. I can't do that to you, and I can't do it to me." Joanne stopped, then continued in an unsteady voice: "I love you, Nickie, more than you have any idea. But I won't be your lover, because sooner or later you would leave me, and then I'd die."

Nickie covered her face with her hands. "I'm going to end up all alone."

"No, honey. Trust me, you'll find someone."

"Who?" Nickie dropped her hands. "Someone like Alex Steward?" With a bitter laugh: "Yeah, right. Nice guys don't hook up with trannies. Once Alex found out about me he lost interest in a hurry."

After a moment's hesitation Jo said, "Nickie...I'm not so sure that

Alex isn't interested."

"What are you talking about? He dumped me and left me standing in the rain."

"I know, but..." Joanne related how Professor Steward had surreptitiously listened to her question-and-answer session with the students. "Alex didn't see me, and he slipped out before you finished. I don't know why, but he was there, Nickie."

"Alex was *there?*" Nickie uncurled herself and sat up straight. "Why didn't you tell me?"

"Because I was furious at Alex for hurting you, that's why! And I was jealous. I can't help it, I still am. But look at you, all lit up like a Christmas tree. You're still in love with him, Nickie. Now can you understand why I made us stop?"

Nickie got out of the chair and embraced her friend. They stayed like that for a long minute. Then she kissed Jo on the forehead and whispered, "Yes, I do understand. You were right. I shouldn't have made such a fuss. That was unfair, and I'm sorry, truly I am. But please, Jo, don't be jealous. Of Alex or anyone else. Because no matter what happens, as long as I live, nobody will ever take your place in my heart. Promise me you'll always be my best girlfriend?"

Joanne Markwith looked up at the woman she loved but could never have. "Yes, sweet Nickie." She sadly nodded. "Best girlfriends forever. I promise."

———— ((●)) ————

Thanks to the Christmas exodus the Windfield College library reference room was deserted save for a lone figure sitting at one of the long tables. Her face set in a frown of concentration, Cinda Vanderhart examined a slim volume through an oblong magnifying glass. After a minute she turned the page and resumed her scrutiny. Finally she closed the book, set it to one side and plucked another from a small stack on the table. A quick look at her watch and she muttered under her breath, "Shit." She jammed the magnifying glass into a stuffed Jansport backpack on the adjacent chair, snatched up three more books from the stack and slinging her backpack over one shoulder, hastened to the reference desk.

"Hey, sister." A heavyset girl stood behind the desk. Cinda recalled having seen her at a meeting of the campus lesbian alliance. "How's it goin'?"

"Busy as hell," the other replied. "What's up with you?"

"Not much. I'm flying home to Indianapolis this afternoon. My roomie's giving me a ride to Dulles in ten minutes."

"Indianapolis, huh? How bad does that suck?"

"You have no idea," Cinda groaned. "Listen, sis, I need a favor. See these?" She held out the three books.

The heavyset woman flicked them a bored glance. "Old senior class almanacs. What about 'em?"

"I need to borrow them over the break," said Cinda.

"Nuh-uh. Can't check out reference books."

"Yeah, I know. That's where the favor comes in. Maybe you can just sort of...not notice? I'll guard them with my life, I swear."

"You know how much trouble I could get into?" The girl picked up one of the volumes. "Nineteen-seventy-seven. Back in the Stone Age." She examined the other two. "Seventy-eight and seventy-nine. What do you want them for, anyway?"

"An article I'm writing for the *Spectrum*. About the first decade of Windfield, what the place was like, where the students came from, that sort of thing. A retrospective. Come on," she appealed. "Please? I'll return 'em the instant I get back from break."

"What the hell. Go for it. But if they don't make it back here I will hunt you down, missy."

"Outstanding." Cinda slipped the class books into her backpack. "You rock, sister. Bye the way, I'm Cinda."

"Kellie," replied the heavyset girl. "Have a Merry Christmas. You do celebrate Christmas in Indy, right?"

"Yeah, but for us dykes it's about as frikkin' merry as Death Row. Thanks again, Kellie. Merry Christmas."

Gloating over her success Cinda left the library. The trip home would be marginally more tolerable now that she could continue with her investigation. She'd already meticulously combed through several years of the earliest Windfield College graduates without finding what she sought. But she wasn't discouraged. She had a hunch that one of the three old Windfield books in her backpack contained a senior photo of a young man with different-colored eyes, who looked remarkably like a certain lady English professor. Discovering that photo was going to be Cinda's Christmas present to herself.

"I know you're in there, Ms. Farrell. Maybe you think you can hide your past, but I'm going to find out who you were." She waved at Heather's white Scion as it drew to the curb. "*And* how you're connected to that townie waiter. Count on it."

————))(())((————

Later that afternoon, at about the same time that Cinda's airplane was beginning its final approach into Indianapolis, Collie Skinner emerged from the general manager's office in the Foxton Arms and went back to the employee's area. He found Robin anxiously waiting for him.

"Well? What did Mr. Demarest want?" The general manager rarely dealt directly with the service staff. "You're not in any trouble, are you?"

"No, nothing like that," Collie shook his head. "Sort of the opposite, actually. He had a special assignment for me."

"What sort of special assignment?"

"Sounds crazy, but Mr. Demarest said that Ambassador Douglass wants the restaurant to cater a whole big seafood buffet at Windfield's spring picnic. Shrimp, crab legs, oysters, the works. No matter what it costs. Can you imagine? For a stupid picnic." Disdainfully: "I guess burgers and hot dogs aren't high-class enough for Windfield kids."

"Okay, but what does this have to do with you?"

"Get this: Old man Douglass told Mr. Demarest he wants *me* to be in charge. I have to set the whole thing up, order the food, arrange the service, everything." Collie looked at Robin. "If it all turns out okay I'll get two thousand dollars. Plus a big tip."

"Two *thousand* dollars?" Robin squeaked, her eyes wide.

"Yup. Beats me. I thought rich old guys like Douglass hate Windfield. Maybe he's getting senile."

"I still don't understand why Ambassador Douglass wants *you*."

"How should I know? Mr. Demarest said he mentioned I had lost my mother, and Mrs. Skinner was a valued employee, it's the least he can do, and blah blah. Robin, he didn't care about Mama one bit. She was scared of him. I mean *terrified*. I never told you, but right before she...before the end, Mama started thrashing around, all delirious, moaning about Mr. Douglass and Doublecross Dingbats. She was dying, but still worrying about that bast–" He bit his lip.

"Doublecross Dingbats?" Robin squinted in puzzlement. "What on earth is Doublecross Dingbats?"

"Who knows? Probably just gibberish." Collie shrugged. "Mama was out of her mind with fever. Anyway, Robin, I really didn't want to have anything to do with that guy, not even for two grand, but Mr. Demarest said I don't really have a choice." He sighed. "The Windfield College picnic. Lucky me. Guess when it is?"

"I don't know. When?"

"April Fools Day." With a humorless laugh: "Can you beat that?"

Robin squeezed his hand. "Maybe it won't be so terrible. You'll do a great job, and two thousand dollars...well, how bad can that be?"

"Two thousand *plus* tip." Collie fondly chucked her under the chin. "I'll buy you a nice present."

Robin clucked, "No, you'll put in right in the bank where it belongs. I don't need any presents. I've got you."

"Not even a pretty dress from Millicent's?" Millicent's was an exclusive boutique on Middleville's main street.

"Nicholas, two thousand dollars is nothing at Millicent's. That's a store for rich ladies. Come on, we better get to work."

The Foxton Arms made it a point every year to have the most beautiful Christmas tree in town. The front foyer was dominated by a flawless tall blue spruce entwined in twinkling gold lights and decorated with satin-finish silver ornaments. To one side of this eye-catching wonder the maitre d' stood behind his podium fussing over the reservation book. Catching sight of Collie and Robin, he beckoned them over with a forefinger.

Clearing his throat: "Mr. Skinner, Ms. Thompson, we are fully booked this evening. Henceforth I'll thank you to postpone your backroom tête-à-têtes until after closing. Understood?"

Robin blushed. Collie said, "Sorry, Mr. Foley. My fault. I...um...got to talking."

"I can imagine." The maitre d' regarded them over his half-glasses. "You spoke with Mr. Demarest?"

Collie nodded. "I did."

"Everything in order?"

"Yes, sir."

"Very well. Mr. Skinner, we're expecting a party of three at six-fifteen. They've requested your service."

One of his regulars, thought Collie. Maybe the Congressman, or Dr. Roberts. "Who is it?"

The maitre d' checked his listings. "I don't recognize the name. Mr. Cale Pittman."

"Pittman?" Collie went pale. "A party of three?"

"Three, yes. You know the gentleman?"

"I won't serve them. I'm sorry, but I can't."

"Collie, no," Robin whispered a warning.

The maitre d' glared. "Mr. Skinner, did I just hear you decline to serve these guests?"

Collie stood his ground. "Pittman is coming here with my father and brother. They're nothing but trash, Mr. Foley. They can rot in Hell."

"Mr. Skinner, I understand that you have been through a difficult time. We have made every effort to be accommodating, but your family issues are of no concern to this establishment. These patrons will be treated with courtesy and you *will* be their server. Is that clear?"

"It's clear, sir." Collie glowered. "I quit." He turned on his heel and stalked into the back.

"Oh, God," Robin exclaimed. "I'm sorry, Mr. Foley. He didn't mean it. Collie's still very upset about his mother. Please, sir. Let me go talk some sense into him."

The maitre d' hesitated. He nurtured a soft spot in his heart for Robin Thompson. And Collie Skinner had always been a good employee. If this girl cared for him, he probably deserved a second chance.

"All right, Ms. Thompson," the maitre d' acquiesced. "Speak with Mr. Skinner. But quickly. And he must serve Mr. Pittman's party, or be terminated."

"Absolutely. Thank you, sir."

In the back room, Collie had already removed his tie. He made a cutting motion with his hand. "Forget it. I won't serve them. Never. Those bastards."

"Nicholas, listen to me..."

"Jay-Bo *hurt* Mama, Robin! For God's sake, I saw the marks on her! Do you seriously expect me to smile and dish up a pepper steak for that fat son-of-bitch? All he ever did was make Mama cry."

"He'll make her cry again, Nicholas." She added quietly, "If you let him."

Collie frowned. "What?"

"Can't you see? They're only coming here to goad you into quitting, get you fired, whatever. Jay-Bo is looking to hurt you like he hurt Luanne because she loved you, not him, and he hates you for it. What better way than to make you lose your job, wreck your life, ruin everything you've worked for?"

Collie hung his arms at his side and stared at the floor.

"Your mother is watching over you this minute, Nicholas. She wants you to be strong, to be successful, to live your life and be happy the way she never was." Robin placed her hands on his upper arms. "But if you quit, then you'll lose everything. Jay-Bo will get the last laugh, and wherever she is, your mother will be crying again. Please, Nicholas, don't let that happen."

"But...I don't know if I have the strength to pull it off, Robin. I just don't know."

"God doesn't give us more than we can handle," she answered. "And you are a lot stronger than you realize." She hesitated. "Remember, we don't know what...what Nick Farrington was like. Perhaps he was a person of great strength, and passed it on to you."

"That's right." Collie set his jaw. "Jay-Bo Skinner *isn't* my father. If I can stay focused on that...Aw, what's the use? I'm sure Mr. Foley has already decided to fire me."

"No, Nicholas. Mr. Foley's a fair man. Just go back in and do your job. It'll be okay, I promise."

"All right. I will." Collie snapped his bow tie back in place. "Besides, what can they do in the middle of a restaurant? Whatever crap they dish out, I'll handle it."

Robin prayed that was true. "If it gets ugly, think about how you won't let your mother down."

"Or you, either." He gave Robin a grateful kiss. "You're my guardian angel. I love you."

"I love you too, Nicholas. Now back to work. And this time," she wagged a stern finger, "behave."

⸺⸺∙((●))∙⸺⸺

After apologizing to Mr. Foley, who curtly nodded and shooed him on his way, Collie went about his duties, steeling himself for the upcoming encounter.

At a quarter past six he saw Mr. Foley lead Jay-Bo, Lloyd, and Cale Pittman to an unobtrusive corner table. The Skinner men were dressed in their black funeral suits. Pittman wore a brown tweed jacket and dark slacks. Catching Collie's eye, the maitre d' inclined his head toward the men with a frigid look.

Thinking, I can do this, Collie presented himself at their table and reeled off the customary greeting: "Good evening, gentlemen. Welcome to the Foxton Arms. My name's Collie, I'll be your server tonight. Before I tell you about tonight's specials, may I bring you something from the bar?"

Jay-Bo looked Collie up and down with a scornful expression. Cale

Pittman studied Collie for a moment then ordered a Bombay Sapphire martini. Lloyd said he'd have the same. Collie looked inquiringly at Jay-Bo. "And for you?"

"Y'all got any Wild Turkey 101 in this candy-ass joint, boy?"

"I believe we do," replied Collie. "Sir," he carefully appended.

"Bring me a double. A real double, hear? And make it snappy, boy."

"I'll bring your orders right away, gentlemen." Collie hastened off, congratulating himself on staying cool. Returning quickly, he set the drinks down in front of the men. "Shall I tell you about our specials now, or would you prefer to enjoy your drinks?"

Cale Pittman tasted his cocktail. "I'd prefer to enjoy my drink."

"Very good, sir. I'll return shortly for your orders." He turned to leave.

"One moment, waiter."

"Sir?"

"I said I'd prefer to enjoy my drink."

Collie looked uncertain. "Yes, sir?"

"How can you expect me to enjoy this? Did you not hear me ask for Bombay Sapphire?" Pittman gestured in disgust at his martini. "That isn't Bombay Sapphire gin. It's cheap house garbage."

"But—"

"Are you calling me a liar?" Cale speared Collie with glittering dark blue eyes. "I don't react well to being contradicted."

Jay-Bo drained half his drink in one swallow. "See what I tole you? Damn boy ain't got an ounce of respect."

"That's the goddamn truth," interjected Lloyd, pushing his cocktail away. "Is that all you do here? Rip people off?"

Collie saw several patrons at nearby tables glancing their way. "If the drinks are unsatisfactory, gentlemen, I'll be glad to bring you something else."

Cale Pittman considered it with pursed lips. "What do you think, men?"

Lloyd shrugged. "Whatever you say, Cale."

Jay-Bo tossed off the remainder of his bourbon. "Gimme a refill on this."

"You heard him," said Pittman. "In fact, just bring us the whole bottle." He gestured at the untouched martinis. "Get that swill out my sight."

Collie gathered up the drinks, acutely aware of the stares being directed at them from other tables.

"What the hell?" The bartender frowned when Collie returned the two cocktails.

"Sorry, Vince. I got some real jerks. Anyway, they want the bottle of Wild Turkey."

"They do, huh? Too damn bad."

"Come on, Vince," Collie pleaded. "I think these guys are troublemakers."

"Screw 'em," said Vince, dumping two ten-dollar martinis down the sink. "You know the rules. No full bottles. What do they think this is, some kind of redneck bar?"

Collie took Jay-Bo's bourbon back to the table and explained that the Foxton Arms didn't allow the sale of an entire bottle of hard liquor.

Pittman shook his head in disbelief. "Outrageous. You call this a restaurant?"

"Nice place you work at, Cockeyes," sneered Lloyd Skinner. To his business partner: "That's what the kids called him in school. Cockeyes. I was always steppin' in to keep him from gettin' his ass pounded. Nothin' like havin' a freak for a brother."

"Jeepers creepers," Cale laughed, "where'd you get those peepers?"

Collie saw Robin throw him an apprehensive look from several tables away. He slipped her a reassuring wink, then gravely answered, "I couldn't say, sir. That's something you would have to ask my father."

"Shoot, don't ask me." Jay-Bo grunted. "Maybe his old lady slung a freebie to the trash collector."

Collie consciously forced his jaw muscles to relax. "For tonight's specials, gentlemen, we start with fresh grilled swordfish marinated in lemon vodka, served with a caper-and-cayenne sauce over wild rice and—"

"Holy shit," interrupted Jay-Bo, "that stuff could turn a man into a faggot. You got any sloppy joes?"

"I'm afraid we don't, sir." Collie pressed on: "Also we have a rack of New Zealand lamb chops, grilled with fresh thyme and rosemary, accompanied by baby parsnips sautéed in apple brandy—"

"Never mind," Cale Pittman cut him off. "Is your chef some sort of European lunatic? Don't you have anything that a normal American male can eat?"

"I'm sure we can find some—"

"Steaks?"

"Yes, sir. Delmonico, Chateaubriand, Porterhouse. All prime corn-fed Black Angus."

"Bring us three rare Porterhouse steaks. *Rare.*"

"Don't go puttin' any kind of homo sauce on mine, boy," Jay-Bo growled. "Hear me? And another bourbon."

At the adjacent table a well turned-out older gentleman dining with his aristocratic silver-haired wife stared at Jay-Bo with haughty repugnance, then bent forward and whispered something which made her smile.

Collie fled for the kitchen. After putting in the order he stood for a moment, calming his nerves.

"Hey." He felt Robin's tentative touch. "Are you all right?"

"Yeah, I'm okay." With a faint grin: "So far."

"You're doing great, Nicholas." Robin kissed her finger and placed it on lips. "I'm so proud of you. Hang in there."

When the steaks were ready Collie carried them out and set them sizzling before the three men. "Here you are, gentlemen. Enjoy."

"Where's my damn Wild Turkey, boy?" Jay-Bo glowered. "The service here stinks, y'know that?"

"Sorry, sir. I'll bring it immediately."

"Make that three." Cale Pittman dourly inspected his picture-perfect Porterhouse. "Doubles."

When Collie returned with the drinks Pittman pointed at his plate, where the steak displayed a perfect pink gash. "This meat is cooked to death. Tough as a shoe. I asked for rare. What's wrong with you? Can't you get anything right?"

Collie flushed. "Sir, I beg your pardon, but that steak is rare."

"Don't you give my partner any lip, Cockeyes." Lloyd pointed: "Mine's no good, either."

"I ain't eatin' this horsemeat," Jay-Bo pushed his plate into the center of the table. "Wouldn't feed it to a dog."

"Pity the dog," said Cale Pittman. "Get rid of these, waiter, and bring us three *rare* Filet Mignons. Think you can manage that?"

At the adjacent table the older gentleman abruptly set down his utensils, muttered something to his wife and left the table.

Feeling sick at the thought of wasting over a hundred dollars worth of prime beef, Collie silently began gathering up the plates. Jay-Bo slurped his third double bourbon, banged the glass down on the table. "It's no wonder our waiter's fuckin' everything up, boys. Cockeyes here ain't got his mind on his work."

"Yeah?" Lloyd grinned. "Why not, Pop?"

"The kid's finally gettin' laid regular," Jay-Bo chortled. "Ain't you, Cockeyes? That little waitress over there, with the sexy ass. Your hot-box these days, ain't she?"

Summoning a supreme effort of will Collie said nothing and placed the last steak on his serving tray.

"I hear them church gals can really throw it around," Jay-Bo licked his lips obscenely, "once you convince 'em to let somebody besides Jesus in their panties. Right, boy?"

Collie bit his tongue so hard he could taste the metallic flavor of blood. As his last ounce of self-control wisped away he suddenly heard Mr. Foley's authoritative voice: "Is everything all right here?"

"No, it isn't." Cale Pittman spoke indignantly: "Our service has been atrocious. This incompetent waiter has mixed up the orders, neglected to bring our drinks, and comported himself in a surly manner. Frankly, he's ruined the entire evening. Your restaurant's excellent reputation is completely unwarranted."

Collie stood by numbly, waiting to be fired. I tried, Mama, he thought. I really did try.

"Excuse me, but that simply isn't so." Collie looked up to see the older gentleman from the adjacent table standing beside the maitre d'. "Conrad, these...people have behaved swinishly from the moment they arrived. They've abused their server in the most barbaric fashion, used foul language in the presence of the ladies, and created an offensive scene. The young man was unfailingly polite and did his best in every way possible. Blaming him is beneath contempt."

"Who the hell asked you?" Jay-Bo snarled. "Think your shit don't stink? Sit your rich ass down and shut up."

By now the entire dining room was looking their way. The hum of voices ceased. Mr. Foley calmly signaled to a watching waiter, who slipped from the room to call the police if necessary. "I must ask you gentlemen to leave the premises. There will be no charge. Please leave immediately, or the authorities will be summoned."

Cale Pittman stared daggers at the maitre d' for a long moment. He shrugged, threw his napkin on the table and rose. Jay-Bo and Lloyd followed suit, roughly shoving back their chairs. Then the three men nonchalantly threaded their way through the tables and exited the dining room.

The instant they vanished from sight the room began to buzz with excited conversation. Standing over the tray of ruined steaks, Collie saw Robin watching from a distance, her eyes huge and frightened. He tried to smile, but his facial muscles had frozen.

The maitre d' addressed the older gentleman who'd spoken: "Mr. Ribble, thank you for bringing this matter to my attention. On behalf of the Foxton Arms I apologize to you and Mrs. Ribble. We will be honored to take care of your meal this evening." He bowed slightly, and turned to Collie. "Please come with me, Mr. Skinner. Mr. Wilson will clear your table."

Collie trailed the maitre d' to a private area off the kitchen. Mr. Foley cleared his throat. "Well. I cannot hold myself blameless for this disagreeable incident, Mr. Skinner. You gave me fair warning. Because of my faulty judgement I placed you in a very difficult position and subjected our guests to a great deal of unpleasantness. Although it was unintentional, I sincerely regret doing so. You handled yourself as well as could be expected under such extreme circumstances." He paused.

"Sometimes one's relatives can be...dreadfully trying." He offered his hand. "You have my sympathies."

"Thank you, sir." Collie shook hands. "I'm awfully sorry that they disrupted the restaurant. If it wasn't for me..."

"Say no more. It's over and done. Would you like to take the rest of the evening off?"

"No, sir. If it's okay, I'd just like to get back to work."

"Very well," Mr. Foley nodded. "I've noticed a positive change in you of late, Mr. Skinner. Setting aside our disagreement earlier, I see more maturity and forbearance. As I recall, not long ago I had to reprimand you for almost savaging some Windfield students."

"Since my mother died I've learned some things, Mr. Foley. Things I never knew. They...make a difference."

"I also suspect that Ms. Thompson may be having a, shall we say, civilizing influence on you."

"She sure is. The best influence ever."

"How fortunate men are," observed the maitre d' with the hint of a smile, "that the good Lord saw fit to bless the world with womankind."

Collie couldn't have agreed more; and when, hours later, he and Robin were able to spend some quiet time together, Mr. Foley's words seemed wise indeed.

"Now listen, Barlow," Ambassador Eamon Douglass tapped his finger on the desk for emphasis. "No matter how freakish this person looks or sounds, you're not to turn a hair. Not one hair, goddamn it. Understand?"

Leaning against the wall in the Shamrock office with his arms folded across his chest, Big Mike shrugged. "Freaks don't bother me."

"I very much doubt," Douglass frostily observed, "that you've ever seen one like this."

The special consultant yawned. "A weirdo's a weirdo."

"Your area of expertise, hey? Freaks and weirdos."

A knock sounded at the door and the store manager stuck in his head. "Um, a Professor Farrell to see you, sir."

"Well, what are you waiting for? Show the professor in, Holt."

When he saw Nickie Farrell the ambassador's immediate thought was that there must be some sort of mistake. He'd constructed a detailed mental image of what the transsexual Windfield professor would probably look like, but he had never been more spectacularly mistaken. The man who coolly walked into the office presented the perfect façade of a comely forty-something lady. He was conservatively dressed in a charcoal business suit, with a plain white blouse. His hemline hung below his knees, his heels were of moderate height, and he wasn't made up like some tart. He had his wavy red hair pulled back with one of those old-fashioned contraptions like that harridan of a First Lady used to wear, but otherwise presented a modern, professional, feminine appearance. It was a flawless deception. Eamon Douglass sat planted in his chair, slightly stunned.

Professor Nickie Farrell approached the desk and said in a voice reminiscent of the actress Lauren Bacall, "Good afternoon, Ambassador Douglass. I trust I haven't kept you waiting."

Almost against his will Douglass rose and extended his hand. "Not at all. A pleasure to meet you at last, Professor." He shook Nickie's hand, which was startlingly soft and womanly. Indicating Big Mike, whose face had remained blank: "My consultant, Mr. Mike Barlow."

"Good day, Mr. Barlow."

"Call me Mike."

The ambassador gestured at the wooden chair where Luanne Skinner had sat only a few weeks before. "Have a seat, Professor."

"Before we start, may I say something?"

Still thrown off-balance by the idea that this creature was a surgically-mutated male, Eamon Douglass nodded. "By all means."

"Ambassador, I believe that people in your position seldom operate in the dark about anything."

"An accurate supposition." Douglass narrowed his eyes. "Go on."

"Would I be correct in assuming that you are aware of my...atypical personal history?"

Goddamn right, thought the ambassador. "As it happens, Professor, I am."

Nickie met his eye. "Sir, some people find it uncomfortable to be around...people like me. What I'm getting at is, if you would rather work with someone else from the college, I certainly understand. So does President Lindsey. I'll be willing to step aside, if you prefer."

The ambassador steepled his fingers and leaned back, staring straight ahead at Professor Farrell's crotch. What sort of medical deviltry had been wrought there? Worse, how many innocent men had been duped into fornication with that manufactured fraud? The idea made the ambassador's blood boil. Such transsexual trickery had to top the Almighty's list of blackest abominations. Nickie Farrell belonged in Hell, and Eamon Douglass was going to make certain that the professor got there.

"My dear lady," he smiled, "I appreciate such forthrightness, but your private circumstances are no concern of mine." To Big Mike: "Any problems working with the professor, Mr. Barlow?"

"Nope."

"Then that's settled." He indicated the chair. "Would you care to sit down, Ms. Farrell?"

"Thank you, Ambassador." The fake woman sat, carefully smoothing her skirt and crossing her legs. Douglass watched, simultaneously amazed and repulsed by the professor's mimicry of a real female. This guy truly belonged in a zoo.

Tearing his eyes from Nickie's profanely sleek legs: "As you know, this project must be completed before April first, the day of Windfield's spring picnic. Today is December twenty-first, which only leaves us a little over three months. I'm not a man who tolerates delays and screw-ups, Professor. The clock is ticking for me, as I'm sure you're aware. We *must* get this done on time. Is that clear?"

"Perfectly clear. I hope you don't mind, but I took the liberty of having these prepared as possible starting points." Nickie unzipped a slim portfolio and handed a sheaf of papers to the ambassador. "These preliminary sketches were drawn by an architect friend of mine named Alain Michaels. He has his own design firm in D.C." The ambassador intently inspected the sketches one by one, laying them face down on the desk. "As you can see, Ambassador, each design incorporates the existing memorial obelisk, as the trustees required. Of course the final choice will be yours."

"These are quite good. I salute your initiative, Professor Farrell. Well done."

"Thank you, sir. Alain is very well-regarded."

The ambassador laid down the final sketch, shuffled through the pile and held one up. "I think we could go with this. Very graceful, solemn and uplifting. First-rate. There is one little thing I want to add. Well," he chuckled, "maybe not so little."

"I'm sure Alain can incorporate whatever additional element you deem necessary..."

"A sundial, Professor."

"A sundial?" Nickie looked surprised, then she smiled. "That's an excellent idea, Ambassador. Sundials provide character."

"I assure you this is a very special sundial, Professor Farrell." He turned to Big Mike, who stood idly chewing on a toothpick. "Mr. Barlow, kindly escort the professor out to the yard and show her my sundial."

"Yep," said Mike, and heaved himself away from the wall. "Follow me, Professor."

Nickie rose. "Ambassador, would you happen to have a tape measure? Alain will want to know the exact dimensions."

"This is a hardware emporium, Professor," replied Eamon Douglass. "I think it likely that we have several hundred tape measures. Feel free to take your pick."

"Oh, gosh, I knew that," giggled Nickie Farrell with a look of girlish chagrin that Douglass might have found charming if the professor been an authentic female. "After you, Mr. Barlow...I mean, Mike."

The ambassador watched them go, his eye on Nickie's rear end and firm calves. When the door closed he muttered, "Goddamn deviant." He picked up the sketch and studied it. Alain Michaels —obviously a homosexual— really knew his stuff. It almost seemed a shame that his elegant memorial would be blown to smithereens, but some things couldn't be helped. Windfield College needed to be wiped out. Meeting Nickie Farrell had only deepened Douglass's resolve. A college that would knowingly hire a transsexual madman to teach impressionable young people...well, any college that committed such an immoral crime was worse than Sodom and had to be destroyed for the good of the country. Come April Fool's Day, at the moment Douglass triggered the Redeemer he would make sure that Professor Nickie Farrell was standing right beside him.

The door to the office opened. Nickie preceded Big Mike into the office. "That is a beautiful piece of sculpture, Ambassador Douglass! It must weigh an absolute ton, but I'm sure Alain can work it into your design."

"Splendid. Tell Mr. Michaels that I want it to sit on a pedestal, two or three feet high. Marble, granite, whatever he decides."

Nickie pulled out a little spiral pad and jotted a few notes. "Pedestal, two three feet. Anything else?"

"As I said, it's imperative that we get started immediately. How quickly can Michaels finalize the design? Money is no concern. I want it done fast."

"Yes, sir. I'll tell him."

"I think," said the ambassador, looking at Big Mike, "that it would be prudent to set the sundial on its foundation while your student body is away on vacation. That's liable to be a somewhat hazardous operation, with heavy lifting equipment, and the fewer idle spectators, the less chance of anyone getting injured."

"Good point." Nickie made another note. "Classes resume on Tuesday the second of January. We'll aim for sometime before that."

"Excellent. You have my telephone number, Professor. Keep me informed, and don't worry about the time of day or night. I don't require much sleep. As I told President Lindsey, I intend this to be a Spring Picnic people will remember for a very long while. With your assistance, I believe I can live up to that promise." He stood and extended his hand. "Thank you for your good work."

Nickie shook hands. "You're welcome, Ambassador Douglass. I'm honored to be associated with your project, and I'll do everything in my power to make sure it turns out exactly the way you want."

"In that case, I'm sure it will. Goodbye, Professor Farrell. And, Merry Christmas."

"Merry Christmas, gentlemen." Nickie picked up her briefcase and left the office.

The ambassador lowered himself back into the desk chair, and addressed Big Mike: "Well?"

"That ain't no guy. No way."

"Fooled you, didn't he? But the professor is as much a man as you or I. That so-called "woman" is a sordid counterfeit, the product of such decadent medical knavery as the world has seldom known."

Big Mike shook his head. "Damn to hell."

Ambassador Douglass laughed and banged his shillelagh down on the desk top. "That's exactly what I'm going to do, Mr. Barlow. Damn *him*, and all the rest of those Windfield perverts, straight to the depths of Hell."

Chapter Twelve
Christmas Eve

Wielding needle and thread, Alex Steward sat at the kitchen island in his eldest son's suburban Atlanta home, painstakingly stringing cranberries into garlands for the family Christmas tree. He'd already managed to puncture his thumb with cranberry juice a half dozen times, and now he did it again.

"*Oww!*" Alex stuck the throbbing thumb in his mouth.

His daughter-in-law Marcie, an athletically-built blonde child psychologist, glanced up from her KitchenAid mixer. "Poor Dad," she commiserated. "Infantile regression, huh?"

"Hah, hah. It's a good thing these berries are red already. The blood doesn't even show."

A tow-headed youngster charged into the kitchen. "Grandpa! You wanna play *Galactic Extinction* with me?" Craig Steward Junior waved a wireless video controller. "C'mon, Grandpa! I'll be Lord Krakenzoid, and you can be the Praxonian Deathbot."

"Grandpa's busy making decorations, honey," chided his mother. "Don't you want everything to look pretty tonight when Santa drops in?"

"Is he bringing me a mountain bike?"

Marcie pursed her lips. "Well, I suppose anything's possible. As long as you don't blow it before he gets here."

"Don't worry, I won't!" The boy scampered away.

"Way to go, Mom. I owe you one." Alex picked a plump cranberry out of a bowl and cautiously threaded it onto the chain. "Do I look like a Praxonian Deathbot?"

"Not really. The Deathbot is covered with iridescent scales," said Marcie. "But you do resemble Lord Krakenzoid."

Alex lobbed a cranberry at her, which she neatly fielded with one hand and popped in her mouth. "No throwing food, Grandpa."

A fleeting smile, then Alex's expression turned serious. "Marcie, may I ask you something?"

"Of course, Dad," his daughter-in-law replied, sliding a trayful of cookies into the oven. Ever since Alex's arrival she'd been wondering when he would choose to unburden himself of whatever was bothering him. "Anything at all."

"You have a brother who's gay, don't you?"

"Uh-huh." Marcie nodded, concealing her surprise. "Damon. He lives out in Santa Cruz with his partner. They breed show whippets. Little barking speed demons. Why?"

"When you were growing up, did he ever seem like...a girl?"

She shook her head and laughed. "My gosh, yes. Dame was a born princess. He used to arrange elegant tea parties for my Barbie dolls, picked out my party dresses, braided my hair, everything. All the girls adored him. They were absolutely crushed when he came out."

"Okay, but did you get the idea that he would rather have been a girl?"

Puzzled, Marcie said, "Well, I've seen him do drag a couple of times. He looks better in high heels than I do, damn him."

"I guess I'm not making myself clear. What I mean is, did he ever say that he wanted to be a girl? Or tell you that he *was* a girl?"

After washing out her mixing bowl Marcie placed it in the dish rack and perched on a stool by her father-in-law. "Dad," she touched his arm, "what's this all about?"

"Nothing, nothing." Alex stabbed at a cranberry with his needle, jammed it into his thumb instead, and winced in agony. "Jesus *Christ.*"

"Give me that." Marcie took the cranberry garland and laid it on the granite countertop. "Now," she said, "talk to me."

Her father-in-law massaged his hurt thumb. Not looking at her he asked, "What do you know about...so-called transsexuals?"

Marcie blinked. "Well, Dad, it's an unusual occurrence. The more modern term is Gender Identity Disorder. It isn't fully understood, and there's a lot of disagreement among health professionals as to how it should be diagnosed, treated, and so forth."

"But they mostly start out as homosexuals, right?"

"Not necessarily," Marcie shook her head. "In fact the general consensus is that true GID has little or nothing to do with sexual preference."

"I don't understand."

"This is far from my area of expertise," admitted Marcie, "but the way I understand it, Gender Identity Disorder has to do with how a person feels inside," she tapped her chest, "while sexual preference simply refers to whether a person likes to sleep with men, women, or both."

Alex Steward rubbed his face with both hands. "I see, said the blind man."

His daughter-in-law gave him a searching look. "Dad," she asked softly, "have you actually met someone like that? A transsexual woman?"

He sat silent for a moment then nodded. "Yes."

Marcie waited.

"She's a new assistant professor of English at Windfield."

"A colleague? Well, that's interesting." Marcie smiled. "What's her name?"

Alex swallowed. "Nickie Farrell."

"Nickie Farrell," Marcie repeated. "Pretty name." She paused. "Has she had reassignment surgery yet? Do you know?"

"Yes, several years ago. Everything's done."

"Good for her. It's a long and wrenching process. Is Nickie nice?"

Alex mutely stared at the countertop.

"Oh, my. You're drawn to her." Marcie covered his hand with her own. "Gosh, Dad. That must be complicated for you."

"I had no clue she was...like that. We went on a few dates, everything was going along fine. Better than fine. And then..." Alex frowned miserably. "Suddenly there was a story about her in the school newspaper. She granted a whole interview to a student reporter, but never said a word to me."

"Well, maybe she was afraid," Marcie suggested. "Think about how difficult it would be for her to tell something like this to a man. And not just any man, but one she found attractive. She'd have no idea how you might react." After a beat: "How *did* you react, Dad?"

Alex hesitated. "I ended our relationship."

"But why?"

"*Why?* " He looked at his daughter-in-law as if she was simpleminded. "Because I can't fall in love with a woman who used to be a man, that's why! Even if she's beautiful and smart and gracious, and... anyway, I just can't."

"Do you think Nickie Farrell is a man?" Marcie asked. "Do you, Dad?"

"No. Maybe. Hell, I don't know what I think," Alex gruffly replied. "Doesn't matter. It's finished."

"Dad..."

He roughly picked up the cranberry chain. "I don't want to talk about this any longer. I'd prefer that you not mention it to Craig, either. Okay?"

"All right." Marcie slid off her stool. "But can I say one more thing? If you're attracted to Professor Farrell it doesn't mean you're weird, or gay, or depraved. All it means is that you like her. Period. She's a woman who just didn't happen to be born female. And, Dad? I really hope you're not throwing away something precious because of shame or fear. That would be a terribly sad waste." She kissed him on the cheek. "For both of you."

<hr>

Hidden a quarter of a mile in among the trees at the end of a brush-choked dirt road –actually little more than two rock-strewn ruts– was a secluded spot where Gander Creek, meandering up against a massive stone escarpment, doubled back on itself to form a deep pool. A broad sandy area created by the swirling current bordered this pool and was known to the locals as Tyler's Beach. Since the saw-toothed ingress road was only navigable by truck and could easily wreck a differential, few people bothered to visit Tyler's Beach except for occasional fishermen or the most determined teenage make-out artists.

Wearing bulky jackets and boots to ward off the afternoon cold, Cale Pittman and Lloyd Skinner squatted on the sand next to a propped fishing pole, sharing a quart of Southern Comfort. Cale had wanted to start a fire but Lloyd had dissuaded him, saying that rangers were always on the lookout for smoke and it wouldn't do to attract their attention with an illegal campfire. The baited line in the water hadn't been touched but neither man cared. The fishing was just an excuse to go off by themselves. Earlier in Stuarton, already well into his Christmas Eve celebration with a twelve-pack of Miller, Jay-Bo had tossed them the keys to his pickup with the observation that they'd catch pneumonia a hell of a lot sooner than any damn fish.

"So anyway," Lloyd passed the bottle to Pittman, "I was thinkin' maybe it's time we head down to New Orleans. Whattya say?"

Cale tipped the bottle back, his eyes on the motionless tip of the fishing rod. "What's your rush, partner? The Big Easy isn't going anywhere."

Lloyd shrugged and blew into his fingers, which ached from the cold. "Yeah, but why hang around here? Virginia sucks, Cale. Always has. Nothin' but white trash, niggers, and rich assholes." He spat on the sand. "Did you see their faces the other night in that fuckin' restaurant? Lookin' at us like we were lower than pig shit."

"Yes, I saw." With a mirthless grin: "We will avenge that affront to our warrior honor. *Übermenschen* cannot allow such disrespect to remain unpunished." He lit a cigarette. "Payback, partner. Very soon."

"Cale, I'm with you all the way, you know that, but..." Lloyd stared at the pool's surface, where random eddies and swirls hinted at turbulence below. "Those richies run things." He picked up a rock and tossed it into the water, where it splashed and disappeared. "You and me..." He paused. "I mean, I wish we could change things, but I don't see how we can."

Pittman puffed smoke and handed Lloyd the Southern Comfort. "Even the bravest Superiorman can suffer doubts. But don't worry, partner. Your warrior spirit is intact." His dark blue eyes crinkled at the corners. "As I can personally attest. Anyway, I'm not ready to leave yet. For one thing, I still have to investigate that transsexual deviant up at the college...Well, will you look there!"

The fishing rod was bending downward in short jerks. Lloyd grabbed it and began reeling in the line. "Probably just snagged a drifting branch."

"Maybe not." Cale Pittman got to his feet. Lloyd wound a few more times and dragged a small pale catfish out onto the sand. It lay there, gasping weakly, the line protruding from its whiskered mouth.

"Looks like he swallowed the hook," Lloyd put down the rod. "Hold on, there's a hook remover in the tackle box."

"What for?" Cale Pittman grasped the sand-covered catfish firmly in one hand and with the other sharply jerked the line. The hook ripped free, along with bloody remnants of the fish's innards. "See? No problem." Picking up the bait knife, Cale laid the spasming fish on the piece of driftwood. With careful deliberation, he jammed the steel point into one of its eyes.

"Now, finish him off." He withdrew the knife and held it out. "You are an *Übermensch*. There is nothing you cannot do."

Lloyd took the knife and stabbed out the catfish's remaining eye. The dying creature flapped its tail once against the driftwood before Pittman hurled it into Gander Creek, where it floated upside down in a stain of blood and was soon swept away by the current.

Cale squatted by the water's edge, scrubbing the knife and his hands with sand to remove the fish residue. Drying his hands on a rag, he stood up and faced Lloyd. "See? *Der Wille zur Macht*." Placing his hands on Lloyd's shoulders. "The will to power, partner. It belongs to *us*. Herr Nietzsche would be proud of you. I know I am." Cale drew Lloyd closer and kissed him on the mouth. Drawing back: "What do you say we go in the truck and celebrate? After all, it's almost God's birthday."

Carefully folding the edges so as not to tear the pretty silver paper, Robin Thompson wrapped Collie's Christmas present and secured the ends with tape. She hoped he would like the sweater she'd picked out. It was a V-neck pullover, blue with light brown markings. She smiled and attached a ribbon bow to the package, thinking of how the colors would perfectly complement his eyes. She felt very blessed this year, and intended to thank God with all her heart at church this evening. Collie would be there beside her, helping to prepare and serve Yuletide dinner for the less fortunate. What better way to spend Christmas Eve? She went to her living area and placed the wrapped present under her small but brightly-decorated tree.

On the television a pastor was preaching about how necessary it was, in this sinful day and age, for God-fearing folks to keep a watchful eye out for the proverbial wolf in sheep's clothing. Backstabbers and liars, cheats and rapscallions were always lying in wait for the unwary. "None of us is immune from being deceived," the pastor cautioned. "Faith alone is not enough. Remember, even our Savior was double-crossed by Judas in the Garden of Gethsemane."

Adjusting an angel ornament on the tree, Robin suddenly paused, then snapped her fingers. "Double-crossed...*That's* what I meant to look up."

She connected her laptop to the Internet and typed "Doublecross Dingbats" into the Google window. The screen instantly filled with listings. She clicked on a site called "Fontstocks.com". Eye-burning orange letters screamed: "THOUSANDS OF COOL DOWNLOADABLE FONTS HERE!!!" Beneath was a bewildering array of hyperlinked indexes: Win, Mac, Postcript, TrueType, Open, Free, Commercial. In another search window she again typed "Doublecross Dingbats".

"What in the world?"

Robin was looking at the oddest set of typeface characters she'd ever seen. They weren't letters at all; instead she could make out little black cats, daggers dripping blood, blackbirds, footprints, playing cards, keys, smoking pistols, martini glasses and skulls. Underneath the characters was a small space labeled "Try Me!" With odd trepidation, she typed in her name and hit the "enter" button:

Robin would never say "I'll be damned", but staring at the bizarre hieroglyphics a similar sentiment crossed her mind. She deleted her name and typed "Luanne Skinner":

Seeing the coffin, she shuddered and tried "Ambassador Douglass":

Guns, coffins, bloody knives...the macabre characters gave her the creeps. Robin closed the window and shut down her computer. Without question, the Doublecross Dingbats were the brainchild of a decidedly offbeat personality. But how on earth could Luanne Skinner have known about them? For the life of her Robin couldn't imagine any possible link between the eerie symbols and Collie's mother. Or, for that matter, Eamon Douglass. On the other hand, it stretched the limits of plausibility to believe that the dying woman had started babbling about Doublecross Dingbats purely by coincidence. There had to be a logical explanation; she felt it in her gut. But with Luanne in her grave, it would likely remain a mystery forever. Which, Robin decided, was just as well. The dead were entitled to keep their secrets.

From her closet she selected a royal blue velvet dress and laid it on the bed. Robin wanted to look special tonight for her man. As for the spooky font she'd found, mentioning it would only remind Collie of Luanne's last moments and make him feel sad again. Under no circumstances would she allow that to happen. Christmas Eve was an occasion for joy, not sorrow. The Doublecross Dingbats had nothing to do with their lives and Robin intended to erase them from her mind. Permanently.

⸺ ◉ ⸺

Some four hundred and fifty miles to the west, in a comfortable two-storey house owned by her parents, Cinda Vanderhart sat cross-legged on the floor of her upstairs bedroom, magnifying glass in hand, examining page after page of the 1979 Windfield senior almanac. Preoccupied with dysfunctional family drama since returning home, she hadn't been free to resume her search until, completely exasperated, she'd slammed into her room and locked the door.

Cinda methodically moved her magnifying glass down the row of photos, taking a few seconds to examine each one. She skipped over the female, black, and Asian students, concentrating on the white male faces. Eyler...no. Ezzell...no. Factor...no. She tightened her grip on the glass, undeterred. Faine...no.

A timid double knock sounded at the door. Cinda called out in an annoyed tone, "Go away, I'm busy." She cast her eyes ceilingward and returned to the class book. Falcone...no. Falmouth...no.

The double knock was repeated. She heard her mother's voice: "Cinda? May I come in, dear?"

"Oh, for Chrissake." Cinda shoved the almanac under her bed, sprang up and unlocked the door. Blocking the entrance: "What is it, Mother? I'm doing research."

Allison Vanderhart, a perfect middle-aged Midwestern cliché, nervously fingered her coral bead necklace. "I don't mean to interrupt, dear, but I wanted to remind you that we're going over to the Kagan's for a little Christmas Eve get-together. Jeremy's home from Notre Dame. Won't it be nice to see him again?"

"Mother, the Kagans are *Jewish*. What the hell are they doing having a Christmas Eve party?"

"Bernice and Ira are very respectful of everyone's beliefs. Not like some people," Mrs. Vanderhart added with a pointed look at her daughter. "They celebrate all the holidays. I think it's lovely."

"Gee, isn't that open-minded of them. I'll pass, thanks. Tell Jeremy hello for me, and ask him if he still eats his own boogers." Cinda stood with her arms crossed. "You can leave now."

"Cinda, please," her mother pleaded. "We don't have much family time together anymore, with you away at school. Would it kill you to come with us just this once?"

Cinda lifted her shoulders in a gesture of utter indifference. "I told you, Mother, I'm doing some important research. Catch y'later."

She made as if to close the door but Mrs. Vanderhart blocked it with her hand and pushed her way into the room.

Cinda glowered, thrusting out her jaw: "*Excuse* me, Mother!"

"You listen to me, young lady. This is still our home, and you'll behave like a civilized person when you're here." Mrs. Vanderhart gestured at her daughter's camouflage sweat pants and ripped t-shirt. Now put on some...some decent clothes, and get yourself ready to go."

"Make me." Cinda threw herself on the bed, raised her knees and spread her legs as wide as possible. "Decent enough for ya?"

Mrs. Vanderhart averted her eyes. "For God's sake, Cinda. Don't you have any self-respect?"

"As a matter of fact, Mother, I do." Cinda closed her legs and hopped off the bed. "But none of it is tied up in phony Yuletide spirit, uptight fundamentalist hypocrisy, or pitiful self-hating Jews like the Kagans. So leave me out of it. You and Daddy and my plastic dimwit sister can go sing "Jingle Bell Rock" and slam eggnog for Jesus until you drop."

Cinda's mother said, her voice shaking with anger: "Why are you so hateful? Where did we go wrong with you? How could you possibly turn out so *different?* "

"Beats me. Did you have a fling with the mailman?"

Allison Vanderhart slapped her daughter hard across the face.

Cinda slowly rubbed her fiery red cheek. "Well, thank you very much for that. Merry Christmas, Mommy Dearest."

Her mother stared in shock for a few seconds, then burst into tears.

"Oh, oh, oh," she cried, covering her face. "What have I done? God forgive me!" She turned away, her head hanging, sobbing as if her heart would break. "I'm a terrible mother. No wonder you hate me. I won't bother you anymore, Cinda. I'm sorry. You do whatever you want."

Seeing her stumble for the door Cinda rushed forward. "No, Mother. Wait. I'm the one who's sorry." She hugged her weeping parent. "I shouldn't have said those beastly things. Don't cry, Mother. Please. I don't hate you. I love you! You're a great mom. The best."

Holding her mother close, waiting for her sobs to subside, Cinda realized with an ache in her heart that the older woman was terrified; terrified of an ever-changing world that grew more confusing every day, a world where daughters pierced themselves and spouted menacing lesbian rhetoric, a world where nothing was sacred anymore, where traditional values were sneered at as benighted and stupid. An inside-out world where, unthinkable as it seemed, a man could choose to become a woman. Cinda's mother could never comprehend these things; but that didn't make her a bad person. It was just that her horizons had always been limited, and she lacked the ability to adapt. Allison Vanderhart lived a conformist life safely bounded by religion, convention, and routine. That was okay. Cinda was younger, stronger, smarter, and freer. Time was on her side, and she didn't need to torment her mother any more. In that regard, at least, she could afford to grow up.

"I apologize for being such a bitch." Cinda kissed her mother. "What the heck, it's Christmas Eve. I'll come with you tonight, okay?"

"You will?" Mrs. Vanderhart looked up, red-eyed. "Are you sure?"

"I'm sure." Cinda kissed her again. "How can I resist the chance to see Jeremy Kagan?"

"Well, I'm so glad, dear." Mrs. Vanderhart pulled out a tissue, wiped her eyes and blew her nose. "I love you too, Cinda. And I don't mean to be such a pushy old..."

"You're not," Cinda interrupted firmly. Taking a deep breath:

"Look, Mother, just for you I'll wear a skirt." She cringed inwardly. "And some lipstick."

Her mother's expression brightened. "A little mascara, too? You have such pretty eyes, dear."

"All right, Mother," Cinda groaned. "Mascara, too. I probably won't even recognize myself."

"Just look for the beautiful young woman," smiled Mrs. Vanderhart. "God bless you, dear. We'll be leaving in about an hour, all right?"

"I'll be ready."

Cinda waited until the door closed, then heaved a dispirited sigh and retrieved the Windfield class book from under her bed. She began scanning more photos through the magnifying glass, but her enthusiasm had dimmed. Fannon...no. Farmer...no. She let the magnifying glass drop, thinking, what's the use? I'll never find it. She raised the glass and looked again. Farquhar...no. Farrington...

"Omigod." Cinda bent and peered closely. Her heart began racing. She carried the book to her desk, laid it flat and shined a gooseneck lamp directly on the page. Another quick inspection, and all doubt vanished. The boyish features had a familiar cast, but the eyes...they were absolutely unmistakable.

"It's *her*," she whispered, chills running up her spine. "Nickie Farrell was Nick Farrington, Class of 1979." She raised a triumphant fist in the air. "Merry Christmas, Ms. Farrell. I *gotcha!*"

———— ◦((◦))◦ ————

Dressed only in her underwear and a peach-colored slip, Nickie Farrell sat on her bed and tried not to focus on the fact that she was alone on Christmas Eve. To a certain extent it had been her own choice; Nickie had declined Joanne Markwith's entreaties to come spend the holiday with them, because she didn't want to become a permanent appendage on someone else's family. No one else had invited her.

Nickie picked up her television remote and flipped through the channels, all of which were broadcasting standard holiday fare extolling the joys of family and friends. After counting four channels playing "Silent Night" she clicked off the television. That afternoon she'd bought a rib steak and she briefly thought about broiling it, but the notion of sitting by herself and consuming a slab of red meat was anything but appetizing. The window beyond her sheer curtains showed black, but a check of her watch showed it was only five-thirty. Nickie picked up the latest sexy thriller by Eileen Waverly, a favorite author, but set it aside after a few minutes, unable to concentrate, and checked her watch again. Five-forty.

With a small groan she got off her bed, went into the bathroom, combed her hair, brushed her teeth, decided that her complexion resembled a relief map of Mars, went back out to the bedroom, stretched out on the bed again and stared up at the white ceiling. Unbidden, an image came into her mind of a small pet gerbil she'd had when she was a boy in grammar school. Roderick Rodent. Roderick had lived in a cramped 3-gallon fish tank too small for him to do anything except dig in the wood shavings and sleep. One morning Nickie found the little creature dead, lying on its side with its tiny mouth half-open. When tearfully asked why Roderick had expired, Mrs. Farrington had replied that he died from loneliness. Young Nick had found it a most unsatisfactory answer. Nobody died of loneliness.

"Shows how much you knew," Nickie said aloud. She sat up and stared at the cordless phone on the night table, her face a mix of longing and reluctance. She held the receiver in her lap, wrestling with indecision. Finally she muttered something unintelligible then punched in a number and raised the phone to her ear.

After three rings there came an answer: "Farrington residence."

Nickie recognized the patrician, faintly aloof voice of her mother, Amelia. "Mom? Hi. It's me." She pulled up a bra strap which had slipped off her shoulder. "Nick," she added in a deeper masculine tone which echoed strangely in the room. "I just wanted to wish everybody a Merry Christmas."

Amelia Farrington said, "Did you, now? Well, how very thoughtful of you, *Nicholas*." The hostile emphasis was unmistakable. "Merry Christmas to you too, I'm sure."

Nickie shut her eyes. "How is everybody, Mom?"

"Your father had another attack. He's only been home from the hospital for three days."

"Oh, *no*. His heart again?"

"Of course. What else?" Nickie had always thought that her mother would have coolly gone down on the *Titanic* without batting an eye. "Dr. Blackstone thinks the next episode might kill him."

"Jesus, Mom. Can I say hello to Dad?"

She didn't reply for several seconds. "I'm afraid that's out of the question. The doctor said he must avoid stress of any kind, and the fact is, *Nicholas*, it's impossible for your father to think about you without becoming apoplectic." Mrs. Farrington had also majored in English, at Bryn Mawr. "So unless you want to take a chance on finishing him off..." She let the sentence hang unfinished.

Nickie's shoulders drooped. This call, like all the others, was a wretched mistake. Her parents regarded their son's gender transition as a self-indulgent outrage, a scandalous stain on the Farrington's good name. "Nickie" was a disgrace, an outcast, and "she" would never be welcomed back into the fold. They'd die first. Literally.

There was a commotion on the line, muffled words which sounded like an argument, then Nickie heard the strident voice of her brother Bennet, coarsened from years of carousing: "Yo, Bro! Whassup?"

"Hello, Ben. Merry Christmas. How are Sandy and the kids?"

"Same shit, different day," answered Bennet. Nickie could tell that her brother had been drinking. They had once been incredibly close. "How's it goin' with you? You're a teacher now at some redneck college in Kentucky, right?"

Nickie knew it was pointless to correct him. "I'm doing fine, Ben."

"Awesome, dude." Despite being forty-four, Bennet always made a concerted –unsuccessful– effort to sound like a twenty-year-old. "Hey, man, you got a boyfriend?" Bennet guffawed. "Christ, I never thought I'd be askin' my brother that. But then again I never thought my *brother* would go mental and chop off his crank, either. Ain't life a bitch?" With an unpleasant snigger: "Bitch? Get it?"

"You've always been a master of witty repartee, Ben."

"Uh-oh. Is that sarcasm I hear? That's hardly ladylike, Bro'."

"Ben, listen. I'm worried about Dad."

"*You're* worried about Dad?" Bennet mocked, his disgust plain. "Say, Boss, who do you think ruined his life in the first place? Mom? Me? Nope, it was good ol' Nick-*key* Farrell, the shemale wonder-fruit, who couldn't wait to go to Canada and have the Farrington family jewels reconfigured into a bearded clam. Worried about Dad, my ass. Eat shit, Nick."

"Stop it, Ben! I never wanted to hurt anybody. I'm sorry if you have unresolved issues but you're not being fair. I love Dad as much as you do!"

"Yeah, yeah. Sure you do. Tell y'what, my dear sister. Why don't you go give some unsuspecting sap a nice Christmas blowjob and make him think he just got sucked off by a real woman?"

"*Shut up!* " Nickie shrieked, but the phone had gone dead in her hand. She flung it away and hurled herself on the bed, bawling, tears soaking into the pillow clutched in front of her face.

After an interval the racking sobs diminished, then ceased. Nickie sat up and pushed aside the sodden pillow. "No. I won't do this."

She wiped her swollen eyes with a tissue and recited aloud: "God, grant me the serenity to accept the things I cannot change, the courage to change the things I can, and the wisdom to know the difference." Then she went into the living room, where a copy of the *Middleville Gazette* lay on the coffee table. In the back pages Nickie found a listing of area churches. She ran her finger along the notices and stopped by the Good Shepherd Community Church, which offered "Christmas Eve festivities and worship service. All welcome." She closed the paper and went to make herself presentable, never having noticed the obituary section on the opposite page, at the bottom of which was a brief commemorative sentence about the passing of a woman named Luanne Jane Skinner.

⫸◆⫷

For as long as anyone could remember, Ambassador Eamon

Douglass had espoused Ebenezer Scrooge's attitude toward Christmas, so famously expressed as "Bah, humbug!" He'd invariably insisted that Shamrocks be kept devoid of traditional holiday accoutrements, dismissing them as "tinsel for idiots." But this year, to the staff's surprise, he had ordered them to erect a Christmas tree in his study. It stood merrily twinkling beside the fireplace now, lavishly decorated with expensive crystal ornaments and countless colored lights.

From his desk chair the ambassador contemplated the lovely tree, an expression of sour amusement on his face. Centered on the green desk blotter rested the cell phone he'd received from "Father George" Volka. Beside it, standing guard, the glass wolf snarled its perpetual snarl.

"I don't know where I'll be this time next year, Barlow," Douglass addressed Big Mike, who sat with his boots stretched toward the crackling fire, "but I doubt it'll be the sort of place to have Christmas trees." He took a sip of whiskey from a crystal tumbler. "So I got this one, just to see if I'll miss the damn things." Brandishing his shillelagh at the tree: "Well, I won't. It's a bunch of pagan tomfoolery."

Big Mike said nothing. He'd never given a crap about Christmas trees. He wanted some whiskey, but Douglass had forbidden it, saying that this was no time for him to be getting liquored up.

The ambassador consulted a gold pocket watch. "Why haven't they called yet?" He moved the glass wolf to the other side of the cell phone. "I hate this waiting. Makes me as crazy as a menstruating woman."

Big Mike looked up, his features contorted with revulsion. "Jesus, don't talk about that."

Douglass squinted at his consultant. "What did you say?"

"Women. That bleedin' thing they do." Mike Barlow's voice cracked. "Goddamn disgustin'."

Ambassador Douglass uttered a harsh laugh. "What's the matter with you, Barlow? How the hell do you think you got here? That's the way their system works. Of course it's disgusting. Almost everything about women *is*."

"Just don't wanna talk about it," grumbled Big Mike, shifting uneasily in his armchair. Unbeknownst to anyone, as a young child he'd once accidentally surprised his parents in the throes of passion, which in Amos Barlow's case took the form of drunkenly raping his wife any-time he felt so inclined, even when she was having her monthly period. Unluckily, this was one of those times. Enraged at being interrupted, Mike's father had grabbed him by the scruff of the neck, and scream-ing "So, you wanna get a taste of it, you little shit?" had jammed the boy's nose into his mother's bloody crotch. Irreversibly traumatized to the depths of his soul, Mike had developed a neurotic dread about a woman's cycle, especially the blood. Tampon commercials made him queasy. In the supermarket he gave the feminine products aisle as wide a berth as possible. Of course no one guessed that a formidable ruf-fian like Mike Barlow suffered from such an extreme –and bizarre– phobia. If they had, he would have killed them.

Ambassador Douglass found it rather interesting that his homicid-al henchman nursed an aversion to this simple fact of human biology, but he was distracted from further speculation by the shrill electronic ring tones which suddenly erupted from the cell phone.

"About damn time!" He carefully lifted the phone, punched a but-ton and held it to his ear. He heard a voice say in a thick down-under accent: "The Redeemer is come."

Eamon Douglass enunciated, "Blessed be the Savior."

"Roit." A brief pause. "Oi'm speakin' with E.D., then?"

"Yes, this is E.D." The ambassador held a Mont Blanc pen poised over a spiral pad. "I'm ready to receive instructions."

Big Mike watched as Douglass wrote with sharp jabbing motions. "Yes...south from Cambridge...past St. Michael's...three miles...Terrapin Lane? Yes...launch ramp...okay. Understood." With a piercing glance at Mike: "My associate will arrive on time, I assure you. Without fail." He set down his pen. "I beg your pardon? Ah, indeed. Merry Christmas to you, sir. Goodbye."

The ambassador laid the cell phone down by the glass wolf. "It's here, Barlow!" His exultant grin stretched horribly beneath the single gleaming eye. "I admit I had my doubts but the damn thing is finally *here*, by Christ. It's time for you to start earning that million dollars. Go get it for me."

"Now?"

"Of course now! Right this goddamn minute," scowled Douglass. "They're expecting you tomorrow at seven o'clock sharp. It's perfect timing. Nobody pays attention to anything on Christmas morning except opening their presents. Hell, an atom bomb could go off and the imbeciles wouldn't notice. I assume you've been down to the Eastern Shore?"

Mike shrugged. "Sure."

"Good. Listen carefully." The ambassador read from the notes he'd written. "Do you think you can remember that?"

"Yeah," said Big Mike. "I go to that abandoned launch ramp and wait for them to call."

"Exactly so." The ambassador handed him the cell phone as if it was made of solid gold. "I suggest you not lose this."

"Yep." Mike stowed the phone in his jacket.

"There is one more thing." Douglass opened a desk drawer and extracted a thick brown manila envelop "I find myself in a generous holiday spirit. This," he brandished the envelope, "is a gratuity for our friendly delivery men. Twenty thousand in cash, which you will give them with my profound best wishes."

Big Mike's eyes narrowed slightly.

"However, if they are unable to accept it for some reason –like being dead, for instance– you may keep the money for yourself." The ambassador leveled a cold look at his special consultant. "Any questions?"

"Nope. I get it."

Douglass placed the envelope in Mike's outstretched palm, and picked up his glass wolf. "I am about to write a great piece of history, Barlow. A piece of history which will change the world. Your part in that history, while ancillary, is nonetheless of considerable import." He shook the wolf at Big Mike. "There better not be any foul-ups."

Big Mike rose from his chair, clutching the manila envelope. "I'll take care of it."

"See that you do." The ambassador set down the wolf. Pointing a forefinger at his special consultant: "If anything goes wrong, if you don't bring my Redeemer back here safe and sound, I will fill a bathtub with menstrual blood and drown you in it."

The color drained from Mike Barlow's face. "Nothing will go wrong."

"Well, what are you standing there for?" Douglass waved his hand in curt dismissal. "Get out of here." As Mike hurried from the study: "Merry goddamn Christmas."

————)(()(————

In the social hall of the Good Shepherd Community Church a Christmas Eve celebration was in full noisy swing. Under cheerful green-and-red garlands, serving tables were piled with platters of roast turkey, stuffing, mashed potatoes, gravy, candied yams, and corn on the cob. An assortment of home-made pies, cakes, and holiday cookies sweetened the air with delectable odors. All throughout the big room people sat talking, eating or singing in a jolly holiday spirit. Children played with toys they'd been given by Santa, a florid-faced old farrier named Hank Stiles. Many of the families came from unfortunate circumstances; but on this night, at least, their cares were temporarily set aside.

Robin Thompson circulated about the hall chatting with the guests, offering more food, exclaiming with the children over their gifts. More than a few young fellows bent lively glances at Robin because she looked very charming in her velvet holiday dress, but she obviously had eyes for only one man. Wearing a white kitchen apron over his coat and tie, Collie Skinner helped Reverend Shorr carve the turkeys and dish up the food. Every so often he would glance up and wink, making Robin giggle with pleasure.

"Have you seen that nephew of mine?" Beryl Jamison stood at Robin's elbow. "I get plumb nervous when he's not in sight. Chuckie gets into scrapes better than anybody alive."

"Boy was born to be hanged," sniffed Mrs. Greene, walking past with a plateful of mashed potatoes. "You mark my words."

"I'll find him, Mrs. Jamison." After a quick search Robin discovered Chuckie out in the back yard. Surrounded by an admiring circle of cohorts, he was demonstrating how to convert a disposable lighter and a can of spray varnish into a makeshift flamethrower.

Robin confiscated Chuckie's deadly contrivance and shooed the boys back inside before they froze or incinerated themselves. On her way back to the social hall she happened to glance into the main sanctuary and noticed a solitary figure seated in the rearmost pew. Wondering who it could be, Robin entered the church and saw that the person in the pew was a lady fashionably dressed in a dark suit and a fedora hat with a scarf-like band trailing off the back. Despite the evening hour she was wearing colorfully-tinted sunglasses.

"Hello," greeted Robin, halting by the pew. "Merry Christmas."

"Merry Christmas," responded the lady in a husky voice.

Something about her struck Robin as familiar. "Have you been with us before?"

"No, this is my first visit. Am I intruding?"

"Not at all," Robin quickly answered. "Everyone's welcome. We're glad you're here." She smiled. "My name is Robin."

"It's nice to meet you, Robin. I'm Nickie." With a melancholy smile: "That's a beautiful dress."

"Thank you." Robin hesitated, thinking, Nickie...? "Is everything all right?"

The lady stared toward the altar for a long moment. "Everything is the way it's meant to be."

"Would you like to join us in the social hall? There's lots of food. Our service doesn't start until later."

"That's very thoughtful, but I'd just like to sit here for awhile, if you don't mind." She added, "I haven't been to church in a long time. Too long."

"May I sit with you?"

The other woman silently nodded.

Robin settled on the pew cushion. "I love Christmas Eve, but sometimes I get a little sad remembering how it used to be with Mom and Dad. They've both passed on. The church is my family now."

At that moment Chuckie Jamison stuck his heavily-moussed head in the door, peering around with mischief-filled eyes. Robin extended a stern finger back toward the social hall, and the lad fled.

"Yours?" With a glance at Robin: "No, silly of me. You're much too young."

"I'm not even married. That's Chuckie Jamison. He's a good boy, just likes to get into trouble. You know how boys are."

"Actually, I don't," the lady named Nickie glumly admitted. "I never did."

"Do you have any children?"

Nickie shook her head. "I didn't when I had the chance, and now I can't." She looked down at her clasped hands. "I wish I did. Then I'd have a family."

Robin quietly asked, "Are your parents gone, too?"

"Gone? No, not gone. But...they don't want me in their life anymore."

"I'm sorry." Robin put her hand on top of Nickie's. "I don't understand that. Why would they not want their own child?"

"I...I changed," said Nickie. "In ways they couldn't understand. I became a different person from what they were used to and it made them terrifically angry. But I never meant any harm, or stopped loving them. I was only trying to find some peace in my life..." Her voice caught, and she fell silent.

Seeing a tear slide down from behind the other's sunglasses, Robin produced a tissue and offered it.

Nickie accepted the tissue. "Thanks." Removing her colored glasses, she carefully dabbed her eyes. "Quite a pity party I'm throwing myself, isn't it? Enough. It's Christmas Eve."

"Y-yes, that's right," Robin stammered. She stared at the lady's different-colored eyes, exact replicas of Collie's. Nickie! *Of course.* This was the woman from the Foxton Arms, the professor who'd had lunch with the white-haired gentleman. The fedora had prevented Robin from recognizing her at once, but it was her, without a doubt. And didn't that lesbian girl, the one to whom she'd stupidly given her number, have a bee in her bonnet about this lady? For no reason that she could pinpoint, Robin began to feel uneasy.

"Please forgive me if I've put a damper on your holiday. I'm fine, really. You should get back to your party. Your friends are probably wondering where you are...see?" Nickie gestured with her glasses toward the door. "I do believe that gentleman is looking for you."

Robin turned and saw Collie standing in the doorway. He waved, a bit uncertainly.

"A special friend of yours?" With a small smile: "He looks like a nice young man."

Suddenly feeling inexplicably spooked, Robin knew she had to prevent Collie from coming anywhere near Nickie the Windfield professor. The thought that these two mismatched sets of eyes might connect raised the short hairs on her neck. Robin quickly stood up and edged out of the pew.

"I'm sorry to leave you alone, Nickie, but I'm supposed to be keeping an eye on the children. I hope you feel better soon. Merry Christmas."

"Thank you." Nickie looked past her at Collie. "Go, enjoy this happy evening. God bless you. Merry Christmas."

Robin made her way up the aisle. She grasped Collie's hand and pulled him out of the sanctuary even as he was gazing curiously at the woman in the pew. "So," she said, "did you miss me?"

"You betcha," Collie grinned. "Who was that lady?"

"Just a visitor," Robin answered. "She's never been here before."

"Why's she sitting there by herself?" Collie halted. "Ask her to come in and have some dinner..."

"No."

Collie looked at Robin in surprise.

"I mean, she'd rather be by herself right now. She's having problems with her family, Nicholas. It's not a very Merry Christmas for her."

"Oh." Collie's face clouded. "I sure remember how that feels. Poor lady."

"I know." Robin took his hand. "But she's in God's house. He'll find a way to give her some comfort."

"Let's hope so," said Collie, and together they walked back to the social hall.

When the services began some time later Robin glanced toward the back of the church, but the rear pews were empty. Nickie the Windfield professor had disappeared.

———⟐———

Conrad Foley lived in a modest but comfortable split level house located on five secluded acres seven miles west of Middleville. His two-bedroom gray-shingled home was situated at the crest of a broad grass-covered hill that sloped down to a small brook bubbling along the property line. Several spreading sycamores and pin oaks dotted the hill, while smaller redbuds and dogwoods grew in profusion beside the water. The wooded slope rose again on the other side, presenting a bucolic vista of trees and greenery as far as the eye could see. A wide wooden deck projected from the house, where the Foxton Arms' maitre d' liked to sit and absorb the serenity of his country setting. As often as not he would see deer, fox, wild turkeys or other woodland creatures gamboling about by the stream. A widower for over thirty years since his young wife died from meningitis, Mr. Foley loved nothing more than this private retreat. His fully-equipped gourmet kitchen, prized collection of cookbooks, and meticulously-tended flower beds and garden provided him with everything he wanted in this world.

Under the deck, carefully stacked along a concrete foundation wall were several cords of seasoned firewood logs. Near them, a squat emergency generator which Mr. Foley had acquired due to the frequent power blackouts was wired into the house's electrical system with a thick black cable. Beside the generator, resting in a welded steel cradle was a twenty-five gallon drum of gasoline. A thin feeder pipe ran from the bottom of the drum to the generator. Although there were no obvious leaks, the gravel beneath the pipe was stained with oily petroleum residue.

Late Christmas Eve the house stood quiet and deserted in the light of a pallid moon. Mr. Foley was enjoying a holiday dinner with his niece's family in Winchester and didn't expect to return until late. But even if he'd been at home he might not have smelled the smoke coming from under the deck, where a Virginia Slim 120 cigarette, carefully folded into an unused Foxton Arms book of matches, was slowly burning down in a dry old bird's nest sitting under the generator's gasoline feed pipe. Nor would the maitre d' have been likely to spot the black Mustang GT parked under a cluster of low-hanging branches by the entrance to his long curving driveway.

The cigarette ash grew longer, gradually dropping off, until finally the glowing end burned into the book of matches, which ignited with a sulfurous *whoosh!* Immediately the old dry nest caught fire and burned fiercely, a blazing ball of yellow flame, directly beneath the feeder pipe.

The subsequent explosion was powerful enough to blow the wooden deck apart and scatter gasoline-soaked firewood in all directions. Within minutes one whole side of the house was a roaring mass of flames. As the conflagration grew, windows began to blow out. The painstakingly shaped holly shrubs by the front entrance shriveled, smoked, and caught fire. Inside the house, the maitre d's beloved cookbooks added fuel to the crackling inferno, blackening and crumbling into whirling spirals of sparking ash. Ten minutes after the explosion the entire house was transformed into a pillar of fire which lit up the tranquil countryside.

Out by the entrance to the driveway, the black Mustang drove out from the shadows and sped off into the night, a ghostly sound of laughter mixing with the engine's growl. As it pulled away an empty quart bottle of Southern Comfort sailed out of the window and smashed to pieces against a roadside boulder, where the glittering fragments wetly reflected an angry orange glow rising over the fiery ruins of Conrad Foley's cherished home.

Chapter Thirteen
Karmic Countdown

On the second morning after Christmas, Ambassador Douglass once again sat with Windfield President Fredericka Lindsey on the long black leather couch in her office.

"I must say, Ambassador Douglass," the Windfield College president commented, gesturing out the big picture window toward where a yellow Caterpillar backhoe was busily excavating the earth by the Randall Windfield Memorial, "your alacrity in getting things done is most impressive." She poured coffee from an elaborate silver samovar into a china cup and handed it to him. "I had no clue you could be ready to begin work this soon."

Douglass accepted the cup. "Madame President, I did not become a wealthy man by twiddling my thumbs or allowing my associates to twiddle theirs. Even when I had all the time in the world, which I no longer do, I abhorred dawdling." Through the window they could hear muffled diesel snorts from the laboring backhoe. "I gave you my pledge to have this project completed by April first." He sipped the rich brew. "This is just some preliminary foundation work, pouring concrete, setting in the weight-bearing steel footings and other mundane construction details." Such as, he didn't add, planting a Cesium 137 dirty bomb surrounded by several sealed heavy-duty PVC pipes packed with commercial-grade explosives. "Routine but necessary steps best taken in case the ground freezes."

Fredericka Lindsey looked out the window. "Seems like an awful lot of work for only one man. Can he do it all by himself?"

"My special consultant is exceptionally capable, Madame President. Over the years he has yet to fall short on any project I assign him." As two Australian smugglers could confirm, were they not at that moment being eaten by blue claw crabs at the bottom of the Choptank River. "Of course, when the above-ground decorative work is under way skillful artisans will be brought in. But for now, my man can handle it. If necessary he'll work nights as well. I assume that won't present a problem?"

"I don't see why it would. No one's on campus now. Except for us executives," she added with a little chuckle. "Work never stops at the administrative level, as I'm sure you know."

"A construction zone can be quite hazardous, Madame President. I suggest it be declared strictly off-limits. After all, I'd hate to see anyone get hurt."

"No need for concern. I'll see to it that your man's work isn't interrupted." Fredericka Lindsey set her cup down on the coffee table and picked up an artistic rendering of the new memorial. "It's sublime, Ambassador. The sundial is a brilliant touch. I'm so pleased. A number of the trustees had expressed misgivings that we'd be presented with something in the overstated style of Albert Speer."

The ambassador clenched his teeth. "That wouldn't do at all, would it?"

"Hardly," agreed President Lindsey. "But this is perfect. Truly remarkable."

More remarkable than you know, you liberal cow, thought Eamon Douglass. "Thank you, Madame President. I'm glad that you and the trustees approve. Of course the credit belongs mostly to Mr. Alain Michaels, who designed it. And to Professor Farrell, who recommended Mr. Michaels. An exemplary choice."

"Are you referring to Mr. Michaels, or the professor?"

"Both," smiled Ambassador Douglas.

"So I take it you're pleased with Professor Farrell?"

"Indeed so. I couldn't have asked for a better liaison. He has been efficient and..." The ambassador stopped in mid-sentence. With a cough: "*She* has been efficient, prompt, and reliable. I wish I could say the same about all of my employees."

President Lindsey gave the ambassador a cool appraising look. "Ambassador Douglass, you don't harbor any reservations about the professor because of her unusual personal circumstances, do you?"

"I do not," retorted Douglass. Seeing the woman's eyebrows shoot up he added in a milder tone, "I admit, Madame President, that when I first learned of Ms. Farrell's...um...status, I was startled. Frankly, such modern-day realities lie well outside my range of experience. But the professor's private affairs have nothing to do with the business at hand. Let me assure you that I have no objections whatsoever to working with the professor. In fact I am counting on her to be by my side on the day your new memorial is dedicated."

"I'm pleased to hear you say that," said Fredericka Lindsey. "Professor Farrell is an esteemed and valuable member of the Windfield community." She glanced at her watch. "Is there anything else we need to cover?"

"No, I think that brings us up to speed," answered Douglass, reaching for his shillelagh. "Ah, there is one more thing: I have taken the liberty of ordering a catered seafood buffet for the picnic. I hope you don't mind?"

Fredericka Lindsey had few passions other than Windfield and work, but seafood was one of them. "That's a wonderfully generous gesture, Ambassador, but..."

Eamon Douglass held up his hand. "But nothing, Madame President. I insist. Of course I respect the patriotic American hot dog, but I would like this year's picnic to be exceptionally well-attended. An array of fresh seafood does tend to attract people, wouldn't you say?"

Bemused, the president nodded. "No doubt, Ambassador. No doubt."

"Splendid. I have arranged for it to be catered by the Foxton Arms Restaurant. You've dined there, of course."

"Many times," said Fredericka Lindsey, thinking that a picnic-sized seafood spread from the Foxton Arms would cost more than a new BMW.

"Good. A young man there by the name of Skinner has been assigned the catering job." He rose and extended his hand. "Once again, Madame President, thank you for your time."

"My pleasure, Ambassador." Fredericka Lindsey shook the proffered palm. "On behalf of the college I want to thank you again for all you're doing. The new memorial will be an enduring legacy."

"The pleasure is mine, I assure you." He gazed out the window at the construction site, wondering if the Redeemer was in place yet. "In a few days I will celebrate my last New Year's Eve, President Lindsey. But I feel no sadness. Knowing what will be here after I am gone fills me with a great sense of joy." With a stiff little bow he walked out of Hendrix Windfield's office for the last time.

⸻ ◉ ⸻

Jay-Bo Skinner stretched luxuriously in his new BarcaLounger, popped another Old Milwaukee, drank deeply, and thought about Karma.

He didn't really understand what Karma was, but as Cale Pittman had explained it, the basic idea seemed to be that after the Universe had given you the shaft for long enough, it turned around and began shafting other folks while you finally caught a break. In this way, Pittman told him, Karma prevented the world from getting out of balance, like a wheel without tire weights. In the old days Jay-Bo would have dismissed this Karma stuff as so much dunderheaded bullshit; but in light of recent events he had to admit that it was right on the money.

He grabbed the remote and turned up the sound on his new television. The toothy miniskirted blonde was back again, this time shrilly lambasting a splinter group of the Ku Klux Klan which was suing her for defamation of character, claiming that she had irreversibly damaged their reputation by calling them closet socialists. Jay-Bo emitted a yeasty belch and guffawed. "Stepped on your dick good this time, you dumb bitch."

Maybe, he thought, the blonde's Karma had gone sour. If so it was long overdue. He remembered the last time he'd seen her, only a few

— 270 —

months ago, riding high on her bestselling book while his life had been the complete pits: stuck in a dead-end marriage with a faded whining wife, supported by a detested brat of a son, having to beg them for a few measly dollars so he could put gas in his truck or go have a beer at Hamburger John's. It had been a humiliating nightmare...Karma at its absolute worst.

And then as if by magic the whiny wife had dropped dead, the brat had gone away, and his eldest son —who'd always had good genes but lousy Karma like his Old Man— had shown up just in time with a right-thinking business partner who seemed to be equal parts saint and white knight. Almost overnight Jay-Bo's life had been transformed from terrible to terrific. The rent was paid, the refrigerator was stocked, and the booze supply was limitless. Instead of being hassled and given grief all day long, Jay-Bo found himself treated with consummate respect. As an agent of Karmic realignment Cale Pittman proved positively messianic. His generosity seemed inexhaustible: he purchased a new television, and then floored Jay-Bo with the new green BarcaLounger as a special Christmas gift. For all of this he asked nothing, saying only that it was his honor to keep company with such fine deserving men. Jay-Bo's suspicious nature might have been tweaked by so much good fortune had not Cale —with his usual deference— made it clear that it was all just Karma at work. After that, Jay-Bo's lingering misgivings evaporated.

He channel-surfed until he found an old western that seemed to be piling up dead Indians at a pleasing rate. Inspired by the incessant gunfire Jay-Bo got out his beloved Colt Python and fondled it, admiring the spotless blue-black finish, the perfectly shaped wooden grips, the deadly sensuousness of the cylinder. The sexiest actress on earth wasn't half as beautiful as this gun, he thought, using his shirttail to wipe a tiny smudge off the trigger guard. Women were essentially useless, whereas a weapon like this...Jay-Bo emitted a satisfied grunt, checked to make sure the revolver was loaded and then slid it back down into the lounger's pouch. He was quite certain that neither Lloyd nor Cale Pittman would touch his personal firearm.

Jay-Bo drank his beer and idly watched the U.S. Cavalry mow down acres of Sioux. Cale and Lloyd certainly did spend a great deal of time together. They were always going off somewhere in Pittman's black Mustang, often not returning until late at night. Lloyd explained that his business partner wanted to check out various investment opportunities in the flourishing Northern Virginia real-estate market, which entailed driving all over the county to inspect different properties. Someone with a sharp eye, said Lloyd, could make a killing buying the right abandoned cow pasture. Jay-Bo knew that this was perfectly true, and he couldn't deny that Cale Pittman was damned sharp. The business partners were out looking for that once-in-a-lifetime bargain this very afternoon. For all he knew, they might find it.

Still, once or twice Jay-Bo had caught Lloyd staring at Cale with an intense admiration that was reminiscent of how the high school cheerleaders had looked at *him* after a big score on the field; sort of dazzled and moonstruck and giggly, which had been great, but they were girls. Guys weren't ever supposed to look like that. Unless, of course, they were faggots.

But there was no reason for concern. Jay-Bo drained his beer and crushed the can in his fist. Lloyd probably just had a case of hero-worship for his business partner. And after everything Pittman had done for them, who wouldn't? Cale was a great guy, a right-thinking man. There wasn't a chance in a billion that he and Lloyd were queering around. If anything, they hated homos more virulently than Jay-Bo himself. He had nothing to worry about. Nothing at all.

It never occurred to Jay-Bo that fickle Karma, having once switched from bad to good, could just as readily revert back the other way.

⸻ ◉ ⸻

"Me? Maitre d'? But...I can't take Mr. Foley's job!"

For the second time in as many weeks Collie Skinner stood in front of the general manger's desk. Mr. Demarest had summoned him to the Foxton Arms an hour earlier than usual for the purpose of having a "brief talk". That sounded ominous enough to make Collie more than a little apprehensive; but Mr. Demarest's proposal took him completely by surprise.

The general manager steepled his fingers. "There's no 'taking' involved here, Mr. Skinner. In order to deal with the consequences of that terrible fire Mr. Foley has requested a leave of absence. Therefore, it's imperative that we find someone to fill his position at once."

"What about Mr. Bellison? He's always been the substitute maitre d' when Mr. Foley isn't here."

The manager rocked back in his chair. "Well, but Mr. Bellison prefers to devote his energies to being food service manager. Dealing with our clientele isn't really his forte. As I'm sure you're aware, Mr. Skinner, some of our guests can be demanding at times."

"Yes, sir, but..." Collie shook his head. "I don't have the experience to be a maitre d'."

The manager leaned forward, his hands laced on the desk top. "Mr. Skinner...Collie, isn't it?"

"Yes, Mr. Demarest."

"Collie, Conrad recommended you himself. He thinks you'd do a fine job."

"Mr. Foley said that?"

"Yes. He described you as diligent and personable. However, if you don't feel up to it, we will look elsewhere." He paused. "What'll it be?"

"I don't have the right clothes." Collie looked embarrassed. "I don't know if I can afford—"

The manager held up his hand. "They'll be provided. I've already spoken with Martin over at Desmond's. He'll see to it that you're properly outfitted. You're familiar with Desmond's?"

Desmond's was the menswear counterpart to Millicent's. Collie had never set foot within twenty feet of its austerely aristocratic entrance. "I know where it is, sir," he gulped.

"Very good. Now, as you doubtless realize, a maitre d' is compensated at a higher level than the wait staff. You will start at—"

"Mr. Demarest, I apologize for interrupting, but..." Collie hesitated. "Sir, I don't want to make more money because of what happened to Mr. Foley. That wouldn't be right. I'd feel like...like I was profiting from his house burning down."

"That's not how it is, but I understand your concerns." Thoughtfully: "What do you make now?"

"I guess about five hundred a week, maybe a little more. Unless I get lucky with some big tippers. Then it can be a lot more."

"I see. Well, since you won't be counting on tips quite as much," said the manager, "does seven hundred and fifty a week sound agreeable?"

"You bet, Mr. Demarest." Collie's pulse speeded up. At seven-fifty a week, he'd have no trouble saving enough to buy Robin an engagement ring. "Thank you, sir!"

"That's settled, then." The manager nodded approvingly. "If Conrad Foley has faith in you, so do I. Let's plan for you to start on January second. Mr. Bellison will carry us through New Year's. You'll go see Martin right away?"

"First thing tomorrow, Mr. Demarest."

"Splendid. Oh, one other thing, Mr. Skinner."

"Sir?"

"Although I assured Ambassador Douglass that you would organize his catered seafood extravaganza at the Windfield College spring picnic, in light of your new status I won't hold you to that commitment. If you'd rather excuse yourself, you may do so."

Collie hesitated. He felt tempted to take a pass. Ambassador Douglass was a cantankerous old reptile and Collie didn't trust him for an instant. But he couldn't responsibly walk away from two thousand dollars, especially now that he had begun to envision a future with Robin Thompson.

"No, sir. I'll still handle that, if you don't mind. I said I would, and I want to keep my word."

"Good lad."

"And Mr. Demarest?"

"Yes?"

"As soon as Mr. Foley's ready he can have his job back. He's the real maitre d'."

The manager smiled. "I can see why Conrad spoke of you as he did. Well, Collie, let's take things as they come. I'm sure you'll do us proud. You may go now."

Collie left the office, his head swimming. He discovered Robin in the back room reading some notices on the employee's bulletin board. Noiselessly creeping up from behind he grabbed her around the waist. She jumped like a startled cat then turned around and scolded, "Don't do that! Lord, you almost scared me to death." She took a moment to smooth her ruffled feathers. "Did you see Mr. Demarest?"

"I sure did," grinned Collie. "Guess what?"

"What?"

Collie assumed a gravely dignified pose and intoned, "Good evening, Mr. and Mrs. Uppersnoot. How pleasant to welcome you again to the Foxton Arms. Reservations for a party of four, I believe? Very good. If you'd care to follow me, I have your usual table waiting."

Mystified, Robin put her hands on her hips. "Nicholas, you're not making fun of poor Mr. Foley, are you?"

"No, never. Robin, I'm the new maitre d'!"

Her eyes grew large. "You are?"

"Yep. It's only till Mr. Foley comes back, of course, but still...*me*. Can you believe it?"

"That's *great*." Robin threw her arms around his neck and kissed him. "You'll be just perfect, I know."

"Mr. Foley recommended me." Collie shook his head in disbelief. "I didn't even think he liked me."

"Of course he likes you. Everybody likes you. Well, except for me."

Collie did a double take. "You don't?"

"No, silly. I *love* you." Seeing his tricked look Robin grinned. "Gotcha!"

"Yeah, you did." The swelling affection he felt made his chest ache. He loved Robin Thompson more than he'd ever loved anyone else, except his mother. Thinking about Luanne, Collie's smile dimmed.

"What is it?"

"I wish I could have shared this with Mama. She never had much to be happy about, and maybe..." Collie stopped, swallowed. "I miss her so much. It isn't fair that she had to die."

Robin hugged him, laid her head on his shoulder. "Your mother would have been so proud of you. She *is* proud of you. And so am I. You're changing every day, Nicholas. Becoming more of a man, a good strong man with a beautiful spirit."

"Thanks to you."

"No." Robin looked into his eyes. "True change only comes from within, Nicholas. It's all your own doing. I just thank God every day for letting me be in your life."

After a short silence Collie said, "I think about Nick Farrington a lot, Robin. It's like he's inside me, where I can't see him or hear him. I guess that sounds crazy, huh? I have no idea if he's even still alive, but I wish I could meet him."

"I don't think it sounds crazy," said Robin, with an obscure look. "Will you ever find him? I don't know, Nicholas. But if it's meant to be, then it will happen. Now come on, Mister Maitre d'," she playfully patted his rear. "Let's get to work."

———•((◦))•———

In all his thirty-two years on the planet, Norris Budge had failed to impress anyone. This was largely due to the fact that he had crapped out in the genetics dice game. He stood barely five-foot-four, with a bulbous nose, weak chin, close-set eyes, straggly black hair, posture like the letter 'S', and a more-or-less permanent case of rhinitis. In addition he early on developed a disposition not unlike one of those teacup-sized dogs that snap and yap at mastiffs twenty times their size. This trait endeared him to no one, including his despairing parents, but it did earn him countless wedgies all throughout his school years.

Upon graduating from Stuarton High Norris Budge set out to find some occupation that would place him in a position of authority. He attempted to enlist in the armed forces, but was rejected by all four branches and the Coast Guard. He made the rounds of law enforcement, and was turned down by the town cops, the county sheriff's department and the State Troopers, whose recruiter, a pony-tailed blonde with eyes like glare ice, told him in no uncertain terms to get lost.

Budge next tried various security agencies and rent-a-cop firms, with no luck. He applied to join the department of animal control, but they declined, afraid that he lacked the physical wherewithal to subdue so much as a rabid skunk. He eventually settled for being a ticket-taker in a movie theater, which at least allowed him to supervise the red-velvet rope and reprimand children for spilling their popcorn.

Then, about the time Norris thought he would go mad from the smell of rancid oil, a miracle: he landed a job with the Windfield College office of campus security. For Budge, it was a dream come true. As a campus cop he got to wear a uniform, including a khaki shirt with epaulets, a black tie, a peaked cap, and an official nameplate over his breast pocket. He was issued a walkie-talkie, a flashlight, a pound of keys, and an Acme Thunderer whistle. On his own he added a Sam Browne belt, which looked asinine, some paratrooper boots from an Army-Navy surplus store and mirror-finish Ray-Ban sunglasses. Best of all, he could prowl the campus at will in one of the security office's electric golf carts. For Norris Budge, life offered no greater satisfaction than humming along the manicured pathways, squinting balefully from under the bill of his cap and keeping a watchful eye out for troublemakers. In no time at all "Budgie" became one of the most enduring jests among the Windfield students, especially the girls, who loved to call his name in a flirtatious singsong, stick out their tongues, pretend to swoon, and wiggle their behinds at him as he drove by.

If Budgie resented the fact that he was regarded with a mixture of derision and incredulity by the entire college, he never let on. He devoted himself to enforcing the rules: ticketing bicycles with out-of-date registration stickers, issuing campus citations for everything from littering to illegal pets, and sternly escorting inebriated students back to their dorm rooms. He was quick to report even the most negligible infraction, as the exasperated security chief soon learned. Still, no one demonstrated a greater dedication to their duties or to Windfield than Norris Budge, who, unbeknownst to anyone, harbored a secret ambition: to one day score a spectacular Big Bust that would earn him universal admiration and respect. He felt positive it would happen someday. All he had to do was remain hyper-vigilant for anything even remotely suspicious.

When the student body left on holiday breaks the security office operated with a skeleton staff. Budge, who had no life beyond the Windfield gates, inevitably volunteered to man the office for the duration. He endlessly patrolled every nook and byway of the abandoned campus, enjoying the feeling of authority that came from being the sole law enforcement person on duty.

A cold drizzle was falling late in the afternoon when Norris Budge, zooming about in his cart, caught sight of the construction underway by the Randall Windfield Memorial. He'd seen the posted memo about staying clear due to equipment hazards, but of course that only applied to civilians. Deciding to inspect things for himself, he drove across the wet grass and pulled to a stop by a portable concrete mixer, which was being loaded with cement and gravel by a bear-sized bearded man.

"Hey, fella," Budge addressed the bear-man, who looked wet and surly, "whatcha got going on here?"

"What's it look like?" Mike Barlow growled, shaking the contents of a cement bag into the mixer.

Norris Budge got out of his cart and walked to the edge of a large hole in the ground set off by strings stretched between wooden stakes. The excavated space was mostly taken up by a big hollow square built from two rows of cinder blocks. "Setting a foundation, huh?"

"Don't give a damn what it is," shrugged Big Mike. "Who are you, anyway?"

"Officer Norris Budge, Windfield College Security." Craning his neck, he peered over the strings into the cinderblock square. "What is that?" He pointed. "There. It looks like...is that some kind of propane cylinder?"

Mike Barlow slung a shovelful of gravel into the mixer. "I just build what I'm told."

"Now why," said Budge, squinting at Ambassador Douglass's Redeemer, "would anyone put a propane cylinder in a foundation?" He rubbed his chin thoughtfully. "Seems pretty peculiar to me. What'd you say your name was?"

"Little Red Ridin' Hood," answered Big Mike. "Look, Fudge, I got no time for yakkin'."

"*Budge*," corrected the campus cop, with a frown. "Officer Norris Budge." He glared up at the big man, who reminded him of all the bullies he'd known in school. "You don't wanna get funny with me, fella. I happen to be in charge here."

Mike Barlow hurled another scoop of gravel into the mixer.

"I think there might be something dangerous going on with this foundation. Propane cylinders have been known to explode. Student safety is my responsibility, y'know," declared Norris Budge. "I'm going to have to report this."

Big Mike glowered at the smaller man. "You sure 'bout that?"

"It's my job to make sure there are no security violations." Budge drew himself up. "I don't make the rules, but I damn well see to it that they are strictly enforced."

Barlow eyed Budge. "Okay." He turned away and started up the mixer, which began rotating with a grinding clatter.

Wanting to have the last word but realizing that he wouldn't be heard above the noise, Budge jumped into his golf cart and drove away. The propane cylinder —or whatever it was— probably wouldn't present any hazard, but Norris Budge didn't take risks. Better to report it than chance overlooking the Big Bust. Besides, he resented the bearman's disrespectful attitude.

He silently motored around the empty campus to make sure nothing was amiss, then headed back toward the security office. The drizzle had stopped and everywhere the lampposts were blinking on. As he passed the front lawn he noticed that the construction site stood deserted, the mixer standing silent and motionless in the gathering gloom.

He was driving across the murky visitor's parking lot when he spotted an unfamiliar black longbed pickup truck by the curb, its engine idling, smoke curling from the exhaust into the damp air. A window rolled down and the big man from the construction site waved at him to stop.

Budge stepped on the brake. "What do you want?"

"It's that propane tank, Officer Budge," said Mike Barlow.

"Somethin's wrong. You better come look."

"Is that right? Well, I thought so!"

"Yep. Get in, I'll drive us back over there."

Budge maneuvered his cart between two white parking lines, then climbed into Mike Barlow's truck. "So what's the matter with it?"

"Dunno. Actin' funny. Sorta fizzin' and lettin' out a stink."

"Hm. Probably a valve defect." Budge knew nothing about pressurized cylinders, but it sounded good. "Hey," he frowned, seeing that they were leaving the campus grounds, "this isn't the right way. Where do you think you're going, Mister?"

He never got an answer. Big Mike reached over and in one quick motion gave his neck a vicious twist that snapped it as easily as a twig. Norris Budge collapsed like a marionette with cut strings. Barlow pulled over, transferred the lifeless body into the truck bed and covered it with a tarp held down by bags of cement. Then he drove back onto the Windfield campus and resumed working under some construction lights he'd brought, mixing and pouring concrete in the winter night until he'd finished encasing the ambassador's Cesium 137 bomb in a snug square cinderblock cocoon.

Many hours later in the dead of night, a weighted broken-necked corpse sank to the bottom of the same West Virginia lake where the last remnants of Moley Fescue had long ago rotted away. A few aquatic creatures stirred from their winter hibernation long enough to sample the newcomer, but they soon lost interest. Consistent to the last, Norris Budge failed to impress.

Fighting a cold, feeling stressed and snappish, Nickie Farrell was sitting in her wing chair trying without much success to work up a class lesson on *The Oxbow Incident*, when the lamp bulb suddenly expired with a sizzling *pop!*

Spitting out a four-letter word, Nickie flung aside her notebook and went to fetch a fresh bulb, only to discover that she had none left. She indulged in a moment of teeth-gnashing frustration, then sighed and shrugged into her coat. Maybe going to the supermarket would help clear her brain. Tearing a shopping list from the magnetized notepad on her refrigerator, she left her apartment and drove the short distance to the Middleville Safeway.

After filling her cart with various foodstuffs Nickie made her way to the housewares section and discovered that they were out of her preferred soft pink bulbs. Balked and angry, she snatched up a box of the plain white variety then huffily set it back on the shelf. No, damn it. She wanted *pink* ones, even if that meant walking half a block to Berensohn's Hardware to get some. After checking out and stowing her groceries in the Accord's trunk, she hurried up the street toward the hardware store, hugging her coat close and brooding over the difference between steely resolve and mule-headed obstinacy.

Berensohn's shelves were stocked with light bulbs of every conceivable variety. Nickie filled her hand basket with enough pink bulbs to illuminate a theater marquee, then stood in the checkout line behind a weathered older black man wearing a ragged blue quilted jacket and a Bull Durham cap. The checkout clerk, a lumpish young fellow with pocked skin and yellowish eyes, craned his neck past the black man and beckoned to Nickie. With a leer from under greasy dark bangs: "Come right on up, ma'am. I'll take care of you."

Indicating the black man Nickie demurred: "No, this gentleman was here first. He's next."

"Gentleman?" The clerk hooted. "Shoot, that's no gentleman, that's just ol' Blue Ridge Harry. He don't mind, do you, Harry?"

The black man turned and addressed Nickie in a low voice, "Don' pay no mind, Miss. I ain't in any hurry. You go ahead."

"I will not." Nickie coldly addressed the clerk, who smirked at her from behind his counter. "This gentleman was in line before me, and it's *his* turn. Do you not know how to be civil?"

The clerk sucked in his cheeks. "Wal, now, lemme see. Is that sumpin' like *civil* rights?"

"It don' matter none, Miss." The man called Blue Ridge Harry regarded Nickie from eyes the color of stained walnut. "You bes' go ahead."

"She ain't from around here, Harry," guessed the clerk. "Never even heard of 'ladies first'. Prob'ly from New York or Boston or some damn place. Bet she's one o' them libber-rated women from the college. Ain't you, darlin'?"

A number of other customers had paused in their shopping and stood listening. A few of them wore grins. One old red-faced woman holding a new garden rake watched with slitted eyes.

Nickie set her basket down on a pile of boxes and snapped, "Don't you dare address me like that! I'd like to talk to the manager. Call him, please."

"He's at lunch, darlin'." The clerk's expression turned hostile. "You fixin' to buy somethin'? This here's a place of business. If you ain't got business mebbe you should just be on your way."

Livid, embarrassed, Nickie fumed, "You're damned right I'll leave!" She turned on her heel and almost barreled headfirst into a heavyset man coming in from the street. He put up his hands. "Whoa, there. Is something the matter, ma'am?"

"Who are *you?*"

"I'm Kurt Berensohn, the manager. What seems to be the problem?"

"Since you ask, the problem is *him*." Nickie pointed at the clerk, who stood sullenly ringing up Blue Ridge Harry's purchases, his eyes darting in their direction. "That employee was unforgivably rude."

The manager's expression hardened. Addressing the clerk: "Ludie?"

"Geez, Dad, I was only tryin' to be nice. All I said was 'ladies first', and she got sore." He added in a plaintive voice: "Some customers don't 'preciate a man bein' polite..."

Kurt Berensohn glared his son silent. "Go out back and start unloading that crate of batteries."

"Dad..."

"*Move* it, boy."

Red-faced, Ludie Berensohn came out from behind the counter. As he passed Nickie he hoarsely whispered: "Nigger-lovin' Yankee cunt." Then he disappeared into the rear of the store.

Momentarily stunned, Nickie gaped after him. Suddenly she felt weakly feverish and shaky. All she wanted was to go home and lie in bed with the covers over her head.

Kurt Berensohn was saying, "...I apologize for any inconvenience, ma'am. Would you like me to ring those up for you?" He indicated her forgotten basket.

"What? Oh, all right. But please hurry. I'm not feeling well."

As the manager bagged her light bulbs, Blue Ridge Harry halted on his way out. "Things 'round here ain't what you're used to, Miss. Lots of folks still believe in the old ways. Bes' be mindful of that." He touched his cap. "You take good care, Miss."

Brushing aside the manager's continued apologies Nickie paid him and left the store. After only a few steps she felt so dizzy that despite the cold she had to sit for a moment on a wooden bench. She lowered her head, removed her glasses, rubbed her eyes and took deep regular breaths.

"Now listen. That Ludie Berensohn ain't nuthin' but a no-account fool. Stayed in fifth grade until he was sixteen. He ain't worth spit."

Raising her head Nickie saw a red-faced old woman holding a brand-new rake standing a few feet away on the cobblestone sidewalk.

"It doesn't matter," she answered. "I just want to go home. If you'll excuse me." Seeing that the old woman was examining her eyes with the piercing intensity of a magpie eyeing a shiny bottle cap, Nickie quickly donned her sunglasses and hastened off. She wasn't about to explain heterochromia to some inquisitive old biddy.

The old biddy –it was actually Mrs. Greene, Empress of Busybodies– watched Nickie hurry away down the street. Then she said aloud, "Well, don't that beat all. What in tarnation is one o' them college people doin' runnin' around with Collie Skinner's eyes?" She addressed the rake, scowling: "Don't you tell me there ain't somethin' mighty fishy goin' on. *I* know it. They can't fool Carlotta Greene."

⊰⊱

"God *damn* it, Barlow!" Ambassador Eamon Douglass brought a fist down on his desktop, making the glass wolf jump. "By what right do you go around bumping people off," his nostrils quivered, "without *my* permission?!"

Unperturbed, Big Mike shrugged. "Didn't have no choice."

"There's always a choice," smoldered the ambassador. "And it wasn't yours to make. Do you realize you may have thrown the Redemption into jeopardy? Who the hell was he, anyway?"

"Campus security asshole. The kind that's always stickin' their nose in where it don't belong."

"Christ on a crutch." Douglass ground his teeth. "That bitch president assured me that no one would interrupt your work. How the devil did he sneak up on you?"

"I was loadin' the mixer. Makes a lot of noise. Little weasel drove up in one of them electric things, don't make a sound. I didn't have a chance to spread the tarp 'fore he walked over to the hole and *saw* it. Right away he's askin' questions and tellin' me he's gonna report hazardous material or some bullshit. Like I said, there was no choice."

"All right. It was a bad situation, I grant you." The ambassador drummed his fingers. "But you can't just make people disappear into thin air, Barlow! There's bound to be an inquiry, questions...not good. Not good at all, goddamn it."

"This wasn't the sorta guy anyone gives a shit about."

"So you say, but what about his car? Did you ever think of that? If it's left sitting around and—"

"Didn't have a car. Rode one o' them little two-wheel scooter things. I dumped it in Sawtell Quarry."

"Very resourceful," Douglass grumbled. "But they have all sorts of goddamn security cameras these days. What if—"

Mike Barlow interrupted, his eyes hooded: "I ain't fuckin' stupid. Think I'm lookin' to get popped for murder? I took care of it. If you're so worried," he added, "go set the thing off right now. Everything's ready to blow. If you don't wanna wait just take that trigger-stick over there and..." He spread his arms. " Ka-BOOM."

Eamon Douglass raised his eyebrows. "By Christ, I could, couldn't I?" He regarded his underling with a thoughtful frown. "Perhaps my concerns were a bit unwarranted, Barlow. Your consulting work has always been above reproach. Help yourself to some whiskey."

While Big Mike applied himself to the bourbon decanter, the ambassador picked up his "trigger-stick", a blackthorn shillelagh nearly identical to his own, which had been cunningly engineered by Volka's technicians to conceal a wireless detonator for the Cesium bomb. All the ambassador had to do was unscrew the tip ferrule, load in a stack of AA batteries, get within a hundred feet of the Redeemer, press a concealed button under the flip-up handle, and, as his consultant had so succinctly phrased it: Ka-BOOM.

Douglass caressed the death-dealing stick, which would be the last object he touched in this world. As he had many times before, the ambassador wondered if he'd feel anything in the split seconds after he pressed the trigger. Given the amount of explosives that Mike had packed in around the bomb, it wasn't likely. His brain would be atomized before it had time to register any sensations. The suffering would be left to those who remained behind, as they watched Windfield College wither and die.

Carefully setting the bogus shillelagh on his desk Douglass demanded, "You're certain that you armed it properly?"

"Yep. Did exactly what that diagram said. It's set to go." Big Mike took a swallow from his crystal tumbler. "The sundial is sittin' on the pedestal right over the bomb. Bastard was some kind of heavy." He took another drink. "Laid a double-thick tarp down with cinder-blocks to hold it. Ain't goin' nowhere. Don't matter if it rains, snows, everything'll stay dry. Like I said, you can go blow it up anytime you want." With a humorless grin: "After you put my million bucks in the bank."

"Oh, you'll get every penny you deserve," Douglass assured him. "That, I promise you. Meanwhile, thanks to your timely intervention with that campus snoop, I think the Redemption can take place as scheduled. I promised those Windfield degenerates a new memorial, and a memorial they shall have. If only for a very brief while." Raising his glass with a coarse laugh: "To brevity, Mr. Barlow."

Early in the afternoon of New Year's Day, waiting expectantly, Robin heard Collie's voice call from her bedroom: "Okay, close your eyes. Ready or not, here I come!"

Robin covered her eyes and heard him enter. "All right, you can look now."

She removed her hands and beheld Collie, resplendent in a new tuxedo from Desmond's, his face showing mixed pride and sheepishness. "What do you think?"

"Oh, Nicholas! You look...you look so stylish, so *in charge*." Robin's brown eyes were as bright as he'd ever seen them. "You have no idea. Oh, my."

Collie smiled uncertainly. "Are you sure? I feel like one of those penguins in that movie." He made an effort to relax his stiff posture. "I hope I get used to it. Mr. Foley does the whole suave and debonair thing, but me? Geez..."

"You'll be fine," Robin assured him. With a rueful frown: "I don't know how I'm going to stand it. The ladies are going to be making eyes at you all the time."

"Let 'em look. There's only one lady I care about." Collie took her hand, bowed and kissed it with a Continental flourish. "Ma'amselle Rawbin, ze most beautiful lady in ze world."

"Let's not overdo it," giggled Robin. "But thank you kindly, handsome sir."

"Handsome, huh?" Collie straightened. "Well, that's good enough for me. Guess I'd better go change. I can't take a chance on getting it dirty before my big debut tomorrow." He walked toward the bedroom, halted as he caught sight of himself in a framed wall mirror. "You're sure I don't look..." He hesitated, swallowed. "You know, gay?"

"Of course not," said Robin. "You look like a movie star. One of those old-fashioned ones, like Gregory Peck or whatzisname, the James Bond man."

"When I went to Desmond's to get the tux, there was this salesman who helped me. His name is Martin."

"Yes?"

"Well anyway, I'm sure he's a gay guy. But he was really cool, you know? He didn't act like I was some low-class fool in a store for rich people. He even called me "Sir", but not in a snotty put-down way. We actually had a great time. Martin kept making jokes and cracking me up."

"That sounds like fun."

"Yeah, it was." Collie stared at himself in the mirror. "But the weird thing is I kept feeling...ashamed. Guilty, like."

Robin tilted her head. "Why, Nicholas?"

Collie made a helpless gesture. "Maybe because I always hated gay people so much. Listening to Jay-Bo calling them faggots, queers, fairies...you know. Even blaming them for what happened to Lissa." He turned and looked at Robin. "It's all bull, isn't it? Hating people like Martin for no reason. He's a good guy. I liked him. And it makes me pretty sick to think about how I used to feel."

Robin nodded, her eyes moist. "Hatred will make you sick, Nicholas. Your mother knew that. See how right she was?" She went to him and straightened his bow tie. "You're not a hateful person, Nicholas. You never were. Don't feel guilty about the past. Let it go, and concentrate on the future. " She stood back at arm's length. "From what I can see, it's looking very *very* good."

Collie's eyes shone. With his forefinger he affectionately beeped Robin on the nose. "Let me go take this stuff off. I'll be right back."

Robin watched him walk into the other room, thinking that Nicholas was the sexiest man she'd ever seen. She smiled at her private thoughts. Robin was a healthy young woman with a very healthy libido. Despite her unshakeable resolve to save sex itself for the marriage bed, on several occasions she and Collie had indulged themselves in some exceedingly heated makeout sessions. His frank admissions of past intimate encounters didn't upset her. Robin accepted that men were different, and Collie's willingness to honor her wishes about waiting only made her respect him that much more. She tingled to imagine a future when they would be able to share their love in all the wonderful ways available to a man and woman...

Her reverie was interrupted by the jangling cordless phone. Still in a bemused state, she picked it up: "Hello?"

"Robin, it's me, Cinda Vanderhart. From Windfield? I'm back from vacation. We need to talk."

Robin cast a nervous glance toward the bedroom. In a low tone: "I told you before, there's no point. I have nothing to say to–"

"Nick Farrington."

Robin's insides knotted. "W-Who?"

"You heard me. Nick Farrington."

"I have no clue what you're talking about."

"Sure you do." Cinda's voice was calm, bold. "In fact, I'd bet my career on it. You know plenty, Robin, and I want to hear all of it. Of course if you won't talk to me I'll just find a way to ask your boyfriend if *he* ever heard of Nick Farrington. What do you think he might say?"

Robin put a hand to her forehead. "Why are you doing this? Why can't you leave us alone?" In an angrier tone: "What gives you the right?"

"The same thing that gives you the right to hide stuff from people who should know the truth."

Robin almost wailed, "I don't know what truth you're talking about! Please, I'm telling you I don't know!"

"That's exactly why we need to talk. To figure it all out. Anyway, I'll be in touch soon," promised Cinda Vanderhart. "Happy New Year. Bye."

The phone clicked dead in Robin's hand. It was all she could do to keep from flinging it across the room. She dropped into a chair, hands over her face. How on earth had the Windfield lesbian come up with the name of Collie's real father? Why was she so interested? And did that lady from the church, Nickie, have some sort of connection? Robin just wanted it all to go away. Nothing good could come of whatever Cinda Vanderhart was up to. She bent forward and began to cry softly into her hands.

"Hey, Robbie, what's wrong?" Collie was suddenly kneeling by her chair. "Why are you crying?"

Robin threw her arms around his neck. He rocked her gently, caressing her hair. "It's okay, it's okay."

After a moment Robin drew back. Wiping some tears away: "Nicholas, you know I'd never do anything to hurt you, right?"

"Of course I know that."

"Or hide things from you, or try to control your destiny?"

"That's not the kind of person you are." He grinned. "But if you want to control my destiny, I really don't mind."

"I only want you to be happy, Nicholas. I want *us* to be happy. You've been through so much already, I couldn't stand for you to be hurt any more."

He kissed her eyelids, tasted the saltiness. "I have you, Robin. Nothing can hurt me now."

"God, I hope not." Robin laid her head on Collie's shoulder. "Just remember that I love you, Nicholas. Whatever happens." She hugged him as hard as she could. "Please, please, don't forget."

Chapter Fourteen
Disclosure

Shortly after daybreak on the morning of February second, in the town of Punxsutawny, Pennsylvania, the annual staged lunacy known as "Groundhog Day" took place with all its attendant traditional hoopla. The luckless rodent called "Phil" was hauled out into the glare of massed television lights before a bellowing throng where, rigid with shock, he failed to notice his shadow, thereby forecasting an early end to winter. According to time-honored custom, this earth-shattering news was immediately transmitted around the world via the global information networks.

At about the same time that Phil's heart was in danger of exploding, Heather Walters jogged through crisp early sunlight along a perimeter path which encircled the Windfield College campus. The morning was so mild that she too might have predicted the early demise of winter had she not been deeply preoccupied with developing the most man-slaying buns on campus. Without doubt she already possessed the raw material to be a strong contender; but resolving to leave nothing to chance, she'd started jogging every morning to further sculpt and refine her sleek California Girl flanks.

Breathing easily, her blonde pony-tail swinging like a metronome, Heather followed the path past the college gates, then turned left to complete her run with a quarter-mile sprint straight up the sloping front lawn. She started up the hill, feeling the fat-burning fire spread in her haunches. As she puffed past the nearly-completed Randall Windfield memorial she noticed several people talking together around the construction site. Seeing who they were Heather almost broke stride but she quickly recovered and finished the climb with a last burst of speed.

A few minutes later she bounced into her dorm room, panting, her face pink from exertion.

"Hey, Roomie," she greeted Cinda Vanderhart. "You have got to come jogging with me some time. Seriously. It'll make you feel, like, so alive."

"I'm too busy to feel alive." Cinda looked up from her laptop. "Do you happen to know how your dad voted on the last redistricting bill? I'm writing an essay called *Fiascos of Government*."

Heather peeled off her damp Hello Kitty sweatshirt. "What was the bill for?"

"Another corrupt manipulation of the system to keep incumbents in power. The unrestricted gerrymandering thing."

"Oh, yeah. I'm sure Daddy voted for it. Listen, you'll never guess who I just saw."

Cinda resumed her typing, muttering, "Have you no sense of decency, sir, at long last? Have you left no sense of decency?"

Clad only in her underwear Heather scrutinized her rear end in a full-length mirror nailed to the wall. "I was running by that new memorial thingie they're building out on the hill, okay, and who's there but Ms. Farrell with President Lindsey and some old dude with an eye patch." She pirouetted and inspected the view over her other shoulder. "An eye patch, like *Pirates of the Caribbean*. What's up with that?" She shook out her blonde mane. "Guess who else?"

"Ambrose Bierce?"

"Who?"

"Never mind. Elvis?"

"No, silly." Heather giggled. "Our waiter from the Foxton Arms. That one with the weird-colored eyes? Even though he's wearing sunglasses I'm positive it's him. So I'm like, what's a waiter doing out there with our trans professor and the president and some old crankcase who thinks he's a pirate...hey, where are you going?"

Cinda had flung aside her computer and was pulling on clothes as rapidly as she could. "Out," she answered, jamming her feet into lace-up boots.

Heather stood in her skivvies, hands on hips. "Cinda, I thought you said you were finished buggin' on Ms. Farrell. You're not even taking her class this semester. Are you going to start this stuff again?"

"Huh? I have no idea what stuff you mean." Not trusting Heather's talkative nature, Cinda had kept mum about her ongoing investigation of Nickie Farrell. She finished buttoning up a discolored winter parka and pulled a knitted ski cap down to her ears, giving herself the appearance of a demented street person. "I'm just in the mood for a little walk. Y'know, to feel more alive."

"Omigod, you are such a liar. Why do I ever tell you anything?"

"It's that built-in Catholic need to confess." Cinda put her hand on the door. "By the way, hot stuff, I know you don't like hearing this from a dyke but your tush is looking cuter by the day. Is that an extra dimple I see?"

With Heather distracted into a further self-examination, Cinda escaped out the door.

⎯⎯⎯◦((◉))◦⎯⎯⎯

"I must say, Ambassador, everything is progressing beautifully." President Fredericka Lindsey gestured at the snowy marble columns extending in two wide semicircles from the original obelisk which, now mounted on a graceful tall plinth, rose more than fifteen feet into the sky. Centered in the encircled area was the massive sundial, also mounted on a pedestal. Along the perimeter, tiered enclosures showed where flower beds would accent the memorial site in a blaze of seasonal colors. "My compliments. It's going to be absolutely stunning."

"Indeed, I think 'stunning' will prove to be an apt description." Eamon Douglass waved his shillelagh around at the edifice. "I am not displeased, Madame President. Not displeased at all." With a gracious nod at Nickie Farrell, who stood by the Windfield president: "And may

I add that the professor has done an exemplary job of overseeing matters. My compliments to *her*."

"Thank you, Ambassador," said Nickie. "It really will be very special, I think."

"More special than anyone can guess," agreed Douglass. "Now, on the day of the dedication, where do you propose to locate the speaker's podium?"

Nickie indicated an area in front of the obelisk. "We thought we'd put up a wooden platform right along here. Not too high, Ambassador, just enough to elevate you above the sundial so that people can see you when you address your remarks."

"Excellent," nodded the ambassador. "Perfect. Naturally, as my liaison and project co-coordinator you will be up there with me. I insist, Professor. It's only proper that you receive your due accolades."

"As you wish, sir," Nickie acquiesced, "although I've done nothing to merit any accolades."

"Never refuse an accolade, Professor Farrell," wryly observed President Lindsey. "They do have their uses."

Nickie glanced at her watch. "Ambassador, will that be all for now? I've got some class work to prepare."

"Just one more thing. You should meet the person who's in charge of catering my little buffet." Douglass beckoned to a young man in sunglasses standing a short distance away. "Come here, Mr. Skinner. This is Professor Farrell, my project liaison. If you encounter any problems, talk to her. Understand?"

"Yes, sir." The young man extended his hand. "I'm Collie Skinner, ma'am. Pleased to meet you."

Nickie shook hands. "Hello, Mr. Skinner. I can't imagine that you'll need me, but if by chance you do please don't hesitate to call." She handed Collie a card. "If there's nothing else, I'd best get back to my office. Ambassador Douglass, President Lindsey, you know where to reach me." She nodded to each in turn and walked away up the hill.

Cinda Vanderhart rushed from her dorm in a highly agitated state. Heather's tidings had thrown her a nasty curve. What possible circumstances could have brought Robin's waiter boyfriend here to a meeting with Windfield's president *and* Nickie Farrell? Was the townie girl up to something? Cinda hurried along the path, gritting her teeth. Over the past weeks she'd left a dozen messages, but Robin never returned her calls. Cinda was out of patience. One way or another she intended to corner the waitress and sit on her if necessary until the other girl spilled what she knew about her boyfriend's history and how it related to a man named Nick Farrington. This was her investigation, her mystery, and she wasn't about to let the puzzle be snatched away when she was so close to solving it.

As she reached the edge of the grass Cinda almost collided with Nickie Farrell, who was walking with her head down, heading back toward the campus buildings.

"Ms. Farrell?" Cinda feigned a surprised grin. "Hey, how's it goin'?"

Seeing who'd addressed her, Nickie's expression became guarded. "Good morning, Ms. Vanderhart. It's been a while." She took in Cinda's ragamuffin appearance. "Are you enjoying the new semester?"

"Oh, yeah. It's great," replied Cinda. "None of my profs are as good as you, though."

"Hm. I see you're still working on your subtlety."

"For sure," said Cinda. "So what's going on out there?" She jerked a thumb at the memorial site. "Isn't that President Lindsey? Who's the old dude with the pirate patch?"

"That's Ambassador Eamon Douglass. He's a well-to-do philanthropist. Why do you ask?"

"Just curious." Watching Nickie from the corner of her eye: "And that other guy?"

"The ambassador's caterer, I gather. Ms. Vanderhart, I'd love to chat, but I must get back to my office. Enjoy your studies." Nickie began to walk away.

Relieved, Cinda thought: Okay, nothing's happened...yet. Then she abruptly called out: "Ms. Farrell? You don't like me, do you?"

Nickie halted and turned around. "That's not so, Ms. Vanderhart."

"It's okay if you don't. Not many people do, y'know."

"Ms. Vanderhart..." Nickie came back and stood before the younger woman. "Cinda, listen to me. It's much more important for you to like yourself. Do you?"

"I don't know." Cinda hesitated. "Maybe not so much. I get tired of being different, Ms. Farrell. It's lonely. Don't you ever get lonely?"

For a long moment Nickie stared toward the distant Blue Ridge foothills. "Yes, I get lonely. I think we all do, sometimes."

But you wouldn't be *so lonely if you suddenly found out you had a—*

Cinda cut off the thought without finishing it. The suspicion was there, but she wanted to be one hundred percent certain before she said anything. And there was only one way to find out for sure. She needed to talk with Robin the waitress.

"Anyhow, Ms. Farrell, I didn't mean to take up your time. I know I've been a pain in the ass, and I'm sorry for that. And whatever you think of me, I really meant what I said before about not having any teachers as good as you."

"All right." Nickie looked around, taking in the blue sky, the sun, and the pretty campus grounds. "I heard on the radio that the groundhog didn't see his shadow this morning. I think he's right." She closed her eyes and inhaled deeply. "Can you smell it? Springtime, Ms. Vanderhart. The season of life, of renewal. It's almost here."

━━━━━•((●))•━━━━━

Later that afternoon Robin Thompson stood at her ironing board pressing the pleats on her formal shirts, watching the Food Channel and laughing at the antics of Chef Emeril Lagasse.

"Now, folks, just to kick things up a coupla notches and make the sauce really happy we add fawdy-seven cloves o' gahlic...BAM!" The chef raised his arms in triumph as the audience went wild.

Chuckling, Robin grabbed her can of spray starch and shot a

quick spray: "BAM!" She ironed the pleat into rigid perfection. "Sooo happy."

The telephone rang. Robin didn't interrupt her work, merely glancing at the used answering machine she'd found in a Stuarton thrift store for five dollars. After two more rings the machine clicked on and she heard her own voice: "Hi, this is Robin. I'm not available right now, but please leave a message after the beep. Thanks!"

"Robin, this is Cinda Vanderhart. Again. I guess you haven't gotten my previous twenty-six messages."

Robin made a face and kept ironing.

"If you're there, pick up." A pause. "No? Okay. Just so you know, I've got my roommate's car and I'm on my way to the Foxton Arms to see you-know-who."

Robin set her iron down and grabbed up the phone. "This is Robin."

She heard a short laugh. "Imagine that. So nice to hear your voice, Robin. You're a tough lady to get hold of."

"Please don't go bothering anyone at the restaurant. There's no—"

"Oh, I only said that to make you answer the phone. I'm not going there. But believe me, I will if I have to."

Robin hit the mute on the television remote. Suddenly Emeril's madcap shtick didn't seem funny. "All right," she spoke into the receiver. "What do you want?"

"Same thing I've always wanted. To talk about things. Seriously, I don't get why you're so uptight." Cinda added, sounding aggrieved: "Anyway, I have some interesting information about Nick Farrington."

Robin cautiously replied, "And I care because...?"

"Don't play games." Cinda's voice turned chilly. "See, Robin, I *know* that both of us suspect there's a connection between your boyfriend and my English professor. Not just because of those weird eyes they have, but something about Nick Farrington. I want to figure out exactly what that connection is. For some reason, you don't. Well, too bad. I'm going to find out what's up whether you like it or not." After an interval she resumed in a milder tone: "But if you would talk to me, maybe we could decide together what we need to do next."

"And all this is because my boyfriend and your professor just happen to have unusual-colored eyes?" Robin tried to sound scornful. "Tell me, if two people have blonde hair do you go pushing your way into their lives, too?"

Cinda laughed. "Nice try, sis, but give me a break. Heterochromia iridium isn't quite as common as blonde hair. When and where do we meet?"

Robin tried to protest but Cinda cut her off: "*When?* Or I swear I'll be at that restaurant in twenty minutes."

Defeated, Robin dropped into a chair. "I'm off on Monday, but I have classes that evening."

"You go to school?" Cinda exclaimed with cruel surprise.

"Part-time," responded Robin with a bitterness she hated to hear in her own voice. "Not all of us get to attend a fancy place like Windfield."

"Huh. All right, next Monday morning. Where?"

"Not in town," said Robin.

"Don't want to be seen with me, huh? Figures. Okay, you come here. I'll tell my roommate to get lost, we can talk in the room. I live in Dickinson East, number one-twenty-eight. Park in the visitor's lot, it's a short walk. Eleven o'clock. Okay?"

Robin leaned her head on her arm. "Whatever."

"Good." Cinda paused. "Don't even think about standing me up. If you're not here by eleven-fifteen, I'll be on my way into town. For real. And just so you know," she added, "that *is* a threat. Bye, Robin."

———※(◉)※———

"So, Mr. Skinner, how did it go at the college? Everything under control?"

Dressed in his new tuxedo, Collie faced the general manager. "It felt weird to be there at Windfield, but no problems so far. If any come up, I'm supposed to call some lady who's in charge of everything."

"I take it Ambassador Douglass is pleased?"

"He sure acted like it, sir." In fact Collie had been more than a little surprised at the old man's avuncular cordiality. Eamon Douglass had waved aside Collie's attempts to apologize for his rude behavior at Luanne's funeral, stating that a young man mourning his mother ought not be held to account and thanking him for overseeing the Windfield buffet. "He did insist that the tent be set up right nearby and he made me promise to stay there until his speech is done." Collie shrugged. "Kind of weird, but easy enough. I guess when you have that much money you're allowed to be a little...uh..."

Mr. Demarest laughed. "At the ambassador's financial level, Mr. Skinner, odd behavior is called 'eccentric', and it's more-or-less *de rigeur*. You seem to have the situation well in hand. Has the order been sent in?"

Collie nodded. "Yes, sir. Mack will drive down to Annapolis that night and bring it to the college early in the morning. I'll be waiting there to set everything up."

"Very well-done, Mr. Skinner. You seem to have a talent for this sort of thing. I hear that you're doing a fine job as maitre d'."

"Thanks, but I'm still just filling in for Mr. Foley."

The general manager regarded Collie thoughtfully. "May I ask you a somewhat personal question? Don't answer if you prefer not to."

"I don't mind, Mr. Demarest."

"You went to work right out of high school, is that correct?"

"Yes, sir."

The general manager paused. "Was your decision not to pursue higher education a matter of preference or necessity? Again, you needn't answer."

"I would have liked to go to college, sir. I had a chance for James Madison or even Virginia State. But...my family couldn't afford it."

"Was there no financial aid available? The universities are well-funded for students in need."

"That wasn't the only thing, sir. I...I needed to be at home."

The manager nodded. "I see. But you know, it's never too late. You can continue your studies at any time, at whatever pace is feasible."

"I know, sir. That's what Robin is doing. She'll get her associate degree next year."

"Ah, yes. Our Ms. Thompson. An uncommonly industrious and decent young woman. I'm told that you and she are, as they say, an item."

Collie felt himself redden. "Yes, sir. As a matter of fact, I plan to ask her to marry me." He hastily added, "But she doesn't know yet, so please..."

Mr. Demarest raised his palm. "Your secret is safe with me. However, I will say –though my opinion is hardly relevant– that if Ms. Thompson sees fit to accept your proposal, you should consider yourself an exceedingly fortunate young man."

Collie grinned. "I will. I mean, I do."

"Not so fast. She hasn't said 'yes' yet." Mr. Demarest raised his eyebrows. "I'll expect to be invited to the wedding, of course."

"Of course," Collie agreed. "Sir."

"Very well, Mr. Skinner. Best of luck. Now, I believe we have a restaurant to run."

On his way back to the front foyer, Collie encountered Robin just as she was coming in from the parking lot. "Hey, beautiful! Welcome to the Foxton Arms."

"Hi, Nicholas."

Something about her tight-lipped expression made Collie ask, "What's the matter?"

"Nothing," she answered, not meeting his gaze. "It's one of those... you know. Female days."

"Oh. Sorry." Collie swallowed, squelched as any male would be. "I have to get out front. I hope you feel better." He started to walk away.

"Nicholas..."

Collie looked back. "Hmm?"

Silently Robin mouthed: "I love you."

"I'm glad. Me, too." He winked his brown eye, blew her a kiss and vanished.

Although Robin never would have spoken it aloud, one phrase kept repeating itself in her mind: "Damn you, Cinda Vanderhart. Damn you, damn you."

A week later Nickie Farrell sat in her office talking on her cell phone and watching a frenzy of avian activity outside the window, where continuing mild weather had attracted flocks of purple finches and chickadees to the bird-feeder.

"I'd love to, Leon. Give Eric my love, and I'll see you Friday night. Thank you *so* much. Bye."

"Hey, birdies," Nickie grinned out her window, "how cool is that?" Leonardo Lanza was an art professor she'd met at a faculty function. A fellow New Yorker, Leon was handsome, gay, and a sweetheart. They'd hit it off at once, ruefully reminiscing about the hedonistic 80's Manhattan disco scene. Leon and his partner Eric were quite taken with her, assuring Nickie that none of the T-girls they knew had transitioned half as gracefully as she had. He'd just called to invite her to dinner and Nickie had happily accepted. She couldn't wait to play with their cute little Yorkshire terriers, Xanax and Prozac.

Smiling, she picked up her red pencil and resumed correcting some essays. After an interval the office intercom buzzed.

Nickie punched a button. "Hi, Jo-Jo. What's up?" She listened for a moment. "Sure, I guess it's okay. Send him on over."

From a file cabinet she extracted copies of her freshman course outlines. She was paper-clipping them together when a knock came at the door.

"Come in, please," she called.

A man dressed in a London Fog-style raincoat and a gray herringbone Downer hat entered her office. He removed his hat and regarded her through bookish tortoiseshell glasses. "Professor Farrell?"

"That's me," Nickie answered. The man appeared to be thirtyish, respectable-looking, with short dark hair and angular features. "I understand you'd like some freshman course syllabuses for your nephew?"

"That's correct," the man nodded. Holding his hat in his hands: "Floyd is a brilliant young fellow, unfortunately confined to a wheelchair because of a tragic accident. He's thinking of applying to Windfield, and since I happened to be in your area on business Floyd asked me to bring him some detailed course descriptions. I'm sorry to bother you, Professor, but I'd really like to help the boy in any way I can." The man smiled and Nickie noticed that he had unusual, almost navy blue eyes. "Floyd aspires to be a writer."

Nickie returned the smile. "No bother at all, Mr....?"

"Forgive me. I'm Carl Pittston," said the blue-eyed man. He stepped forward and extended his hand. "A pleasure to make your acquaintance, Professor."

"Mr. Pittston." They shook hands over Nickie's desk, and then she handed him the paper-clipped copies. "Your nephew should find these illustrative of our academic expectations."

Accepting the papers without taking his eyes off her face Carl Pittston said, "I'm sure they'll be very helpful. You know, Professor Farrell, from what I've seen of your college I think my nephew would do well to come here. There seems to be such a laudable emphasis on cultural diversity."

"Yes, Windfield prides itself on providing educational opportunities to scholars of every background and circumstance. There's no discrimination or prejudice here, Mr. Pittston. Everyone is a respected member of our community. And, as you may have seen, we are fully equipped to provide for the needs of our handicapped students." She folded her hands atop her desk. "I'm sure that your nephew...is it Floyd?"

"Floyd, yes."

"I'm sure Floyd would find the Windfield experience most enjoyable."

"I daresay. Especially if he had you as a teacher," observed Pittston with a light laugh. "Well, Professor, I needn't take up any more of your time. I'm very much obliged." He put on his hat. "Maybe some day we'll meet again."

"At Floyd's graduation, perhaps." Nickie smiled.

"Indeed." Carl Pittston's navy blue eyes widened a bit. "If not before. Have a good day, Professor Farrell." Replacing his hat, he opened the door and went out.

As Alex Steward passed by Nickie Farrell's office, he slowed his steps and glanced at the closed door, wondering what she was doing at that moment. For the umpteenth time he thought about popping his head in to offer a friendly greeting, then decided against it. He didn't want her drawing any mistaken conclusions from an innocent "hello". They were cordial colleagues, nothing more, and he intended to keep it that way.

At that moment Nickie's door opened and a man he'd never seen before came out into the hall. Startled and displeased, Alex stared at the younger man, who wore a trench coat and hat and carried some papers in one hand.

The man nodded an untroubled greeting. "Such an agreeable lady," he gestured with the papers back at the closed door. "So very accommodating. Undoubtedly a first-rate instructress. Well, good day." With a genial tip of his hat he walked off down the corridor.

Alex hurried to the departmental office. Joanne Markwith greeted from her computer: "Well, if it isn't Professor Steward. What can I do to make your day?"

"Hi, Jo. Checking my messages." He made a show of inspecting the contents of his mail slot. "I just saw some fellow come out of Ms. Farrell's office. I've never seen him before. Do you know who he was?"

Jo narrowed her eyes. She liked Alex, but this silly charade of his was becoming idiotic. No matter how hard he forced himself to deny it, the man was still hopelessly hung up on Nickie Farrell. Joanne knew for a certainty that all Alex had to do was offer one word, one gesture of reconciliation, and Nickie would be in his arms. How could the big boob possibly not know that? And if he did know it, how could he resist? It drove her crazy. Joanne wished she could give Alex a piece of her mind, but she resisted the impulse.

"Actually, Alex, he was a potential applicant's uncle. He dropped by to ask Professor Farrell for a sample course syllabus." She smiled sweetly. "Why do you ask?"

"Oh, no reason." Alex paused. "Except..."

Jo raised her brows. "Hmm?"

"I don't know." Alex frowned. "Something about that guy didn't feel right."

"Why? Did he do anything wrong?"

"Not at all." Alex shrugged. "Well, it's none of my business."

Yes it is, you male donkey! Joanne had to clamp her jaws to keep from shouting at him. Everything about Nickie could be your business if you didn't have your head wedged so far in the dark that you can't see your nose in front of your face!

After a calming moment: "Alex, I'm sort of buried, here. Dr. Silverman needs these budget allocations as soon as possible..."

"Yes, of course. See you later, Jo. He retrieved his briefcase and left the office.

Joanne expelled her breath and irritably snatched up the computer mouse. Sometimes, she thought, men could be stunningly dense. Didn't Alex realize that Nickie's visitor had made him feel jealous? Probably not. Lately Professor Steward had made a career out of being clueless.

⊷⊷⊷⟪◉⟫⊶⊶⊶

Robin Thompson had never set foot on the Windfield College campus. Nor would she ever have done so, if not for Cinda Vanderhart's outrageous blackmail. Robin steered her Kia through the elaborate stone-and-wrought-iron gates and followed an arrowed sign which read 'Visitors'. She drove along the smooth macadam roadway, trying not to feel intimidated by the sophisticated surroundings. It was an alien world, she thought; the people here were as different from her as Martians. Robin pulled into the visitors' lot and cruised along the rows, failing to find a space until a black Mustang backed out right in front of her.

It took many minutes of asking for directions and negotiating the maze of pathways, but she finally found Dickinson East. Standing before the door labeled '128', she took a few breaths to quiet her hammering heart and knocked twice.

"Well, right on time." Cinda Vanderhart swung the door wide. "C'mon in. Never mind the mess, our cleaning lady didn't show up yesterday." She laughed and pointed to a chair with a bra draped over the back. "Just kidding. Sit there," she invited, snatching away the bra. "Wanna take off your coat?"

"I'm fine." Robin sat, her purse in her lap. "You said you want to talk. Well?"

Cinda dragged over a second chair and straddled it backwards. "I don't get this hostile attitude. Face it, we're both here to figure out the truth about– "

"No," interrupted Robin. "I'm here to keep you from hurting someone I love. So can we get this over with?"

"Suit yourself." Cinda peered closely at the townie girl's stiff features. "Tell me how you heard the name Nick Farrington."

Robin shifted in the hard chair. "It wasn't long ago. The beginning of December. My boyfriend's mother was in the hospital. She was terribly sick..."

"What's your boyfriend's name again? Carlie? Carlin?"

"Collie. It's a nickname from Colin, his middle name. But his real name is Nicholas."

"No fooling!" Cinda leaned forward over the back of her chair. "Go on."

"Luanne –that was his mother– knew she wasn't going to make it, and..." Robin looked down and cleared her throat. "Anyway, before the end, she told us a secret she'd kept hidden all these years. She said that her husband Jay-Bo wasn't Collie's father. His real dad was a man named Nick Farrington."

"Holy shit," murmured Cinda Vanderhart. "I *knew* it."

"She said he was a student here at Windfield," continued Robin. "A senior. Luanne and Nick Farrington had an affair. By the time she found out she was pregnant Nick had graduated and was gone. She had no way of finding him or letting him know. There was nothing she could do. So Collie was born, and his mother hid the truth for all those years. Until she knew she was going to die." Robin dug a tissue from her purse and wiped her eyes. "Even though she never saw Nick Farrington again, Luanne told us that she loved him more than anyone else she ever knew. And he loved her, too." She crumpled the damp tissue in her fist. "That's why she named her baby Nicholas. That's all I know."

Cinda nodded, eyes agleam. "It all fits. Incredible. God, what a great story!"

Robin frowned. "What do you mean, 'story'? You make it sound like some stupid movie. And I still don't see why this is any of your concern. It happened more than twenty-five years ago. We weren't even born yet. None of these people have anything to do with you. It's all in the past."

"No, it's *not* in the past!" Cinda sprang up from her chair. "That's what you don't know, Robin. It's very much in the here and now."

"That's impossible. Luanne is dead and there's no telling if Nick Farrington is even alive. Why must you stir things up?"

"All right, listen." Cinda turned the chair around and sat facing Robin so that their knees almost touched. "Don't freak out, okay?"

Robin shrank into herself but said nothing.

"Nick Farrington isn't dead. Well, not exactly. I mean the man is gone, but not the person."

Robin looked at her as if she was babbling.

"Robin, do you know what gender transition is? They used to call it a 'sex change'. It's when someone goes from being a man to a woman."

Robin scraped her chair to the side and stood up. "I have no idea what kind of things you Windfield people like to talk about, but I don't want to hear it. I'm going home now."

"Wait a minute, goddamn it! I have to tell you what—"

"Cursing, too? Very nice." Robin slung her purse over her shoulder. "Goodbye. Don't call me again."

Cinda sprang for the door and placed a palm flat on it. "No, you're not going to run away! Nick Farrington was a *transsexual*. He had a sex change, Robin. He became a woman. Do you hear what I'm saying?

He became a woman. And that same woman is a professor right here at Windfield! See that brick building over there?" She pointed out the window. "That's the English Department. Her office is on the first floor. She's probably there right this minute."

Robin backed slowly away from the door, clutching the little gold crucifix she wore around her neck. "You're crazy," she stammered.

"I swear, it's the truth!" Cinda spread her palms outward. "Think about it, Robin. What reason would I have to lie? Nick Farrington –your boyfriend's father– is now a woman named Nickie Farrell. Nick, Nickie. Farrington, Farrell. Come on! How can you doubt it?"

"Nickie Farrell?" Robin sank back into the chair. Nickie...the lady professor she'd served at the Foxton Arms...elegantly-dressed and sad in church on Christmas Eve...the lady with Collie's eyes...*she* was Nick Farrington? Collie's *dad?* Robin put a hand to her forehead and moaned.

"Hey, girl, you want some water or something? You don't look so good." Cinda opened a compact refrigerator and pulled out one of Heather's bottles of Evian. Handing it to Robin: "A shock, isn't it? I was pretty floored when I first figured it out, too. But Robin, trans-sexuality is becoming more recognized all the time. Gender transition isn't such big a deal a deal anymore. It happens all the time. And now your boyfriend can finally get to meet his real father. How awesome is that?"

Robin choked over the water. "Have you lost your mind?!"

"What?" Cinda blinked. "You can't not tell him. Ms. Farrell is his *father.*"

"In a skirt! And high heels! With...with..." Robin's eyes inadvertently dropped to her own chest.

"Boobs," suggested Cinda.

"*I know what they are.*" Robin's voice shivered near hysteria. "How can I tell him something like this? Can you imagine how he'll feel? How on earth would you feel?"

"I'm probably not the best one to ask," Cinda dryly replied. "I'd give two arms and a leg if my Old Man was a T-girl like Nickie Farrell."

"That's ridiculous," Robin snapped. "Anyway you're not a man.

Men look up to their fathers as male role models. If Collie ever found out that his real father had an operation to become a woman, I don't know if he could take it. And my God, what the people around here would say..." She shuddered. "You don't have any idea."

"Screw 'em. Nickie Farrell is worth a thousand pea-brained bigots. She's one classy lady."

"I know. I met her." Seeing Cinda's astonished expression: "At our church on Christmas Eve. She seemed awfully lonesome. I spoke to her for a little while. She said she didn't have a family anymore. I couldn't understand that." Robin looked at the water bottle in her hand and set in on the desk. "Now, maybe I do."

"Except that's not true. Ms. Farrell *has* a family. She has a son, with her birth name and her heterochromia eyes. And I'm going to make sure she knows it."

"You are, huh?" Robin's voice was weary, resigned. "Whether or not it's the best thing for Nickie and her son. No matter who gets hurt." She slowly shook her head. "It must feel nice to be so positive about everything."

"Look, Robin," Cinda countered with some heat, "I'm not the bad guy here. All I want to do is re-unite a parent with her child. A child she never knew she had. You just said Ms. Farrell seemed lonesome. Can't you see how this could make her happy?"

"Or not. You have no way of being sure."

"Uh-huh. But *you're* sure that it's right to keep this from your man Collie. His mother lied to him his whole life, but now that you have a chance to tell him the truth, the incredible amazing truth, you're going to carry on her tradition and keep lying? That's plain chickenshit. I'll bet you think I'm a spoiled Windfield dyke bitch who should mind her own business, right? Too bad. You do whatever you have to do, but I *am* going to tell Ms. Farrell about her son, whether—"

"Before you do, let me talk to my pastor."

"Huh?" Cinda scowled. "Why should I?"

"Because I'm asking you." Robin stood up and faced the Windfield girl. "Please. I need spiritual guidance. Let me talk to Reverend Shorr, and then..." She hesitated. "I'll go with you when you tell Nickie Farrell the truth. It'll be better that way. For one thing, I know Collie, I knew Luanne, and I can answer all kinds of questions that you can't. Maybe she'll remember me from church, and that might help. It's going to be difficult enough, but if this has to happen, can't we try to do it in the least hurtful way?"

Cinda narrowed her eyes. "This isn't another dodge?"

"No. I promise." Robin leveled her gaze at the other woman. "I'll talk to my pastor, then call you."

"When?"

"Give me a week."

"Don't try hiding behind your answering machine," warned Cinda. "That won't work anymore, Robin. I'm serious. This clock is ticking."

"Just because I don't go to Windfield doesn't mean I'm stupid. Or dishonest."

"Yeah, whatever. Call my cell, 317-580-7839. That's an Indy area code."

Robin programmed the number into her phone, then walked to the door. Grasping the knob: "I hope this all turns out all right. I wish I wasn't so sure that it won't."

She opened the door and left the room without another word.

———◦《◎》◦———

Side by side, Lloyd Skinner and Cale Pittman gazed silently out over the wide-open spaces of the Manassas National Battlefield Park. Although the fields wouldn't be cloaked in their summertime green for months, they nonetheless gave off a vernal sense of quickening earth. Late afternoon sunshine provided no palpable warmth, but the windless air was mild and both men's jackets were unbuttoned.

"Think of it." Cale swept his hand at the vista. "Thousands and thousands of volunteer militia, hard-hitting warriors clashing in a fury of battle, cannons, grapeshot, bayonets, and blood...rivers of blood. Were they afraid? Hell, no. They were iron. Real *men*. They came here to fight and kill and die for their cause." The setting sun's rays glinted in his navy blue eyes. "It all happened right here, partner. Not once, but *twice.*"

"Must've been one hell of a mess, huh?"

"Yes. A beautiful, glorious, blood-soaked hell of courage, bravery, fearlessness, and male guts. The kind of guts that don't exist anymore. There were no pussies here. No pussies, no queers, no transsexuals."

"I don't guess ol' Stonewall let any faggots in his Confederate army," observed Lloyd. "We oughta head back, place closes up in fifteen minutes."

Cale Pittman nodded and placed a hand over his heart. "Gentlemen soldiers...rest peacefully, with honor."

They drove out of the park and turned north toward Graymont County, sharing nips from a pint of Jack Daniels.

Lloyd took a healthy swallow. "Get this: fuckin' Disney tried to buy the battlefield a few years ago. Wanted to build another Mickey Mouse park."

"If that had happened I would've personally torched the entire place."

"Damn straight." Lloyd drank another mouthful of whiskey. "Cale, partner, I'm gettin' really sick of Virginia. Sick of the Old Man, too. Whattaya say we take off? I'll go anywhere you want. New Orleans, Florida, hell, even back to Ocean City. But it's time to move on."

"Partner, I hear what you're saying, and I'm with you. New Orleans beckons, and we should be on our way."

Lloyd grinned with relief. "Great! When? Tomorrow? No, tonight. The sooner we hit the road the better."

"Not yet." Pittman shook his head. "I still have business."

"What business?"

"With that transsexual professor."

Lloyd's shoulders drooped. In a peevish voice: "Jesus, Cale. Forget it, willya? Why waste any more time on that asshole? Fuck 'im. Besides, you can't just keep sneakin' in there like last time. They'll nail your ass for sure. Let's blow this shithole."

"No. And I'll find a way. Vigilance is always rewarded with opportunity. You'll see."

"But why?" Lloyd Skinner drained the bottle and slung it out the window. "What's so important about one goddamn trannie teacher? There's queers and pervs all over the place." He slouched in his seat, glowering.

Cale Pittman patted Lloyd on the thigh. "Let me explain. As you point out, there are perverts everywhere. But of all the deviants in the world, partner, nothing is worse than a shemale. It is the worst desecration of the natural order that has ever polluted mankind."

"Aw, hell. Who gives a rat's ass if some sissy faggot wants to cut off his nuts and wear a dress?"

"I do," hissed Cale Pittman. "Especially if that sissy faggot is encouraged to make innocent young men believe it's *okay*." Pittman grimaced. "It isn't 'okay'. It's a defilement of everything normal, and no right-thinking *Übermensch* can permit it to remain unchallenged. If we ignore something like that," Cale banged the steering wheel for emphasis, "we might as well spit on the graves of those brave warriors back on the battlefield. They did not spill their red blood so that future generations of American males would feel at liberty to transform themselves into cunts."

"But–"

"Femininity is destroying the world. Women were never meant to dominate or rule. Why do you suppose God is a 'He'? Why do little boys think the worst insult of all is to be called a girl? Because it's the natural order, partner. This creeping feminization of everything must be stopped in its tracks, like the Ebola virus, or we –I mean *men*– are doomed. We might as well all slice off our dicks and go shopping for pantyhose and bras."

"Not me," Lloyd rumbled. "I'll kill 'em first."

"Of course. Because you are a Superiorman." Pittman paused, then inquired: "Would you like to hear a story?"

"Yeah, sure."

"All right." Cale drove in silence for a moment. "Some years ago, there was a boy, let's call him...Max. Max was a pretty ordinary kid. After third grade he got transferred to a strict all-male school because his father, who always made a big deal of his own macho masculinity, insisted that Max learn to be a real man. Max wasn't much of a tough guy, but for a while he got along all right."

"Okay."

"One day after school Max and his friend Dub sneaked up into the attic of Max's house to smoke some Kools they had boosted. There was a footlocker up there that had always been locked before, but this time Max saw that the padlock wasn't latched. Naturally he was curious, so he and Dub opened it."

"Oh, man." Lloyd lit a cigarette. "What was in there?"

"At first Max thought it was just a bunch of his mother's old clothes. Dresses, blouses, ladies' underwear, high-heeled shoes, that sort of thing. Boring. But then, on the bottom, he discovered some magazines. Magazines with titles like *He-She, Trans Fantasy, SheMale Exotica.* Max and Dub were almost afraid to look inside, but of course they did, and saw things..." Cale's jaw clenched. "Things they couldn't have imagined in a million years."

"Shit."

"That wasn't all. There was a brown envelope with pictures. Old-style Polaroids, you know, the kind that used to develop themselves. The pictures were of Max's father, who was proud of being so damned manly, all dressed up in women's clothes, made up like a cheap whore. Other pictures of his mother, dressed in strange costumes with chains and boots..." Pittman stopped speaking, his features a cauldron of hatred.

"Son of a bitch," muttered Lloyd.

The Mustang growled along in silence for a few minutes. At length Cale Pittman continued: "Max made Dub swear on his life that he would never say anything. But of course Dub blabbed as soon as he could. For Max, life at school became an endless nightmare of teasing. He fought back as hard as he could, but mostly he got the shit kicked out of him. The more it happened the angrier his father got, yelling at him whenever he came home all beat up, calling him a weakling faggot pantywaist. Eventually the fighting got so bad that the school kicked Max out."

"Goddamn." Lloyd shook his head in disbelief.

"After a while Max began to realize that discovering the photos had been a good thing. His parents' depravity had sharpened his perceptions. He began to recognize how males everywhere were being deliberately turned into girls. He saw how the line between the sexes became increasingly blurred. Men were becoming nurses and airline attendants. Women were becoming sportscasters. Traditional men's clubs were being forced to admit women or close their doors. Male rock stars started appearing in makeup and corsets. Men who tried to preserve traditional male values were derided as barbarians. It got to the point that if a guy didn't act like a fairy the women called him a Neanderthal. Max saw all this, and he swore that it would never happen to him. He would never, *never* be like his father, standing there in nylons and mascara with a shit-eating grin on his face so his bitch wife could turn him into a living Barbie doll." Cale turned and stared into Lloyd's eyes. "In the end, Max did fine. He learned to kick ass, made himself tough as nails, and became a Superiorman. An *Übermensch*, partner. Like you. Like me."

"What happened to Max's parents?"

"Actually, they died in a house fire." Cale winked at Lloyd and laughed.

Lloyd's jaw dropped and his eyes widened. "*You're* Max. And you *did* set the fire!"

"Crispy critters. Got a million bucks for it, too. The Will to Power, partner."

"Jesus fuckin' Christ." Lloyd leaned back against the headrest. "I need another drink."

"Absolutely. Something to eat, too. A juicy rare steak, maybe."

AAfter a mile or two they came to a dilapidated roadside joint marked by a red neon sign that read 'Olde D Bar & Grill'. As they pulled into the lot Lloyd sat up. "New Orleans can wait. We got business to take care of. You n' me, partner. All the goddamn way."

Chapter Fifteen
Occurrence at Gander Creek Bridge

The Reverend Calvin Shorr, pastor of the Good Shepherd Community Church, sadly contemplated the tearful young woman sitting across from him in his book-lined study. In all his years of ministry he had never encountered anyone with a gentler heart than Robin Thompson. Now, when she most needed his counsel, he felt helpless. Her dilemma was so far outside his experience that he could give little solace beyond sympathetic bromides. Reverend Shorr was a caring man, and his inability to offer Robin any meaningful guidance caused him much distress. He couldn't imagine where he might find answers to the questions she had asked him. The Reverend was well-versed in the Holy Scriptures, but except for a few murky Mosaic references to the problematic ritual purity of androgynes he could think of nothing in the sacred texts that seemed even remotely relevant.

"The worst part," Robin cried, "is I'm afraid that Collie –Nicholas– might ask me to help him find Nick Farrington. If that happens, Reverend Shorr, what am I going to do? I can't lie to him. Not about his own father. That would be the worst kind of sin. But if I tell him the truth, what then? He's liable to lose his mind." She paused. "I'm having a very hard time not thinking bad thoughts about that Windfield girl, Reverend. This mess is all her fault. She should have left it alone. It's none of her business."

"Well, but that can't be undone now. Robin, you said Collie's father was here in our church on Christmas Eve? You spoke with him?" The Reverend's brow creased. "Um, I mean, *her?*"

"Yes. She seemed like a nice lady, but very sad." Robin lowered her voice. "There's no way you would ever *know*, Reverend. I'm a woman, and I had no clue."

Reverend Shorr sipped a glass of water. "Sometimes I think that the scientific community has taken us all much too far, much too fast. Life was complicated enough before...things like this were made possible. But we mustn't second-guess our Lord, Robin. He will never saddle us with greater burdens than we're able to bear."

Robin nodded assent.

"Now, about your situation. I agree with you that it makes sense to break the news to Professor Farrell first. However, I don't think it's wise to hazard a guess as to what her reaction might be. The possibilities seem almost endless. One might naturally assume that the discovery of her long-lost child would be a source of great joy, but..." Reverend Shorr frowned. "These circumstances are so extraordinary. The professor may not choose to embrace anything from her previous life. Not even a son."

"Nickie's family threw her out, Reverend. She told me that she wished she had children."

"Any breakup of a family is tragic, and I grieve for her suffering." The Reverend's expression grew firm. "But wishing in the abstract is very different from the reality. The prudent course is to tell her and see how she responds. We'll hope for the best. But," he added with a cautionary lift of his forefinger, "whatever Professor Farrell decides, Robin, you must respect her decision. Even if it means concealing the truth from her son."

"But Reverend," Robin's voice quavered, "wouldn't that be the same as lying to the man I love?"

Reverend Shorr laid his glasses on the desk and rubbed his forehead. "Sometimes, Robin, our only choices are between bad and worse. All right, assume for a moment that Professor Farrell tells you she doesn't want to meet her son. If Collie then somehow discovers the truth, in addition to the shock of everything else he will have to deal with parental rejection. After losing his mother so recently, how could we possibly expect him to endure that?" He replaced his glasses. "I'm sorry, Robin. You came to me for answers, not more questions. But I feel lost, too. This is an instance, I believe, where the best course is prayer. Go speak with the professor, and have faith that the Lord will guide you onto the proper path."

"All right, Reverend." Robin lifted her bowed head. "Thank you for seeing me. I'll do what you say, and I will trust in God. He hasn't let me down yet."

"Nor will He," smiled Reverend Shorr. "You can count on Him. Bless you, my dear girl. Please keep me informed."

———

Cinda Vanderhart lay sprawled on her bed, laptop propped against her knees, composing an article for the school paper titled *U.S. House of Representatives: Closet Chapter of NAMBLA?* Deep in thought, she let her cell phone buzz three times before she impatiently snatched it up.

"Yeah, what?"

She heard a restrained female voice say, "It's me. Robin Thompson."

"Coolio!" Cinda shoved aside her laptop. "I didn't think you'd call."

"I don't break my promises."

"Whatever." Cinda rolled her eyes at her reflection in Heather's mirror. "So, are you ready to go talk to Ms. Farrell?"

"On one condition."

"We journalists don't really do conditions, y'know," said Cinda, picking at a ragged toenail. She heard nothing but silence. "Okay, what condition?"

"We'll leave it up to Professor Farrell to decide whether or not she wants to meet Collie. If she doesn't, that's the end of it. You just let the whole thing go, and leave us alone. All of us. *Forever.*"

"Don't be ridiculous. He's her son. Of course she'll want to meet him."

"There's no way to be sure of that. You may be awfully smart at figuring out other people's business, but I don't think you're all that good at figuring out their feelings. Anyway, if you won't promise me that much, you can just go talk to Nickie by yourself and see if she even believes you. She might not, y'know."

Knowing this was true Cinda squirmed a bit. "But what if she does want to meet him?"

"That's her business," replied Robin. "You stay out of it."

Annoyed, Cinda protested, "Y'know, if it weren't for me your boyfriend might not even be in a position to find out who his father is!"

"Do you think I could ever forget that? Am I supposed to *thank* you?"

"Fine," Cinda snapped. "We'll go talk to her..." She grabbed a calendar from the mess on her desk. "How about next...no wait, I have a lab report and a politics paper due. Week after next. Wednesday, March first."

"All right."

"Ms. Farrell has office hours from one to three. Just come to my room around twelve-thirty and we'll go over there."

"You're sure you won't change your mind about this? It's not too late."

"Change my mind? Get real. I'll see you at twelve-thirty, Robin. Wednesday March first," said Cinda. "Ciao for now."

She snapped her cell phone shut and with a contented sigh grabbed the laptop and went back to her article.

⸻

Ten days later, at the stroke of midnight, Ambassador Eamon Douglass looked up as the massive grandfather clock in his study began tolling its sonorous twelve-count marking the transition from February to March. He laid his pen on the holographic will he was composing and silently counted the booming notes until the final echoes died away.

"One more month," he addressed the glass wolf. "One short month before I –and Windfield– both cease to exist." He winced. Recently his internal pain had been getting worse. It wasn't debilitating; Douglass had endured more severe discomfort from an abscessed tooth. Still, the metastasis was accelerating and making its fatal presence known. The ambassador reluctantly opened a bottle of MS Contin and swallowed a tablet. He hated popping pills like a damned hippie, but the pain was a distraction and he didn't have time to be distracted. His health didn't matter, anyway. As long as he could stand on his two feet and press the button a month hence, that was enough.

Within minutes the opiate anesthetized his twinges, and Eamon Douglass returned to the task of re-writing his will. He already possessed a complex legal instrument as thick as a phone book; but the ambassador had decided to alter it in a way that would, in addition to ensuring a fantastic amount of legal chaos, set off an unprecedented maelstrom of avarice.

Douglass knew that certain insidious provisions of the blasphemously-named Patriot Act made it inevitable that in the aftermath of Windfield's destruction the Feds would designate him a "terrorist" and seize all his assets. In order to gum up the works of this socialist banditry, the ambassador had decided to apportion his estate among certain attorney-rich entities that would, without question, fight Uncle Sam to the death over Eamon Douglass's fortune. First on his list: the American Civil Liberties Union. For a possible shot at a gargantuan monetary windfall, Ambassador Douglass reckoned that the ACLU would eagerly enmesh the government in court proceedings on a more-or-less permanent basis. So would the Church of Scientology, the United Negro College Fund, the Brady Campaign, the American-Arab Anti-Discrimination Committee, NORML, and AIPAC. Other beneficiaries would include the Natural Resources Defense Council, CNN, the Association for the Preservation of Virginia Antiquities, the National Organization for Women, and just for the hell of it, Al Jazeera.

Cackling in an MS Contin haze at the thought of precipitating a greed-fueled scramble such as the world had seldom seen, the ambassador scribbled and scratched on his legal pad late into the wee hours, divvying up his vast estate among people he'd spent a lifetime hating. He had never been happier.

———⊳◉⊲———

The following afternoon, Nickie Farrell found herself in a state of emotional conflict. Her position as assistant professor had been elevated to permanent status; on the other hand, Dr. Silverman's news that Professor Hal Whitman had finally succumbed to his illness diminished the gladness she might otherwise have felt.

Rounding a turn in the corridor she saw two women waiting outside her office door. One was Cinda Vanderhart. The other was the young lady she'd met on Christmas Eve at the Good Shepherd Community Church.

"Well, if it isn't Ms. Vanderhart." Unlocking her office door, she apologized to the second girl, who seemed ill at ease: "I'm afraid I don't recall your name, Ms...?"

"Thompson. Robin Thompson."

"Robin, of course. Forgive me." Nickie looked from one to the other. "I had no idea you two knew each other. Small world, isn't it?"

"Like you wouldn't believe," agreed Cinda. "Can we talk to you, Ms. Farrell? Just for a few minutes."

"I'm a bit busy..." Nickie hesitated, then pushed open her door. "Well, sure. Come on in."

She sat behind her desk and indicated the lone chair. "Sorry, I've only got one."

"Take it," Cinda told Robin. "I'll stand."

"Well, now. What's on your mind?" Nickie raised her eyebrows. "I admit I'm a bit curious. You ladies make an unexpected pair."

Robin Thompson looked at Cinda. "Go on. This is your idea."

"Okay. First off, Ms. Farrell, Robin knows all about you being trans." Cinda stood with her arms crossed, leaning against a tall file cabinet. "Back in 1979, when you were a senior here, your name was Nick Farrington, right?"

"That's none of your business, Ms. Vanderhart!" Nickie whipped off her sunglasses to level a furious glare at Cinda: "I'm getting damned tired of you violating my personal privacy!"

"I know, but you need to hear this."

"Says who?" Turning fiercely on Robin: "Why are you here, anyway?"

Before Robin could respond Cinda interjected, "She'll tell you in a minute. What do you remember about a woman named Luanne Skinner?"

Nickie grew rigid in her chair and the color drained from her face. "*What* did you say?"

"Luanne Skinner," repeated Cinda. "Actually, you had an affair with her. At the end of your senior year."

Nickie grated through clenched teeth: "I'm not going to sit here and listen to thi—"

"What you don't know is that right after you graduated, Luanne Skinner found out she was pregnant."

"Pregnant?" Nickie faltered, then her anger flared anew. "So what? Mrs. Skinner was married. She had two children already."

"Yes, she did. But *this* child wasn't her husband's."

Nickie rose up from her chair. "That's enough. I want both of you out of my office. Now."

Cinda ignored her. "Luanne Skinner had a baby boy. He's grown up now, he lives right here in Stuarton, and he has one blue eye, one brown. Heterochromia iridium, exactly like yours. His name is Nicholas. Nicholas Skinner. Luanne named him for you, Ms. Farrell. Nicholas Skinner is your son."

Nickie weakly subsided into her desk chair, covering her mouth with a trembling hand.

"Tell her, Robin," Cinda prompted. "She needs to hear everything."

Nickie's imploring eyes turned to Robin. "This is a joke, isn't it?"

With as much compassion as possible Robin said, "No, Nickie. It's true."

"See?" Cinda spread her hands in an I-told-you-so gesture. "Would I lie?"

"How can you possibly know about this?" Nickie's whisper was more of a gasp.

"Luanne showed me an old Windfield book," Robin answered. "It had Nick Farrington's picture in it. She told me about the affair and said Nick was Collie's real father."

"Collie? I thought you said his name was Nicholas?"

"It's a nickname from Luanne's maiden name. Colin. He didn't like being called 'Nicholas', so..." Robin gave a tiny shrug. "Collie."

Nickie's glance darted back-and-forth like a rabbit surrounded by wolves. "How would you even know Luanne Skinner? She has to be twice your age."

"Luanne and I were friends from church. The one where I saw you on Christmas Eve."

"Dear God." Nickie squeezed her face between her palms. "Don't tell me she was there that night?"

"No." Robin hesitated. "Last fall Luanne suddenly got terribly sick. She told Nicholas and me the secret about his father just before..." Robin's voice broke. "Just before she died. It was awful. Luanne said Nick Farrington was the only man who'd ever truly loved her."

Nickie collapsed her head onto her arms and began to cry. Robin glanced up at Cinda, who lifted one shoulder with a "what now" expression.

Looking away, Robin spoke in a quiet voice: "Luanne loved Nicholas more than anything in the world. I'm sure it's because of who his father was. *Is,*" she amended. "Your son's a wonderful man, Nickie. His life hasn't been easy, and losing his mother almost killed him, but he's doing well now. We work together at the Foxton Arms Restaurant. I love him very much, and someday I hope we'll be married."

"Even though I was a mess I would have come back," Nickie choked out. "But I didn't know. *I didn't know.*"

"Luanne had no way of finding you," said Robin. "And she was petrified of her husband. If he'd ever found out..." She left the thought unfinished.

Cinda piped up, her voice cheerful: "But now you have a chance to make up for all those lost years. You have a *son,* Ms. Farrell! How cool is that? Aren't you excited? He's finally going to meet his real dad..."

Nickie lifted her head so suddenly they heard the bones in her neck crack. "What? Did you tell him about me?" Her voice became shrill. "*Did* you?"

"No," said Robin. "He doesn't know anything about Nickie Farrell."

"Thank God." Nickie pointed a warning finger: "I want it to stay that way. Not a word to him or anyone else about me being his parent. Not one word, do you hear? The last thing he needs is a transsexual father. I can't, I won't do that to him. Let him live his life in peace."

"If that's what you want," Robin said, with a sharp glance at Cinda, "that's how it'll be."

"Hold on a sec," Cinda objected. "How can you not want to meet your own child? It's unnatural. You're his *dad*. Seriously, Ms. Farrell. How are you going to teach class all day knowing that your son is practically living right next door?"

"*Cinda*," Robin hissed, "let it *go*."

Nickie picked up her sunglasses and donned them. "That's a good question. Thanks to your wretched investigative snooping, it's probably going to be impossible. Even though I really did want to stay at Windfield." With a bitter grimace: "Funny, I found out just a few minutes ago that my job's been made permanent. Another of life's endless ironies."

"But you have to reunite with your son! You can't run off and pretend that he doesn't exist!"

Nickie leaped to her feet and crashed both fists down on her desk. "Don't you *dare* tell me what I can and can't do. It's *my* life. I'm sick of your meddling! Keep your nose out of my business! You've caused me nothing but trouble, Ms. Vanderhart. First you broke your word and ran that story before you said you would. Then I told you my old name was none of your affair, but you dug it up anyway. And now *this?*" She banged her fists again. "I'll move to Tierra del Fuego if that's what it takes, but *no more lives* are going to be messed up because of me. Especially not my son's. Oh, Jesus...my son." She placed her hands over her temples. "Luanne...why? Why?" Her anguished wail echoed in the cramped office: "*I would've come back!*"

Robin got up from her chair. "Let's *go*," she commanded Cinda in a tone that precluded argument. "Nickie...I swear to you I'll never tell Nicholas."

"If you love him you won't. No one needs a freak for a father." Nickie sat and swiveled her chair away from them. "Please leave."

Robin followed Cinda out of the office. Nickie began sobbing anew, the sounds contrasting sadly with the cheerful March sunshine beyond the window.

———— ◉ ————

Neither girl spoke until they emerged from the building. Standing on the stone steps, squinting in the bright light, Cinda Vanderhart let out a regretful sigh. "Well, that sucked."

"Sucked?" Robin echoed, with an incredulous stare. "Do you have any idea what just happened up there?"

"Don't patronize me," Cinda snapped. "Count on a God-Squadder to lay a guilt trip faster than the speed of light."

Robin clenched her fists at her side. "You may have ruined Nickie's life. Don't you realize that? Don't you care?" Around them groups of Windfield students chattered and laughed as they strolled through the springtime climate. "Never mind that you've forced *me* into a lifelong lie. I'll cope with that. But Ms. Farrell can never be the same after this. You've changed her world forever. And for what? Why was it so important to force this down her throat?"

With a faraway look Cinda answered, "Believe it or not, I honestly thought that reuniting her with her son would bring some joy into her life. She doesn't have much, believe me. You think I'm a selfish lesbian Anti-Christ piece of shit, don't you? Well, that's nothing compared to what most people think about someone like Nickie Farrell. Transsexuals spend their whole lives being targets of contempt, ridicule, hatred, you name it. There are some seriously evil assholes out there who would love to tie Ms. Farrell to a tree and set her on fire. All in the name of God, of course." Cinda sourly added, "Some of them might even be in your own church."

Robin flushed. "Insulting people doesn't take away from the fact that what you did was wrong. Messing around in another person's life is wrong. Making me go along with it was *wrong*. You say your intentions were good, but even if they were, so what? Nickie is still devastated. I hope she doesn't decide to leave Windfield because of this, but if she does...well, I wouldn't want that burden on my soul."

"Oh," sneered Cinda, "I'm sure Jesus knows this was all *my* fault. Don't sweat it. Your spiritual purity is still starched and clean."

"So much anger." Robin shook her head. "You must be a very unhappy person."

"Spare me the condescension," Cinda retorted. "I'll survive."

Robin nodded. "People like you always survive. No matter how many others they hurt." She readjusted her purse on her shoulder and descended from the steps. "Don't call me again. Don't leave messages. That was our agreement, so just forget that we exist." She turned and began walking away.

"Hey," Cinda called after her, "this story isn't over."

Robin halted and looked back. "Maybe not. But your part in it is. There's nothing you can do for Ms. Farrell anymore, except apologize. Not that I think she'd listen. I wouldn't."

Robin walked away and vanished among the students crowding the pathways. Tight-lipped, Cinda started toward her dorm, but after a few steps she hesitated, looked over her shoulder at the English Department, then reversed direction and went back inside.

———— ((◉)) ————

Joanne Markwith stood over the copy machine, humming to herself as she ran off a pile of classroom handouts. The office door opened.

"Hi, Madame Professor." Jo's smile faded the instant she saw Nickie's face. "What's wrong, hon?"

"I can't teach my afternoon class. Post a cancellation notice."

"Nickie, what is it?" Alarmed by the other's bleak expression: "Are you sick?"

"No. I need to leave for a while. Just cancel my class. Please."

"Where are you going? Talk to me, sweetie. Something's wrong.

Maybe I can help."

"No one can help me." The dismal hopelessness in her friend's voice gave Joanne Markwith goose bumps. Before she could reply Nickie opened the door and went out.

Joanne ran after her into the corridor. "Nickie, wait! Come back..."

At that moment Jo saw Cinda Vanderhart appear around a corner. Cinda caught sight of Nickie and immediately exclaimed, "Ms. Farrell! Hey, I'm really sorry. Honestly I am. I didn't mean to–"

Nickie's voice was tinged with panic: "*No.* I don't want to hear it! I can't take any more. Just *leave me alone* already."

Holding an arm out as if to fend off an attacker she rushed past Cinda Vanderhart and disappeared.

Joanne glared at the freshman girl. "What in God's name did you do?"

"N-nothing."

"Answer my question." Joanne strode forward. "*What did you do?*"
Cinda fled.

Joanne had no chance of catching the fleet-footed young woman. She returned to the office and resumed copying, filled with foreboding. Something bad was in the offing, she thought. Something very bad.

"Nickie, be careful," she silently prayed. "For heaven's sake, *be careful.*"

⊸⊶《◉》⊷⊶

Nickie Farrell steered her car out through the stone gates of Windfield College onto the county road. She drove without purpose, taking no notice of the golden forsythia blooms along the shoulders, the clusters of daffodils stirring in the mild breezes, the budding dogwood trees. Her mind had traveled back to a springtime twenty-five years past when she had been a brash college boy trying to subdue his internal demons with reckless behavior; behavior which had culminated in a short-lived love affair with an unhappy married woman. The wife of an abusive brute, she'd glowed with happiness whenever they were together, as if sensing that their few precious moments of shared joy would have to sustain her for a lifetime. And the tormented young man had found in the ill-fated country girl a purer love than he'd ever known. In the way of such encounters it had come to an end with nothing remaining of their bygone love but bittersweet memories. Or so Nick Farrington had assumed.

She drove past some elaborate iron gates next to a big painted sign proclaiming 'Damascus Farms, Est. 1842', but Nickie took no notice. "Luanne," she wept, grasping the steering wheel with both hands, "Oh, God, Luanne. I'm sorry. I would have come back, if I'd known. I loved you. I would have tried my best. Why did you die? I should have been the one to die. Nobody needs me, but our son needed you." Tears ran down her cheeks and dripped into her lap, staining her skirt with makeup. "Nicholas. My *son*. But I'm no good to him. I won't ruin his life, Luanne. He'll be better off without a circus freak father. I'll go away, far away. I wish you hadn't died. You were so good, so loving. It's not fair."

The fenced-in pastures on both sides gave way to overgrown woods as the road began to descend and curve steeply to the right. A yellow sign pocked with rusted bullet holes warned 'Single Lane Ahead'. The road gradually narrowed to one lane which led onto a stone bridge marked with a green sign atop a rusty length of pipe: 'Gander Creek'.

A sudden torrent of long-ago memories coursed through Nickie's head. "Gander Creek," she breathed. "It was here. This is the place. Oh…my…God."

She hit the brakes and pulled the Accord onto a sandy shoulder.

"It couldn't still be there. Not after all this time." Nickie scrambled from the car, heedless of her keys and purse, and hurried toward the bridge. At that moment a black Mustang GT came barreling across from the opposite end. It roared by and rapidly disappeared up the hill.

She walked out onto the stone span. The stillness was broken only by the bubbling sound of Gander Creek flowing by underneath. Rays of sunshine slanted down through overhanging branches and illuminated the worn stone parapets. Nickie bent down, carefully inspecting every inch, brushing aside the occasional leaf or clump of dirt. After a minute or so she found what she was looking for: two faint letters crudely scratched into the stone surface inside a heart shape:

She crouched down as a huge sob welled out: "Luanne!"

Then Nickie Farrell laid her head on her hands and cried as if her heart would break, a red-haired woman in a blazer and skirt, alone in the middle of a deserted stone bridge at the bottom of a country hollow.

———◦《◉》◦———

Bluestone gravel sprayed from the driveway of Damascus Farms as the black Mustang GT made a hasty turnaround. Twin exhausts bellowing like prehistoric beasts, it swerved onto the road and accelerated back the way it had come.

Inside, Cale Pittman slammed through the gears, revving the engine to the redline with every shift of the stick. He grinned at Lloyd Skinner, his eyes burning blue like a submerged nuclear core. "Opportunity, partner! Didn't I tell you? *Übermenschen* always get their opportunity. *Der Wille zur Macht.* We're in business now!"

Lloyd stared at the speedometer. "You're sure it was him?"

Cale Pittman let out a whoop of pure glee: "Oh yeah. Not a doubt in the world, partner. I'd know that fake cunt anywhere. It's him, all right. The transsexual professor. Only *he's* going to be the student for a change. And *we* are going to be the teachers."

Nickie was brought back to awareness by the rumble of a car engine. She looked up and saw a black Mustang pulling in behind her Accord. Quickly she got to her feet, wiping her tear-streaked face and pushing at her disheveled hair.

The driver's door of the Mustang opened and a man wearing a leather jacket and dark sunglasses got out. He stood looking at Nickie for a moment then called out with kindhearted concern: "Having car trouble, ma'am?"

"Oh, no. Not at all." Nickie smoothed her blazer and walked toward the man. "I was just...looking at the stream. It's so beautiful."

The man wrinkled his nose at her Honda. "Y'know, these Jap vehicles are supposed to be so reliable, but they break down all the time." He pointed at the Mustang. "Now there's a solid piece of American engineering. You ought to get yourself one of those. Pretty lady like you would look sexy driving a pony car." His lips pulled back in a smile. "Yep, mighty sexy."

The disquieting realization suddenly hit Nickie that she was isolated on a deserted road with a strange man who had twice used the word "sexy". Trying to hide her nervousness she replied in a careless tone, "Well, I'm not really the sports car type." She took a few steps toward her car then stopped as a second, much bigger blond man emerged from the Mustang.

"No?" The man in the leather jacket looked puzzled. "What type are you?"

"The boring type. A schoolteacher. And actually I have an afternoon class I'm late for, so..." To her dismay Nickie saw the big blonde man stroll to her car and casually lean against the driver-side door. She swallowed and finished her sentence, "...I really should be on my way. But thank you for your concern."

"Oh, don't mention it," grinned the first man. "Professor Farrell."

Nickie felt the short hairs on her neck rise and a surge of adrenalin flooded her system. "I'm afraid I don't...Have we met, Mr...?"

"Just call me Friedrich," chuckled the man, removing his sunglasses and folding them into his jacket. "You know, like Nietzsche."

Badly frightened now, Nickie stared at the man's navy blue eyes and recognized him as the one who'd come to her office for a sample syllabus. There was no doubt it was the same person. What had his name been? She was too scared to recall.

Nickie drew herself up. As firmly as possible she stated, "I really need to be going now." She walked up to her car and addressed the big blonde man, who didn't move. "Excuse me, please."

"You ain't goin' nowhere." The blonde man crossed his arms, leaned forward and laughed in her face. The sour smell of whiskey enveloped her as he added, "Bitch."

"How thoughtless of me," said the man who called himself Friedrich. Indicating the blonde ruffian: "Allow me to introduce my colleague, Dr. Cutter. He's a very famous surgeon. Do you know what his specialty is?"

Nickie dumbly shook her head. She had never before experienced such a feeling of helpless dread.

"Sex-change operations." Friedrich nodded solemnly. "It's true. You know, he takes little boys and turns them into little girls. Did you ever hear of such a thing?"

"Let me go," Nickie's voice shook so badly she could barely articulate the words. "I haven't done anything. Please. I want to leave now."

At that moment a rusted-out Oldsmobile Cutlass came wheezing down the hill. Behind the wheel slouched a shrunken old woman who resembled the crone in Grant Wood's famous painting, *American Gothic*. Nickie suddenly broke toward the old car, waving her arms and pleading at the top of her voice, "Wait! Stop! Please, *help me!*"

The woman didn't even glance her way. The Oldsmobile crossed the bridge and clattered away. Nickie ran a few more steps, panting, still calling after it, "Don't leave me, for God's sake, please..." Then she felt herself grabbed from the rear. A muscled hairy forearm encircled her throat, and again she smelled rancid whiskey breath. "I *said* you ain't goin' nowhere, you fuckin' dirtbag."

Nickie tried to punch free, but her flailing arms were grabbed in an iron grip and twisted up behind her back until she gasped with the pain. As a last resort she kicked backward with her shoe and heard a curse as the heel of her pump connected with something solid. The forearm tightened around her neck until she saw stars, and she felt herself almost lifted off the ground.

"Now, was that nice?" Through a fog of terror she heard Friedrich's disapproving cluck: "Really, Professor. You should know better than to disrespect a great surgeon like Dr. Cutter. I think we need to find somewhere private where we can all have a friendly chat." After a short pause: "Why, look there! A nice cozy space under the bridge. Almost like a little operating room, in fact. Dr. Cutter, if you would be so kind as to bring our guest?"

Powerless as a ground squirrel in the jaws of a hungry fox, Nickie Farrell felt herself being half-carried, half-dragged off the side of the road. Down a short incline, and then the sunlight was blocked out by a dank-smelling concrete slab. With odd detachment she noted that the rushing noise of the creek sounded weirdly amplified under the bridge. Then she was thrown to the ground amidst a tangle of dead brush and leaves, and a sudden vicious blow to the side of her head made everything go black.

⸻ ◆ ⸻

"Stop!" Cale Pittman barked at Lloyd, who was drawing back his heavy work boot to deliver another kick. "What's wrong with you, partner?"

"Goddamn it, that motherfucker hurt me!" Lloyd rubbed his bruised shin.

"Get a grip. A Superiorman laughs at pain. Who's the pussy here, you or him?" Pittman bent over Nickie's motionless form and roughly rolled her onto her back. After a moment: "Okay, he's just knocked out. No harm done."

"Bastard really does look like a woman," Lloyd scowled. "Lookit those damn tits."

"Fake, partner. Everything's fake. It's all a sick, evil deception."

Nickie's colored sunglasses lay on the ground where they'd been dislodged by the kick to her head. Cale picked them up and donned them. "Cute," he laughed, peering around. "Okay, let's revive our sleeping beauty." He pointed to a discarded beer bottle sticking out of the mud. "Get me some water."

While Lloyd complied Pittman searched around until he found a long stick of driftwood. He snapped off one end, leaving a sharp point. "In case our trannie needs a little persuasion. Remember Mr. Catfish?"

Lloyd smirked. "Give it here." Cale handed him the stick and took the filled bottle. "All right. Lesson time." He poured a thin stream of icy creek water down onto Nickie's upturned face. "Wake up, Princess. It's time to play. Come on. Don't keep Uncle Friedrich waiting..."

———— ◉ ————

Nickie regained consciousness in a whirl of disjointed sensations. She felt cold, and wet, and she was lying on her back. An iron spike of agony throbbed in her left temple while a strange swooshing sound echoed all around. She couldn't remember where she was. Maybe, she thought, she'd had another operation and was coming out of the anesthesia. She opened her eyes but immediately shut them as water poured all over her face. Choking, gasping for air, she became aware of a taunting voice above her: "Come on, *Mister* Farrell, time to wake up. You've been a naughty boy, haven't you? Running around in Mommy's clothes again. Tsk, tsk. I'm afraid that's just not acceptable. We don't tolerate little transsexual faggots. This is a man's world."

A menacing growl threatened: "Wake up, you sorry-ass sack of shit, before I stomp your throat in."

Nickie opened her eyes and couldn't suppress a moan at the sight of the big blonde man straddling her supine body. He stood holding a sharp stick, the point poised a few inches above her face. His companion stood to one side, wearing her sunset glasses and holding a dirty old beer bottle. Paralyzed with fear, Nickie couldn't move a muscle.

"Willya look at that? This asshole's got two different-colored eyes."

The blonde man waved the pointed stick in front of Nickie's nose. "A goddamn mutant, just like my shithead brother."

"Hm! So he does. If he gives you any trouble go ahead and gouge out the brown one first. It's unsightly anyway."

"Good idea," grinned the blonde man.

"All right, Fluffy, listen up." The blue-eyed man knelt by Nickie's head. "Here's the program for today's entertainment. First, you're going to lose those ladies' clothes. I can't allow a transsexual fraud to wear real women's fashions. That wouldn't be decent. On the other hand, since I'm such a good sport, I'm going to help you feel like a woman in other ways." He flipped the bottle into the air and caught it again. "You went to an awful lot of trouble and expense turning your prick into a cunt. I think it's important we find out how good a bargain you got." He reached out and patted her shoulder. "Doesn't that sound fun?"

"Why are you doing this to me?" Nickie's piteous whine echoed in the dank space. "*Why?*"

"Shut the fuck up, trannie," said the blonde man, kicking her in the thigh. "Or this ends up in your brain." He held the pointed stick an inch above her left eye.

"Thank you, Dr. Cutter." The man in the leather jacket reached down and roughly pulled up Nickie's skirt, exposing her legs and underwear. He slipped his hands inside the waistband of her pantyhose and yanked hard. They ripped free, and he pulled the shreds away, tossing them aside. "My, what pretty blue panties," he commented. "Sorry, but they've got to go."

There was a sudden rumble as a vehicle crossed the bridge overhead. Nickie's chest shook with suppressed sobs as the noise faded away.

"Now, were you thinking that some brave knight was going to come to your rescue?" The blue-eyed man laughed. "Sorry, but that only happens to real princesses." In one motion he slid Nickie's panties off her naked legs. Inspecting them through the colored sunglasses: "Victoria's Secret. You deviates never get enough, do you?" He wadded them into a little ball, forced Nickie's jaw open by squeezing with two fingers and jammed the panties down into her mouth, nearly suffocating her. "Much better," he nodded, and reached for the beer bottle. "Now let's see how you like being fucked, girlyboy."

Nickie felt her legs being pulled apart. The cold air on her exposed privates almost hurt. Knowing what was about to happen, her conscious mind ran into a small dark corner of her brain and huddled there, shivering, like a small furry creature waiting to be eaten.

Lloyd Skinner watched approvingly as his partner inverted the bottle and took aim at their captive's phony vagina; which, he had to admit, looked exactly like the real thing. The sight of the trannie professor lying gagged and helpless on the ground, about to be violated with an old beer bottle, was actually quite stimulating. Here at last was payback for all the bullshit and indignity visited on his family by Windfield College.

Leering and waving the sharpened stick: "Nail him good, partner! Give that goddamned Windfield trannie something he'll remember forev-"

The words lodged in his throat as they heard the unmistakable ratcheting sound of a shotgun being cocked. Cale dropped the bottle and jumped up, his face distorted in a rictus of rage and fear: "*What the fuck?*"

Silhouetted in the sunlight just under the edge of the bridge, a grizzled black man wearing a Bull Durham cap stood with an over-under 12-guage shotgun leveled at their heads. In a firm voice he ordered, "Back off. I ain't likely to miss." He raised the weapon and sighted along the barrel. "You got 'bout two seconds to do s'I say."

Cale and Lloyd slowly retreated as Blue Ridge Harry came forward, keeping the shotgun steadily trained on them. When he reached Nickie, who lay motionless on the ground with her eyes closed, he crouched and pulled her muddy skirt down over her nakedness. Then he stood back up, never taking his eyes off the two *Übermenschen*.

"*Nigger,*" hissed Cale Pittman, "I swear you are one dead motherfucking nigger."

"I been hearin' that from no-account white trash for a long time." Blue Ridge Harry aimed the shotgun squarely into Pittman's face. "I ain't dead yet. Take off that lady's glasses. Set 'em down easy."

Glaring horribly, Cale removed Nickie's sunglasses and dropped them on the sand.

Behind them on the ground, Nickie coughed the wadded-up panties out of her mouth and rolled onto one side, drawing her legs up into a fetal position and weakly moaning.

The black man gestured with the gun barrel: "All right, now climb up to the road, real slow like. You first," he nodded at Lloyd. He added without turning around: "I'll be right back, Miss. Ain't nobody gon' hurt you."

When they reached the top, Harry motioned with his shotgun at the Mustang, behind which stood a beat-up orange pickup. "You boys git. Don' think 'bout comin' back."

"So what're you gonna do, call the cops?" Cale Pittman spat on the ground. "Think they'll listen to a lying old nigger?"

Blue Ridge Harry actually laughed. "You two ain't gon' be 'round long enough t'go bothering the po-lice. The good Lord'll see t'that." His smile faded. "I ain't gon' tell you again. Git yo' sorry white asses out of here."

"Come *on*, Cale," Lloyd urged, his eyes glued on the yawning shotgun muzzle.

"Shut your trap, *partner.*" Pittman threw him an enraged glance. He sauntered to the Mustang and opened the driver's door. "Nigger," he snarled, "This isn't over. I'll see you again. Count on it, boy." He got in, fired the engine, and fishtailed up the hill in an acrid cloud of tire smoke.

Blue Ridge Harry kept his shotgun pointed at the black car until it had disappeared. Then he ran to the orange pickup, grabbed an old blanket from the front seat, locked the weapon in a rusty cross-bed tool box and scrambled back under the bridge.

Nickie still lay curled on her side, feet drawn up. Blue Ridge Harry knelt beside her with the blanket. He could see her whole body shivering.

"Miss," he said quietly, "Le's get you warm, now." He gently draped the blanket over Nickie, feeling her flinch at his touch. "They's gone, Miss. But we best be gettin' you some help. Hospital ain't far."

"N-n-no," cried Nickie through chattering teeth. "No hospital. No d-doctors."

Harry retrieved Nickie's sunglasses and her wadded-up underwear. Placing both in his pocket he said, "Can you stand up, Miss? Come on. We got t'get you out from down here."

Keeping her wrapped in the blanket, with surprising strength he helped Nickie up and assisted her to climb the embankment. In the fading light he saw that her face was almost white, the eyes wide with shock, an angry raised bruise on her left cheekbone. Her outfit under the blanket was streaked with mud and ripped in several places. Harry eased her into the Accord's passenger seat then hurried around and got in behind the wheel.

"Miss, I can't give the kind o'help you need. Womenfolk got to care for you. Tell me where to go, Miss. Please. Otherwise we goin' to the hospital."

Holding the blanket tightly around her shoulders, Nickie stuttered: "No. N-no hospital. My purse...cell phone. P-push 5." Her lips trembled as she began to sob.

"You safe now. Jus' hold on, Miss, for a li'l while longer." Blue Ridge Harry started the car. "Ol' Harry ain't gon' let nuthin' happen to you."

———— ((◦)) ————

Alex Steward dropped some student evaluations on the counter in front of Joanne's desk and casually observed, "I noticed that Nickie cancelled her afternoon class...?"

Still distressed by her friend's earlier demeanor, Jo was in no mood to put up with Alex's ham-handed fishing. "Yes, she did. Don't ask me why because I have no idea, and anyway it's none of your concern."

Alex blinked at her bristly tone. "No, of course not. I was only wondering..." He fell silent under the secretary's withering look. "Um,

I'd better go get ready for my seminar."

"Yes, do that." Jo clamped the jaws of her stapler on Alex's papers and tossed them in an overflowing basket just as a Big Ben ring tone emanated from her purse. She extracted her cell phone and looked at the message window. Eagerly: "Hey, Nickie! Are you all right? I've been..." She froze in mid-sentence. "Wait...Who is this?"

Alex paused with his hand on the door.

Joanne's mouth fell open. "Oh, no. Oh, God. When?" Clutching a handful of her hair: "Is she badly hurt? Oh, my *God*."

Alex rushed over. "What is it? What's happened? Is it Nickie?"

Joanne stared at him, unseeing, and spoke into the phone. "My place? Yes, of course. Whatever she wants. It's 1018 Willow Lane. I'll meet you there in twenty...no, fifteen minutes. Thank you, Mister... Harry? Okay, Harry. Take care of her."

Jo snapped her phone shut and started to cry. As she jumped to her feet: "Shit, shit, *shit*."

"For God's sake, Joanne," Alex pleaded, his face pale, "what happened? Tell me!"

"It's Nickie." Joanne snatched up her purse and coat. "She was... she's been attacked."

"*Attacked?*" Alex put a hand on the counter to steady himself. "Who? Where?"

"I don't know. I've got to leave. Tell Dr. Silverman I had a sudden emergency. I'll call him as soon as I can. And you *keep quiet* about this, hear? It's nobody's damn business. Don't hurt Nickie worse than you already have."

Alex looked stricken. "I want to see her. I want to help..."

Instantly Jo was in his face like a bantamweight facing off an opponent. "*Don't you even think about it!*"

Cowed, Alex held up his palms. "Please, Joanne. Can't I just–"

"No, you *can't*." Joanne's eyes showed white all around. "Where were you when Nickie needed you? You had your chance. *I'll* take care of her now. Keep out of it." Joanne yanked open the office door. "Oh, God. Why are men such *savages?*"

With a slam, she was gone.

"Jo?"

The sound of Nickie's beaten voice almost made Joanne lose it, but she got a grip and helped the black man ease her friend out of the Accord. "Come on, baby," she whispered to Nickie, whose glazed eyes searched her face. "It's okay, sweetheart, I'm here. You're safe now." In a low aside to Blue Ridge Harry: "Do you know if..." Jo couldn't say the words. "Has she been...?"

Harry shook his head. "Don' think so. Not like that." He handed Jo Nickie's sunglasses, underwear and car keys. "Seem like I mebbe got there in time."

"Thank God. Bless you, Mr. Harry." Seeing the raised bruise on Nickie's face: "Whoever did this is going to pay."

"Bes' not think 'bout that right now. Jes' take care o' her." He paused, his brown eyes sorrowful. "She's a mighty good lady." Then Blue Ridge Harry touched a finger to his cap and walked away down the sidewalk.

Joanne put both arms around Nickie and slowly assisted her to the front door. "My poor angel," Jo murmured as her tears again flowed. "What sort of monster would do this to you? I'm so sorry, baby. So terribly, terribly sorry."

Aware that Nickie had sustained a blow to the head, Joanne made sure that she could stand on her own and focus her eyes properly, then gave her a set of soft gray sweats and showed her to the bathroom. While Nickie showered Joanne folded the sullied clothes into a shopping bag and stowed them away, knowing that Nickie would never wear them again. She brewed some Chamomile tea and carried a steaming mug back to the bedroom, where she found her friend sitting droop-shouldered on the bed, dressed in the sweats, wet hair hanging. As Joanne entered the room Nickie looked up with the expression of a little girl who'd been severely whipped for something she didn't do. Jo smiled bravely and handed her the tea. "Here, sweetheart, try and sip this, okay?"

"Okay," Nickie barely whispered. "Thank you, Jo."

"This will help the swelling." Joanne gently rubbed some Arnica salve on Nickie's facial bruise. "Would you like me to blow-dry your hair?"

A faint nod. "Thank you, Jo."

Joanne spent the next fifteen minutes carefully drying and brushing out Nickie's long red locks. She kept up a muted but cheerful hairdresser's patter, telling Nickie how pretty her color was, how so many girls would be envious, what a chore her own curls were, and which conditioners she liked and didn't like. During the grooming Nickie sat with her eyes closed, taking occasional sips of the tea, responding only in occasional soft monosyllables.

When Joanne finished she lightly fluffed Nickie's hair with her fingers. "There, gorgeous as ever."

Without looking at her Nickie said in a subdued voice, "I don't want to talk about it."

Jo set aside the dryer, sat on the edge of the bed by Nickie and gently hugged her. "You don't have to do anything you don't want, hon. Just take it easy. You can stay here for as long as you need to. Days, weeks, anything. Or I'll come be with you at your place, if you'd rather. Whatever makes you most comfortable." She kissed Nickie on the temple. "You don't have to worry about school, while you were showering I called Dr. Silverman..."

Nickie started with alarm.

"Don't worry," Jo soothed her. "I made him swear not to say anything. Except to President Lindsey, if she asks. He'll keep his word, hon. Larry's a good man. We'll say there was a family emergency and you had to leave for an indeterminate period. Someone will sub for your classes. It's going to be all right, I promise."

"I'm useless." Nickie stared down into her lap. "A trannie freak."

"Oh God, Nickie, no." Jo held her friend close. "Don't say that. Never."

"I am. You don't know..."

"You're a smart, beautiful, courageous woman, and people admire you so much. Nothing can change that, not for a minute. You need a little time to bounce back, that's all." Jo tenderly lifted Nickie's chin. "And remember, we're best girlfriends forever."

A brief tiny spark seemed to illuminate Nickie's different-colored eyes.

"That's my brave girl." Jo kissed her again. "Would you like some more tea?"

Nickie shook her head. "Can I rest a little?"

"Sure, sweetie." Joanne stretched out against her pillows and patted the bed. "Here, let's cuddle like two teenagers having a slumber party."

Nickie snuggled up against Jo like a cat seeking warmth. After a while her breathing slowed and became regular. Warm tears slid unheeded down Joanne's cheeks as they lay side by side in the silent room. For a long while Jo continued to tenderly pet her wounded friend, quietly weeping for the cruel and irrecoverable loss of Nickie Farrell's feminine innocence.

Chapter Sixteen
Love Over Power

The insistent buzz from President Fredericka Lindsey's intercom rasped on her Monday-morning nerves. "What is it, Del?"

"Ambassador Douglass, line three. The man sounds pretty cranky."

"He's not the only one," muttered the college president. She pushed the blinking button on her phone bank. "Good morning, Ambassador."

"I have very few good mornings lately, Madame President, and this isn't one of them."

President Lindsey closed her eyes. "I'm sorry to hear that."

"Can't be helped. Madame President, I have been trying for days to reach Professor Farrell, with no success. My messages have been ignored. I am displeased and somewhat surprised, because heretofore Ms. Farrell has been unfailingly responsive. Can you explain this lapse?"

Fredericka Lindsey knew the precise explanation but she would never discuss it with anyone, let alone Eamon Douglass. "Ambassador, Professor Farrell had to leave campus very suddenly last week due to an unexpected family emergency."

"She *left?* " There was no mistaking the outrage in his tone. "It's imperative that Professor Farrell be here for the Redemp...for the Windfield Memorial dedication. I *insist*."

Fredericka Lindsey bit her lip for a five-count. "Ambassador, I appreciate your enthusiasm with regard to this upcoming event, but unexpected circumstances do occasionally arise. Professor Farrell had... no choice in the matter."

"Madame President, are you telling me that Ms. Farrell has left Windfield permanently?"

"That's not what I said, Ambassador. I've spoken with the professor, and she will be back on campus next week." Consulting a desk calendar: "Monday, the thirteenth of March."

After an irritated silence: "Does Ms. Farrell intend to remain incommunicado until then?"

"I think that's likely, since she's devoting her attention exclusively to personal matters," replied President Lindsey. "But as I say, Professor Farrell will return to Windfield in a week's time. In the meantime, I can assure you that everything is proceeding smoothly. The new memorial is magnificent." She glanced out the window. "I can see everything from here, Ambassador. They are beginning to arrange the flower beds. It's a breathtaking achievement."

"Good. As you know, Madame President, excellence is my standard. Everything must be perfect."

"And so it is, Ambassador Douglass. We are indebted to you."

"I'll let you go now. See to it that Professor Farrell contacts me immediately upon her return."

Fredericka Lindsey thought about saying 'Have a nice day', but then realized she didn't care whether Eamon Douglass had a nice day or not. "Goodbye, Ambassador."

—————◦((◦))◦—————

That evening, Collie Skinner paused outside Robin's apartment for a moment's reflection. He expected –hoped– that by the time he came back out his life would be changed, though not because today was his twenty-sixth birthday. Birthdays came and went, but tonight...well, tonight would be a once-in-a lifetime moment.

"Get a grip, dork," he admonished himself. "Remember that you're the man, and don't mess it up." After a final pat of his carefully-combed hair Collie tapped the little metal knocker.

"Hello, Nicholas!" Robin opened the door wide. "Come in, my handsome birthday boy. Are you hungry? Guess what I made! Some of your favorite–" She broke off, blushing. "Why are you staring at me?"

Collie thought Robin had never looked more enchanting. She wore a form-fitting white sweater and green plaid skirt, with her hair swept back on the sides and affixed by faux pearl clips. She'd put on a bit more makeup than usual, which accentuated her brown eyes and made them look huge and luminous. In his dazzled view Robin was the quintessential good girl: demure, sweet, feminine, chaste, and achingly sexy.

"Because," he managed not to stammer, "you're the most beautiful girl...*woman* in the world."

"Oh, Nicholas." With a love-filled smile: "It makes me happy that you think so." She led him by the hand to her living area, where a small table had been set with linen, silverware, glasses, and two tall red candles.

"Wow! You didn't have to go to all this trouble." Collie sat on the couch as Robin lit the candles and turned the lights down. "This is like the Arms." He sniffed the savory aromas wafting from the kitchen. "Except the food smells even better." With a grin: "Don't tell Chef Yves I said that. Beef Bourguignon?"

Robin's eyes danced. "Patience, Mr. Maitre d'! Dinner isn't served yet. Wait there." She disappeared into her bedroom, then came back out bearing a colorfully-wrapped package with a blue bow on it.

"Happy birthday, Nicholas." She handed him his present. "I hope it's something you can use."

Collie shook the package near his ear. "Hmm," he teased her, "I don't hear anything."

"Well, aren't you going to open it?"

Collie carefully undid the wrapping. "Omigosh...a cell phone!" Admiring the box: "Just like yours. How cool is that!"

"Do you like it?"

"Yes, of course...but geez, Robin," he worried, "don't these things cost an arm and a leg?"

"Not necessarily. I'm a pretty good bargain shopper. Besides," she gently chided, "you're not supposed to worry about that."

Collie studied the list of features. "I'll need a degree in engineering just to figure out how to turn it on."

"No, silly. It's really easy. Here, let me show you."

For the next quarter of an hour she familiarized Collie with his new phone. As a ring tone he selected ZZ Top's "She's Got Legs" in honor of Robin, who colored with pleasure and ordered him to behave.

Collie snapped the phone into its plastic holster. "What a stellar gadget! I push and hold this button to turn it off, right?"

"Yes, but don't do that, Nicholas. Just leave it on standby. If the power's off you can't receive calls. How am I supposed to reach you that way?"

"Oh, now I get it," he chuckled. "This is like one of those electronic collars they stick on bears and stuff. So you girls can always know where your guys are."

"Why, Nicholas," Robin pouted from under arched brows, "you don't really think that, do you?"

"Here's what I think." Collie pulled her into his arms. "I think you're the most fantastic girl I've ever known, and being kept track of by *you* is the luckiest thing that could ever happen to *me*." He kissed her for a long luscious moment. "I love you, Robin. Thanks for the phone."

"You're welcome," said Robin. "And I love you too, Nicholas, very much." She stood and pulled him up. "Come on, birthday bear. You must be starved. Let's eat."

After a dinner of Beef Bourguignon, Robin brought out a chocolate cake decorated with 26 flaming candles. Collie extinguished them all with a mighty whoosh and received 26 traditional swats on his bottom along with one extra "for good luck". The cake was richly delicious, and Collie ate two pieces. Full to bursting, he helped Robin clean up and then they snuggled together on the couch, exchanging kisses and endearments in the warm candlelight.

At length, his heart pounding, Collie said, "Robin, I'd like to ask you something." He repositioned himself to see her face. "Is that okay?

Do you mind?"

"Of course not, Nicholas. You can ask me anything."

"The thing is, there's something I really want to do, but without your help it's going to be impossible."

"Oh?" Robin looked uncertain. "Well, I'll help you in any way I can."

Collie nodded. "You don't know how glad I am to hear you say that." He reached into his pocket, pulled out a small square box made of maroon velvet and handed it to her. "What I want, Robin, is for you to say you'll marry me." His different-colored irises shone. "Please?"

Robin's eyes expanded in astonishment. She opened the box with shaking fingers and regarded the solitaire diamond engagement ring with awe. "*Nicholas!*"

"I picked it out myself," said Collie with shy pride. "Well, Mrs. Jamison helped me a little, but..." He smiled. "It's almost as pretty as you are. What do you think?"

"Think?" Robin echoed in a tremulous voice. "This is the most beautiful ring I've ever seen, Nicholas. Are...are you sure you can afford it?"

"Hey, you're not supposed to worry about that." Collie winked his blue eye. "Would you like to try it on?"

Robin nodded and handed him the box. "Will you do it?"

"Sure." Collie took her left hand and held the engagement ring poised in front of her fourth finger. "Does this mean the answer is 'yes'?"

"Yes, Nicholas," Robin answered, her face alight. "I want to marry you more than anything else in the world."

"Me, too." Collie slid the ring on her finger. "There. We are now officially engaged to be married." With boyish elation: "You and me, Robin! Together forever."

Gazing wide-eyed at the radiant stone on her hand: "Forever, Nicholas. I promise." Robin threw her arms around his neck, kissed him, then again held up her hand to look at the ring. "Oh, God, I love you so *much!*"

"I love you too, Robin. You make me happier than I've ever been before." Collie added in a quiet voice, "I'm not even sad that Mama isn't here. She knows, and she's happy for us."

"Yes, she is." Robin caressed his cheek. "I feel it, too. God bless her."

"I was thinking it might be nice to have the wedding sometime next fall. You know, when the leaves turn colors. That was always Mama's favorite time of year. Does that sound like a good idea?"

"Of course, Nicholas. I'll marry you tomorrow, if you want." Robin's eyes sparkled like the diamond on her finger. "Well, maybe not tomorrow." She giggled and began to prattle: "I need some time to find a dress. A wedding gown! Nicholas, can you believe it? And I have to talk to Reverend Shorr, and choose the right date, and figure out who's going to walk me down the aisle..."

"Well," Collie smiled at her excitement, "maybe by then we'll track down Nick Farrington and *he* can walk you...hey, what's the matter?"

Robin's eager chatter had cut off abruptly. She stared at Collie, her face pale.

"What is it?" Collie was bewildered to see her eyes suddenly spill over with tears. "Did I say something wrong? "I didn't mean to tease you about Nick Farr—"

Robin clapped her hands over her ears, jumped up and ran into her bedroom. Collie heard the bathroom door slam. He sat where he was, utterly at a loss, heart thumping hollowly in his chest. Maybe, he thought, she was having a delayed emotional response to becoming engaged. Even though Robin was the most level-headed person he knew, she *was* a female, and they often reacted to things in irrational ways.

Five nerve-wracking minutes elapsed before Robin reappeared. Although her face was calm Collie could tell that she'd been crying. She looked pensively at the ring on her finger and for a horrid instant Collie feared that she would give it back to him. But instead she rested her hand on his arm and said, "I'm sorry if I upset you, Nicholas. It's just...I need to say something. All right?"

"All right," replied Collie, trying not to sound panicked.

Robin looked him in the eyes. "Nothing could possibly make me happier than to be your wife, Nicholas. We're engaged, and we'll be married. But..."

"But?"

"But if anything happens to make you change your mind, and you don't want to marry me, I won't try to hold you to it. I promise I won't bother you any more."

"'Bother' me? That's impossible," Collie objected. "I *love* you, Robin. I'll never be with anyone else. Nothing could make me change my mind."

"Nicholas," Robin took his hand and raised it to her cheek, "life is unpredictable sometimes. There can be surprises, which might make us see things in a different light. It could happen."

"Not to you and me," Collie stubbornly insisted. "We're going to be married, Robin, and we're going to live happily ever after. I promise." He pulled her close and kissed her. "So no more talk about changing our minds. Okay?"

Robin hesitated, then smiled and nestled against him. The diamond on her hand reflected glints of flame from the still-burning candles. "All right, Nicholas. I really like that part about living happily ever after. Can we start right now?"

———— ((◊)) ————

Joanne Markwith was finding it difficult to concentrate on her usual mid-week backlog of administrative bumpf. She kept thinking about the things Nickie had finally told her, not only concerning the horrific assault but also the stunning revelation which had driven her to Gander Creek in the first place. It was a testament to Nickie's extraordinary resilience that she hadn't withdrawn into catatonia. The attack itself had been unthinkably brutal, but the other...Jo still could hardly believe it. Nickie had a son! A son, with her birth name and her extraordinary eyes, sired from an illicit affair back when Nickie was a reckless college boy named Nick. A *son*, living right here practically on the doorstep of Windfield College.

Jo shook her head. Professor Nickie Farrell, of the luscious red hair and killer legs, was a *father*. The notion boggled her mind. It was easy now, in retrospect, to understand why Nickie had looked so shattered that afternoon. Joanne couldn't imagine how she herself might react to such a shocking disclosure. She involuntarily shivered. Of course, only a transsexual woman could be surprised by a child she never knew she had. As Nickie had once solemnly observed, if one's destiny was to be a girl, there were substantial advantages to being born that way.

More than anything else, Jo felt reassured by how readily Nickie seemed to be recuperating. Her resilience was astonishing. The facial bruise was almost gone, and her appetite had returned. Last night as they ate popcorn and watched Jonathan Winters demolish the gas station in *It's a Mad, Mad, Mad, Mad World*, Nickie had dissolved in a convulsion of giggles. Although her slumber was still interrupted by periods of restlessness, for the most part she slept soundly. And so far, to Jo's immense relief, Nickie had given no indication that she intended to quit Windfield. She'd revealed no intentions with regards to her son; but Joanne knew enough to let that alone. Nickie would eventually work it out in her own fashion, and the best way Jo could help her was to just go on being her loving friend.

Joanne sighed, then turned to the task of untangling the upcoming year's classroom scheduling conflicts. Absorbed in highlighting and relocating a Hemingway seminar, she didn't immediately look up when the door opened. After a moment she lifted her gaze and felt a cheery greeting die on her lips when she beheld Cinda Vanderhart standing in front of her desk. Despite the younger woman's penitent expression Joanne narrowed her eyes and demanded in a cold monotone, "What do you want?"

Cinda shifted her stance and spoke in a contrite voice: "Well, I know that you're friends with Ms. Farrell, and I was just wondering if... if maybe you know when she's coming back?" Discomfited by Joanne's unfriendly aspect, Cinda swallowed. "The reason I ask is, there are some weird rumors going around, and—"

"Rumors? What sort of rumors?"

"Bad stuff. Like she got hurt, or...or something." Cinda hesitated. "Nobody really knows, though. It's not true, is it? Everyone really likes Ms. Farrell..." her voice trailed off.

Looking at the girl's aggressively butch attire, with her nose stud, spiky hair and prominent labrys pendant, Joanne Markwith found herself wondering if the antipathy she felt arose solely from the way Cinda had disrupted Nickie's life. Was it also possible that her anger was charged with personal resentment? Jo couldn't help but think of her own angst-ridden teenage years, back when things had been so much worse for homosexual people. Modern little Cinda, so accustomed to flaunting her gayness, couldn't possibly understand how it had been back when queer folk were forced to live in secret shame and constant fear of exposure. Like most assertive young dykes Cinda thought being cut from a different cloth was cool, but hardly a big deal. This callow *sang froid* had allowed her to root around in Nickie's past without once stopping to consider that perhaps to Nickie and others it *was* still a big deal. Jo didn't believe that Cinda's intentions were malicious, but the girl did have a woefully juvenile disregard for possible repercussions to her actions. Like most of her contemporaries Cinda affected a blasé attitude which expressed itself in the omnipresent mantra of the young: What*ever*. It's none of your business...what*ever*. Someone might get hurt...what*ever*. Ms. Farrell might freak out so badly she'll run off and be assaulted by wild beasts...yeah, well, what*ever*.

Lost in her thoughts, Joanne didn't realize that she had been leveling an unblinking stony glare at Cinda until the freshman dropped her eyes, mumbled some words of apology and began to slink away.

"Ms. Vanderhart...wait. It's all right, I won't bite your head off." Seeing Cinda hesitate: "I just want to talk to you for a minute."

Cinda trudged back and stood with downcast eyes, hands stuffed in her jacket.

Joanne said, "I know about the thing you told Professor Farrell."

Cinda nodded but didn't look up.

"It was an enormous shock, Ms. Vanderhart. Didn't you ever wonder how something like that might affect her?"

"I swear I thought it would make her happy," Cinda whispered. Jo saw a tear running down her cheek. "I really wanted Ms. Farrell to like me." She swatted away the tear. "Instead she'll hate my guts forever."

"No, she won't. Professor Farrell isn't capable of hating anybody,

Ms. Vanderhart. She's much too good-hearted and kind. Don't you know that? You were in her class. Was she ever harsh or unfair?"

"No. Ms. Farrell was the best. But now she's gone and it's all because of me," Cinda sniffled. "What if she never comes back? What if—"

Jo held up her hand. "Professor Farrell will be back next week. She just needed to take some time off, that's all. And by the way, there's nothing to those rumors you've been hearing. Ms. Farrell is doing okay, but..." Jo paused for emphasis, "you *have* to quit interfering in her business. Ever since that snotty midterm paper you have been on her like white on rice. I don't know why you turned her private life into a pet project of yours, but it has got to stop. It *will* stop. Because if it doesn't you'll have to deal with *me*. And sister, I'm not nearly as good-hearted as she is."

Cinda gulped. "I'll leave Ms. Farrell alone, I swear."

"And her son."

"Him, too."

"Have you blabbed about any of this to your friends?"

"No." Cinda earnestly shook her head. "I haven't said a word. Not even to my roommate. Honest."

"All right. Keep it that way," said Joanne. "From now on you never even heard of Professor Farrell. Got it?"

"Got it." Adding in a small voice: "I'm glad Ms. Farrell isn't leaving. I never meant to hurt her, but I know I did, and I'm sorry. Could you maybe tell her that? You're so lucky to be her friend. Thanks for not yelling at me." Cinda slipped out the door before Jo could say anything else.

Joanne sat still for a long moment, grateful that she wasn't young anymore. The youthful years were chaotic and confusing, a mélange of mistakes and pain. Middle age had a lot of drawbacks, but on the whole it was much safer and saner.

"Mixed-up kid," she muttered, and went back to her work.

After a while Alex Steward walked into the office. Joanne hadn't seen him since the day after Nickie's ordeal, when he'd humbly volunteered to take over her classes. Knowing his busy schedule Jo gave him credit for assuming the extra duties, although she'd refrained from telling Nickie about it.

She greeted him with a friendly grin: "Hi, Alex. How's it going?"

"Busy as a one-armed paper-hanger with the hives," replied Alex, returning her smile. "You know Oliver Wendell Holmes' poem *The One-Hoss Shay?* Well, that's me. I'll keep going and going and one day collapse into dust."

"No doubt. You're such an ancient relic." With an inquiring look: "So, what can I do you for?"

Alex reached into his breast pocket and pulled out a sealed white envelope. "If you don't mind, I'd like to ask a favor?"

Seeing the envelope Joanne thought to herself, well, what do you know. It's about damn time, Professor Steward! Couldn't you have seen the light *before* Nickie got hurt?

"In the event you happen to see Professor Farrell," Alex's look contained an unspoken message, "will you please give her this?" He held out the envelope. "If you don't see her," Alex quietly added, "just put it back in my mail slot. I'll completely understand."

Joanne silently nodded, and he placed the envelope in her outstretched hand. "Thanks. Listen, can I say something?" Alex stopped, weighing his words. "I've been a damned fool, Jo. A benighted, obtuse fool." He grimaced. "Of course you've known that all along. I imagine you think I'm a donkey, and I don't disagree. I treated the lady abominably." Jo perceived in Alex's blue eyes a great fear that he'd lost something precious and unrecoverable. "You've been a better and more loyal friend to Nickie than I ever was."

"We all make mistakes, Alex. Lord knows I've made some beauts in my time. I'm in no position to judge." She looked at the envelope. "You *are* a donkey, but a nice one. I'll make sure Nickie gets this."

Alex exhaled with relief. "Bless you, Jo. You're a better man than I am."

She archly addressed an imaginary audience: "Is he kidding?"

Alex blushed. "You're a better *woman* than I am. I mean, than I am a man. I mean..."

"Maybe you should get out of here, Professor Steward, before I change my mind. And make sure you keep Nickie's students up to speed. She'll be back next Monday."

"She will?" Alex's features lit up like a little boy contemplating a banana split. "*Great!*" Making an effort to collect himself: "Er, that's wonderful news. Terrific. I'm sure her students will be delighted. We'll *all* be delighted."

"Professor Steward," said Jo, not unkindly, "you need to go away now."

"Sorry. I'm gone." Alex placed his hand over his heart, blew her a kiss and exited. Jo glumly inspected the white envelope, which was addressed in precise cursive handwriting to "Professor Nickie Farrell." She wondered if Alex knew just how much he was asking of her. He really was a decent fellow, but men didn't think about things like that. For a desperate instant Jo considered shredding his letter, but the impulse passed. She couldn't possibly do that to Nickie. If there still remained a chance for her and Alex to find bliss together, Jo would never stand in the way.

"You deserve to be happy, sweet Nickie." Jo stowed the letter deep in her satchel. "I hope this will bring it to you."

Blinking the blurriness from her eyes, she swallowed the lump in her throat and forced her attention onto the English Department's fiscal spread sheet.

Jay-Bo Skinner popped his fifth beer of the afternoon and took a long pull. For some reason the usual alcoholic glow wasn't kicking in. Recently Jay-Bo had been troubled by a gut feeling that his Karma might turn sour again. It wasn't anything overtly obvious; he had plenty of booze and food, the rent was paid, his Python was polished and loaded, and the new BarcaLounger was developing a depression that comfortably cradled his butt. Jay-Bo was free to laze around, drinking beer while watching war movies on the television, with an occasional foray out to Hamburger John's for a night of inebriated fraternizing with scrofulous barflies. Life seemed downright peachy.

However, lately this wonderful existence was increasingly shadowed by Jay-Bo's hunch that Lloyd and Cale Pittman had been up to no good. His police instincts hadn't yet totally evaporated, and Jay-Bo could have sworn that his son acted like a guilty perp. Lloyd had always been a truculent lout, but this was different. He constantly darted his eyes as if half-expecting the law to pounce at any minute. It was a look Jay-Bo well remembered from hundreds of collars, and seeing it on Lloyd's face made him edgy.

But it was Cale Pittman's demeanor that most unsettled Jay-Bo. For the past week Lloyd's business partner had seemed lost in thought, his dark blue eyes vacantly fixed in what Jay-Bo's Vietnam comrades had referred to as "the thousand-yard stare." Any words directed at him drew little response beyond a distracted "Hmm?" Something was obviously weighing on Pittman's mind. Along with Lloyd's jumpiness, Cale's withdrawn reticence had caused Jay-Bo's Karmic antennae to twitch in anticipation of an impending change; one which would almost certainly be for the worse.

What galled Jay-Bo the most was that he couldn't do a damned thing about it. Trapped by his reliance upon Cale's free-flowing money, he was powerless to throw his weight around. Raising any objections would risk rocking Jay-Bo's free-ride boat, exposing him to the horrid possibility of being homeless, penniless, and starving. If that ever happened, Jay-Bo swore, he would eat a .357 round. Having worn the proud uniforms of the Marines and State Police he'd damn well rot in Hell before flipping burgers or standing in line with welfare niggers.

And besides, even if the boys had gotten themselves involved in some sort of criminal misbehavior, it wasn't any of Jay-Bo's concern. Thanks to the liberal fags and assholes who'd gotten him unfairly tossed off the force, he was no longer responsible for policing the citizenry. Screw 'em. Cale and Lloyd were right-thinking men, worth more than all the self-righteous pricks who'd ever gone to Windfield. Whatever they'd done, Jay-Bo told himself, it was no big goddamn deal.

He drained the rest of his beer and started to feel better. The Karma would straighten itself out. Everything was going to be fine.

———»((()))«———

In Joanne's kitchen the two women sat eating Chinese takeout. Nickie enjoyed hers with great appetite, but Jo mostly poked her chopsticks at the food.

"Are you sure you're ready to go back to your place? There's no rush, Nickie. You can stay here as long as you like."

Hearing Jo's doleful tone Nickie looked up from her plate. "That's sweet, but I'm better now. It's time for me to go home. I'll be all right, really."

"Sure you will." Jo forced a smile. "Can't keep a good woman down."

"I just want to put it all behind me and get on with my life. I can't wait to get back to my classes." Nickie added with a small laugh: "Do you suppose anyone missed me?"

"Honey, everyone missed you." Joanne's eyes darted toward her satchel, carelessly hung on a chair by the front door. "*Everyone.*"

Nickie cracked open a fortune cookie and peered at the little paper slip. "Hmm...'New beginnings will bring great happiness.' If you say so." She crumpled the paper and popped a piece of cookie in her mouth.

"Nickie, Cinda Vanderhart came by the office today. She wanted to know when you were coming back." Joanne shrugged. "It's hard to be sure with these kids, but to me she seemed genuinely upset that you were gone."

"God knows I was furious with Cinda, but now..." Nickie dropped the remnants of cookie on her plate. "I feel sorrier for her than anything else. Smart as a whip and reckless with ambition, but I don't think she's a happy girl. That in-your-face bravado is a defensive front."

"I think you're right," Jo agreed. "When I asked her why she did it, she said she just wanted you to like her. It was pitiful, actually."

"It's so confusing at that age." Nickie shook her head. "At least, it was for me. How about you?"

"Don't ask. I used to wonder what it would be like to kill myself."

"I was too chicken for suicide, but I came close a few times by accident. Quaaludes and tequila." Nickie cringed at the memory. "I elevated stupidity to an art form."

"No, hon, you weren't stupid. Just desperate. Same as me." Jo wanly smiled. "We've been through a lot of stuff for a couple of old broads, huh?"

"I guess we have. But look: We're still here! Like in the old Stephen Sondheim song."

Jo didn't speak for several seconds. "Someone else was in the office asking about you today."

"I had no idea I was so popular. Who?"

"Alex Steward."

Nickie's pupils widened. "Alex? What did he have to say?"

"Not too much. I never actually told him that you were staying here, Nickie. But he was in the office last week when Mr. Harry called me, so he's aware that something happened."

Nickie put a hand over her eyes.

"He doesn't know any details, Nickie. I'm positive of that. Anyway..." Joanne retrieved the white envelope from her satchel. "He asked me to give you this."

Nickie stared at the envelope. "He didn't tell you what it was about?"

"No, sweetie. I'm sure he meant it for your eyes only."

"Oh." Nickie swallowed. "I suppose I should read it." She began to slide a fingernail under the flap but Joanne put out a restraining hand.

"Not now, Nickie. Take it home and read it there."

"I have no secrets from you, Jo," Nickie protested. "After everything that's happened you're like my sister."

"That letter should be a private moment between you and Alex. I'm sure he'd prefer it that way. I don't want to be a third wheel, Nickie. *Please* don't read it here." Jo's voice cracked. "Oh, drat, what's wrong with me? Too much MSG in the Kung Pao Chicken...no, no, I'm fine, you don't need to..."

But Nickie had already taken Jo in her arms. "Sshh," she whispered.

"I do understand, you know."

"I'm sorry I'm s-such a pathetic old f-fool," Joanne choked out, and then she cried desperately while Nickie held her, swaying slightly and running fingers through Jo's curly hair.

After a few minutes her sobs slackened. Jo snatched up one of the takeout napkins, wiped her eyes and blew her nose. "Okay," she sniffled, "that was nearly as satisfying as the fried wontons. Thank you, dear, for letting me make an ass of myself."

"Don't call my best girlfriend an ass." Nickie grasped Joanne by the shoulders and looked straight into her eyes. "Listen to me, Jo. No one has ever been as kind, as supportive, as accepting of me –*Ms.* Nickie Farrell– as you've been. Not my family, not my friends, no one. From the first day I came to Windfield you treated me like one of the girls. You even invited me into your family. Do you have any idea how priceless those things are to a transsexual like me? It's so easy for us to feel like outcasts, or zoo exhibits, or aliens. No matter how successfully we make the change, we're always insecure, constantly looking over our shoulder for smirks, sneers, pointed fingers. Mostly we survive, although some of us don't. But if we're really *really* lucky we get to have a special woman in our lives. A woman like you, Jo. Believe me, there's no greater blessing. Not even finding a man. Men are marvelous in their own ways, but they cannot replicate the mystery, the joy of bonding, really *bonding* with another female. You gave me that joy, and it's the most precious gift I'll ever receive." She paused for breath. "I'll always love you, Jo. So this is for you, from me, until the end of our days, and no one will ever, ever be able to take it away."

Nickie pulled Joanne close and kissed her on the mouth, tenderly at first, then with increasing intensity, pressing her lips into Jo's as if to brand there forever the memory of a secret woman-to-woman love that no man would ever know.

When at last it was over Nickie drew back and whispered, "Okay?"

"Okay," Joanne smiled, because it was. "I will always love you, too, darling Nickie. Now go home. Go home and read your letter."

"Hello there, Collie!" Congressman Walters shook hands with practiced gusto. "Or I should say, Monsieur le Maitre d'. Moving up in the world, I see."

"Just filling in while Mr. Foley is on leave, sir," Collie explained. "It's good to have you with us, Congressman. Ladies," he greeted Heather Walters and Cinda Vanderhart with a little bow. "Nice to see you again."

Heather, in a *sotto voce* aside to her roommate: "Hello-o, does *he* clean up well!"

Cinda made no response as Collie escorted them to their table.

"Kudos on your advancement, my boy," observed the congressman after they were seated. "Speaking from a purely self-interested standpoint, I'll miss your exemplary service."

"Not to worry, sir. Ms. Thompson will take excellent care of you. She's far more accomplished than I am. In fact," he shyly smiled, "Robin's my fiancée."

Heather and Cinda exchanged quick looks as the congressman enthused: "Getting married, eh? Congratulations, Collie. To you and your bride. Despite what you may hear, marriage is still a wonderful institution."

"I'm counting on it, Congressman. Robin will be right with you. Enjoy your evening." He smiled and departed.

Congressman Walters had begun to expound on the joys of matrimony when Robin arrived at their table. "Ah, you must be the lucky lady who's going to marry my friend Collie," greeted the congressman. "Allow me to offer my sincerest best wishes. He's a fine young man, very fine."

"Yes, sir, he is," responded Robin, gazing straight at Cinda Vanderhart. "I feel very blessed. Thank you so much." The engagement ring flashed on her hand as she held up her pad. "What may I bring you this evening?"

No sooner had Robin disappeared with their orders than Cinda pushed her chair back. "Ladies room," she said, and left the table.

"Heath, your roommate seems a bit...subdued," Congressman Walters said to his daughter. "She hasn't challenged me once on my voting record. And she almost looks respectable tonight. What happened to that rock in her nose?"

"I don't know." Heather frowned. "Cin's been acting totally abnormal. Like, hormonal. I told her she should take birth control pills. They help a lot with mood swings and stuff."

"Seems like a waste of some perfectly good birth control pills," opined the Congressman with a broad wink.

"Omigod, Daddy." Heather closed her eyes and shuddered. "Do you always have to be such a *caveman?*"

"Your mother wouldn't have it otherwise, dear." He plucked a hot sourdough roll from a basket set down by a goggle-eyed busboy. "Now see here," his voice grew stern, "what's all this I hear about you writing a term paper on creeping fascism in the Democratic Party...?"

———— ⁕ ————

Cinda Vanderhart hovered by the ladies room until she spied Robin emerging through the swinging kitchen doors. She hurried over and addressed the startled waitress: "Hey, girlfriend. Listen—"

"I'm not your girlfriend, and I'm really not interested in anything you have to say."

"I get that, and I don't blame you, but I thought you should know about Ms. Farrell, she—"

"Not here." Robin ushered Cinda into the plushly-decorated powder room. "What about Ms. Farrell?"

Cinda described Nickie's sudden disappearance from Windfield. "She's supposedly coming back soon, but people have been saying that something ugly happened to her. I heard one rumor that she got mugged in D.C."

"Oh, no!"

"It's only a rumor. Nobody knows for sure. But I asked one of her friends in the English department about it, and she told me Ms. Farrell is all right." Cinda flushed with shame. "This whole thing was my fault. I'm awfully sorry, Robin. Especially for dragging you into it. I know that doesn't help much."

"Not much, no. Are you done? I need to go."

"Does...*he* know anything?" Cinda inclined her head toward the door. "Your fiancé?"

"Of course not! Didn't you hear me promise Nickie I'd keep it secret? But if he ever does find out what I've been keeping from him I'm sure he'll never speak to me again." Robin added in a tone of bitter reproach: "Thanks to you."

"What I did stinks. I don't know how to apologize more than that, Robin. Believe me, if there was any way I could make it up to you—"

Robin raised her hands in alarm. "Don't even think about it! There's nothing you can do. Just please, *please* leave us alone. Go back to your table."

Cinda nodded, her face stiff, and exited.

As she returned to work Robin prayed that the Windfield girl would finally disappear from her life for good. Many of her prayers had been answered in the past; this, however, wasn't destined to be one of them.

———————

Nickie hadn't been in her apartment since the morning of the attack. Everything was the same as she'd left it: Her rinsed-out coffee cup upside down in the drying rack; last week's unread TIME magazine on the table by her wing chair; the snagged pair of pantyhose in the bathroom wastebasket. It was all familiar, but for some reason Nickie felt a little detached, as if she'd been absent for a very long time. Suddenly she found herself reviewing the sequence of events that awful day: Dr. Silverman's news of her job status, finding Cinda and Robin waiting outside her office, the monumental shock of their revelation about her son, the distraught drive to Gander Creek, the devils in the black Mustang...

"Stop it, Farrell," she exclaimed aloud. "I won't dwell in the past. I will *not* give my power away."

So saying, she slipped a Haydn concerto into the CD player, then went to her bedroom and changed into a long mint-green cotton nightie. She took Alex's letter out of her purse, and after holding it for a long moment, slit the flap with her nail. She removed the handwritten sheets, curled herself on her bed and began to read.

Dearest Nickie,

I love you.

Doubtless you think I've got a lot of damn nerve to say such a thing. Well, you're not wrong. After the way I behaved you have every right to tell me to get lost, or something even more emphatic. But I hope you won't do that, Nickie, because I'd like another chance. I'm not saying that I deserve it. In fact, I probably don't. Still, the magic we shared —before I wrecked everything— was so special, so powerfully sweet, that I can't let it die forever without making an effort at resuscitation, and hoping for a miracle.

You are one of the kindest, gentlest, most caring souls I've ever encountered, which makes my mean treatment of you all the more atrocious. To say that I'm ashamed of myself is such a paltry understatement that it seems weak and whiny even as I write the words. Literature is full of idiots and fools, Nickie, but I do believe I've been a more colossal ass than any of them. Nor will I offer any excuses for what I did to you. It was cruel, unfair, heartless and shortsighted. Yes, I was surprised to learn your truth, but nothing you ever said or did warranted my extreme reaction. I could have listened, I could have made an effort to understand, but instead I chose to feel victimized. Walking away from you the way I did that night, well, it makes me sick to think of it. That was a sin, Nickie, a bad one, and I will have to answer for it whenever and wherever we flawed humans are called to account. I don't know if the Lord will forgive me, but I hope you can.

What tears at me the most is that something terrible had to happen to you before I came to my senses. I don't know the details, nor do I claim a right to know them. All I know is, when I realized that you had been assaulted I felt as if I might break into little pieces. Nickie, it was the same feeling I had when my wife was pulled out of the surf. The same helpless panic, the horror, the ice-cold dread in my guts. The idea of someone deliberately hurting you almost drove me mad, especially since I couldn't help but wonder if it would have happened at all had we still been together. That's an impossible question to answer, I know, but it will gnaw at me for as long as I live. I realize I can't change the past. What's done is done. All I want now is to love you, care for you, and make absolutely certain that nothing like this ever happens again.

I always thought of myself as an enlightened man, Nickie. Progressive, modern (if never hip) and freethinking. I rode into Windfield on a high horse of liberal broadmindedness. None of that lowbrow intolerance for Alex Steward! No, indeed. I celebrated everybody: blacks, whites, yellows, reds, Jews, Christians, Muslims, atheists, gays, straights, Democrats, Republicans and animal-lovers. Except then I fell in love with a beautiful transsexual lady, tripped right over my own hypocrisy and fell headfirst down a well of fear, prejudice, and ignorance. And there I skulked, willfully marinating in my own folly, letting the beautiful lady suffer because I was too blind and stupid to appreciate her for what she had always been: a gift from heaven.

Nickie, words cannot express how deeply, deeply sorry I am. I want to have you in my life, every day, every hour, every minute. Please take me back. I think we belong together, don't you? Let's make it right again.

I'll end the way I began, my darling:

I love you.

Alex

Her heart pounding, Nickie re-read the letter twice, then clutched the written sheets to her breast. "Alex," she breathed, "Oh, Alex!"

She got off her bed and began waltzing barefoot around the room, humming, her face alight in a way it had never been before. No human eyes were present to watch her, of course; but had there been, they surely would have glowed with gladness to see Nickie Farrell so very, very happy at last.

———=•((•))•=———

After an entire weekend of listening to the incessant sounds of argument and conflict emanating from the right-thinking men's bedroom, Jay-Bo was going crazy. Booze had lost its ability to dampen his exasperation. All he heard of their muffled voices were a few random phrases and words: "Forget the bastard"; "fuck Virginia"; "New Orleans." The clamor seemed to be mostly generated by Lloyd, whose strident remonstrations were distinguishable from Pittman's measured retorts. Jay-Bo had no idea what was going on, but he was almost at the end of his rope. It was like listening to a couple of squabbling women, which in Jay-Bo's mind ranked as pure living hell.

"Son of a *bitch*," Jay-Bo seethed as more bickering noise resounded from their room. He pointed his television remote and maximized the volume on *Hamburger Hill* until the racket of heavy machine-gun fire, exploding mortars, and screaming soldiers shook the walls. Although it wasn't yet four in the afternoon Jay-Bo had already downed a six-pack of Miller Genuine Draft and most of a pint of Old Crow. Surly, frustrated, and drunk, he glowered from bloodshot eyes at the television, wondering if he could kick the shit out of Lloyd and Cale without having the rent money cut off.

The bedroom door opened and Pittman emerged. His navy blue eyes were flat with obstinacy. Lloyd's features wore a peevish thwarted expression.

"Jesus Christ, Old Man, think that's loud enough?" Lloyd complained. "How many times can you watch the same goddamn flick, anyway?"

Jay-Bo hit the mute button. "If you two weren't in there squealin' and yammerin' like a coupla women on the rag, maybe I wouldn't need it so damn loud." He growled: "You got a problem with watching how real men fought over in 'Nam? What'd *you* ever do, boy? Don't hand *me* any shit."

"Some people need to dwell in the past, partner," Cale said tersely. "It's all they've got."

"That's a real wiseass comment there, Mr. Pittman." Jay-Bo thrust out his jaw. "Feelin' pretty high n' mighty, ain't you? Must make you feel awful smart to disrespect men who answered the call."

"Let's get the hell out of here, Cale." Lloyd glared at his father. "Go to Tyler's Beach, fish for cats."

"Shit, all the time you two spend there, y'ain't never caught squat," sneered Jay-Bo. "You even know how to bait the damn hook?" He coarsely laughed and took a swallow of Old Crow. "Catfishin', my ass. More like pussyfishin'."

Lloyd reddened. "Gimme your truck keys."

"Fuck off. I'm headin' over to Hamburger John's."

Pittman pulled out his Mustang keys and contemptuously tossed them to Jay-Bo. "Take my car. Try not to roll it."

"Mister, I was drivin' a police cruiser when you were still shittin' your pants." Jay-Bo swallowed more bourbon, and threw Lloyd his key ring. "You girls have a good time."

Cale and Lloyd exchanged disgusted glances and walked out of the apartment without a word.

"Snot-nose punks," Jay-Bo groused in a sodden undertone. "Who the hell they think they are, givin' me lip? Teach 'em some god-damn manners, s'what I oughta do..." He turned up the sound on his movie then suddenly frowned, remembering that his latest issue of *American Handgunner* was still in the truck. Cursing, he rolled off the BarcaLounger and hurried out the front door, intent on retrieving his magazine before the two fishermen drove off with it.

Rounding the side of the building into a narrow alley, Jay-Bo saw Lloyd and Cale standing by his truck. His eyes bulged and he shrank back around the corner, pressed against the wall, not believing what he'd seen. After a second or two he cautiously stole another look. Sure enough, Cale Pittman stood right next to Lloyd, one hand stuck into the back pocket of his partner's jeans, nuzzling and whispering in his ear. As Jay-Bo stared in horror Cale gave Lloyd's buttocks a lov-ing squeeze and planted a kiss right on his lips. Through the sudden roaring in his ears Jay-Bo heard his eldest son titter like a girl. Unable to watch any more, he staggered back toward the apartment, grasping his head, making strangled sounds.

Jay-Bo slammed the front door and began clenching and unclenching his fists. "*Fags*," he choked, his voice black with fury. "*Here*. In *my* house." His whole body shook. He grabbed a nearby lamp and hurled it against the wall to disintegrate in a tinkle of glass. "Fuckin' queers!" He began to rage, stomping around the room, snatching up objects at random and throwing them in all directions, roaring "Cocksuckers! Faggots! Cornholin' fairies!" With a bellow, he picked up the television Cale Pittman had bought and smashed it down onto the floor. He ran into the kitchen, returned with a wicked carving knife and stabbed it repeatedly into the BarcaLounger, ripping the leatherette into green shreds. "Homos," he croaked, his face bright purple. "Goddamn buttstuffers."

Finally he stopped and stood panting in the midst of the wreckage, still clutching the knife. Everything was clear now. He had been made an unwitting dupe by two limp-wristed flit gayboys, one of them his eldest son. He'd welcomed them as equals, as right-thinking men, and all the while, right under his nose, they'd gleefully indulged in the same depravities as the Windfield vermin who'd ruined his life. But Jay-Bo Skinner wouldn't let them win. This time, the final victory would be his.

Jay-Bo dropped the blade and crunched across broken glass to where the old photo from his Vietnam days still hung on the wall. He lifted it off the nail and held it in his hands, staring into the fierce countenances of his long-vanished warrior comrades. Life had been glorious back then. But for no reason everything had turned against him and his world had dissolved into shit. A listless bitch wife. A queer daughter who killed herself in disgrace. A no-good insolent brat who split at the first opportunity. And now his firstborn son, bringing it all home to roost with a "business partner" who was nothing but a faggot fuck buddy.

Jay-Bo straightened and addressed the photo. "Okay, grunts, listen up. You know the drill. Take no prisoners. You got that? No prisoners."

Then, carrying the precious photo, he retrieved his Colt Python from the shredded BarcaLounger and went to get ready for one last search-and-destroy mission.

As the husband of her son's late mother prepared to embark on his final sortie, Nickie Farrell closed the door to her office and set out for the Reflection Garden to meet Alex Steward.

This first day back at school had warmed her heart more than she could have imagined. Everyone Nickie encountered welcomed her with a smile and said how much she'd been missed. Her students expressed their pleasure by being extra attentive and decorous during class. Several of the girls gave her hugs and even some of the boys offered comments like, "Ms. Farrell, you really gotta stick around. Professor Steward's an okay sub but he's kinda out to lunch, y'know?"

Smiling at the recollection Nickie wended her way across the Windfield campus. It was a perfect evening: the blue sky paling into lavender was striated with contrails dyed orange by the setting sun, while mild honeysuckle-scented breezes gently wafted among trees and flowers prompted into vigorous early bloom by the mild weather. On the front lawn, surrounded by flowerbeds filled with blossoming tulips, she could see the white pillars of the Randall Windfield memorial, which —as she'd earlier reassured the fractious ambassador in a protracted phone conversation— was essentially completed and awaiting April first's grand dedication. As she had countless times over the years, Nickie marveled at Windfield's never-ending loveliness.

Approaching her destination, Nickie felt her pulse accelerate. After reading Alex's letter she had called him; but, unwilling to get into a prolonged discussion on the telephone or to rush matters, she'd suggested that they postpone a face-to-face meeting until this evening. Unable to hide his disappointment at having to wait, Alex had nevertheless acceded to her wishes. Nickie wasn't entirely sure why she'd chosen to meet in the Reflection Garden. Perhaps, since that was where her heart had been broken, going back to the same place would help it be mended.

At the point where the pathway entered the enclosure Nickie halted. The last time she'd been here everything had been dead and dismal, but now the garden was bursting with renewed life. The ornamental crabapple trees, ugly brown talons back in November, were transformed into soaring pink puffballs. The flowerbeds were a riot of multicolored jonquils, narcissus, iris, and lilies. A stand of lilac bushes in one corner perfumed the air with a heavenly fragrance. Four short months ago the Reflection Garden had seemed as grim as Tolkien's Mordor, but now it was an inviting haven of surpassing beauty.

Nickie saw Alex Steward sitting on a stone bench under one of the blossoming crabapple trees, leaning forward as if lost in thought, his hands clasped together. He was dressed in a blue blazer and tie, with light-colored slacks and polished shoes which softly gleamed in the violet dusk. Alex's snowy hair and beard framed his face in a way that made Nickie's heart race. She took a few steps into the garden, and the crunch of her heels on the gravel made Alex look up. He got to his feet but didn't rush toward her, instead remaining where he was, his hands at his sides.

Nickie slowly walked toward him until they stood within arm's reach of one another. They looked at each other for a silent moment, then Nickie spoke: "Hello, Alex."

"Hello, Nickie," Alex replied. "Thank God you're all right."

Nickie's expression briefly flickered. "Your letter was wonderful. It meant a lot."

"Everything I said is true, Nickie. Thank you for agreeing to see me. It can't have been an easy decision, after everything I put you through. I hope you'll accept my apology, inadequate though it is." The blue eyes studied her face. "I didn't know how to cope, Nickie. I heard the word 'transsexual' and I ran. It was shameful and ignorant of me, but that's what happened."

"And now, Alex? Is my being transsexual a problem?"

"No." Alex shook his head. "But it never was, Nickie. I'm the one who made it into a problem. I didn't understand that some women aren't born female. But I know it now. As Heaven is my witness, Nickie, I do."

A lilac-scented zephyr stirred the air, and she smiled. "It's a beautiful evening, isn't it?"

"Yes, it is. To be honest, I don't think I've ever seen one quite so beautiful."

Feeling herself tingle with pleasure, Nickie dropped her eyes. "Springtime is always so lovely. Everything comes alive again." She looked up and met his gaze. "A time for new beginnings."

"Yes, pretty lady. New beginnings. I'd like that." With a questioning look: "Can we?"

"I want to." Nickie came forward, felt his arms enclose her. "Oh Alex, I want to so much." She laid her head against his chest, tears running from under her closed eyelids, hugging him as hard as she could.

"Nickie, my sweet beautiful Nickie," Alex murmured, pulling her as close as possible. "Don't cry, my love. I'm sorry I hurt you. What a dunce I was! But I'll never, ever leave you again."

"Do you promise, Alex?" Nickie raised her tear-streaked face. "Truly promise? Because I can't survive it another time."

"I promise, Nickie." Alex looked deeply into her enchanting mismatched eyes. "If you'll let me, I swear I'll stay and love you until I die."

"Don't you *dare* die," said Nickie, and then they were kissing, their hearts finally coming together there in the flower-scented twilight, as occasional blossoms floated down and swirled about them like pink snow.

———— ◄((●))► ————

Jay-Bo Skinner arrived at the turnoff which led to Tyler's Beach and cautiously backed Cale Pittman's Mustang a dozen yards down the rutted road, blocking the enemy's route of escape. There would be no fuckups on Jay-Bo's final action. He was armed, deadly, and merciless; the rock-hard jarhead killing machine of thirty years ago.

He switched off his headlights, killed the engine and carefully stowed the car keys deep in the pocket of his old camouflage jacket. When his eyes adjusted to the twilight dimness he addressed the framed Vietnam photo resting on the front seat: "You boys cover my ass. I'll take point." He opened the door and eased himself out, holding the Colt Python in his hand.

Jay-Bo began to creep his way along the barely-visible dirt road, setting each foot down with stealthy care, making almost no noise. On both sides, closely packed tree trunks stretched away into a blackness of tangled underbrush. The thick blanket of silence was disturbed only by the occasional rustle of some small frightened creature. Pointing the Python straight ahead, his combat instincts heightened to a keenness not felt for many decades, Jay-Bo made steady progress. He began to hear the faint hiss of rushing water. Halting for a moment, he took several controlled breaths to dissipate the tension in his muscles, then cautiously rounded a slight bend and froze. Not more than fifty yards away he spotted his pickup truck parked in a broad open space. The water sound was loud enough to muffle any stray noise as Jay-Bo inched forward, stooping down as he crept up on the truck. Crouched behind the tailgate, he peered around the pickup's bed, noted the driver's closed door and rolled-up window. A quick check on the other side revealed the same thing. Squatting by the rust-eaten tailpipe, Jay-Bo pondered the best way to achieve tactical surprise. The enemy would be entirely unprepared; still, a smart soldier never took chances. Deciding that the steering wheel might obstruct his line of fire, he decided to launch his assault on the passenger door. Checking the Python's cylinder one final time, he clicked it back into the frame, placed his forefinger alongside the trigger guard and duckwalked around the pickup until he was just below and behind the passenger's window. He softly reached up with his hand, grasped the handle, then in one fluid motion stood, yanked the door back and dropped into a combat stance, the revolver aimed into the cab.

Lloyd let out a screech of fright. Cale's head jerked up from his lap, the dark blue eyes growing huge as comprehension set in. "Oh, *shit.*"

"Stinkin' cocksucker." Jay-Bo thumbed back the Python's hammer. "You're dead, gayboy."

"*No,* Dad!" Lloyd squealed, his exposed flesh wilting like a daisy thrown into a furnace. "You don't understand. It's not what you think!"

Jay-Bo's crazy laughter echoed eerily about Tyler's Beach. "It ain't, huh? Was that goddamn faggot just gobblin' your root or wasn't he?" As Lloyd gaped in dumbstruck terror his father screamed "*Answer me, you fuckin' fairy!*"

"It's man-love." Lloyd wept with fear. "Like Richard the Lionheart, Alexander the Great–"

"Forget it, partner," snarled Pittman. "You think this old fart can appreciate the glories of being an *Übermensch?* " Cale contemptuously spat on the dashboard. "He probably has trouble finding his own asshole after he takes a shit."

"Jesus Christ, Cale," moaned Lloyd, staring at the cocked Python. "Shut the fuck *up*."

"Why, partner? We're *Übermenschen*, Superiormen! We have nothing to fear from a drunken peasant."

"Big talker, ain't you, Pittman?" Jay-Bo slitted his eyes. "Always spoutin' off. Real smooth, too. Yessir. Even had me fooled for a while. Well, you ain't nothin' but a dick-lickin' scumbag like all the rest of 'em. You need killin', boy, like a foam-mouth skunk."

"Sure I do," Cale sneered. "And you think *you're* man enough to do it?" With a wild laugh: "Fat old losers like you don't have *Der Wille zur Macht!* The Will to Power is *mine*. Tell you what, Daddy-O. Why don't you take that silly gun and piss off? My partner and I are busy." He winked. "Or do you want a blowjob, too?"

Jay-Bo fired. A concussive blast, a quick flash of flame, and a small black hole appeared just to the left of Cale Pittman's nose as a good portion of his brains splattered like red stucco across the spider-webbed window. Wrenched sideways by the impact, Cale's body draped itself across the steering wheel and hung there like a grotesque puppet, the eyes fixed and staring at the floorboards, dark fluids dripping from a massive crater in the back of his head.

Lloyd Skinner screamed and screamed, his ears ringing, only dimly aware that he had soiled himself. His father cocked the revolver again and leveled it at his nose. "I should've known you would turn out just like your goddamn dyke sister. Lucky me, huh? I ended up with twin queers, one cunt and one pussy."

"Don't, Dad!" Lloyd howled. "I'm your son! Please don't shoot me!"

"Quit yer damn blubberin', faggot," said Jay-Bo, and fired again. The jacketed hollowpoint bullet blew out most of his eldest child's skull. Lloyd's body rebounded off the seat cushion and toppled from the truck onto the coarse sand of Tyler Beach, one hand splayed out across his father's boot.

Jay-Bo lowered the Python. He peered into the pickup's blood-spattered cab, making sure that the adversary within was absolutely deceased. Too many unwary troops had been taken out by supposedly "dead" foes. Stepping back, he nudged the corpse on the ground with his toe. Nodding, he turned away, reentered the woods and headed back the way he came. Jay-Bo felt nothing but a sense of satisfaction. Mission safely accomplished. No casualties. The enemy was slain, and now nothing remained but to join his fallen comrades-in-arms. They too had been men of valor, honorable men who'd always done their duty. And so it would be for him. Life hadn't been fair, but that no longer mattered. Jay-Bo Skinner was ready. *Semper Fidelis.*

On Tyler's Beach, nothing moved. A faint smell of gunpowder lingered in the damp air as Gander Creek tumbled and flowed by on its timeless nocturnal journey.

———⟫⟪———

"Nineteen more nights." Ambassador Eamon Douglass shook his fist at the distant lights of Windfield College. "Nineteen more nights until I rain fire and brimstone on that modern Sodom and wipe it from the face of the earth."

The ambassador and Big Mike Barlow stood on a narrow stone balcony which opened out from the study. During the daytime it commanded an inspiring view of the estate grounds and the lush surrounding countryside; but tonight, as always, Douglass only had eyes for the object of his obsessive hatred. "I've been alive for almost thirty thousand nights, Barlow, but having to wait these final nineteen...it's bloody inconvenient."

Big Mike lifted a tumbler of sour mash whiskey to his mouth. "Ain't you even a little bit scared?"

"Scared of what?" With a derisive snort: "What do you take me for, Barlow? Scared! Was Nathan Hale scared when those blasted redcoats were tying the rope around his neck?"

"Dunno. Who's Nathan Hale?"

"Christ, didn't you learn anything in school?"

"Nope," admitted Big Mike.

"It shows." The ambassador scowled at his special consultant. "My only fear is that there might be some last-minute screw-up. Which goddamn well better not happen."

"Nothin's gonna go wrong. I told you, it's all set. Unless that Russian guy screwed you. Maybe all you got is a big can of dog food sittin' under that sundial with them explosives."

"My Russian colleague is beyond suspicion," snapped the ambassador. "No one has a keener understanding of the patriotic principle involved here...what the devil?"

From somewhere out in the remote darkness they heard an unmistakable gunshot.

"West Virginia poachers," Douglass fumed. "Breed like rats, and just as stupid."

Big Mike shook his head. "Ain't poachers. That's a handgun. Magnum, sounds like."

"What kind of cretin goes pistol shooting in the dark?"

Another distant report echoed across the nightscape.

Douglass ducked down. "Sonofabitch! All I need is to be accidentally gunned down by a demented hillbilly. Get inside." Cursing under his breath, he stumped back into the study. Mike Barlow followed, pulling shut and securing the heavy glass doors.

The ambassador settled behind his desk and pointed Big Mike to a nearby chair. "Sit."

Mike took another swallow of icy whiskey. "So, what now?"

"Unless and until I say otherwise, go serve beer to the rednecks and wait. There's only nineteen days to go and I don't want any goddamn surprises."

"Like what?"

"Like anything. Like you going off and killing somebody. *None* of that freelance mayhem, hear? Keep your head down and your nose clean."

"What about my million bucks?"

"Never mind." With an imperious wave: "I'll tell you everything you need to know when the time is right."

"When's that gonna be?" Mike frowned. "Gettin' kinda close."

The ambassador glared fiercely with his good eye. "Are you presuming to question *me?* "

His special consultant muttered a sullen, "No."

"Very wise." Eamon Douglass picked up his glass wolf and studied it. "I understand that you may be feeling a bit restive. Don't be. All I require is that you present yourself here on that historic morning at eight sharp."

"*What?* " Big Mike exclaimed in dismay. "I have to be *here* when you set off that atom-bomb?"

"When will you get it through your thick skull that it's just a modest radiological contamination device?"

"Great," groaned Big Mike. He added: "*Fuck.*"

"I need you to deliver something to the *Middleville Gazette* on your way out of town. But don't worry. You'll still have plenty of time to be well gone before the actual Redemption takes place."

"That million bucks won't be worth shit if I end up glowin' like a lightnin' bug!"

"Relax," said Douglass, looking amused. "I've arranged everything for you. Plane tickets, credit cards, driver's license, passport, a whole new identity."

"But my identity is Big Mike," objected Big Mike.

"Not for much longer. Need I point out that the authorities are going to scour the entire world looking for a certain Mike Barlow who not only planted the bomb but happens to run a saloon I own?"

The special consultant grimly poured himself more whiskey. "What's the new identity?"

"Cyrus T. Bolt," said the ambassador.

Big Mike choked on his sour mash.

"Euphonious, isn't it?" Douglass nodded with satisfaction. "The 'T' stands for Timothy."

Barlow's expression resembled that of a cornered grizzly: resigned and murderous.

"You'll adjust," promised the ambassador. "It's remarkable how much better things look on the far side of a million dollars, Mister Bolt."

Mike Barlow glared at his whiskey glass as if he might eat it, then knocked back the contents in one ferocious gulp.

Eamon Douglass winced and reached for his bottle of pain pills. "Damn guts are killing me. The end can't come soon enough." He shook out two tablets and swallowed them. "Well, Bolt, you're dismissed. Be here *promptly* at eight o'clock on the morning of April first. We'll conclude our business at that time. Under *no* circumstances are you to contact me before then. There's too much at stake now. Is that clear?"

Big Mike growled an affirmative and lumbered for the door.

"One more thing, Bolt. I mean it about staying out of trouble. The slightest foul-up and I will throw you to the wolves. Understood?"

"Yeah, sure," Barlow grunted, and left the ambassador's study. Neither of them had any way of knowing that they'd seen the last of each other.

Jay-Bo Skinner drove through the night, guzzling from a bottle of Wild Turkey 101 and steering Pittman's Mustang GT with one hand. The still-warm Colt Python was wedged securely under his thigh where he could access it in an instant. With no fixed destination in mind Jay-Bo followed one road after another, turning whenever a familiar place name nudged his memory: Earlsville, where as a boy he'd been jumped by some bullies at a cheap carnival and kicked their asses until they ran off howling; Graymont, where at the age of fifteen he'd gotten his first blowjob from an opposing cheerleader after crushing her boyfriend's football team into the mud; Clover Hill, where he'd won a high school bet that he could chug a full quart of beer without stopping; Cranston, where he'd encountered the spit-polished Marine recruiter who eventually convinced him to enlist. Speeding along the dark country roads with his high beams on, energized by the thunder of the dead enemy's car, Jay-Bo grinned as he recalled these high points in his life. There'd been some good times, damn good, before he stupidly married Luanne Colin and it all fell apart.

Growing drunker by the minute, pumped up in belligerent defiance of everything and everyone, he drove faster and faster. As he flew past turnoffs to the hated blueblood enclaves of Middleville and La Forge he flashed an upraised middle finger. Catching sight of an arrowed road sign which read "Windfield College: 6.5 miles", he stomped on the brakes, smoked his tires in reverse, screamed "Fuckers!" and blasted two gaping holes in the sign with his Python. Laughing insanely, half-deafened, he slammed the Mustang into gear and roared off again, heading south.

After a few miles he gunned the car into an access road and rocketed onto the westbound lanes of Highway 66. A favored hunting ground during his State Trooper years, he had chased down countless speeders on these broad asphalt ribbons. Oh, those had been the days! Forcing the hapless lawbreakers over with a jerked thumb, swaggering to where they cowered in their cars, one hand on the butt of his pistol, his scowl merciless and terrifying...

Jay-Bo tilted the bottle back, gulping, feeling the whiskey burn down his gullet. Some of the overflow trickled down his chin and dripped on the Python in his lap. "Aggghh!" He coughed, spluttered, then tossed the bottle over his shoulder. As the speedometer needle climbed past ninety he began to hoarsely shout training chants from his boot camp days:

> *I don't know but I've been told*
> *Bayonet steel is hard and cold*
> *I love battle, I love war*
> *Most of all I love the Corps...*

At a hundred miles per hour the black Mustang raced past other cars as if they were standing still. Singing and hollering, Jay-Bo glanced in his rear view mirror and saw distant flashing lights.

"Whoo! Let's go, boy," he bellowed. "Think you can catch the Old Man?!" He stamped the accelerator to the floor. "Come on! Let's see if y'got any fuckin' balls!"

The car began to vibrate as it passed the hundred-and-ten mark. Perhaps a mile ahead Jay-Bo saw an overpass that he knew well; it had been the scene of his single greatest bust when he nailed a posse of Haitians transporting a carload of hash oil. Holding the wheel with his left hand, he picked up the Python.

"*Semper fi!*" He shouted over the screaming engine, and placed the gun under his chin.

"Do or die!" Jay-Bo pulled back the hammer and placed his finger on the trigger. The overpass, set on huge concrete abutments, was ballooning in his windshield with terrible swiftness.

"Gung ho! *Gung ho!* GUNG HO!"

He wrenched the wheel to the right and pulled the trigger.

A bright flash illuminated the interior as Cale Pittman's black Mustang arrowed into the concrete abutment and exploded in a gigantic fireball. Three cars collided on the overpass as a frightful billow of flame licked skyward before them. Charred fragments of metal and glass from the disintegrated car made little tinking sounds as they dropped onto the pavement.

James Robert Skinner was utterly, completely gone.

There would be no mourners.

Chapter Seventeen
Quickening

Nickie Farrell and Alex Steward sat in Fenwick's coffee shop, an unpretentious but much-favored breakfast spot renowned for its fresh coffee and huge fluffy omelets.

"Do you realize what today is?" Alex gestured for the waitress to bring their check. "The Ides of March."

"How ominous." Nickie looked up from fixing her lipstick. "Must I beware, or will you protect me from dagger-wielding conspirators?"

"With my life, dear lady," Alex declared. "Have I told you this morning how much I love you?"

"Not yet," said their waitress, a buxom middle-aged blonde with false eyelashes, "but I'm listening." She set the check down and winked.

"After everything I went through to land him," Nickie told her, "I'm afraid he's all mine."

"Story of my life," sighed the waitress. "Y'all have a good day, now."

They rose from the booth and went to pay the cashier. As the woman handed Alex his change she suddenly inquired, "Ma'am, is something the matter?"

Her face drained of color, Nickie stood staring at a rack of folded newspapers by the entrance.

"What is it, Nickie? What's wrong?"

In a strained whisper, pointing at a rack filled with copies of the *Middleville Gazette:* "Those pictures."

Alex grabbed one of the newspapers. The front page featured adjoining grainy black-and-white photos of two men under the headline "Double Murder Linked to Ex-Cop Suicide." Nickie turned away and buried her face in his shoulder. "Alex, it's *them.*"

He tucked the paper under his arm and ushered Nickie out to his Buick LeSabre. Inside, tapping a finger on the *Gazette:* "You recognize those photos?"

"They..." Nickie shuddered and bit her lip. "They're the two men who attacked me."

Glancing at the front page, Alex reddened with anger. "There's something about a murder." He hesitated. "Do you want me to read the story? I won't if it'll upset you."

Nickie let out a deep breath. "Read it."

Alex nodded. "A spokesman for the Graymont County Sheriff's Department today released the identities of two individuals found dead of gunshot wounds Tuesday morning. Caleb Pittman, 33, and Lloyd Skinner, 29, were discovered by a lone fisherman along an isolated stretch of Gander Creek known as Tyler's Beach. Sources in the Coroner's Office declined to speculate pending completion of the official autopsies, but said the bodies appeared to have been dead for at least twelve hours..."

Nickie repeated in an odd tone: "That was the name? 'Lloyd Skinner'?"

"Yes." Alex contracted his brows. "Shall I continue?"

"Please."

"At this time authorities refuse to speculate on any possible connection between the Tyler's Beach homicides and Monday night's fiery crash on Highway 66 which claimed the life of former Virginia State Trooper James Robert 'Jay-Bo' Skinner, father of Lloyd Skinner. Sheriff's Deputy Harlan Scrapp stated that pending completion of tests on a .357 magnum revolver found in the wreckage ballistics experts will not be releasing any further information."

Nickie passed a hand across her eyes. "It can't be. It *can't.*"

Alex folded the paper and slung it into the back seat. "You don't need to hear any more."

Nickie touched his arm. "But you do."

"What? No, I don't. Obviously someone took it into their head to rid the world of these *scum*," he spat the word, "and good riddance. There's such a thing as divine retribution, after all. Let's leave it at that."

Nickie shook her head. "There's so much you still don't know. But it's time now. I want...I need to tell you the truth. It's the only way, Alex. No secrets, ever." She paused. "That man, Lloyd Skinner—"

"Goddamned son-of-a-bitch..."

"He wasn't a son of a bitch. He was the son of a sweet woman named Luanne. Luanne Skinner. I fell in love with her, long, long ago. She's dead now." Nickie's eyes grew moist. "Luanne had another son, too. Lloyd's half-brother. She named him Nicholas."

"Okay, but what does that have to do with—"

"Luanne named him after me, Alex. My male name was Nick Farrington. I was —I *am*— the boy's father."

Alex stared openmouthed. "God almighty, Nickie! Are you telling me you have a *son?* "

"I didn't know until a few weeks ago. The day I found out was the same day those men assaulted me." Nickie leaned back against the seat and closed her eyes. "Drive, Alex. It doesn't matter where. Just drive, and I'll tell you everything."

———— ⊂《○》⊃ ————

Ambassador Douglass looked up as his secretary entered the study. "Well?"

Holmes placed a small brown Shamrocks bag on the desk. "Your batteries, sir." If the secretary harbored any curiosity as to why his employer had suddenly demanded a fresh boxful of AA Energizers, it didn't show. "Will there be anything else, Ambassador?"

Douglass peered into the paper sack, then put it into a desk drawer. Leaning back in his chair he studied the other man for a moment.

"Holmes, my time is growing short. Without beating around the goddamn bush, I assume you're aware that I won't be around much longer?"

"A regrettable state of affairs, sir," replied Holmes. "The entire staff is deeply concerned over the precariousness of your health."

The ambassador emitted a tart laugh. "No doubt, since you're all out of a job the minute I kick the bucket."

"Let's hope it won't come to that, sir."

Douglass flipped his hand in irritation. "Spare me the cheap sentiment, Holmes. I'm more than ready to go. Looking forward to it, actually."

"I understand, Ambassador."

"Believe me, you don't. But never mind." He picked up a sheaf of envelopes and extended them. "Anticipating my imminent demise, I've written references for you and the others."

Holmes accepted the envelopes. "Extremely considerate, sir. Thank you."

"Let's hope they prove to be of some value." Most likely as souvenirs on eBay, he thought. After all, what right-thinking patriot wouldn't pay handsomely for a handwritten letter signed by the infamous architect of Winfield College's destruction? It was a pleasing notion. "That's all for now, Holmes. You'll not mention the batteries."

With the rejoinder "I don't know to which batteries you're referring, sir," Holmes left the study.

The ambassador smiled at his glass wolf. In the wake of the Redemption, with their faces covered in official egg, the maddened authorities would subject the Shamrocks staff to the fiercest grilling this side of a gas barbecue. They'd probably draw-and-quarter the unfortunate Holmes simply for providing the batteries. Eamon Douglass chuckled aloud, his reedy cackle echoing in the empty study. What spectacular disruption he was about to cause! The country would never be the same. Which, of course, was exactly the idea.

Unless something went wrong. The laughter died on Douglass's lips. To his knowledge all the elements were in place. Still, the best laid plans...He frowned and drummed his knuckles. Was it conceivable, as Big Mike had theorized, that the Russian had double-crossed him? The ambassador had Volka's solemn word that the Redeemer *was* a so-called "dirty bomb," but nothing more. If he pressed the button and nothing happened...

"Unthinkable," he snorted. "Egor Antonovich is a patriot, a man of his word. It *will* work."

The ambassador got up and began to pace. The transsexual freak liaison had finally telephoned to reassure him that everything was proceeding on schedule. Still, with only seventeen days left he wanted to personally review the preparations to make certain there weren't any last-minute glitches. The best way to ensure absolute perfection was to carry out a hands-on inspection.

He snatched up his phone. "Holmes? Get me Professor Farrell."

<hr />

"It's the most incredible story I've ever heard." A faint breeze ruffled Alex's white hair. He and Nickie sat on an oak-shaded bench in Middleville's delightfully landscaped town square. "You were dragged under a bridge and tortured by the half-brother of a son you didn't know you had until that same *day?*"

"I know. But it must be the same Lloyd Skinner. Luanne and Jay-Bo's son. I hadn't seen him since 1979, when he and his twin sister were just babies." Nickie watched a plump sparrow joyfully splash in a nearby stone birdbath. "He couldn't have known about me and his mother, though. Luanne kept the secret all these years."

"But you said the other one actually came to your office. These creeps were specifically stalking *you*. Why?"

"I guess I'll never know." Nickie swallowed. "Just as well. I don't want to think about them any more." As Alex started to protest she laid a hand on his arm. "Please, let it go. For my sake."

Alex pulled her close. "Whatever you say."

"You're such a good, decent man."

"Except when I'm being an obtuse fool."

"Even then, too."

After some happy snuggling in the balmy air: "I must say, Nickie, this Miss Vanderhart sounds like a piece of work."

"Seriously, Alex. That girl is more tenacious than a giant squid. Heaven help us if she does go into investigative journalism. She'll root out who really shot Kennedy *and* what the government's hiding in Area 51."

"She wrote that story about you in the *Spectrum*, didn't she? The one I saw and..." He stopped.

"Yes, that was her handiwork. Cinda figured out that I was trans before anyone else had a clue. Don't ask me how, but she did."

"And she unraveled the connection between you and your son just because of the eye color thing?" Alex squinted. "How on earth did she do that?"

"She somehow latched onto his girlfriend, and...well, she just did, that's all. Frighteningly smart, is our Ms. Vanderhart. Wait'll she takes one of your courses. She'll probably uncover evidence that you're a long-lost cousin of the Java Man."

Alex's snowy eyebrows flew up. "See here, Professor Farrell, are you looking to get spanked?"

"Why, Professor Steward," purred Nickie, wriggling her bottom and sticking the tip of her tongue out, "I thought you'd never ask."

"Don't tempt me." He looked around. "I have a feeling the town fathers would object."

"Alex, what am I going to do about Nicholas? I made up my mind to pretend that he doesn't exist, but...it's not working." With a miserable expression: "He's the only child I'll ever have. My *son*. I've already missed so much of his life. Am I being selfish? Is it wrong of me to want to know him?"

"Of course not, sweetheart," Alex assured her. "It's the most natural thing in the world."

"But I couldn't live with myself if I caused him any sort of distress." She looked down at her lap. "Good lord, Alex, can you imagine some strange woman walking up to you and saying, 'Hello, dear, I'm your long-lost father, except I had a sex change.'" She shook her head in frustration. "How can I do that to a normal young man without ruining his life?"

Alex looked thoughtful. "If someone talked to him first, maybe explained a few things..."

"Who?"

"Me," replied Alex.

"You?"

"Me," he firmly repeated. "Think about it, Nickie. I have recent experience at falling to pieces over the notion of a transsexual woman. But I've also been able to get past my prejudices and accept the idea." He smiled and stroked her cheek. "Such a lovely idea, too. Thing is, if I could get your son to relate to me on that level, you know, man-to-man with another guy who's already dealt with this, maybe he'd be able to absorb the truth a little more easily. Bottom line, you *are* his father. Of course there's a chance he might figure me for a perverted old goat and end up flipping out anyway. But if you think it's worth a try, I'll be happy to give it my best shot."

Nickie's face lit with hope. "Oh, Alex, I would give anything in the world if you could make that happen...hold on, my phone's going off." She looked at the cell's message window and rolled her eyes. "Happy, happy, joy, joy. Ambassador Douglass." She flipped the phone open. "Good day, Ambassador."

Alex took her free hand and began playing with her fingertips. Nickie fixed him with an impish grin, listening and nodding. "Yes, sir... The perennials are in, the last sod was put down yesterday...It looks magnificent, Ambassador, truly...What? When?" She pulled her hand away. "Well, if you really think that's necessary...yes, sir." Pushing her lower lip out in a pout: "Sunday? But...all right. Call who? Oh, the catering fellow from the restaurant. I'm afraid I've forgotten his name..."

Alex saw her spine stiffen as she sat bolt upright. *"Collie Skinner?"* She stammered, her eyes wide, "N-no, nothing's the matter. I'll be there, Ambassador. Good day." She slowly let her arm drop, the open phone hanging unnoticed in her hand.

"What is it, Nickie? Who's Collie Skinner?"

"It's *him*, Alex! Nicholas, my son. Collie is just his nickname. He's in charge of the ambassador's buffet." In a tone of horrified realization:

"Dear God. I'd completely forgotten. I *met* him, Alex! I thought he was only a restaurant employee. I gave him my card. My card," she cringed. "Oh, Jesus."

"You didn't know, Nickie." Alex took the phone from her fingers and returned it to her purse. "You couldn't possibly know."

"I gave my own *son* my stupid *card*," Nickie wailed. "How am I supposed to deal with that? And now the ambassador wants to inspect everything and he wants us both there!" She grabbed his arm in a panic. "I can't do this, Alex. I'll lose my mind, I really will."

"No, you won't. You'll be strong, like always. Remember, Nicholas doesn't have any clue who you are. He thinks you're just some officious Windfield lady."

"I'm *not* officious," Nickie sniffled. "And I'm not some lady, I'm his dad."

"Yes, you are." Alex smiled and lifted her chin. "The prettiest dad in all of Virginia. And when the time is right I'll talk to Nicholas, and help him understand, and then he'll love you as much as I do."

"You really think so?"

"Yes, my darling, I do." Alex kissed her. "I mean, what's not to love about Nickie?"

"Collie, we're all shocked and saddened by the tragic events in your family. If you need some time off, by all means take whatever—"

"I don't want any time off," Collie interrupted the general manager. "I'll be fine, Mr. Demarest."

"Well, yes, but the loss of a brother and father...terrible."

"He was *never* my father," Collie emphasized in a flat tone, his eyes cold and level.

"I'm aware that you weren't on the best of terms. That regrettable incident we had here..."

"Mr. Demarest," Collie stated, "as far as I'm concerned they got exactly what they deserved and it has nothing to do with me or my life. And that's really all I have to say, sir. If you don't mind."

The general manager decided to let the young maitre d' handle his own grief. "As you wish. On a far more pleasant note, I'm told that Ms. Thompson has accepted your marriage proposal." He stood and offered his hand. "Sincerest congratulations. She's an exemplary young lady, and you are a very lucky man."

Collie's dour demeanor evaporated. "Thank you, sir! She sure is, and I sure am."

"Have you decided when the happy day will be?"

"Sometime in the fall, sir. After I've saved up some more. Being married can cost a lot, y'know."

The general manager laughed at Collie's earnestness. "That it can. Very wise of you to think in those terms. Speaking of which, if I'm not mistaken you have a big payday coming up shortly. The Windfield picnic business. How's that going? Any problems?"

"So far, so good." Collie briefly summarized the arrangements. "It's costing the ambassador a fortune, sir. Our seafood wholesalers couldn't believe it."

"Couldn't believe their good luck, you mean," wryly observed Mr. Demarest. "I wouldn't worry about the ambassador. This was his idea. Besides, he could buy up every last shrimp on the east coast without batting an eye."

"Must be nice," said Collie.

"You're not doing this all by yourself, are you?"

"No, sir. I drafted Tommy Wilson to help me out."

"Perfect," approved the general manager. "Perhaps some of your motivation will rub off on young Mr. Wilson. It sounds like you've got everything under control, Mr. Skinner. Keep up the excellent work."

"I will, Mr. Demarest."

"And again, best wishes to you and Ms. Thompson."

"Thank you, sir."

Collie left the office and went to change into his formal maitre d' attire. He was pushing at a recalcitrant shirt stud when Robin walked into the room to get ready for her shift. "Hi, beautiful," he greeted her.

"Here, let me." Fastening the stud: "I tried to call you on your cell phone. Have you left it at home again?"

Collie's sheepish look was all the answer she needed. "Oops," he grinned.

"Nicholas..." She put her hands on her hips. "There's no point in having a cell phone if you don't keep it with you."

"I'm sorry, Robbie. I put the dang thing on the charger and then forgot to grab it on the way out."

"Won't you please try and remember?" Robin straightened his bow tie. "It's not just a toy, Nicholas. What if I really needed to get in touch with you? It could happen, you know."

"Gosh, makes you wonder how we ever got along without 'em."

"Wiseguy." Robin swatted him on the seat of his tuxedo pants. "Get out there and charm all the lady customers, you bum."

"Yes, ma'am." Collie gave Robin a quick smooch on the end of her nose. "See you later."

He had no sooner stationed himself behind his podium when the telephone rang. He picked it up. "Foxton Arms, good evening."

"Hello. I'd like to speak with Mr. Collie Skinner, if he's available?"

"This is Mr. Skinner," Collie replied. "How may I be of service, sir?"

There was a short pause. "Mr. Skinner, this is Professor Nickie Farrell speaking. From Windfield College? We met briefly. I'm the one assisting Ambassador Douglass with the memorial dedication, if you recall."

Terrific, Collie thought, I just addressed a lady as 'sir'. "Yes, ma'am. I apologize for the mistake."

"Quite understandable, I have one of those...um...throaty voices," said Nickie Farrell. "Mr. Skinner, Ambassador Douglass wants to meet with us this Sunday at the college, to go over all the arrangements. I'm sorry to disrupt your weekend, but the ambassador can be rather insistent."

"Yes, ma'am, I know," said Collie. "What time?"

"Noon. I hope that's not too inconvenient."

At that moment Robin hurried in from the dining area, saying, "The Kellers just told me they want to come back again Friday evening with two more couples. Do we have any...oh." Seeing Collie on the phone she fell silent.

Collie held up his finger and mouthed "one sec." Into the phone he said: "That's fine, Professor Farrell. Tell the ambassador I'll be there."

"Thank you, Mr. Skinner. See you then."

"Have a good evening, ma'am." Collie replaced the receiver and turned to Robin. "Now what about the Kellers..." He frowned. "Hey, are you all right?"

Robin's brown eyes were huge as a startled cat's. "Who...who was that?"

"Some lady from Windfield. Professor Nickie Farrell. She's in charge of that memorial dedication thing they're having at the picnic. She called to tell me we have to meet Ambassador Douglass this Sunday so he can check everything out and—"

"You and *her?*" Robin's voice sounded like a plucked violin string. "*This* Sunday?"

"Yes." Collie regarded her in puzzlement. "Twelve o'clock. After church. Don't worry, it shouldn't take that long. We can still go to the movies afterwards."

"The *movies?* Oh, *God!*" Robin clapped a palm over her mouth, turned and fled.

Collie stared after her in astonishment. He'd never seen Robin run off like that. Something must have distracted her. She'd even forgotten to tell him about the Kellers.

⸻ ◈ ⸻

After closing up the Knights Inn Tavern on Saturday night, Big Mike went back to the cramped office and sat at a rickety desk, brooding. Two weeks from tomorrow the madman ambassador was going to blow himself sky-high along with Windfield College, in the process transforming one Mike Barlow —a.k.a. Cyrus T. Bolt— into possibly the most wanted man on earth. Even to Big Mike the prospect loomed large. Clearly the authorities didn't give a rat's ass if he occasionally disposed of trash like Moley Fescue or Norris Budge, but nuking a college full of rich kid fruits would unquestionably infuriate them. With the ambassador atomized, they'd be rabid to crucify *somebody*.

Not that the government always succeeded in hunting folks down. They still hadn't managed to snag that Bin Laden asshole. But unlike Osama, Mike couldn't command an army of berserk towel-heads to hide him in the bowels of some godforsaken mountain. In the aftermath of the Windfield attack he'd have to vanish without a trace, on his own, armed only with a handful of forged identity papers. A million bucks would be waiting for him in some foreign bank, assuming he got there safely. But that, Big Mike had begun to suspect, was a goddamn big assumption. The longer he thought about it the more he felt like a lone cowboy who trots over a rise and sees an entire prairie black with Indians: free, but fucked.

Cursing under his breath he opened a drawer and took out his most beloved possession: a monstrous grayish-black revolver he'd acquired at an illegal swap meet. Even in his outsized paw the gun looked colossal. Mike gazed at it regretfully. He might find riches and refuge in some banana republic, but how the hell was he ever going to lay hands on another Ruger Super Redhawk .454 Casull? The thought of leaving it behind caused his stomach to hurt. A weapon like this, which made Dirty Harry's famous .44 magnum look like a bubble wand and could blast a hole in reinforced concrete...damn it, that was something a man couldn't help but revere. Abandoning it, even for a million dollars, seemed treasonous.

Holding the Redhawk, Big Mike went to a closet in the back wall and unlocked it with a key. A bulb blinked on overhead as he went inside. Amidst a clutter of dusty boxes squatted an ugly black safe. Mike twirled the lock and swung the thick steel door open. Stacked willy-nilly on the shelves were bundles of bills, carelessly bound with rubber bands. He grabbed a thick sheaf of twenties, pondered it gloomily and tossed it back. He hadn't counted the money lately, but the last tally had been more than thee hundred thousand dollars. Years of nightly skimming plus the ambassador's various consulting fees had added up to a healthy pile of loot, all of which had to be left behind along with the magnificent Redhawk. If discovered, that amount of cold cash would touch off almost as much pandemonium as the giant gun itself.

"Shit *fire*." Slamming the safe shut, he went out to the darkened bar, drew himself a beer, dropped in a shot of Jack Daniels and poured the whole thing down his throat. He felt trapped by this Windfield business, and feeling trapped made Big Mike almost as nuts as the thought of menstrual blood. He quaffed another boilermaker then perched atop a barstool, drawing beads on the arrayed liquor bottles and dry-snapping the Redhawk.

There had to be a way out. Maybe he could pack up his gun and money and just drive until he found some backwoods redoubt where no one gave a squat about colleges or ambassadors. The problem was, once Eamon Douglass triggered his Redeemer and the Feds realized that Big Mike had disappeared with suspicious suddenness prior to the bombing, they would upend the country looking for him. He would become almost as radioactive as the Windfield campus. Running away was no solution.

Of course if the damn bomb never went off in the first place he'd be home free. But that would only happen if Douglass somehow died before the appointed day. Big Mike flipped open the revolver's cylinder and studied the yawning polished steel chambers. The thought of personally shooting the ambassador had a lot of appeal, but any likelihood of getting away with it was nonexistent. Of course he could always claim that he'd performed a noble deed by preventing a terrorist incident; but even the cops weren't stupid enough to buy that. No, the Commonwealth of Virginia would rapidly park him on Death Row where he'd be given a choice between being needled or fried. So that option was out.

Mike consumed a third boilermaker, which did nothing to soothe his troubled soul. He glowered into the deserted saloon dimness, aiming his Super Redhawk at phantom customers, wishing over and over that he had never gotten mixed up with the Honorable Eamon Douglass.

⸻ ((◉)) ⸻

At a quarter before noon on Sunday morning Nickie and Alex

stood by the new Randall Windfield Memorial waiting for Ambassador Douglass to arrive.

"Well, it's certainly magnificent." Alex admired the massive granite sundial atop its polished marble pedestal. "I can't imagine the ambassador finding fault with any of this."

Nickie pulled her collar up. Under overcast skies the breeze carried a chill. "I hope you're right." She glanced at her watch. "Where's Nicholas?"

"I'm sure he'll be here." Alex squeezed her shoulders. "And remember not to call him 'Nicholas'. That could prove...awkward."

Nickie replied with a hint of irritation, "Geez Louise, Alex, I'm not a *complete* ditz. Can you tell that my eyes are different colors? He mustn't see that."

"No, your rainbow specs hide it just fine." Alex gazed about at the gleaming memorial. "Do you remember when we came out here, after the freshman dance?"

"Seems like a lifetime ago."

"That was the night I realized I was falling in love with you."

Nickie's mouth compressed. "I was still hiding the truth from everybody."

"You had good reason," said Alex. "As I proved."

"Bygones, Alex." Nickie pressed his hand. "Uh-oh," she nodded at a Windfield security cart motoring toward them across the lawn, "here comes the ambassador." Pointing to a distant grouping of benches at the edge of the lawn: "Wait for me there? I'll try to get this over with as quickly as possible."

"Take your time." With a swift kiss: "Hang in there, milady. I love you."

Arriving at the benches Alex spied a well-dressed couple approaching from the opposite direction, holding hands and conversing in the self-absorbed manner of young romantics. He felt a surge of excitement; the man had to be Nickie's son. He seated himself and nodded a pleasant greeting. "Good morning."

"Good morning, sir," politely replied Collie Skinner. Alex's heart jumped; the different-colored eyes were an uncanny replica of Nickie's own. Her son had the same cheekbones, a similar arch to the eyebrows, and hair that was straighter than hers but a comparable shade of dark red. "If you young folks would like some privacy," he offered, "I can go sit somewhere else."

"No, that's okay." Nickie's son turned to his companion, who looked pale and tense. "Why don't you wait here with this gentleman? I'll be back soon." He hurried away toward the memorial.

Robin lowered herself onto a bench and sat hugging her purse, looking unhappy. From the distant chapel a sound of church bells echoed across the grassy expanse.

"I suppose your friend is involved in the upcoming festivities?" Alex inquired.

With a nervous glance: "Uh-huh."

"So is my colleague. She's that lady down there. Professor Nickie Farrell."

"Yes, I know," said Robin in a mechanical way, then grew rigid. "I...I mean, that's nice."

"Have you two met before?"

She turned and looked at him with such apprehension that Alex felt a pang of guilt. The poor girl was vibrating with tension. In a gentle voice, "You're Robin, aren't you?"

For a moment he thought she was going to take off like a spooked feral cat. "*Excuse* me?"

"Robin, my name is Alex Steward. I'm a professor here at Windfield. An English professor like Ms. Farrell. She and I are friends." After a meaningful pause: "Good friends."

Robin's brown eyes blinked rapidly. "My God," she hoarsely breathed. "You *know*. She told you."

"Yes," Alex said. "I know." Seeing the girl's look of panic: "I'm the only one, Robin. Believe me. Nickie hasn't breathed a word to anyone else."

"Is she going to tell *him?* " Robin glanced tearfully toward the memorial. "I thought Nickie didn't want him to find out. She made me promise to keep quiet. Has she changed her mind? Where does that leave me? What happens when Nicholas finds out that I knew the truth? He'll *hate* me!" She began to cry.

"No, no. Take it easy. Nickie won't say anything, not today or anytime soon. The last thing she wants is to cause either of you any problems." Alex moved to sit by the weeping girl. "That's the truth, I promise."

"I *hate* secrets," Robin sobbed. "I *hate* lies. We're engaged to be married!" She displayed her engagement ring. "I can't stand having to conceal the truth! Every time Nicholas wonders who his real father is I feel like I'm going to throw up. It's driving me crazy!"

Alex patted her shoulder. "You're right. Hiding the truth inevitably gets people hurt. Nickie and I have talked about this. Yes, she did change her mind. She's desperate to know her son. Can you really blame her? But she won't go off half-cocked. Trust me. Nickie knows the kind of emotional upset this can cause, and she won't take a chance with Nicholas." He paused. "I told her I'd try to help."

"You?" Robin dabbed at her eyes with a tissue. "How?"

"I can speak with him," Alex answered. "Even though I'm an old guy, Robin, I'm still a guy. Men find it easier to talk about...well, embarrassing stuff with other men. I'm positive Nicholas would be better off hearing about this from another male. Better for you and Nickie, too. At first he might become angry, ask crude questions, say some unpleasant things. Things he'd probably regret later. I could deal with that, but would you want to?"

"All I *want* is not to lose my man."

Alex squinted toward the memorial where the silver-headed ambassador, standing beside Nickie up on the wooden speaker's platform, was gesticulating with his walking stick as if rehearsing a speech. "I wouldn't worry too much, Robin. If Nicholas takes after Nickie –and to look at him he certainly does– then he's as forgiving and kind as she is." He smiled. "Smart, too. And only a fool would let someone like you get away."

Robin swallowed. "I hope you're right, Mr. Stewart."

"Steward. But please, call me Alex."

"What made Nickie change her mind about wanting to know her son?"

Alex didn't respond at once. "Nickie had a very horrible experience, Robin. A life-changing one that altered her outlook. It made her realize that some things in life are too precious to let go." After a moment he added: "I needed to learn that lesson, too."

"Sometimes when bad things happen, good things come along to balance everything out. I think God made it that way."

"My dear, I don't doubt it for a minute."

"When Nicholas's mother died, it was sad and awful. But ever since then he's been getting stronger, becoming more of a man every day. I'm really proud of him and I love him with all my heart, you know?"

"Yes, Robin, I do know. I love his father just as much." They looked at each other and laughed. "Um...that sounded a bit odd, didn't it?"

"Maybe a little," conceded Robin. "Life can be pretty surprising, can't it?"

"More than any of us can anticipate." Alex inclined his head at the security cart bearing the ambassador away. "Looks like they're all done." Seeing Nickie and Nicholas walking their way: "Now, I don't want you to worry. Nothing is going to happen. There's too much going on here at Windfield. Nickie has midterm exams to get through, and then this picnic business. She'll be too busy for anything else. I have a feeling that it'll all work out fine, but in the meantime I promise your lives won't be disrupted. You have my word."

"Thank you, Mr. Stew...Alex." As father and son drew near she stood up to greet Collie: "Hey, you. Back so soon?"

Collie smiled. "See? That didn't take so long. Oh, Robin, this is Professor Nickie Farrell. Ms. Farrell, my fiancée Robin Thompson."

Nickie smoothly replied, "A pleasure, Ms. Thompson. Congratulations on your engagement. Mr. Skinner is a very capable young man. You're a lucky lady."

"Thank you, Professor," said Robin, deeply grateful that Nickie's eyes were obscured by the rainbow lenses. "I feel very lucky, yes."

Alex extended his hand. "I'm Alex Steward, young man. Thanks for sharing Ms. Thompson with me. She's a treasure."

"Yes sir, she is." Collie pumped Alex's hand as Robin blushed. "Well, we're going to take off. See you at the picnic, Ms. Farrell. We'll get everything set up nice and early."

"Excellent. The ambassador seems very pleased with all your arrangements, which makes my job a lot easier." Nickie smiled. "Now, go enjoy your Sunday."

Hand-in-hand Collie and Robin walked off across the grass. Nickie waited until they were well out of earshot then grabbed onto Alex's arm. In a faint voice: "I need to sit down."

"Easy, honey," Alex lowered her onto the bench. "How are you doing?"

Nickie removed her glasses and took a few slow deep breaths. "It's beyond surreal, Alex. As if Salvador Dali is suddenly orchestrating my life. I'm talking to my own child and he probably thinks I'm just some fussy academic spinster." She paused. "He's so much like his mother was, Alex. It's unearthly. He has Luanne's way of talking, her gestures... God." She looked after the dwindling figures. "I've got to have him in my life, Alex! I can't survive otherwise. He's my *boy*."

"Yes, he is. He's a very handsome young man. Is that what Nick Farrington looked like?"

"What? Don't be absurd. Nicholas is much better-looking."

"Hmm. Now that you mention it, he would make a gorgeous woman," Alex mused. "Just like his Old Man."

Nickie gave Alex's ear lobe a sharp yank. "Don't you even *think* it!"

"Ow," he ruefully grinned, rubbing the offended ear. "Joke misfire."

"Anyway it's pretty clear where his compass is pointing and it isn't Gender Identity Disorder, thank heaven."

"Ms. Thompson is a sweetheart. She's miserably anxious about all this, poor creature."

"As well she should be." In a remorseful tone: "I put Robin in a terrible spot when I told her keep silent. It's the same as asking her to lie. I should never have done that."

"You were trying to protect your son from being hurt." Alex took her hand. "Don't second-guess yourself in hindsight, Nickie. We'll work it out somehow. I told Robin I would talk to Nicholas. Let's get past midterms, the picnic, and then we'll figure out the best way to proceed. What do you think?"

"Yes, that's a good idea." Nickie looked into Alex's blue eyes and a smile slowly replaced her troubled look. "My son. He really is a handsome young devil, isn't he?"

"An absolute heartthrob," Alex confirmed. "Exactly the same as his dad."

⎯⎯⎯⎯◆⎯⎯⎯⎯

Robin didn't break her silence until they were driving out the Windfield gates. "So," she said, expertly shifting the little Kia through its gears, "was everything okay? Did Ambassador Douglass give you any problems?"

"Not really," replied Collie. He watched Robin's skirt nudge upwards as she pumped the clutch. "He just kept insisting that we set the buffet tent up close by, so that everyone can hear his speech." Collie pantomimed waving a shillelagh: " 'A huge crowd, Mr. Skinner, we *must* have a *huge* crowd!' He seems awfully jazzed about this whole thing. It sort of gives me the creeps. I mean, how come a grouchy old billionaire is getting all psyched over some college picnic? What's up with that?"

Robin lifted her shoulders. "Who knows? Maybe he wants to have some fun for once."

Collie shook his head. "Eamon Douglass isn't about having fun, Robin. Mama was terrified of him. She warned me to stay away from people like that." His expression grew somber. "Mr. Douglass, Doublecross Dingbats! Remember? That's what she was crying right before the end. I know it meant something, but we'll never know."

"No, I don't suppose we will." Robin kept her eyes on the road. She'd never told Collie about the bizarre computer font. Luanne was gone, the ambassador wasn't their concern, and she had far weightier matters on her mind. "That lady, Ms. Farrell...she seemed nice."

"Yeah. She acts sort of...conservative. I guess reading all those books can make you a little uptight."

Robin smiled despite herself. "That's silly, Nicholas. I'm sure Ms.

Farrell is very intelligent." Casually: "Her hair is almost the same color as yours."

"I didn't notice."

"Well, it is. She's really kind of cute."

Collie looked at Robin. "No, *you're* cute. Professor Farrell is an old lady."

"Old? For heaven's sake! When I'm fifty are you going to call *me* an old lady?"

"Aw, you know what I mean." With a sly laugh: "Y'know, I think she and that white-haired dude might be getting it on. Didn't you see the way she was looking at him, all secretive and everything? Just goes to show, you're never too old to–"

"*Nicholas.*" Robin's tone silenced him. "That's enough."

"Geez, Robin." Collie pouted out the windshield.

"I'm sorry, I didn't mean to snap. It's just that...how would you like it if someone was talking about me that way?"

Collie thought it over. "I'd kill 'em."

"Well, then. Let's respect her feelings, too."

"Okay. No problem. Anyway in two weeks the picnic will be done, I'll get paid my two thousand bucks and we can forget about Windfield and Ambassador Douglass and Professor Nickie Farrell." He grinned, his humor restored. "Sound good?"

"Of course, Nicholas." Robin trained her unblinking gaze straight ahead. "Whatever you say."

"That's my girl. Hey, did anyone ever tell you how sexy you look when you step on the clutch pedal?"

On the afternoon of March thirty-first, her last midterm safely passed, Heather Walters bopped into her dorm room in a happy upbeat mood. "Cindaaa," she trilled to her roommate, who as usual sat pounding her laptop. "Look what I just bought!"

Cinda deigned to glance up. "A hankie. So what?"

"It's not a hankie," Heather giggled, "it's some short-shorts. For the picnic tomorrow."

"Are you sure they aren't too big?" Cinda wrinkled her nose and resumed typing.

"Oh, hah. For your information they look really hot on me. What are *you* gonna wear? Wait, don't tell me. Military fatigues. Or maybe carpenter's overalls? They're, like, sooo flattering."

"I'm not wearing anything," retorted Cinda, "because I'm not going."

"What do you mean? Everybody's going. It's like traditional and everything. A big deal."

"Whoopee," Cinda sniffed. "I have better things to do."

"Like what? Midterms are over. You've got straight A's again, of *course*. All you ever do is work, work. Can't you even take one day off to goof around like a normal person?"

"Look, Roomie. Go to the picnic, okay? Wear your little hankie, expose your ass for all the bozos and Neanderthals to drool over, scarf hot dogs, have a real traditional blast. But leave me out of it."

Heather persisted, "Come on, Cin. Don't be such a grouch. Maybe you could write it up for the paper? The new memorial dedication and all..."

Glaring at her roommate Cinda snarled, "I'm a *journalist*. I don't write fucking *puff pieces* about *picnics*. Do you get that? Or has all the hair bleach finally short-circuited your bimbo brains?"

Hurt and anger flooded Heather's blue eyes. "Go to Hell, *Roomie*. Just because I'm not as smart as you doesn't mean you can call me names. Since when is it a crime to want to have a little fun? I don't know what's wrong with you. You've been crabby and bitchy for the past month. You hardly talk to me. It's like, I've tried to be there for you but all you do is shut me out." She crossly blinked away tears. "We always had good times together. I thought you were way cool and totally outrageous. But now you've turned ugly. It's no fun being your friend any more. You want me to leave you out of it? *Fine*. I'll go enjoy myself at the picnic while you sit here and write sarcastic essays about how everything sucks and everyone's no good. I hope it makes you feel real superior." She marched to the door. "If you ever decide to get over yourself, let me know. Oh, and for your information I *don't* bleach my hair. It's just a highlight rinse." She slammed out.

Cinda stared at the closed door as one tear slid down from the corner of her eye. She brusquely wiped it away with the back of her hand. "Yeah, well," she muttered. "Whatever."

That evening in the parking lot of the Foxton Arms, after a delightful repast of Cointreau-glazed goose breast and a bottle of Stags' Leap Ne Cede Malis, Peter and Gladys Deighland climbed into their Lincoln Continental Town Car for the short trip home to their modest little seventy-acre equestrian ranch.

"Are you sure you don't want me to drive, dear?" Mrs. Deighland delivered her customary straight line. "Two martinis, you know."

Her husband at once replied, "No need, Gladdie, I'm as sober as a judge," whereupon she obligingly tittered since Peter Deighland was, in fact, a judge. Basking in his wife's *pro forma* esteem, he slowly backed the big Lincoln, cutting his steering wheel sharply to swing the vast front end clear of an adjacent Mercedes CLS 63. There came a barely perceptible jolt as the rear bumper contacted something.

"Hell's bells," exclaimed the annoyed judge. "And here I just had Miguel polish the car." He frowned into his side mirror. "Ah, good. It's one of those flimsy Asian death traps. No harm done." He put the shift lever into drive and pulled out of the lot.

Robin's little Kia showed nothing more than a barely-visible grayish smudge on its rear bumper. Everything was as before, except that a small black floppy disk now rested on the floor mat behind the passenger's seat.

After closing, Collie and Robin walked out to the deserted parking lot hand-in-hand. Standing by her car, they indulged themselves in a prolonged good night embrace.

"Are you feeling okay, Robin? You look a little puny, as Mama used to say."

Robin sighed. "Cramps. It's that time again."

"Sorry," said Collie, holding her car door open. "Painful, huh?"

"You don't want to know." Robin added with an inscrutable look: "Do you?"

"Do I what?"

Robin slid into the car and fastened her seat belt. "Do you ever think about what it might be like to be a woman?"

Collie regarded her uncertainly. "Uh...is this a trick question? Like, where I end up getting myself in trouble?"

"No, no." Robin gave her head a shake. "Don't mind me, I must be retaining water on the brain. Come over tomorrow after you're through with the picnic. I'll fix you something special for dinner."

"It's a date," said Collie. "Just no shrimp or seafood, okay? I have a feeling I'll be sick of it by then." Glancing at his watch: "Uh-oh, I better haul my butt out to the Knights Inn. Big Mike has been awful cranky the past few days. Maybe it's his time of month, too." He closed her door. She blew him a kiss through the window, backed out, and drove off.

Not more than five minutes later her cell phone emitted the special ring tone she'd reserved for Collie alone. She smiled and flipped open the phone. "Ye-ess?"

"Robbie? I knew there was something I forgot to tell you. It's really important, too."

"Mm-hm," answered Robin. "And what might that be?"

"I forgot to tell you how much I love you."

"And how much is that, Nicholas?" They'd been playing these nocturnal phone games ever since becoming engaged. "Give me a number."

"Well, I can't count that high, but it's a lot. A *whole* lot."

"Smart answer," Robin approved. "No wonder I'm going to marry you."

"It's a good thing, because...hello? Robin? What's that beeping noise?"

"What beeping noise? I don't hear anything."

"Damn, the screen says my battery is low..."

Robin made an exasperated sound. "Uhh! Nicholas, when was the last time you charged your phone?"

"I don't know. Last week? I thought these things are supposed to hold a charge."

"Not forever, Nicholas!"

"Robin? I can't hear...tomorrow...love you..." She heard the connection go dead.

"For heaven's *sake.*" Irked, Robin tossed the phone toward her purse. It missed, caromed off the cushion and disappeared under her seat.

Sufficiently PMS-ed to silently think *shit!* without actually vocalizing it, Robin drove home drumming her fingers on the steering wheel and trying to think positive thoughts. She parked the Kia, gathered her purse and coat, then opened the rear door and stooped to retrieve her cell phone, which lay behind the driver's seat. She was about to close the door when she noticed a small dark square on the floor. Bending down, she picked up a black floppy disk and looked at it in mild surprise. She didn't recall losing any disks. Besides, she always kept her car neat and clutter-free. If it had been here before she would have noticed. She turned it over, but there was no identifying label.

Robin closed the car door and walked off toward her apartment, a puzzled frown on her face. A floppy disk couldn't materialize from thin air. It had to have come from someplace. And what was on it? She had no idea, but she intended to find out.

⎯⎯⎯⎯•«(•)»•⎯⎯⎯⎯

Collie had just begun serving drinks and pizzas to the boisterous Saturday night crowd when another Knights Inn server, a shave-headed beanpole known as Stick, gestured with an extended thumb and pinkie held to his ear: "Phone, Skinner. Some guy, says it's important."

Collie went into the kitchen and grabbed the grimy receiver dangling from the wall phone. "Yeah, who is this?"

He listened for a moment, then: "*What?* Are you telling me those idiots shipped my entire Windfield order to fucking Red Lobster by *mistake?* Jesus Christ!" He looked at his watch. "You realize I'm supposed to start setting everything up in seven *hours?*" Collie closed his eyes for a minute, one fist pressed to his forehead "All right, listen. I'll drive down there tonight with Mack. I know the order by heart, it's the only way I can be sure those guys don't screw it up. Tell Mack to pick me up here, we'll save some time. Yeah, the Knights Inn Tavern. As soon as possible."

Steeling himself, Collie went out to the bar where Big Mike filled pitchers and mixed cocktails with a fearsome glower clearly meant to forestall conversation. But Collie had no choice.

"Boss," he said, "I'm sorry, but I gotta take off. I have to drive down to Annapolis tonight. I'm in charge of that big spread for Ambassador Douglass at the Windfield picnic tomorrow, and something's gotten all screwed up at the seafood supplier. I need to go take care of it. The truck driver's picking me up in a few minutes. I'm real sorry, Big Mike, but it's an emergency. If anything goes wrong I'll be toast at the Foxton Arms, and Ambassador Douglass will murder me."

Mike Barlow narrowed his eyes at Collie, the pupils redly glowing like warning lights at a railroad crossing.

"Okay, I'm fired. I don't blame you." Collie untied his apron. "Stick will take up the slack, don't worry." He laid the apron on the counter. "I better go out and wait for the truck." He thought about offering his hand, changed his mind. "Seeya."

Then the big man did something Collie could hardly believe. He actually grinned. "You have yerself a good ol' time at that picnic, boy. Yep, you an' the ambassador."

Collie blinked. "Sure, Big Mike. Uh...does this mean I'm not fired? Should I come to work again?"

"Don't matter one way or th'other, Skinner."

"Great! I'll make it up, Boss, I swear. I'm leaving my car in the lot. I'll pick it up tomorrow."

"Skinner," Big Mike glared, his customary truculence restored, "Get the fuck outa here."

After taking off her work clothes, Robin donned an oversized "Virginia is for Lovers" t-shirt, ran a brush through her hair, got herself a carton of low-fat raspberry yogurt and carried it to her desk. Waiting for her laptop to boot up, distractedly licking her spoon, she contemplated the enigmatic floppy disk with a vague apprehension. Robin didn't like mysteries; they upset her practical sense of order.

When the computer's desktop presented itself Robin inserted the floppy and clicked on her 'A' drive. The disk window opened to reveal a single icon. Peering closer, she saw that the icon bore an unsettling label: "POP goes the Redeemer!"

"What on earth?" Robin checked the icon's properties and saw that it was a GIF file, which meant that the disk contained an image rather than text. She hesitated, her finger poised above the touch-pad. In this irreverent age, 'POP goes the Redeemer!' might be a pornographic anti-Christian photo. Could some hate-monger have slipped the disk into her car just for the nasty fun of it? Robin wavered. Maybe the smartest move would be to throw it in the trash.

No, she decided. Two quick finger taps and the icon disappeared, replaced by an array of weird but familiar symbols:

Below this heading, in smaller font size, the window was filled to the margins with line after line of the bizarre pictograms.

Robin recognized the Doublecross Dingbats at once. But it made no sense. What possible connection could there be between Luanne Skinner's death-babble and this mysterious floppy disk?

Robin studied the screen. Then: "Of course," she muttered. "It's a message."

For whatever reason, some unknown person had written a message in Doublecross Dingbats, turned it into a graphics file and copied it onto a floppy disk. Then, inexplicably, the disk had ended up in her car. In order to decipher the cryptogram she needed a character map that would match the alphabet to the corresponding symbols. Then she could translate the message one letter at a time.

As she had done once before, Robin typed "Doublecross Dingbats" into her Google window, producing more than five hundred results. She selected one at random and was taken to a site which offered to sell the font set for thirty-five dollars but contained no character map. She tried another site, then another, with no success. Discouraged, she opened a site called 'fontbazaar.com' and saw, alongside the Doublecross Dingbats sample, a hyperlink labeled 'Test Drive!' A quick finger tap and to her delight she arrived at a key grid which matched each symbol to a letter of the alphabet.

She immediately printed the grid out. Holding the sheet in her left hand, she set about deciphering the lines, writing each letter down on a notepad and softly speaking aloud as she worked: "Scaredy cat, a D... running cat, E... pistol, an A..."

In short order she had converted the first several lines. Robin picked up her notepad and re-read the unsettling words:

DEATH DECLARATION
AND STATEMENT
CONCERNING
MY PATRIOTIC
APRIL FOOL ERADICATION
OF WINDFIELD COLLEGE
BY
AMBASSADOR EAMON DOUGLASS

What on earth was a "Death Declaration"? Or a "Patriotic April Fool?" Robin frowned at her desk clock. It indicated a few minutes after midnight, which meant that April first –April Fools Day– had already started. The Windfield College picnic would be starting in just a few hours; but how did any of this tie in with Eamon Douglass, the eccentric picnic-loving tycoon whose name Luanne had linked to the Doublecross Dingbats? And that menacing word, "eradication"...it sounded like something to do with pest control.

Robin picked up her pen and started translating again, letter by letter. After the first few sentences her eyes widened. As the minutes passed her emotional state evolved from dismay, to dread, to horror. Cold chills raised gooseflesh all over her body.

By the time she finished the last sentence, the clock showed one-fifteen. She closed her eyes, trying to gain control of her thoughts. The translated "Death Declaration" was so mind-boggling that Robin feared for her sanity. Calm down, she told herself. It had to be a deranged hoax. She opened her eyes and re-read some passages: "...In the hallowed footsteps of Captain Nathan Hale...Stamp out the pestilential blight of Windfield College...Modern Sodom of unrepentant depravity...My friend Hendrix III...Fiery Redemption...Cesium 137...Irradiate the honorable soil of my beloved Commonwealth...Fifty short years... Patriotic Death...God bless the home of the brave."

With a sudden icy certainty in her gut Robin *knew* that this was not the work of some prankster. Luanne's involvement –whatever it had been– no longer mattered. The floppy disk, the Dingbats, the death-dealing "Redemption"; they were all elements of a suicidal scheme cooked up by the billionaire madman Eamon Douglass. "Jesus save us," she gasped as the realization hit home. "April Fools...He's going to do it *today*." Then a split second later: "The picnic...*Nicholas!*"

Robin sprang up so forcefully that her desk chair toppled backwards. She paid no attention and ran to the phone. Frantically she punched in 911, then abruptly slammed down the receiver before the connection went through. What on earth would she tell them? The emergency dispatchers had zero tolerance for anything but immediate crises. Robin remembered an occasion when one of her babysitting charges had playfully dialed 911. A brace of granite-faced sheriff's deputies had shown up and sternly described for her the fearsome penalties awaiting citizens who misused —or allowed improperly supervised *kids* to misuse— the emergency system. With a sinking feeling Robin realized that if she reported something this outlandish on April Fools Day it would raise a red flag of suspicion. What chance would a simple country waitress have of convincing law enforcement that a former United States ambassador was about to set off a radiological bomb at a college picnic? They'd probably trace the call, break down the door and bury her in some nut house. She couldn't do it alone. She had to find somebody to help her...

Of course! Jay-Bo Skinner had been a state trooper; Nicholas would know exactly how to make the police listen. Robin quickly dialed his number.

"We're sorry, but the number you have dialed is not available..."

With a whimper of dismay she remembered that his cell phone battery had died. Fighting a surge of panic, she resolved to drive out to the Knights Inn and tell him in person. It would be hopeless trying to explain it over the bar telephone. Even if Nicholas could hear her over the tavern din he'd think she'd lost her mind.

Robin quickly pulled on a pair of stone-washed jeans. Not bothering to change the oversize t-shirt or even put on a bra, she stuffed her feet into a pair of loafers, grabbed the handwritten sheets and rushed out to her car.

The Knights Inn Tavern was located along an isolated stretch of country road perhaps twenty minutes away. Robin had never set foot in the place but she'd driven past it many times. As she sped through the night she glanced at the glowing digital numerals of her dashboard clock and saw that it was just past one-thirty. She knew the saloon closed at two, which left her enough time to get there before Nicholas left. She would show him the ambassador's insane message and then let him decide how best to sound the alarm. "Nicholas, Nicholas," she prayed, "for God's sake, we've got to stop him. He's going to kill all those poor innocent people..."

The gravel lot by the Knights Inn was deserted except for one longbed pickup truck and the red Camaro. Robin ran to the front door and pulled on the handle, but it was locked.

"Hello," she pounded on the door with her fist. "Hello, is anybody in there? Open up!" She pounded some more. "Please, I have to see my–"

The door swung inward and Robin found herself facing a massive bearded man. He favored her with an inhospitable scowl: "We're closed."

As he began to shut the door Robin begged, "Wait, please! Are you Mr. Barlow?"

The bearded man's black eyes narrowed. "Who wants to know?"

"I'm Robin Thompson. Nicho...I mean, Collie Skinner's fiancée. I've got to see him!"

"He ain't here."

"But..." She gestured at the Camaro. "That's his car!"

"No shit, lady. He still ain't here. Beat it."

"But where is he?" Robin's voice became desperate. "He's supposed to work until two o'clock!"

"He had to go somewhere. Some kind of fuck-up. We closed early tonight. Now get lost."

"Oh, God," Robin wailed. "What am I going to do? I *have* to see him!"

"Not my problem," shrugged Big Mike. "Go home."

The door had almost closed when Robin cried, "You've got to help me! Please, Mr. Barlow! *Something terrible is going to happen at the college!*"

Big Mike squinted at her. "Say what?"

Robin gulped. "Someone is going to...to set off a bomb at Windfield College. It's a radiation thing, to kill as many people as possible and make sure the college is destroyed forever. It's going to happen today!"

"Who says?"

"I found a computer disk in my car, and there was this coded message..." She pulled the sheets out of her purse and held them out. "Read it for yourself. Have you ever heard of Eamon Douglass? Ambassador Eamon Douglass?"

Ignoring the proffered papers: "What about him?" Big Mike sidled out the door.

"He's the one who's behind it! He's completely crazy. Somebody's got to tell the police. I would, except they'd never believe me." She hesitated. "Can *you* call them? I'm sure they'll listen to someone like you."

Big Mike stroked his beard. Thoughtfully: "Who else knows 'bout this?"

"Nobody. I just found out. That's why I came to see Collie."

"Maybe you better come inside, lady." Big Mike stood aside and held the door wide. "Sheriff Dewitt comes here all the time. Yep. We're fishin' buddies. We best give him a holler. Ambassador Douglass, you say? Ain't he the one got all them millions?"

"Yes! That's him." Robin walked into the Knights Inn Tavern. All the lights were off except for some garish neon signs. A sour smell of beer pervaded the air. "You can't believe how filled with *hate* he is, Mr. Barlow." Placing her purse on the bar: "He wrote this thing he calls a 'Death Declaration'. She heard the front door close and turned around. "I've never seen anything like–"

She didn't get a chance to finish the sentence. In one stride Big Mike stepped forward and with a backhanded swat of his huge paw, knocked her senseless.

Chapter Eighteen
April Fool

Robin opened her eyes to blackness. Dazed and disoriented, she stirred her limbs and felt them come into contact with dusty squarish objects. Whatever space she was in felt cramped and airless. It smelled of old papers and dirt. As she struggled to upright herself a sharp pain in her cheek brought memory flooding back in a sudden rush: The floppy disk...Ambassador Douglass's hellish plan...the Knights Inn...Mike Barlow's huge arm...

Robin desperately groped about in the dark for some means of escape. Her fingers came in contact with a cold metal surface in the middle of which rose a round protuberance. She explored with her hands and realized that she was feeling the front of a large safe. A scream was rising in her throat at the thought that she might be trapped in some sort of vault when she noticed a faint line of light running along the floor. Clamping her mouth shut, she determined that it was coming from under a closed door. Apparently she wasn't locked in a vault but some sort of storage area or closet. Not that it made much difference; either way, she was a prisoner.

She bent her head as close as possible to the light, listening for any noises. Nothing at first, then she heard heavy footsteps, the scrape of a chair, and some guttural sounds that might or might not have been words.

Robin beat her fists against the door: "Is anybody there? Let me out! *Please!*"

"Shut up, bitch," came a surly growl.

Undeterred, Robin pounded some more. "Mr. Barlow! Why are you doing this? Ambassador Douglass is getting ready to blow up Windfield in a few *hours*. We've got to stop him! Let me out of here!"

She heard a grating rumble, like boulders in a rock crusher, and realized that Big Mike was laughing.

"You think it's *funny?* Those people are going to *die.*" Robin hammered on the door in a frenzy: "*Let me out of here*, or you'll be sorry, I swear you will!"

A sudden sledgehammer blow on the other side of the door made Robin scream and recoil backward in the darkness. She landed on what felt like some piled boxes and tumbled onto the hard wooden floor, coughing and choking in an invisible cloud of dust.

"One more word, you fuckin' cunt, and I'll cut out your tongue and make you eat it."

The heavy footsteps thumped away. Robin curled on her side, muffling her terrified sobs in her hands. She was alone, trapped by a grotesque barbarian, powerless to prevent an unthinkable terrorist act from claiming hundreds of innocent lives including that of the man she loved.

"Jesus help me," she cried in the dark. "I love you, Nicholas, oh God, I love you forever."

⇒⋙●⋘⇐

At a few minutes past three o'clock on the last morning of his life, Ambassador Eamon Douglass awoke with a smile on his face. He lay still for a few moments, savoring the sensation of being on the threshold of history. By this time tomorrow —hell, in less than eight hours— the Commonwealth of Virginia, the United States, in fact the whole sorry world would be irrevocably changed; and he, Eamon Douglass, would be forever enshrined in the pantheon of great patriots who had sacrificed themselves for the betterment of their countries. Of course it might take a while for the true nobility of his actions to become clear to his countrymen, since most of them were idiots. Their initial reactions were more likely to resemble an anthill being kicked: hysterical bugs running in all directions. The image amused Douglass, and his hoarse laugh punctuated the darkness. April Fools, indeed!

"I regret that I have but one life to give for my country." The ambassador threw back the comforter and switched on his bedside lamp. "So, let's get to it."

Feeling buoyant, Eamon Douglass climbed out of bed for the final time, put on his Sulka robe and shuffled into the ornate black-tiled bathroom to begin readying himself. Every cell in his old body seemed to hum with the electric certainty that both he and Windfield College would shortly cease to exist. The long-awaited Day of Redemption had arrived at last. Nothing could stop him now.

⊶⊷◉⊶⊷

Hearing no further sounds from his captive, Big Mike went out to the bar and tossed down a double shot of Booker's. The incendiary 126-proof bourbon ignited a calming fire in his innards, which was a good thing because he needed to stay cool while he considered his next move.

He still found it hard to believe that the little snatch had discovered the ambassador's secret scheme and then come running to blab it all to her boyfriend. Even for a woman that had been incredibly stupid. She claimed she'd discovered the truth on some computer thing, but Big Mike didn't give a shit whether or not that was true. The crucial thing was that the bitch *knew*, which saddled him with the immediate problem of what to do next.

The obvious choice was to strangle her. Quick and simple. The idea of murdering a helpless girl didn't bother Mike in the slightest, assuming it served a purpose. But did it? He wasn't sure. Eamon Douglass had made it very clear that there was to be no spontaneous killing. On the other hand, his whole Windfield scheme was obviously coming unraveled. If one meddling twat had managed to sniff it out, what was to stop a dozen others from doing the same thing?

Big Mike downed another dose of liquid fire. He could kill the twat, collect the loot in his safe and light out for parts unknown. But then the ambassador would blow up the college, and once that happened Mike's ass would be targeted by every lawman in America.

"Sonofabitch!" He slammed his fist in rage. Life had been going along just fine. He'd been perfectly content running the tavern, skimming the nightly till and performing the occasional maiming or homicide. Everything was peachy until that goddamn crazy old fart went crackers and decided to irradiate a bunch of college faggots.

Mike Barlow picked up the shot glass and shattered it against a wall. He'd been a jackass to go along with the billionaire lunatic. Hell, Douglass had probably never intended to give him a million bucks. Why on earth would he? It suddenly seemed embarrassingly obvious that he'd hang Big Mike out to dry and merrily blow himself to atoms, laughing all the way.

"Fuck that shit," Big Mike seethed. If it all had to end, okay. But it would damn well end on *his* terms, not the ambassador's. Screw the Windfield queers. First he'd dispose of the nuisance girl, then he'd go to Shamrocks and shoot Eamon Douglass –and anyone else who happened along– into little pieces. He would doubtless die too, but at this point he didn't care so long as the two-timing old bastard ended up dead.

As he walked back into the office Big Mike suddenly halted, and a calculating glitter lit up his black eyes. He stood in deep thought for a moment, absent-mindedly twisting his beard. Then he picked up the gigantic revolver and walked over to the closet.

"Wake up, bitch." He beat the gun butt on the door. "You n'me gotta talk."

—◦《◉》◦—

Huddled on the filthy floor, Robin shrank back as the closet door flew open. Shielding her eyes from a bare light bulb that clicked on overhead, she cowered among several grimy cardboard boxes.

"Get up outa there."

"Why?" Robin quavered, not daring to raise her eyes.

"Get the hell up, bitch. I ain't gonna tell you again."

Realizing she had no choice Robin slowly stood and beheld the bearded giant pointing a mammoth revolver between her breasts. Her knees went wobbly. "Wh-what are you going to do?"

"Shut up." Big Mike grabbed Robin's arm and yanked her out into the room. "I'll tell you when to talk." He shoved her toward the desk. "Sit down."

Robin sank into the beat-up swivel chair, quivering with fear. She looked for some means of escape, but a quick glance around the small office inspired nothing but a renewed sense of hopelessness. Big Mike outweighed her three-to-one, had muscles the size of Buicks and could probably snap her neck with a flick of one finger. The idea of overpowering him was ludicrous. But she couldn't lose her faith. Miracles happened all the time. And if not...Well, Jesus had remained strong in the face of death. Robin raised her chin, doing her best to look unafraid. "Are you going to shoot me?"

Big Mike approached her chair and before Robin could flinch he jammed the massive gun in her face so that the tip of her nose was actually inside the cavernous barrel. A burnt metallic smell flooded her nasal passages. Convinced that she was about to die she closed her eyes and reached up to grasp her little gold cross. "Father, into Your hands I commit my spirit..."

"None of that prayin' shit, bitch." The chain was rudely ripped away, scoring her tender skin. "Open your goddamn eyes."

Robin made herself obey.

"This here's a Ruger Super Redhawk .454 Casull," she heard Barlow say. "Turn a grizzly bear's head into applesauce. What'll it do to yours?"

Robin saw no point in answering. After eternal seconds of waiting for death, to her astonishment the gun was removed from her face. Shaking uncontrollably from the adrenalin coursing through her blood Robin rubbed her neck where the chain had been torn off. Big Mike retreated backwards and sat on the edge of the desk, which creaked a splintery protest under his bulk.

Keeping the gun trained on her: "Listen up, bitch. You wanna stop that fuckhead from settin' off his bomb?"

Robin couldn't believe her ears. Was this God's prayed-for miracle? "You'll let me call the police?"

Big Mike squinted at her in disbelief. "Think I'm crazy, you dumb snatch?"

Robin thought the answer was obvious but remained mute.

"I'm gonna let you kill him."

Robin nearly choked. "*Me?* "

"We're gonna go over to his mansion, and you're gonna shoot him. In the balls would be good. Then all our problems go away. You'll be a big hero for savin' them college fags, I'll be a hero for helpin' you, and there ain't no bombin'. It's perfect."

"Perfect?" Robin shrieked, her eyes wild: "You are insane! I can't kill anybody!"

"Sure you can." Big Mike flourished the revolver. "It's easy."

Robin felt herself slipping close to the edge of madness. "*I'm not a murderer!*"

"Listen, I'm gettin' tired o'yer squawkin'." Mike slitted his eyes. "I'm tellin' you to shoot that old fuck."

"*No!*" Robin clapped her hands over her ears. "I won't do it!"

Mike Barlow heaved a sigh. "Damn women always hafta be a pain in the ass." Keeping the gun leveled he opened a desk drawer and drew out a gleaming knife with a wickedly hooked blade. "They call this a fang knife. Works great for guttin' a big buck." He waved it in her face. "Wonder if it's any good at cuttin' off tits?"

Robin's nerve broke. With a cry of terror she ran out of the office and threw herself at the front door, scrabbling at the latch in a panic, screaming at the top of her voice: "Help! Somebody! Please, help me!"

Meaty fingers buried themselves in her hair and she felt herself almost lifted off the floor. Robin struck out with her fists, tried to kick, but it was like flailing at the Rock of Gibraltar with drinking straws. She felt herself dragged backwards and slammed face up across a bar table. The grip on her hair was replaced by one around her windpipe.

In the reflected glow from the neon bar signs she could see that Mike Barlow had her pinned like a beetle to a specimen board. The fang knife flashed in the dimness. He's going to do it, her brain screamed; he's going to disfigure me.

"*Stop*," she clawed at the hand constricting her throat. "Get away, you bastard!" As the blade descended toward her chest she reflexively drew her knees up toward her chin to try and shield her body.

Robin suddenly felt the grip on her throat release. She heard footsteps retreat from the table, and an odd strangled sound. Forcing her eyes open, she saw her tormentor standing a few feet away, staring toward her crotch with a look of pure horror. Pointing the fang knife at her bottom he gasped like an idling steam locomotive: "*Blood!*"

Hearing the frightful word Robin wondered if she'd been mutilated already but was too shocked to feel it. She lowered her knees and raised up on two elbows, dreading to ascertain the truth.

In a high-pitched squeal like an animal being slaughtered Big Mike repeated: "Blood!" His eyes bulged like eggs. "You filthy cunt! *You're on the rag!*"

Robin flushed and looked down to see the top inseam of her jeans discolored with a dark stain. To her mortification Big Mike was correct: her menstrual period had suddenly started in a big way, causing what females everywhere obliquely referred to as "an accident".

Traumatized, horribly embarrassed, she closed her legs and quickly rolled off the bar table. Big Mike followed her with his eyes, his features contorted with revulsion. Robin began to back away. "I can't help it," she gulped. "I'm very regular, this is when I always..."

"*Shut the fuck up*," Big Mike screamed. He flung the fang knife away and pulled the Redhawk from his waistband. Aiming it at her head, he pointed with his other hand toward the rest rooms, respectively labeled in crude letters 'HENS' and 'PECKERS'. "Get in there," he almost gagged. "Most fuckin' disgustin' thing in the world—"

"I need a tampon."

Mike Barlow trumpeted like a tyrannosaur: "*Does it look like I carry 'em around in my goddamn pocket?*"

Robin indicated her purse, still sitting on the bar where she'd set it.

"I have one. Can I get it?"

Big Mike cocked the hammer on the revolver. "Just the...thing, not the whole damn bag. Make it fast."

Robin retrieved the tampon and walked toward the ladies room. Big Mike threw her a tattered bar apron.. "Put this on. I don't wanna see...anything. You hear me? And don't try to be smart. You're still gonna shoot that fuckin' ambassador."

With a haughty look of contempt remarkable under the circumstances, Robin went inside and locked the door.

———)(()(———

The grandfather clock in the ambassador's study had just finished bonging four o'clock when, dressed in a tailored gray Savile Row three-piece suit, a black-and-gold club tie, custom-made wingtips and a brand-new eye patch, Eamon Douglass sat down at his desk to enjoy his final breakfast. In contrast to what most people might have done, he hadn't ordered anything fancy or extreme. He'd always resented as a waste of taxpayer money the fact that condemned felons were permitted to demand things like Lobster Thermidor or chocolate-covered frogs' legs. His own gentlemanly refection consisted of freshly squeezed orange juice, two poached eggs, English muffins, thinly sliced Scottish smoked salmon, and rich black coffee. The ambassador ate slowly, savoring every mouthful without becoming maudlin or sentimental, and finished every bite. The pain in his gut throbbed unpleasantly, but he would not take an MS Contin pill unless it became absolutely necessary. The Redemption was only a few hours away, and he wanted his mind to remain crystal clear.

After his breakfast had been cleared away the ambassador unlocked a desk drawer and took out a document labeled "Countdown Checklist." He ran his finger down the list of items, two thirds of which had precise red check marks in front of them.

He nodded with a tight-lipped smile. Everything was proceeding without a hitch. The revised bequests had been sent off the day before by Federal Express. As an extra precaution and to ensure maximum disruption, copies had also been sent to the Attorney General of Virginia, an unctuous self-serving mountebank who could be counted on to make any legal mess infinitely worse.

The ambassador slipped the replacement floppy disk into his laptop and checked to be sure the coded Final Statement opened properly. As expected, the Doublecross Dingbats were intact. Douglass was very proud of his Death Declaration. It really was a lucid and logically irrefutable masterpiece, destined to become one of the most famous —or infamous, hell, he didn't care– exit screeds of all time. He removed the disk and shut down his computer, wondering how quickly the dummies at the *Middleville Gazette* would unravel it once Mike Barlow —no, Cyrus T. Bolt– brought them the disk and gave them the clue. It wasn't all that difficult a puzzle, but newspaper people could be denser than black holes. Still, as long as they leaked it to the public before the government clamped a lid on everything, he was content. Once his Declaration escaped onto the Web, of course, everyone on earth with a computer would read it. The ambassador relished the notion of a worldwide audience feverishly analyzing every syllable of his masterpiece. What a triumph! Not to take anything away from the great Nathan Hale, but it would certainly equal anything the hanged revolutionary had ever achieved. Douglass picked up a red felt-tip pen and placed another checkmark on the list.

The ambassador's eyebrows contracted as he contemplated the next item: his obligingly unprincipled "special consultant" Big Mike Barlow, a.k.a. Cyrus T. Bolt. Of course the ambassador had taken pains to make sure that the forged papers contained so many hidden red flags that Barlow/Bolt would set off sirens the instant he tried to use any of them. There was no million-dollar payoff waiting in a Georgiana bank. Douglass marveled at the fact that Big Mike had ever bought that lie in the first place; although, when Mike had saved the day by spontaneously snuffing Norris Budge, the ambassador, temporarily deranged by a sense of gratitude, had briefly considered keeping his word. But in the end, Douglass simply could not leave behind any living souls who believed they'd successfully hoodwinked him. It wasn't a question of megalomaniacal ego, but principle. Barlow's years of skimming

–although meaningless in monetary terms– represented an audacity for which he had to pay with his life. To ensure that outcome, a registered letter containing explicit details of Mike's long criminal career had been mailed to the federal and state police.

Nonetheless, recognizing that Barlow/Bolt might be feeling apprehensive when he came by in a few hours to pick up the disk for delivery, Douglass had readied an extra envelope with five thousand in cash as a calmative. He placed it to one side of his desk blotter, with the floppy disk sitting precisely on top, and placed another red mark on his checklist.

As he contemplated the next item his expression became somber, and a small sigh escaped his lips. Two blackthorn shillelaghs rested side-by-side atop his desk: one concealed the detonator which would trigger the Redeemer, and the other was his constant companion of more years than he could remember. He reverently picked up the latter and carried it over to the fireplace where, as always, a pile of seasoned logs flamed and snapped.

"I'll not let you end up in some damned federal evidence locker," he murmured. "Farewell, loyal friend." He tossed the shillelagh into the fire. Almost immediately it began to burn. Douglass stood silently, one hand on the carved mantle, his head bowed, watching the varnish bubble and smoke as the metal ferrule on the tip slowly turned cherry red. After several minutes the long tube of grey ash broke into pieces and fell among the other embers. The ambassador straightened, returned to his desk and lifted up the glass wolf. "Don't worry," he addressed it. "I won't leave you for the vultures, either." He placed the figurine in his coat pocket, then turned his attention to the detonator shillelagh.

As he had practiced many times before, he carefully unscrewed the tip. Then the ambassador opened the fresh package of batteries that Holmes had brought him the previous week, and began loading them one-by-one into the hollowed-out shillelagh, meticulously eyeballing each as it was inserted to make certain that they were correctly stacked anode-to-cathode all the way. When he was done he replaced the tip and hefted it in his hand. The new stick was noticeably weightier than the one he'd burned, but not so much that it would present a problem. Holding it in his right hand he flipped aside the top half of the cane's head to expose the firing button. He repeated the maneuver half a dozen times. Then, nodding in satisfaction, he laid it across his desk and made a check mark near the bottom of his list. Everything was in readiness.

———《《◎》》———

From the look and smell of the lavatory Robin could tell that management did not prioritize feminine sensibilities. The chipped sink had a crusting of hair and dried-on soap, the fingerprinted mirror was cracked at both ends, and from the malodorous puddles in front of the commode it was obvious that impatient male patrons didn't hesitate to enter and defile the women's domain. Some drunk had left the seat up, neglected to flush and, after depositing a cigarette butt to delaminate in the yellow soup, forgotten his pack of Kools on the toilet paper dispenser.

Robin hurriedly took care of her personal business and made an effort to clean her jeans with half a roll of toilet paper. Desperate to escape or at least find some sort of weapon with which to fend off the psychopath barkeeper she began searching every inch of the small room. A grimy window in the back wall offered a tantalizing possibility, but Robin soon determined that it had been nailed shut.

On the floor behind the toilet, liberally splattered with misdirected male urine, Robin spotted a spray can of Raid Ant & Roach Killer. Fighting her rising gorge she picked it up and quickly rinsed it under the tap. The can felt full; Robin pressed the nozzle and a sickly-sweet-smelling cloud of poison shot out several feet. Her heart leaped; if she could spray Barlow in the face maybe it would buy her enough time to unlatch the front door. But then Robin recalled a news report about teenagers purposely inhaling this stuff to get high; if so, how incapacitating could it really be? It was formulated to dispatch ants, not buffalo-sized homicidal maniacs.

A series of thunderous blows shook the bathroom door in its

frame. "What the fuck you doin' in there, cunt?"

"Give me a minute, will you?" Robin yelled, casting about for anything else she could use. Her eye fell on the abandoned pack of Kools, and she picked it up. The pack felt curiously weighty in her hand; looking more closely, she saw that a disposable lighter had been shoved down among the cigarettes. She shook out a red plastic Bic, threw the smokes aside and flicked it. With a little hiss of escaping gas a yellow pencil of flame shot up.

Robin stared at the can of Raid, then at the lighter, and a vivid image exploded into her mind: Chuckie Jamison, behind the church on Christmas Eve, wowing a circle of admirers with his improvised flamethrower.

With a sharp intake of breath: "Oh, my *God*." Would it work? More importantly, could she bring herself to do such a thing? The very idea made her skin crawl. But there was no time for dithering. If she didn't get away and sound the alarm very soon, Windfield –and her sweet Nicholas– would be exterminated.

Robin's pretty face took on a stony cast. She had prayed to the Lord for deliverance; if He chose to offer it in the form of some bug spray and a Bic lighter, then so be it.

More thudding sounds of heavy fists on the door: "Come out of there, you stinkin' bitch! I'm countin' to three...*One!*"

Robin took up a position to the left of the door.

"*Two!*"

She raised the can of Raid in one hand, and flicked the lighter with the other. The flame wiggled like a hula dancer in her trembling grasp.

With an earsplitting crash, the door slammed inward. Holding his Super Redhawk out in front of him, Big Mike Barlow stormed into the 'HENS' room.

"Forgive me, Jesus." Robin brought the flame next to the can, and pressed the spray valve.

A huge plume of fire blossomed forth and enveloped Mike Barlow. His beard, head and shirt front became a mass of flames. He dropped the revolver and fell back, bellowing like a foghorn and beating at his face with his hands. Screaming at the top of her lungs Robin followed, hosing him down with the burning bug spray. A horrific stench of burning hair and insecticide filled the air. Robin somehow lost her grip on the lighter's trigger and the flame winked out. She threw aside the can, hoping that Big Mike would burn up like a dried-out Christmas tree, but to her horror she saw that the flames were quickly subsiding and that he was charred but very much alive and evidently still able to see. With an unearthly roar he began to lurch toward her.

Knowing that she had only seconds before he would tear her to pieces Robin lunged for the huge revolver lying on the floor. She grabbed it up, swung the massive barrel around and pulled the trigger just as Mike Barlow reached his arms to rip her head off.

A titanic blast shook the Knights Inn Tavern to its foundations. Big Mike spun backwards through the air with a smoking hole in the left side of his chest and landed on a wooden chair, collapsing it into kindling. Robin shrieked in agony, her wrist broken by the gun's ungodly recoil. Deafened, reeling with shock, she staggered toward the saloon's entrance. After a few wobbly steps she lost her balance and fell, striking her head on the edge of a table and landing hard on her wounded hand. She screamed again as a lightning bolt of pain slashed through her entire body. Then a swarm of reddish comets obscured her vision, her eyes rolled up and she sank out of consciousness and lay unmoving on the dirt-caked bar floor.

————))(((————

A blare from an eighteen-wheeler's air horn jolted Collie awake. He sat up, rubbing his eyes. "Shit. What time is it? Where are we?"

"Just crossed the Potomac," replied Mack Woodhull, the Foxton Arms' burly delivery driver. "Been movin' along pretty good. We should make it back by six, maybe a little after." He glanced at his passenger. "Didja manage to catch some winks? You crashed before we even got to Bowie."

"I guess." Collie rubbed his face, trying to clear the cobwebs. Reassembling the Windfield order in the middle of the night had been an experience he never wanted to repeat. But somehow they'd gotten it done, and the truck was now freighted with enough fishy-smelling delicacies to satisfy an army of ravenous picnickers. "Mack, can we find a drive-through and grab some coffee? I gotta wake up. I can't let that old grouch catch me falling asleep on his job."

"Old grouch?"

"You know, Ambassador Eamon Douglass. The guy paying for all this." Collie jerked a thumb over his shoulder. "Mean as a water moccasin but richer than God, and he's going to give me a big chunk of change...*if* I don't screw up."

"After all you done last night, he oughta pay you double. Those seafood guys were bein' pricks. You handled 'em real smooth." Mack snorted. "I prob'ly would've just kicked their asses."

"I thought about it," Collie admitted. "But what good would it do? Besides, I'm not into fighting anymore since I got together with Robin."

"Your girlfriend?"

"Fiancée." With a weary grin: "We're getting married in the fall."

"Good for you." Mack's eyes twinkled. "Nothin' better than a good woman. What's she like? Pretty as a picture?"

Collie visualized Robin lying asleep in her neat little bedroom dreaming Technicolor girl dreams and found that he couldn't speak.

Mack's rugged features softened. "You love her a whole lot, don't you?"

Collie cleared his throat. "Robin's the most beautiful girl in the world, but that's not the main thing. It's the way she..." He paused. "Being with her always makes me want to be a better person, Mack. I feel glad to be alive. I've never been religious, but because of Robin I know there's a God." Collie swallowed. "Does that make any sense?"

"Oh, yeah." Mack nodded. "I know exactly what you mean."

"Are you married?"

Mack's eyes grew sad. "Lost the wife to cancer a coupla years ago."

"I'm really sorry." Collie shuddered. The mere thought of something happening to Robin froze his blood.

"Alicia was the best," said Mack. "Just old-fashioned decent, y'know? A real lady. I miss her every day." He swerved the truck onto an exit ramp. "There's a Mickey D's here. Let's get that coffee."

After loading up on caffeine and breakfast junk they headed back out to the highway. Chewing on a large bite of Egg McMuffin Mack asked: "You wanna go by the Knights Inn and pick up your car?"

Collie checked his watch. "No time. I told Tommy Wilson to be at the restaurant by a quarter to seven, and then we gotta haul this stuff over to the college. It's gonna take a while to unload and set up. I can always get my car later." He smiled, suddenly remembering. "Tonight, after Robin makes me dinner."

Mack looked with distaste at his Egg McMuffin. "She's probably a great cook, too."

"Like you wouldn't believe."

"Lucky you." Hoisting his paper coffee mug: "Here's to all the good women in the world. Especially Miss Robin."

Collie raised his coffee. "Amen, brother. I'll definitely drink to that."

<hr />

Robin's consciousness returned in irregular flickers, brightening and dimming like a light bulb during a brownout. She became aware of lying on a hard surface. Her head throbbed in agony, her ears were filled with a high-pitched ringing noise, and one side of her face seemed to be numb. Most frightening, any movement caused an explosion of pain in one arm such as she'd never felt before. She heard herself whimper as thoughts began to clarify out of the mental mists: I'm hurt. I'm alone. I need help...

As her eyes came into focus and she saw where she was, Robin's memory came crashing back with horrific suddenness and she almost passed out again. But she fought the blackness coalescing behind her eyes, and panting with the effort, raised herself to a sitting position by pushing against the floor with her uninjured hand. She sat still for a moment, cradling her right arm in her lap, waiting for the savage pounding in her head to let up. Her right wrist, she saw, was grotesquely swollen. Her left cheek felt sticky; when she touched it her fingers came away coated with blackish globs of dried blood. She discovered a swollen knot above her ear and more stickiness in her hair. Robin wondered if she'd suffered brain damage. At the very least she had a double concussion, both from the fall and from being knocked out earlier by that monster...

She cast her eyes around and saw a large indistinct mound amidst the wreckage of a chair several yards away. A wave of nausea gagged her as the reality hit her that she'd shot –*killed*– another human being.

"Oh, no. No."

Even assuming that her action proved to be legally justified, the fact remained that she, Robin Thompson, had broken the divine Sixth Commandment. But whether –or how– she could learn to live with that was irrelevant right now. Only one thing mattered: finding a way to prevent the looming Windfield tragedy. She'd taken one life; perhaps by saving many others she could earn some small bit of redemption in God's eyes.

Robin looked at a wall clock over the bar and noted with dismay that it was nearly eight o'clock. She had obviously been lying unconscious for hours. The Windfield picnic was supposed to start around ten with Ambassador Douglass's dedication speech, which meant that she had only a short while left to do something. But what? Even if she could drag herself out to her car, which she doubted, the injuries to her hand would make driving impossible. Her only option was to get to her phone and call...

Nicholas! Surely he had recharged his cell phone by now. If she could just talk to him, she was positive he'd find a way to thwart the ambassador's deadly plan.

Not daring to stand up lest she stumble and knock herself out again, keeping her eyes averted from the sprawled corpse nearby, Robin painfully slid herself across the floor in the direction of the bar. Clutching one of the stools as a support, she managed to pull herself to her feet. The room began to spin and her vision wavered, but she took a few slow deep breaths and the whirling sensation subsided. Pulling her cell phone from her purse, she thumbed the preset numeral for Nicholas's number. Please, she silently begged, be there. Four rings, five, and then she heard the automated voice: "We're sorry, but the number you have dialed is not available..."

"Nicholas," she moaned, *"where are you?"* Overcome, Robin lowered her forehead onto the bar, which smelled of sour rags. She felt woozy, and the agony in her wrist was worsening with every passing minute. If she blacked out again without getting through to someone, Windfield and Nicholas were done for.

Whining with pain, she raised her head and started scrolling through her preset numbers. Reverend Shorr? Mrs. Jamison? Neither of them would be able to do anything except call the police...still on April Fools Day.

From outside the tavern Robin heard the noise of a passing car. Someone was liable to show up at any moment and discover what had transpired. The instant that happened she would become a murder suspect with a credibility rating of zero. Her pleadings about a bomb at Windfield would be met with a Miranda warning and handcuffs.

In desperation Robin resumed scrolling through the list. One had an unfamiliar area code: 317. Robin stared at it. Then her bloodshot eyes lit with a tiny ray of hope. It was a long shot, but just maybe...

With a quick prayer she pressed the send button and lifted the cell phone to her ear.

———— ⟨⟨◍⟩⟩ ————

At ten minutes past eight o'clock, with still no sign of Mike Barlow, the ambassador's impatience turned to wrath. True, Barlow/Bolt had always been an unhurried sort of ruffian; nonetheless, on this morning of all others Douglass had expected his special consultant to be prompt. He sat at his desk, grumbling and drumming his fingers, glancing from his watch to the door and growing more incensed by the second.

At eight-fifteen, beside himself with rage, the ambassador rose and began to pace back and forth, grinding his teeth. Where *was* the cretinous thug? Here he stood on the verge of changing the world forever, ignominiously waiting around for a dirt-ignorant brute who'd never heard of Nathan Hale! How was it, Douglass fumed, that the stratagems of great men were so often impacted by imbeciles?

By eight-twenty the ambassador began to consider the possibility that something had gone amiss. Could Barlow/Bolt have chickened out and fled? Even worse, might he have turned canary and decided to save himself by singing to the authorities? For one blood-freezing moment Eamon Douglass feared that the Redemption had been compromised. But no, if that had happened Shamrocks would already be filled to the rafters with feds. There was no need to panic...yet. As often happened during battle, the course of action would have to be adjusted according to minute-by-minute circumstances. Mike Barlow had ultimately proven worthless, which was exasperating but not tactically vital. In short order, the ambassador knew, his special consultant would be hunted down and executed. In the meantime Douglass would improvise...with certain precautions.

He went to a bookshelf, pushed a hidden latch and swung out an entire panel filled with leather-bound volumes of William Makepeace Thackeray. From the recess behind he pulled out a wooden box. Opening it, he withdrew a palm-sized blue Walther THP .25 ACP semi-automatic pistol. Extracting the clip from the handle he inspected the stacked cartridges, then snapped it back into place. He racked the slide, engaged the safety, and placed the weapon in his coat pocket. The ambassador doubted that he would need the weapon, but in the unlikely event that someone tried to interfere, he'd be ready.

The grandfather clock sounded a single sonorous note to mark the half-hour. Eamon Douglass walked to his desk and, ignoring the cash envelope, picked up the coded floppy disk and slipped it into his breast pocket. Punching the intercom: "Holmes!"

The secretary appeared at once. "Yes, sir?"

"Have my car brought around immediately. I'm running late."

"Llewellyn is already waiting, Ambassador."

"Very well." Douglass grabbed his shillelagh. "I hope this damn dedication doesn't take too long."

"Yes, sir. Will you be wanting lunch when you return?"

The ambassador shot him a sharp glance. "Of course. Why wouldn't I? Today's no different from any other. See to it."

Holmes nodded. "Very good, sir. Anything in particular?"

The ambassador grunted. "No goddamn salad. Something different for once. Deviled eggs."

"Deviled eggs. Yes, Ambassador."

"Holmes," said Douglass, "there may come a day when you decide to write a book about your service in my employ."

"I'd never consider it, sir," demurred the secretary, looking mildly surprised.

"I don't give a damn if you do write it. Just one thing," he shook his shillelagh for emphasis. "You make sure and tell them that Ambassador Eamon Douglass was never afraid of anything or anyone. Is that clear?"

"Indeed it is, sir."

The ambassador looked around at the familiar space for one long moment. Then he walked to the door, which the secretary quickly opened. Shillelagh in hand, he strode from the room without a backward glance.

———————————

Heather Walters happily studied her reflection in the full-length mirror. "Omigod, girl, you are so hot." Repeating for the sheer joy of it: "Hot!"

As killer as she looked in her picnic outfit, Heather decided, the only males who wouldn't drool at the sight of her were either blind, gay, or afflicted with that E.D. thing. Her white micro-shorts allowed a glimpse of butt-cheek, the cropped pink-and-black top was molded to her bosom like a surgical glove, the 18k bellybutton bling accentuated her tiny waist and iron-flat tummy, and the ribboned Victoria's Secret wedgies transformed her sleek legs into a magazine fantasy.

She checked her eye makeup to make sure that it was suitably bewitching, ran a few fingers through her fluffed-out hair and laughed with pure *joie de vivre*. What a perfect day this promised to be! Fun, food, boys, dancing, sunshine...

She winced as Cinda's cell phone went off. Instead of a melodic ringtone her roommate favored an obnoxious rasp that sounded like an angry rattlesnake. It was just one more thing Cinda did to set herself apart.

The phone buzzed several times, fell silent, then renewed its insistent noise.

Annoyed, Heather picked it up. "Hello?"

A sick-sounding voice said, "Cinda?"

"Cinda's in the shower. I'm her roommate. Who's calling?"

"I've *got* to speak with her. Right away. It's an emergency."

"Oh, puh-leeze. That dog won't hunt." Heather loved Dr. Phil's Texas colloquialisms. "April Fool, okay? I get it. Is that you, Angela? I am *so* gonna spank your butt!"

"I'm not Angela. Please listen..."

"Who, then?" Heather frowned.

"My name's Robin. I work in town. At the Foxton Arms. Please get Cinda. I think...I think I may pass out. I've been hurt."

"Wait a sec...I remember you. You're the one who has that boyfriend with the funny eyes." Heather's tone became chilly. "Uh-huh. Y'know, it was right after we were there that Cinda started acting a little weird. Not good weird, more like crazy weird." She paused. "Why do I have a feeling you had something to do with that? Anyway I don't think she needs to be talking to you right now. We've got a big picnic here today, and I finally convinced her to come with me, and I don't want you getting her all stressed out again. I'm sure your little emergency can wait."

"*No it can't!*" The other girl's desperation sounded very authentic. "For God's sake *don't go to the picnic.*"

"As if," sniffed Heather. "Why not?"

"Because something terrible is going to happen. People are going to get killed. *Please* let me speak to Cinda!" The voice was becoming a frantic wail. "Tell her...tell her it's about Nick Farrington."

"Oh, I'm sure," Heather scoffed as Cinda came through the door, rubbing her hair with a towel. "For your information she isn't interested in guys, and she doesn't know anyone named Nick Farrington, so—"

Cinda leaped across the room like a leopard pouncing on a springbok. Snatching the phone from her startled roommate's hand: "This is Cinda. *What about Nick Farrington?*"

"Thank God, thank God," she heard a sob. "It's me, Robin Thompson. I don't think I have much time left. Listen..."

———— ((●)) ————

"Good morning, Professor Farrell. Please, come in." Fredericka Lindsey beckoned Nickie into her office. "Would you care for some coffee?"

"Thank you, but I'm supposed to rendezvous with Ambassador Douglass in about twenty minutes."

"Of course." The president gestured out the window, where early-birds were already beginning to circulate around the soon-to-be-dedicated Windfield Memorial, the food and drink areas, and the dance floor where later everyone would boogie to D.C.'s latest hip-hop sensation, Run n' Soar. "It promises to be a most festive occasion."

"Yes." Nickie's eyes drifted toward the blue-striped tent where her son Nicholas was doubtless putting the final touches on the ambassador's seafood buffet. "It does, indeed."

Fredericka Lindsey settled onto the black leather couch and patted the cushion beside her. "Please, sit. Just for a moment. Don't worry, I won't make you late."

When Nickie complied: "I wanted to tell you how much I –all of us in the administration– appreciate everything you've done. The new memorial is stately and appropriate, more so than any of us anticipated. Dealing with Ambassador Douglass cannot have been easy, yet you did so with grace and efficiency." She paused. "Even despite your ghastly ordeal. I'm so terribly sorry you had to suffer something like that."

Nickie gave the tiniest shrug. "Life goes on." She looked out the window. "I have many, many blessings to count. More than I ever knew."

"Do you like it here at Windfield, Nickie?" Fredericka Lindsey studied the other woman's face.

"I love it here, President Lindsey." In a soft voice: "I feel like Windfield is my family now. I don't ever want to leave."

"As to that," replied the president, taking her hand and giving it a gentle squeeze, "although there are no guarantees in life, I think it's safe to say that a long-term teaching career here is definitely in the cards, if that's what you want."

"Nothing would make me happier, Madame President."

"I'm glad." Fredericka Lindsey smiled. "Woman-to-woman, I hear that you and Professor Steward have become somewhat close."

Nickie colored and dropped her gaze, then looked back up, her features aglow. "Yes, we have. Alex is...just wonderful."

The president's eyes twinkled. "I've always thought so, too. That gorgeous white hair of his...! Well. I couldn't be more pleased. For both of you." She released Nickie's hand, and they both stood. "You look divine, by the way." With an envious glance at Nickie's lilac twin set and gauzy white skirt: "I wish I could go casual, too. However," she resignedly straightened her blue suit jacket, "as befits my exalted position, I'm obliged to be perpetually attired in administrative drag."

"Madame President," Nickie assured her, "you never look anything but formidably distinguished."

"Now there's a compassionate euphemism," laughed Fredericka Lindsey. "Leave it to an English professor. Thank you for coming by, Nickie." She checked her watch. "On your way. Mustn't keep our benefactor waiting. I'll see you down at the dedication." She sighed. "With any luck, he'll keep his remarks brief."

———※《◊》※———

Standing with the cell phone jammed to her ear, damp hair spiking in all directions, Cinda's face showed incredulity, then awe, finally settling into a look of wild excitement. Heather impatiently extended her arm and tapped her watch, to which Cinda responded with a fierce glare and a finger across her lips.

Rebuffed, Heather plopped down in a desk chair and sat crossly swinging one foot. Ignoring her, Cinda listened intently, exclaiming: "No way...You're positive? My God! Jesus, Robin! Holy shit...Christ... *shit.*" She ran to the window and looked out. "What? You want me to tell him about that? You're sure? Okay, but...Robin? Are you all right? *Hello?* Damn it!" She snapped the phone shut and turned to her sulking roommate. "Get in your car and drive to D.C. *Now.*"

"And miss the picnic? I'm sure. Oh, that's right, I forgot. It's an emergency. Puh-leeze! Tell me you are not actually going to listen to some lame townie waitress who—"

"You have to get the hell out of here, you stupid fucking airhead!"

Heather's jaw dropped, and she burst into tears.

"Oh, Jesus. I'm sorry, girlfriend. I swear." Cinda dropped to her knees by Heather's chair. "I suck. I don't know how to kick my own ass but I would if I could." She grabbed her roommate's hands. "I didn't mean it, Roomie. I didn't."

Heather blinked her big blue eyes, from which depended little mascara rivulets. "Why are you so mean to me? What did I ever do to you? I'm *not* an airhead. I got almost a B-plus average on my midterms!"

"Yes, I know. You're a smart girl. So pay attention, okay? Robin —the waitress— found out there's going to be a terrorist attack at the picnic. A dirty bomb. Do you know what that is? A big explosion full of radioactive waste, to kill as many people as possible. You know that old fart with the pirate eye patch, who donated the new memorial? Ambassador Douglass? It's his idea. He's planning to blow himself up too, like those nutbags in the Middle East. Robin says she read some kind of coded suicide note. She tried to get help last night but this asshole kidnapped her and she had to shoot him. The gun broke her arm and—"

Heather interrupted, in the chary tone someone might use to soothe a lunatic: "Come on, Cinda. Do you hear yourself? You can't seriously believe something so crazy. It sounds like one of those moronic flicks the guys love. Have you forgotten what day this is? It's

April *Fool*, Cinda! I don't know what's up with you and that waitress, but..." She paused, frowning. "Omigod, have you guys been hooking up?"

"What?" Cinda released her grip and stood. "*No.*"

"You seemed awful interested in her that time at the restaurant. Whatever. She is so pulling your chain. As if that little goody-goody could ever shoot anybody!"

"She's not lying!"

"Get real. Everyone lies."

"Not Robin. She's religious. To her lying is a big deal." Cinda stripped off her bathrobe. "And if it's true, Heather? Is a stupid picnic worth dying for?"

Heather wrinkled her nose. "It *isn't* true."

"If you're willing to stake your life on that, I guess I can't stop you." Rapidly donning a sleeveless black sweatshirt and cut-off jeans: "I gotta go."

"What do you mean, 'go'?" Heather jumped up from the chair. "Go where?"

"I have to try and stop it."

"Cinda! Have you gone completely nuts? Do you have any clue what'll happen if you go down there and start yelling about a terrorist attack? You won't just get kicked out of Windfield. The *government* will come after you. I mean the FBI and Homeland Security and the CIA. They will *so* throw your butt in jail!"

"Only if I'm wrong," retorted Cinda, lacing up a boot. "If I'm not..." She left the sentence unfinished.

"Use your head for a minute," Heather begged. "Why would this old guy want to do something so horrible? We're just a school!"

"Listen, do you remember I once told you never to underestimate the power of hate?"

"Yes, but—"

"He hates us, Heather! To him we're all faggots, niggers, kikes, chinks, spics, and dykes. Liberals. Free-thinkers. Everything Windfield stands for and celebrates, he hates. No different from every other big-oted turd in the world except he's so rich and powerful that he thinks he can kill us all. Well, *fuck him*."

"But he's an ambassador. An American! Terrorists are...y'know, Middle Eastern."

"Is that so. Where do you think Timothy McVeigh came from? Yemen?"

Heather stared. "You...you really think it might happen?"

"Not if I can prevent it." Cinda embraced her roommate. "You know how much I love you, right?" A quick kiss, and she was gone.

As the long black limousine approached the front gates of Hendrix Windfield's former country estate, Ambassador Eamon Douglass leaned forward, his shillelagh clutched tightly in both hands, and demanded of Llewellyn the chauffeur: "Are you absolutely clear on what to do?"

"Yes, sir." The chauffeur held up a floppy disk. "Take this down to the *Middleville Gazette* and personally hand-deliver it to Mr. Gerard DuPree."

"Correct. What else?"

"Inform him that it's vitally important to national security."

"And?"

"And tell him that Ambassador Douglass says 'Doublecross Dingbats'." The chauffeur's deadpan expression didn't change. "Sir."

"That's exactly right." Douglass sat back. "I am relying on you, Llewellyn. Disappoint me at your peril."

"I won't, Mister Ambassador."

They glided through the imposing stone gates and began driving along the perimeter road. To their left, acres of sloping manicured lawn were dotted with milling groups of young people in colorful picnic attire. Gleaming in a semicircle near the top of the hill stood the snowy marble pillars of the new Windfield Memorial. Close to the monument, a striped canvas party tent had been erected alongside an array of big-bellied black barbecue grills. On all sides, blooming flowers and trees lent the scene an Eden-like pastoral splendor.

"Looks like quite a turnout, sir."

The ambassador's eye gleamed as he looked out at the doomed Windfield campus. "Yes, it appears so. Of course these rambunctious youngsters would rather indulge themselves in their hedonistic ways than listen to an old man's speech." With a sharp bark of laughter: "I may bore them to death."

"Not at all, sir." Llewellyn turned into the visitor's parking area. "I'm sure they'll give you their full attention."

"Perhaps they will, at that." Douglass pointed out the windshield. "You see that individual in the white skirt? With the red hair? That's my escort. Pull up there."

As they drew to a stop the chauffeur inquired, "What time shall I return to pick you up, sir?"

"That won't be necessary. These college things always run late, so I'll arrange to get home on my own. You just run that disk over to the *Middleville Gazette* and then take the rest of the day off. It's Sunday. Nothing ever happens on Sunday."

"Yes, sir. Thank you. I hope you enjoy the picnic, Mister Ambassador."

"Oh, I intend to. Goodbye, Llewellyn."

⸻ ⟨◉⟩ ⸻

Cinda burst through the door, skipped down the steps of her dormitory and hastened along the stone path, her thoughts tumbling over each other like acrobats. Assuming Robin's story was true, Cinda was putting her life in peril by rushing down to the picnic area. If the bomb exploded she might die a frightful death. But if she helped avert the disaster she would save Windfield *and* score one of the biggest exclusives in the history of journalism. She was risking her life, yes, but investigative journalists couldn't be wimps. If she'd wanted to play it safe she would've gone to some holy roller college and majored in Bible-thumping.

On the other hand, if it turned out that Robin had been playing her for a dupe, Heather's scenario might well come true: Cinda could find herself expelled from Windfield, facing federal charges, her future in ruins, universally scorned as a pariah and fool. That awful possibility, more than the notion of being killed, slowed her steps. She halted and stood to one side of the walkway, irresolute. A stream of students passed by on their way to the picnic grounds, laughing and joshing, as unmindful of the world's evil as newborn kittens. How many might soon lie dead or fatally maimed if she did nothing and the bomb detonated? Cinda had no way of knowing. It all came down to whether or not she believed Robin's warning. The whole thing did sound like a bad movie. Could an overwhelming hunger for a journalistic coup have rendered Cinda's common sense inoperable...?

No. She wasn't some credulous gull. Her reporter's instincts were guided by a strict maxim: "Consider the source." Robin Thompson was an old-fashioned highly-principled *good girl*. Cinda vividly recalled Robin's anguish at having to conceal Ms. Farrell's true identity from her boyfriend. Was it plausible that a person like that would concoct wild tales about dirty bombs and homicidal kidnappers just for a lark? Never; not in a million years. With a start Cinda realized that she wouldn't believe such a story from anyone else she knew: not her friends, her family, her teachers; nobody. But she absolutely trusted that the petite waitress had been telling the truth. With her last strength Robin had reached out to the other girl in an eleventh-hour attempt to avert the carnage. Whether Cinda could succeed remained to be seen; but she was determined to make the effort or –literally– perish in the attempt.

She started running along the pathway in the direction of the new Randall Windfield Memorial.

"Welcome, Ambassador Douglass. It's good to see you again." Nickie greeted the old man as he exited his limousine, clutching the inevitable shillelagh. She indicated a security cart waiting nearby: "I've arranged transportation, if you like."

Eamon Douglass waved aside's Nickie's offer. "I'd rather not be trundled about in some motorized tumbril today, Professor Farrell. It's such a magnificent morning, a stroll will be invigorating. Get me revved up, so to speak, for my little address."

"As you prefer, Ambassador." Nickie gestured at the pebbled pathway. "After you."

Eamon Douglass began to walk, shoulders erect, head held high, the shillelagh wedged protectively under one arm. Nickie fell in step beside him as they gradually wended their way past dormitories, academic halls, and the cafeteria. They were traversing a broad rectangular court when the ambassador suddenly drew up and gazed around with a questioning expression.

"This is Randall Quad, Ambassador," explained Nickie. "It's where our graduation ceremonies take place every year."

"Ah, yes." The ambassador gazed up at a stately old magnolia tree. It had been here, he realized, beneath these spreading branches, that Hendrix Windfield III had righteously banished his scapegrace son Randall. "Many years ago, Professor, before this institution or its graduations existed, I stood in this very spot on an occasion of some significance." Eamon Douglass could still hear the rage-filled curses; still see the champagne dripping down the debased young man's face as the assembled guests gaped in amazement. The father's actions had been so honorable, so *proper*, so perfectly in alignment with the gentlemanly order of things. But then the world had gone mad and all that was righteous and upstanding had dissolved into moral rot.

"What sort of an occasion, sir?"

Eamon Douglass shook his head. "A family celebration. It's ancient history now, long forgotten except by me. No one else cares or remembers. *Tempus fugit*." He saluted the magnolia with his shillelagh and Nickie overheard a cryptic mutter: "Courvoisier and Monte Cristos, Hendrix. To celebrate the Redemption. I'll be with you shortly, old friend."

"I beg your pardon, Ambassador?"

"Never mind." With a sharp glance at Nickie, the ambassador tucked the shillelagh securely under his arm. "*À la recherche du temps perdu*, Professor."

"Remembrance of lost time." Nickie quietly added: "I've seldom found it to be a pleasant exercise."

"No? I revere the past, myself. The 'good old days' are mostly spoken of with contempt, but I recall a time when people were expected to live by accepted values and standards. All that has vanished. Nothing is sacred anymore. Nowadays everything is so damned...flexible. Well, my allotted span is almost done. I'll be dead soon, but I have a feeling that Windfield College will be talked about for a long time to come."

"As will your generous contribution to it, Ambassador. The new memorial will ensure that."

"Indeed." Eamon Douglass straightened his shoulders. "Let's get down there, shall we? The ceremonies mustn't be delayed."

———— ((◐)) ————

In the buffet tent Collie watched a horde of squealing picnickers swarm the tables the instant the platters were uncovered. Collie had seen nature films of marauding yellowfin tunas crashing through shoals of baitfish in a devouring frenzy, but those marine predators had nothing on these Windfield kids.

"Jesus, Skinner," whispered his assistant Tommy Wilson, opening an ice chest to refill a large metal bowl with more shrimp, "you'd think they hadn't eaten in a month."

"Free food makes people go nuts, even this early in the morning. And here I was worried that we'd brought too much."

"Are you kidding? At this rate it'll all be gone in an hour."

"Maybe." Collie shrugged. "Ambassador Douglass kept saying he wanted to attract a big crowd. Well, this oughta make him happy."

Standing up with the refilled bowl Tommy looked past Collie's shoulder. "Uh-oh. Isn't that the guy? Old dude with an eye patch?"

Collie turned and saw Eamon Douglass approaching through the gluttonous hubbub with Professor Nickie Farrell at his side. "Yeah, that's him. Make sure to keep the food coming." He met Douglass and the professor near one end of a long serving table.

"Good morning, Ambassador. Better not shake hands, sir." Wiping his palms on his apron: "I'm kind of fishy."

"Understood," acknowledged the ambassador. He looked around at the feasting throng. "It seems to be going as planned, wouldn't you say, Professor?"

Nickie Farrell smiled at Collie, who noted that in fact she did have hair the same color as his. "Mr. Skinner has done an excellent job of carrying out your wishes."

"Yes, yes. Ably done, Mr. Skinner. My compliments."

"Thank you, sir," grinned Collie, envisioning a two-thousand-dollar check. "You sure got that crowd you wanted. Would you or the professor care to try anything?"

The ambassador declined, as did Nickie Farrell. Collie thought she was watching him rather intently, but that wasn't really surprising; she was the one in charge, and if anything went wrong it would be her butt in a sling.

Nickie checked her watch. "It's getting close to ten o'clock, Ambassador."

"So it is. Time for my little speech." To Collie: "You'll stay right here, of course."

"I will, sir."

"See to it that you do. Goodbye, Mr. Skin—*oof!* " An involuntary grunt escaped his lips as someone suddenly bumped into him from behind. Jarred from his grip, the shillelagh fell to the ground.

Collie exclaimed, "Oh, shit!"

The person who'd run into the ambassador exclaimed, "Oh, shit! Sorry, Mister."

Seeing who it was Nickie Farrell exclaimed, "Ms. Vanderhart! For heaven's sake, watch where you're going!"

As Cinda bent to retrieve the shillelagh the ambassador snarled: *"Don't you dare! "*

Cinda yanked her hand away and backed off, staring at Eamon Douglass with a horrified expression. "I...I wasn't going to..."

The ambassador stooped, seized his shillelagh and painfully straightened, glaring at Cinda. "This is a sacred Douglass heirloom. No one outside the family has *ever* been permitted to touch it."

"I'm sure Ms. Vanderhart meant no harm." Nickie cast a reproving glance at Cinda. "Are you all right, Ambassador?"

"I've absorbed worse hits, believe me," he grumbled, jamming the shillelagh back under his arm. "As for you, young lady, I strongly suggest that in the future you refrain from this sort of rash blundering about before you get hurt."

Cinda goggled at him as if he were a fanged vampire. "Uh, yeah."

"Ms. Vanderhart is one of our more...impetuous young journalism students, Ambassador." Nickie wryly added: "Rashness is a specialty of hers."

"A reporter?" Douglass shook his head in disgust. "Infernal nuisances, all of them. This one will undoubtedly excel. Come along, Professor."

When they walked out of the tent Collie addressed Cinda with more than a little hostility: "Do you know that was Ambassador Eamon Douglass you almost knocked over?"

"No shit. Jesus, what a psycho! What's up with him and that stick? You're Collie Skinner, right? I've gotta talk to you. Now!"

"Sorry, I'm busy. Go have some crab legs."

As he started to turn away Cinda grabbed his arm. "Fuck the crab legs! I've got an important message from Robin. Will you just *listen?*"

"Robin? How do you know Robin?" Frowning: "Wait a minute... yeah, I've seen you before. You've been to the Foxton Arms, haven't you?"

"*Yes,* but never mind about that." She spoke in an urgent whisper: "I got a call from her a few minutes ago, okay? Robin told me that the ambassador is planning to blow up this picnic with a suicide bomb! A dirty bomb, full of radioactive waste. Do you hear what I'm saying? He's going to kill himself and everybody else too! We've got to stop him!"

From outside the tent came a loud screech of feedback, followed by an amplified voice: "Testing...testing...one two three..."

"I get it. The ambassador's going to bomb Windfield...*April Fool!* Okay, very funny. See? I'm laughing. Hah, hah." Collie rolled his eyes. "I can't believe you and Robin thought this up. She never even told me she knew you. I am so gonna get her back for this."

"It isn't April Fool! This is *no joke*. Robin's been hurt! Some creep named Big Mike kidnapped her, but she shot him, and I think the gun broke her wrist..."

Collie grabbed Cinda by the arm and pulled her behind some stacked crates of seafood. "Tell me what kind of bullshit you're up to, and I mean *right now.*"

Cinda angrily shook off Collie's hand. "Don't get male macho with me, you idiot. Just shut up and listen, goddamn it!" Breathlessly she summarized how Robin had found the mysterious disk, deciphered the Doublecross Dingbats, read the ambassador's Death Declaration, then gone to get Collie only to be snatched and imprisoned by Big Mike. "He was in on the whole thing, don't you see? When Robin found out he tried to kill her. She somehow set him on fire with a can of bug spray and shot him but the gun was so powerful it broke her arm. Robin only called me because she couldn't reach *you* on your cell phone."

Collie smacked his forehead with a fist. "*Damn.*"

"I'm *not lying*, I swear! Can't you use your brain? How would I possibly know any of this unless she told me?"

Collie's lifelong mistrust of Windfield showed on his face. "I don't know. *I don't know.*"

They heard a rolling wave of applause from the picnic area, followed by the amplified voice of President Fredericka Lindsey over the loudspeakers: "Hello, students, faculty, friends and neighbors. Welcome to Windfield College's annual Spring Picnic..."

Frantic, Cinda persisted: "Robin told me your mother *warned* you about Ambassador Douglass."

Collie's eyes narrowed. "Mama said he was full of hate."

"*Yes.* She was right, don't you see? He *is* full of hate, so much that he's decided to destroy Windfield and kill us all."

Collie locked stares with her for a long moment. "You're not making this up?"

"It's all true. I swear to God!"

"I *knew* that rotten bastard was up to something," Collie seethed.

"Well, he isn't gonna bomb anybody. I'll tear his head off first."

"Wait! There's one more thing Robin wanted me to tell you, in case...in case she doesn't get the chance."

"What?"

Cinda hesitated, exhaled a deep breath. "There's a secret Robin's been keeping from you. It's about your—"

Collie angrily interrupted, "That's bullshit. Robin would never lie."

"She didn't lie. She just...couldn't say anything."

"But she told *you?*"

"No. Actually I'm the one who found it out in the first place. It's about Nick Farrington. Your father. The man you're named for... *Nicholas.*"

Seeing Collie's stunned expression: "Yes, I know your real name. Never mind how, it's too long a story. And don't blame Robin because it wasn't her fault. I was the one who dragged her into everything."

"Dragged her into what? You're not making any sense."

"Never mind. What you have to know is that your father's *here.* Today. This minute, outside at the picnic!"

"My *father?*" Collie gasped. "Nick Farrington? Who...where is he?"

Cinda hesitated. "Don't freak out...there's no time for that."

Collie grabbed Cinda's shoulders. *"Tell me!"*

"He was just in here. You saw him. Only he's not a 'him' anymore."

"What are you talking about?"

"Nick Farrington was —is— a transsexual. He underwent a sex change and became a woman," said Cinda. "A woman named Nickie Farrell. *She's* your father, Nicholas."

Collie staggered and retreated a few steps, hands clutched to his head, mind blank with shock. His stomach knotted. The buffet tent swirled around him and his vision took on a whitish tinge. He squeezed his eyes shut, panting, mouth hanging open. Impossible, he thought. *No.* It couldn't be true. Far better to die than have a father who was one of...*those.*

Then, from somewhere, his mind was filled with the ghostly voice of his dying mother: "Don't hate, Nicholas. Hate destroys everything. Don't let it destroy you. Will you remember?"

"Mama," Collie whispered. He opened his eyes to see Cinda staring at him with a pleading frightened look, and felt an unexpected surge of strength and determination. "Yes, Mama. I remember."

He ripped off his apron, threw it aside, and ran.

"President Lindsey, honored trustees, Windfield students, ladies and gentlemen, good morning, and welcome to you all." From her vantage point up on the wooden speaker's platform Nickie Farrell looked out over the pink sundial with its shark-fin brass gnomon at a sea of upturned faces. The sound of her own voice thundering from the loudspeakers was disconcerting but she gamely smiled and spoke into the microphone, her hands demurely folded in front: "On such a lovely day I'm certain that the last thing any of you want to do is look at me while I give a speech..."

From somewhere a male voice shouted, "Says who? I do!" This was followed by a piercing wolf whistle. The subsequent swell of laughter was punctuated by a very audible observation from Professor Alex Steward, who was sitting with Joanne Markwith in the third row of folding chairs behind the trustees: "Hey, that's *my* line!"

Blushing to the roots of her hair Nickie waited until the hilarity had subsided then continued: "At President Lindsey's behest, it has been my privilege over the past several months to work closely with a gentleman whose extraordinary generosity has funded the design and construction of this magnificent tribute to our school's beloved founder. We are deeply honored that he is with us today to officially dedicate the new Randall Windfield Memorial. And so without further ado it's my sincere pleasure to introduce Windfield's great friend and benefactor, the Honorable Ambassador Eamon Douglass."

She began clapping her hands as Douglass rose from a lone chair at the side of the platform. He coolly walked up to the microphone, the perfect picture of wealth and rectitude. Holding his shillelagh like a scepter he calmly waited until the last echoes of applause faded away and then addressed the crowd: "Distinguished ladies and gentlemen of Windfield College..." The ambassador paused and smiled. "We meet at last."

Before Collie could run out of the buffet tent he felt his legs kicked from under him. He hit the ground hard and knocked the wind out of his lungs. Struggling to catch his breath, he heard a mocking voice say: "Well, well! If it isn't our pugnacious little friend with the color-challenged eyes. I did *so* hope we'd get a chance to renew our acquaintance. And here you are. Perfect timing!"

Collie glared up at a handsome young stalwart wearing immaculate white shorts, a pink Oxford shirt carefully rolled to the elbows and new Sperry Top-Siders. His face looked vaguely familiar. The college boy stood, arms akimbo, looking down his nose with contempt. "Don't remember me? Hm. I'd be wounded if you weren't such a shitty townie twerp." He spat a sticky globule, which arced through the air and splattered Collie's trouser leg.

From somewhere behind him came a sycophantic snicker: "Oh, Phillip, that is *so* cold."

In a sudden flash Collie recollected the brawl he'd gotten into at the Knights Inn, the night this jerk and his buddies had tormented Robin at the Foxton Arms. He angrily leaped to his feet. "I remember you now, *sir*. I never forget a dickhead. Sorry I don't have time to kick your butt *again*." He tried to dash around Phillip, but felt himself seized and thrown roughly to the ground.

"Leave him alone, you dumb-ass flamer!" Cinda Vanderhart rushed forward with upraised fists. Phillip easily stepped aside and shoved her so hard that she tripped, went down, and rolled halfway under a buffet table.

"Worthless dyke," he sniffed to one of his cohorts. Turning his attention back to Collie: "Funny, you aren't nearly as brave without that trigger-happy Neanderthal waving his big boom-stick to save your inbred ass."

A circle of picnickers stood watching the confrontation as they happily munched their crustaceans and cephalopods. Unnoticed, Cinda crawled out from under the table and stood up, her brows contracted in a deep frown.

Phillip advanced on Collie, who had regained his feet. "Now don't run away," the pretty boy taunted. "Come and take your whipping like a good little redneck..."

Flushed with rage, Collie was preparing to charge when he saw Phillip's head disappear under a torrent of red goo as the air was split by a banshee female shriek: "How *dare* you push my *roommate*, you disgusting *pig!* "

Phillip emitted an ear-splitting screech as the bowlful of seafood sauce that Heather Walters had dumped on him coated the upper half of his body. Immediately the enclosed space was filled with the pungent odor of horseradish as the spectators roared and whooped with delight.

In a pose of unrepentant indignation, still holding the dripping bowl, Heather contemplated her handiwork with great satisfaction: "Like, don't make me mad."

At that moment a prolonged rumble of applause resounded from the picnic grounds. With a cry of dismay, Collie sidestepped his still-squawking antagonist and bolted from the buffet tent.

Cinda Vanderhart, who'd stood in silent perplexity throughout her roommate's performance, suddenly shouted "Boom-stick...Omigod!" Her brooding look was replaced by one of terrible comprehension. With the swiftness of a sprinter exploding from the blocks, she raced after Collie.

>◦(◦)◦<

Up on the platform, the ambassador addressed Nickie Farrell, who stood beside him: "In recognition of your steadfast commitment to this admirable project, which has succeeded so brilliantly, I'm honored to present you, Professor Farrell, with a small token of my appreciation."

With a courtly bow Douglass handed Nickie his glass wolf. As she blinked at the figurine in surprise he continued: "As you know, Professor, the wolf is a creature that has been unjustly despised and feared. Albeit in different ways, people such as you and I have also been greatly misunderstood. Therefore, as we dedicate this glorious memorial together, let it be an occasion when, in the honorable tradition of Windfield College, old notions of intolerance and prejudice are forever laid to rest."

"Thank you, Ambassador," replied Nickie. "What a lovely sentiment." As the spectators erupted into applause, she withdrew to the chair and sat very straight, her ankles crossed, holding the wolf in her lap.

Eamon Douglass waited for silence, then began to speak: "More years ago than I care to contemplate, long before many of you were alive, it was my great privilege to be personally acquainted with Mr. Windfield. I speak not of Randall Windfield –although I encountered that headstrong young man on more than one occasion– but his father, my esteemed comrade and neighbor, Hendrix Windfield the Third. He was an extraordinary gentleman of the old school, an upstanding blue-blooded Virginia patriot, and since the day of his tragic demise not a single hour has gone by that I don't mourn his loss."

A puzzled buzz rippled through the onlookers. Jo Markwith leaned toward Alex Steward and muttered, "What on earth, is the old goat losing it?"

"Lord, I hope not. The last thing we need is some reactionary polemic about the good old days." Alex directed a questioning look toward Nickie, who caught his eye and returned the barest hint of a shrug.

Pointing his shillelagh to the east the ambassador continued: "Just beyond those hills lies my estate, Shamrocks, from where, for the past thirty-seven years, I have nightly contemplated this former estate of my friend Hendrix and wondered when –if ever– the great injustice perpetrated here would ever be rectified. For the longest time I gave in to despondency. But I was wrong to do so, ladies and gentleman. The hour has finally arrived. To me, in my final days, has fallen the glorious task of setting things right."

Not taking her worried eyes off Eamon Douglass, President Fredericka Lindsey whispered to Maudelle Chesterfield, "I have no idea what's happening here, Del, but it's not good. Not good at all."

Her administrative assistant nodded grimly. "I *knew* this was a mistake. You want me to go up there and stop it?"

President Lindsey hesitated. "I don't...let's give it another minute."

"During the American Revolution, so much of which occurred in and around this hallowed land, many valiant men of integrity and honor stepped forward to sacrifice their lives for the cause of freedom. Of these patriots, none was more heroic than Captain Nathan Hale, whose brave words in the face of death have resounded down the decades with undiminished power: 'I regret that I have but one life to give for my country.' So it shall be for me, as I—"

"*You goddamn son-of-a-bitch!*"

A white-faced young man elbowed his way through the crowd and stood in front of the sundial. He pointed a trembling finger up at Eamon Douglass. "I know what you're trying to do, you asshole! But you're not gonna get away with it!"

Staring aghast at her son, Nickie Farrell felt her stomach collapsing inward. This isn't happening, she prayed. Please, God, make it a dream.

Collie turned around and shouted at the mesmerized multitude: "Run! Get out of here! *He's got a bomb!*"

Before anyone could react the sound of hearty laughter boomed from the loudspeakers. "Hah, hah, hah! Beautifully played, Mr. Skinner. Very well done. You've earned your bonus, my young friend." The ambassador stood merrily tapping his shillelagh on the platform, chuckling with obvious enjoyment. "By George, I do believe we gave them all quite a turn. 'He's got a bomb!' Hah, hah, hah!" He spread his arms wide, the shillelagh dangling in his hand. "April Fool!"

A surge of relieved laughter swept through the crowd, along with scattered applause and appreciative echoes of "April Fool!"

President Lindsey sagged in her chair and put a hand to her

forehead. "Jesus, Mary and Joseph. I need a double scotch."

Clutching the ambassador's glass wolf in a death grip, Nickie tried to control her hammering heart. April Fool? Was it possible?

Collie turned back toward the platform. "Bullshit! It isn't April Fool, you bastard!"

"Now, Mr. Skinner," the ambassador admonished, baring his teeth in a grin, "let's not prolong our little joke, shall we?"

Collie raged: "*Doublecross Dingbats*, you fucker! My mother was on to you! Robin read your suicide note! Big Mike tried to kill her!"

Eamon Douglass's face turned scarlet. His gray eye burned with mad malevolence as he bent and hissed at Collie, "Your *mother* was a worthless piece of ignorant scum, you little shit! You're too late. You can't stop me."

From somewhere in the crowd Cinda Vanderhart's voice screamed out: "Nicholas! He's going to trigger the bomb with his stick! *Get the stick!*"

Collie leaped onto the sundial, skirted the gnomon and lunged upward toward the platform. Douglass fell back, but not before Collie fastened his fist around the bottom of the shillelagh. Shrieking curses, the ambassador sawed the cane back and forth with both hands as hard as he could, but he couldn't break Collie's vise-like grip.

"*Goddamn you!*" Maintaining his grip on the shillelagh with one hand Douglass plunged the other into his jacket pocket, withdrew the pistol and fired downward. Collie yelped and released his grip on the shillelagh as a crimson stain blossomed on the shoulder of his white shirt. He slid from the platform's edge, tumbled off the side of the sundial and sprawled onto the grass.

As the screaming spectators began a panicked stampede the ambassador pointed his pistol down at Collie's prostrate form.

Nickie Farrell shrieked and rushed at Eamon Douglass. He swiveled and raised the pistol just as she swung with all her strength and smashed the glass wolf into the side of his head.

It shattered in a spray of crystal shards. The pistol flew out of the ambassador's hand as blood poured from his temple. Swaying drunkenly, his eye patch knocked askew to reveal a shriveled dark hole,

Douglass snarled with black hatred: "Goddamn...trannie...*bitch!*" His fingers fumbled at the shillelagh.

Cinda's frantic yell rose above the uproar: "Ms. Farrell! *Watch out for the stick!*"

"You shot my *son!*" Nickie screamed at Eamon Douglass and threw a roundhouse punch that smashed solidly into his chin. The ambassador staggered backward from the force of her blow. For perhaps a second he wavered on the edge of the platform, flailing at the air with his shillelagh. Then with a howl he toppled over and dropped straight down onto the sundial's gleaming brass gnomon. He was instantly impaled. The sundial became awash in gore, which flowed over the carved numerals and dripped down the sides of the pink granite. The bloodied point of the gnomon projected above the ambassador's chest as his body jerked and quivered for several seconds, then stopped moving. The shillelagh, its top hanging open in an odd way, slid out of his gnarled lifeless hand and clattered onto the stained grass.

Ignoring the surrounding pandemonium, Nickie scrambled off the platform and hurled herself beside her unmoving son. Flinging aside her sunglasses: "Oh, no, oh, no," she sobbed. "Nicholas! My darling boy! *For God's sake, somebody get some help!* Don't die, please, please, you mustn't die."

She cradled Collie's head in her lap, bending down to kiss his face. "Nicholas, I love you. Please, hold on. Help is on the way. Don't leave me, oh, please don't die, Nicholas, my beautiful son."

⎯⎯⎯⎯◉⎯⎯⎯⎯

Collie could feel a weird hot pain beside his neck, and it was difficult to breathe. He was aware of a lot of yelling and noise, and his left arm tingled with the same pins-and-needles sensation he got from sleeping on it wrong. He wasn't tired, exactly, but sort of unfocused and confused. Something pretty bad had just happened, he knew, but he couldn't remember exactly what. He tried to move, but stopped because it hurt.

"Nicholas?"

That's *my* name, he thought, and slowly opened his eyes. He saw a woman's face leaning over him, a nice face he didn't immediately recognize, although it did seem familiar. The woman was crying, which made him sad. Then Collie noticed something else, something most extraordinary and wonderful. She had eyes exactly the same as his. It was like looking into a mirror. One blue, one brown. Beautiful, amazing eyes. And then, suddenly, he remembered.

"Nick?" It was hard to speak; he had no breath to make his voice work. "Nick Far...Farring..." He coughed and gagged on some warm stuff in his throat.

"Don't try to talk," the woman softly said. "Yes, Nicholas. I'm Nick Farrington. I'm your father." She tenderly stroked his forehead, her tears falling on his face like warm gentle rain. "It's me, my dear brave son, and I love you very, very much. We're together now. I promise I'll never, ever leave you."

"Cool," Collie whispered. "Robin didn't lie." As his vision began to dim, he smiled and with great effort lifted one hand: "Hi, Dad. Nice to...meet...you."

The last things he saw were his father's different-colored irises. Then the darkness swept in and he knew no more.

EPILOGUE

In spite of the fact that only a single death resulted from the thwarted attack of April first, the popular media organizations, perhaps to assuage their disappointment over such a negligible body count, defiantly began referring to the incident as "The Windfield Massacre". Though no massacre had occurred, editorial consensus held that as a headline, "The Windfield Near Miss" didn't have legs. Lacking a pile of radioactive student corpses, the media instead whipped up a doomsday meringue of "what-ifs", offering one grisly speculative scenario after another to the jittery public. This was easy to do in light of the discovery by Homeland Security ordinance experts that there had indeed been a so-called "dirty bomb" concealed under the sundial; one which, had it been detonated, would have caused a catastrophic mess. Not only was there a considerable quantity of Cesium 137 in the phony propane tank, but the frightening amount of explosive surrounding it might conceivably have spread the radioactive contamination as far as Dulles airport, causing almost incalculable economic devastation. Naturally the television and print news magazine worked this theme with enormous gusto, offering up apocalyptic visions of Northern Virginia as an irradiated wasteland straight out of *Mad Max*, replete with marauding bands of charred mutant cannibals.

Holed up on Pennsylvania Avenue with an approval rating in the teens, the U.S. President, after checking the polls with his political cabal, issued a powerful statement in which he stoutly condemned the attempted bombing and stressed that Eamon Douglass had been given his ambassadorship by a Chief Executive from the other party. He pledged a thorough investigation, meanwhile assuring the citizenry that they were safe from foreign and domestic terrorists. His opponents on Capitol Hill immediately rebutted these assurances, instead suggesting that due to years of bumbling ineptitude in the White House, no one in America was safe from anything.

From sea to shining sea, the Blame Game was played out at an unprecedented level of vitriol. The Congress blamed the administration. The administration blamed the Congress. The press, in its fair and balanced way, blamed both the President and the Congress. Democrats blamed Republicans, Republicans blamed Democrats. Conservatives and liberals blamed each other. Church-goers blamed non-believers. As a matter of principle Muslims were also targeted for blame, along with the usual blacks, Jews, Hispanics, illegal aliens and homosexuals.

The talking heads had a field day. Right-wingers –prominent among them Jay-Bo's toothy blond– maintained that it was all the fault of the so-called social progressives and their insane excesses, saying that while the ambassador had been somewhat out of line in plotting to blow up a college, it wasn't at all surprising that he had been driven to that level of desperation by the scandalous goings-on at Windfield. The left-wingers countered that anyone who thought with their brains instead of a Bible could see that this incident represented the beginning of a backward slide into a reactionary Dark Age of intolerance. How long, they rhetorically thundered, before the country became dotted with internment camps run by corporate bundists and Evangelical Christians? The arguments of both sides were taken to heart and loudly repeated by their respective adherents, resulting in innumerable shouting matches, insults, fist fights, and a couple of knifings.

Federal law enforcement investigators wasted no time in tracking down the source of Eamon Douglass's lethal Cesium 137. A posse of Marines from the U.S. embassy on Georgiana was dispatched to collect Egor Antonovich Volka, only to find that his estate had been sold to a twenty-eight-year-old multimillionaire software geek from Stuttgart.

Despite a frenzied international manhunt and an offered ten-million dollar reward, the elusive Russian was never apprehended.

As more of the incident's odd details became public, the ever-inventive community of conspiracy theorists enjoyed a boomlet of prosperity, rushing into print several books which presented some eye-popping hypotheses. The most popular of these quickie bestsellers claimed that the government was covering up a dastardly plot involving several disaffected former KGB agents in cahoots with a coven of transsexuals, who'd framed a distinguished American businessman as part of an illicit Northern Virginia land-grab scheme by the North American Man/Boy Love Association.

Although Eamon Douglass hadn't been able to exterminate Windfield College, some of his plans did bear fruit. The multiple bequests he'd sent out precipitated a maelstrom of legal chaos that even the ambassador would have found hard to believe. When the government, as expected, declared Douglass a terrorist and seized all his assets, a mercenary brigade of the most avaricious attorneys in America filed an array of gargantuan lawsuits on behalf of their aggrieved clients. Dour legal experts predicted that the courts couldn't possibly untangle the muddle in less than ten years.

Also as the ambassador had hoped, despite the government's earnest efforts to keep it under wraps, his Doublecross Dingbats "Death Declaration" found its way onto the Internet and did indeed become one of the most infamous and widely-read documents in the long and colorful history of criminal insanity.

As for Windfield College itself, in the immediate aftermath of the picnic the school was evacuated and quarantined for three weeks while hundreds of assorted government agents and officials combed through the campus. Every last bit of the Randall Windfield Memorial was confiscated, dismantled and hauled away, including the flowers. Eventually the original obelisk was returned and erected in its old spot, the trustees having banished for all time any further notion of a grand edifice.

When the college finally did re-open, everyone made a concerted effort to ignore the countrywide ruckus so that they could return to their normal routines as quickly as possible. The campus was declared strictly off-limits to the public. A couple of pushy reporters ignored the ban and were arrested for trespassing, which stopped the press incursions. Even so, more than sixty students felt uncomfortable with the amount of public scrutiny Windfield had attracted and chose to transfer to less notorious schools. The college administration allowed them to withdraw without imposing any financial penalties. Fearing a mass pullout, the admissions office braced for a rush of cancellations from the already-admitted incoming freshman class, but relatively few of those materialized. To make up for the ones who had departed an extra batch of admission letters was mailed out and the vacancies were quickly filled with new students.

With the heartfelt endorsement of the trustees President Fredericka Lindsey personally awarded two all-expenses-paid scholarships to Robin Thompson and Collie Skinner, whose last-ditch heroics had saved Windfield from being obliterated. And, in appreciation for her timely actions at the picnic, Professor Nickie Farrell was granted full tenure.

Collie suffered a collapsed lung, internal bleeding, and the loss of his spleen; but being a strong young man in excellent health, he quickly recovered from the gunshot wound. During Collie's convalescence Nickie Farrell and Robin Thompson took turns spending as much time with him as they could. Despite being constantly hounded both of them refused to give any interviews, and staying at the hospital with Collie provided them a safe sanctuary since reporters and other busy-bodies were strictly barred.

Nickie sat for hours with her son, holding his hand and making it plain with every word and gesture how much she loved him and cherished the miraculous circumstances which had finally brought them together. Collie quickly adjusted to the paradoxical reality of the charming lady professor being his father. He couldn't help being drawn to her. Nickie was everything that Jay-Bo had never been: sweet, kind, thoughtful, smart, funny, and tender. Best of all, she didn't harbor the slightest trace of hatred for anything or anyone, not even the madman who had shot her son. As they became better acquainted Collie found it easy to understand why his mother had fallen for Nick Farrington all those long years ago. They shared intimate memories of Luanne, and Nickie wept for a long while when Collie described her death. Collie learned about Nickie's rejection by her family, and he told her about Lissa's tragic suicide. The more time they spent talking together the clearer it became to them how much sadness they had endured in their lives, and how fortunate they were to finally have a chance to be happy.

As for Robin, Collie was less concerned about his own condition than hers. As a result of her injuries she wore a cast on her broken wrist and had her arm in a sling. Not wishing to upset him she tried to downplay her ordeal at the Knights Inn and her subsequent arrest for Big Mike's murder. She had spent many harrowing hours in custody being subjected to rigorous interrogation, first by the police in connection with the shooting, then by a phalanx of forbidding federal agents concerning her admitted foreknowledge of the unsuccessful Windfield bombing. When it finally dawned on them that the wounded little waitress was a heroine instead of a terrorist, she'd been allowed to call Reverend Shorr, who immediately came and arranged for her release. As Robin related these things Collie sensed a shadowy sorrow beneath her upbeat demeanor, and his heart ached to think of the terrors his gentle-spirited good girl had been forced to endure. He kept repeating how much he loved her, promising to protect and take care of her for the rest of their lives. Then Robin would smile, say that she loved him too, and lie quietly next to Collie on the bed, her head resting on his good shoulder as they helped each other to heal.

United by their love for Collie and realizing how near they had come to losing him, Robin and Nickie found themselves forming a strong affectionate bond. They agreed to consign their previous history to the past where it belonged, although Nickie apologized to Robin for making her withhold the truth from Collie and Robin expressed her remorse for the cruel manner in which Nickie had been forced to learn of her son's existence.

On the day the two women finally wheeled their fully-recovered young man out the hospital's front door into the warm sunshine, he stood up, breathed in a deep lungful of sweet springtime air and made it known that he never again wished to be addressed as Collie Skinner. From that moment forward, he declared, his name was Nicholas Colin Farrell.

⸺◈⸺

Over the ensuing months innumerable columns and features were written about the incident at Windfield, but of all these, only one was officially sanctioned by the college. Cinda Vanderhart's detailed re-counting of the affair, entitled *The Hating*, was the sole article to con-tain direct quotes from the principal people involved. Cinda's piece first ran in several Sunday magazine sections of major newspapers, and then was re-printed and appeared in many smaller publications, including the special graduation issue of *The Spectrum*, of which she had been made assistant editor. After a meticulous chronicling of the event's facts, she concluded:

> So in the end, Eamon Douglass failed to kill me or my college. I'm very glad, of course; but lest you think otherwise, there are more than a few individuals –and you know who you are– who secretly wish it had turned out differently.
>
> Which leaves us with the question: How long before the next attempt?
>
> That's the terrifying thing about this demon called Hate. Sooner or later it always comes back for another try. Oh, the demon may lose a skirmish now and then –I'm alive because it lost this one– but there's always a next time, whether it's another Lockerbie, or Oklahoma City, or 9/11, or Windfield. Throughout history, nothing has proven as tenacious as the human capacity for hatred. Except, just barely, our will to sur-vive. But in the end, if we don't wise up, that too will succumb and we'll all destroy each other in one final blazing sacrifice to Hate.
>
> Is there any hope? What if, as the do-gooders like to preach, we can all somehow learn to be tolerant of others?

⸺ 452 ⸺

Frankly, that's not good enough. Tolerance is nothing but hate held in abeyance. If you doubt that, think of the term "pain tolerance." Sure, you might be able to tolerate a dentist yanking out your molar without Novocain, but do you like it? Hell, no. The fact is, you can tolerate me and still wish me dead at the same time. Thanks, but I'll pass.

The same holds true with so-called "acceptance." Acceptance is nothing but Tolerance Lite. All the 12-step programs incorporate into their liturgies a desire to "accept the things I cannot change." To me, the clear implication is that if you could change them, you would. How is that any better? Perhaps you can force yourself to "accept" the fact that I'm a gay woman, but you'd be a whole lot happier if I wasn't. There's old Hate again, only deeply hidden and dormant, like a virus.

The only way it'll ever work is if we simply allow our fellow human beings to be the way they are. No condemnation, no judging, no trying to control. Live and let live. I'm okay, you're okay. You allow me, and I allow you. Does that mean I should allow you to stick a shiv in my navel? No, but the only reason you'd do it in the first place is because you're not allowing me to be who I am.

I'm no Pollyanna. It's unrealistic to think that we'll all love each other, or even like each other. Call it the Kumbaya Fallacy. But if you can find it in your heart to just allow me to be me, and I allow you to be you, and everyone else does the same thing, maybe, maybe, we can finally conquer the Hate demon and never again face a horror like the one Eamon Douglass had planned for us all.

Can such a thing come to pass? Will you allow it?

I don't know, people.

You tell me.

October 2007
Near Stuarton, VA

Another summer fades away, and once again the Virginia countryside is painted in the brilliant autumn colors that Luanne Skinner so loved. Nestled among flaming red and yellow trees, the Good Shepherd Community Church rears its white spire into the rich blue sky as a stream of guests files inside to watch Robin Thompson and Nicholas Farrell exchange their marital vows. Standing on the front steps, Reverend Shorr welcomes each new arrival with a handshake and warm greeting. He has officiated at many weddings in his time, but never one where the groom's father is a woman. Not that it matters. Professor Farrell has joined his congregation, and over the past several months Reverend Shorr and most of the other church members have come to know and admire her. And of course he loves Robin and Nicholas. Presiding over their union is a source of great pride and happiness for him.

Inside, the flower-decked pews are quickly filling. Several unfamiliar faces are mixed in among the church regulars. Congressman Walters, whose daughter Heather is one of Robin's attendants, has taken a seat up front along with Windfield President Fredericka Lindsey and Dr. Larry Silverman of the English department. Behind them Joanne Markwith sits with her girlfriend Connie Russo, a sassy green-eyed real estate agent who has recently sold Nickie Farrell a beautiful home. Across the aisle from them Conrad Foley, newly-returned to his job as maitre d' at the Foxton Arms, quietly converses with Mr. Demarest. Nearby, Mrs. Greene, wearing an outfit of the most astonishing tangerine color, has seated herself beside a venerable gray-headed black man, who is none other than Blue Ridge Harry. It is almost time for the ceremony to begin, and a hum of excited voices reverberates throughout the sanctuary.

In a private room next to the Reverend's office, Robin is being groomed and fussed over by Heather, Cinda, two other girlfriends and Nickie Farrell. The young women are dazzling in their pink-and-black bridesmaid's gowns, and Nickie is striking in a sage green tailored suit.

Finally, after a last flick at Robin's nose with her powder brush Heather announces, "Okay, girl, you are like *so* ready."

Robin nods, then says, "I'd like to speak to Nickie for just a minute. Do you mind?"

When the others have left Robin asks in a shaky voice, "Do I really look okay?"

"Absolutely stunning, sweetheart," Nickie assures her. "Nicholas is the luckiest man in the country."

Robin contemplates her image in a full-length mirror. "I wasn't sure this day would ever come. Everything that happened...we almost didn't make it, Nickie."

"But we did. You and Nicholas are going to have a wonderful life together."

"I wish Luanne was here," Robin says, her voice sad. "She should have been part of this. I miss her so much."

"Yes," Nickie murmurs. "I do, too."

"Nickie..." Robin swallows. "You don't think Luanne had anything to do with what the ambassador was planning, do you? They found her fingerprints on that disk, you know. All those books with their stupid conspiracy theories..."

"Impossible," says Nickie. "Not Luanne. No one ever had a more pure soul. Put it out of your mind, Robin. Please. It's over and done with."

"But how did the disk get in my car?" Robin's voice trembles. 'How, Nickie?"

"We'll never know." Nickie puts her arms around her future daughter-in-law. "And in the end, it doesn't matter, does it?" She pauses. "Maybe God put it there so you could save the college."

Robin is silent for a moment. "I think you're right." She looks at Nickie and smiles. "I'm glad you're going to be my father-in-law."

Nickie kisses her on the forehead. "Don't make me cry, for Heaven's sake. I'm still lousy at putting on mascara."

"And I'm so happy Alex is going to walk me down the aisle."

Adjusting Robin's veil: "You can't believe how thrilled he is. He doesn't have any daughters, and this is his big chance."

"I love Nicholas more than anything in the world, Nickie. I promise I'll be a good wife."

"I know you will, darling." Nickie kisses her finger, lays it on Robin's lips. "It's time for me to go now. I'll see you at the altar."

Nicholas is waiting in the rear of the church when Nickie joins him. "How's Robin doing?"

"She's perfect," replies Nickie. "The prettiest bride you'll ever see, God bless her."

Nicholas grins, his eyes sparkling. "At least until you and Alex get hitched."

Nickie laughs and takes her son's arm. "One thing at a time, dear boy. Shall we?"

They walk into the sanctuary and begin to make their way up the aisle, stopping to exchange greetings with acquaintances and friends.

As they proceed Nicholas suddenly hears a shy little voice say, "Who's that lady with the man getting married?"

He stops and sees a beautiful young girl with long honey-colored hair sitting next to his mother's old friend Beryl Jamison. Beryl smiles at him and says, "Did you ever meet my niece, Stephanie? Seven years old, and still never met a question she wouldn't ask."

Nicholas bends down. "Hi, Stephanie. Do you really want to know who this lady is?"

Beryl's niece solemnly nods.

"Well," Nicholas confides, "it used to be a really big secret. Even I didn't know for the longest time. But I finally found out. Should I tell you?"

Stephanie blinks huge gray eyes. "Uh-huh."

"Okay." Nicholas Farrell winks and whispers: "She's my Dad."

ACKNOWLEDGEMENTS

First and foremost, I must salute my wife and soul mate, Joleene. Her steadfast encouragement and willingness to allow my many eccentricities made it possible for this novel to be written. I love you, Wolf.

Nowadays, because of the current health care crisis, those who work in the medical profession are not always given their due respects. In light of that, it's important that I recognize and express my deepest gratitude to the following physicians, without whose help I would have been lost: John Aliapoulios, for listening and believing; Richard Horowitz, for his excellent care and unwavering support; Mitchell Atlas, for his technical assistance with the medical elements of my story; and the late Donald T. Lunde, compassionate counselor and family friend, whose untimely passing I mourn every single day.

Finally, heartfelt thanks to the Venerable Lion, who opened my eyes to the power and majesty of the written word and in so doing, enriched me beyond measure.

Iolanthe Woulff
March 23, 2007

CPSIA information can be obtained
at www.ICGtesting.com
Printed in the USA
BVHW031538131119
563718BV00001B/7/P

9 781432 743772